Unbound

Also by Celeste Bradley

THE RUNAWAY BRIDES
Devil in My Bed
Rogue in My Arms
Scoundrel in My Dreams

THE HEIRESS BRIDES
Desperately Seeking a Duke
The Duke Next Door
The Duke Most Wanted

THE LIAR'S CLUB
The Pretender
The Impostor
The Spy
The Charmer
The Rogue

THE ROYAL FOUR
To Wed a Scandalous Spy
Surrender to a Wicked Spy
One Night with a Spy
Seducing the Spy

And by Susan Donovan

I Want Candy
Cheri on Top
Not That Kind of Girl
The Night She Got Lucky
Ain't Too Proud to Beg
The Girl Most Likely To . . .
The Kept Woman
He Loves Lucy
Public Displays of Affection
Take a Chance on Me
Knock Me Off My Feet

Unbound

Celeste Bradley and Susan Donovan

St. Martin's Griffin
New York

UNBOUND. Copyright © 2011 by Celeste Bradley and Susan Donovan. All rights reserved. Printed in the United States of America. For information, address St. Martin's Press, 175 Fifth Avenue, New York, N.Y. 10010.

www.stmartins.com

ISBN 978-1-250-03264-5 (trade paperback)

Previously published in mass market format under the title *A Courtesan's Guide to Getting Your Man*

First St. Martin's Griffin Edition: January 2013

10 9 8 7 6 5 4 3 2 1

Acknowledgments

The authors thank Vicki L. Boone for information on museum operations and Frank Mangine for information on airport security. Also, the input of Darbi Gill and Joy Stefan was most appreciated.

And to our agent, Irene Goodman, go our heartfelt thanks for the unfailing support and for repeatedly scraping us off our respective ceilings.

Warning:

The book you hold in your hands is a naughty, decadent fantasy, a challenge to what it means to be a female sexual creature—but that's not all it is.

Unbound is more than just a sexy adventure. It is the story of two women, in two different times, searching for self-expression and empowerment in a world that doesn't approve of good girls gone bad.

Writing this novel together proved to be a sometimes shocking, sometimes stimulating, always outrageous journey of our own. This new edition is our own dream come to fulfillment—a previously published tale in a sexy new wrapping!

Please join us on this wild ride!

Rebelliously yours,

Celeste Bradley

Susan Donovan

What would happen if one woman told the truth about her life? The world would split open.

—Muriel Rukeyser

VOLUME I

One

This time, she really meant it. She would read just one more page and call it a night:

> *A large, masculine hand ran up the bare flesh of my thigh. The masked lover I knew only as "Sir" whispered into my ear, his breath hot. "I have taught you everything I can. Tomorrow you will choose your first protector."*
>
> *My teacher kissed me then, more tenderly than at any time during his instruction in the Seven Sins of the Courtesan. "Are you certain this is what you wish?" he asked. "Once you enter this world you may never return to the life you've always known."*
>
> *"I know what I want," I told him, luxuriating in the nest of silken sheets, a woman now, not the girl who had come to this bed a week prior. "Only as a courtesan can I be truly free to decide my own destiny."*

Piper Chase-Pierpont placed a white-gloved finger on the musty diary and slid it to the far edge of the museum workroom desk, providing some distance between herself and the devastatingly erotic secrets of a woman long dead. She needed to think. She needed to figure out how to handle this unexpected development, this sudden twist of truth.

Obviously, the first shock was that these diaries existed at all. But the story they told was nothing short of . . . well . . . frankly . . . this was the most triple-X, crazy-assed, explicit tale she'd ever read.

Piper's head buzzed. She craved a large alcoholic beverage, and she didn't even drink. She wanted to wolf down a Three Musketeers bar, though she knew it would only disrupt her endocrine system with free radicals, preservatives, and high-fructose corn syrup. She needed a little fresh air. Water. An ice-cold shower. She was short-circuiting. She tried to calm herself. It wasn't working.

Oh God! What am I supposed to do with this stuff?

Through the broken lenses of her glasses, Piper glanced at the clock on the basement workroom wall. It was after 1 A.M., which meant she'd been held spellbound by these documents for more than five hours, her thighs clenched together in the desk chair, barely moving, breathing hard. She'd only skimmed through the three diaries—out of order, she now realized—but it had been enough to understand that she'd unearthed a secret so outrageous it would rock the known historical record, jeopardize the reputation of her museum, and maybe even give her boss the excuse he needed to cut her position.

And let's face it, Piper thought—if she let this information out, everyone in town would hate her. What city wants to learn that their most beloved and righteous folk heroine spent her youth as a high-class hooker and accused murderess? Not Boston, Massachusetts, that was certain.

Maybe she should just pretend she never found the journals. She could simply take the diaries and run. But how would she live with herself? Piper was a senior curator at the Boston Museum of Culture and Society. Her job was to interpret history, not shove it in a shoebox and hide it under her bed.

Oh, but that wasn't even the worst of it. The story she'd just read hadn't only left her shocked—she was restless.

Overheated. It felt as if the two-hundred-year-old words had been written just for her, Piper Chase-Pierpont, Ph.D., a sex-starved, uptight, overworked, and underpaid woman standing alone, looking down into the abyss of her thirtieth birthday.

God help her, but she wasn't ready to share these journals with anyone. Not yet. Not until she understood the full historical—and personal—import of what she'd stumbled upon. Literally.

Piper's glance went to the center of the basement workroom floor, where it all began. It had been seven in the evening. A Friday in midsummer, which meant the rest of the staff had long ago gone home to their lives. She'd been sitting cross-legged with her notes and sketches for the Ophelia Harrington exhibit spread out around her. Filling the room's shelves and floor were nearly four hundred catalogued family artifacts on loan to the museum. Piper had been soaking it all in, desperately hoping a theme for the exhibit would gel in her mind. The Fall Gala was only three months away, and that made her nervous. She began to chew on an ink pen.

Sure, it was a terrible habit (one that her mother abhorred) but it's what she'd been doing since middle school—when she thought hard, she chewed on a pen.

But this time, the pen snapped. Foul-tasting ink trickled into her mouth. One violent shake of her head and her glasses went flying. Piper jumped to her feet and lurched toward the restroom, stepping on her glasses in the process. In her half-blind state she tripped over Ophelia Harrington's 187-year-old leather and cedar travel trunk, and when she returned from her scrubbing sojourn at the bathroom sink, she discovered that she'd knocked the trunk on its side, exposing a secret compartment. And the journals.

Piper smiled to herself at the irony. Despite her years of experience and a doctorate from Harvard, she had only luck to thank for this particular bonanza. Luck and clumsiness.

And now there they were, three small, innocent-looking journals bound in cracked brown leather, their powder-fine deckle edges ragged with age, their pages packed with historical dynamite.

She considered her options. Piper could follow standard procedure and copy the journals in the museum's document center. But since it was locked on weekends, she'd have to wait until Monday, when someone was bound to peer over her shoulder as she worked. And boy, wouldn't that be fun? They'd see phrases such as "rosy red nipples," and "the dark curls of my pubis peeked from between his fingertips."

No, thanks. Piper had barely been able to read those words alone in her basement workroom in the middle of the night. No way was she about to share them in a 9 A.M. staff meeting. The thought made her shudder.

What she'd do instead, she decided, was find an office-equipment vendor to deliver a professional-grade copier to her apartment on a Saturday. She'd pay out of pocket for it. Then she'd copy the diaries in private and study them at her leisure. She wouldn't tell anyone a damn thing about the journals until she was good and ready, and that would be only once she'd verified the recounted events and could place the outrageous story in its proper historical context. Besides, at home she could apply cold showers as needed.

Piper frowned, suddenly aware of the appalling lack of professionalism in that line of reasoning. How could she even *think* of doing something so outrageous? What if she got caught? She'd always been more milquetoast than maverick. Certainly, these diaries weren't worth losing her career and reputation over, were they?

She tipped her head and wondered.

Well? Were they?

The distant *ping!* of the basement elevator shocked Piper back to the here and now. The night security guard was on his way! *Oh God. Oh no.*

Oh, the heck with it!

And her decision was made.

Piper shoved herself to a sudden stand on bloodless legs, nearly toppling over. She stomped her feet to get the circulation going, shook her arms and hands, rolled her head from side to side. *Get organized, fast. Get the journals and get out of here.*

Footsteps came down the hall. Closer now. Heading her way.

Moving as fast as she could on feet that felt like concrete stumps, Piper began gathering everything she'd need—artifact tweezers, several more packages of lint-free white cotton gloves, acid-free paper, and Mylar storage sleeves, her favorite soft horsehair cleaning brush. Sometime in the future, she'd oversee the proper deacidification of the documents. Right now, she just had to get them home and get them copied.

And to think! Up until a few hours ago, her biggest challenge had been choosing a narrative theme for the Ophelia Harrington exhibit, finding a way to smoothly combine the public and private lives of one of the city's most beloved nineteenth-century icons.

She kept moving. Gathering. Thinking.

Ha! Thanks to this shocking *wormhole* in history she'd just discovered, she was now faced with an inscrutable mystery: *how had a much-desired Regency London courtesan known as "the Blackbird" become the most fiery female abolitionist in America's history?*

Piper gathered all three journals into one big sheet of acid-free paper, and shoved the entire bundle into her brown leather messenger bag. It made her cringe to handle them like that, but there was no time for delicacy.

She staggered toward the travel trunk still lying on its side, righting it. Then she plopped down amid her notes and sketches, pretending to be lost in thought, only this time without a pen.

"Miss Piper?"

"Yes?" Piper looked up and smiled as the door to the basement workroom opened.

Night security supervisor Melvin Tostel poked his head inside and frowned. "You still here?"

"What?" Piper tried to adjust her skewed eyeglasses. She wished she'd had a few extra minutes to retape them. She probably looked like a madwoman. If she was lucky, she looked like the same nerdy, workaholic curator she always had been, just a little, well, *nerdier.*

"Are you okay there, Miss Piper?" Melvin's frown deepened. "You got an exhibit opening or something? I haven't seen you here this late since—" He stopped himself. Even the security guards at the BMCS knew that Piper's last exhibit—one of the more costly in recent museum history—had "fallen short of expectations." That's how her father described the fiasco. Everyone else just called it what it was—a flop. A disaster. An embarrassment.

It was common knowledge that the Ophelia Harrington exhibit was Piper's last chance. The museum trustees had already cut several vital positions, and they'd made it clear that one of the two remaining senior curators would be next— herself or the brown-nosing weasel boy Lincoln Northcutt.

Piper was savvy enough to understand why the trustees had approved her idea for the Harrington exhibit. First, it would be dirt-cheap to install, because she'd already convinced prickly family matriarch Claudia Harrington-Howell to loan all of her ancestor's personal effects to the museum without compensation. Second, the subject matter would offend no one. And then there was the fact that the trustees had long sought to lure Claudia—and her deep pockets— into the museum's fold.

Somehow, Piper didn't think revealing that Claudia's beloved ancestor was a hot mess of a slut would help with that.

The security guard cleared his throat. "So what are you up to, then? You're here awfully late." Melvin began to glance around the room—with suspicion in his eyes, Piper noticed.

Was he on to her? How? It was only moments ago that

she'd decided to violate every ethical guideline of her profession and remove antiquities from the museum premises. *Without permission.* She'd never done anything without permission.

"Nothing!" she announced, louder than necessary. She pushed herself to a stand, still wobbly from the restricted blood flow. "I just lost track of time, I guess. You know how I can be. Well, I should probably get going home now."

Piper stumbled to her desk to grab her messenger bag. She turned off her desk and worktable lamps. She limped toward the door.

"You know your lips are blue, Miss Piper?"

"Oh, right." She shrugged. "An ink pen. What a mess." Piper clomped toward the elevator on her concrete stumps.

"You hurt your legs or something?"

"No! They fell asleep. Sitting for too long in one position can compress the arteries, thereby preventing nutrients and oxygen from reaching the nerve cells."

"Huh." Melvin cocked his head and produced a quizzical smile as he held the elevator door open. "I'll get you safely to your car. Half the lights are out in the parking garage—budget cuts and all."

"Oh, that's not necessary," Piper said, trying to sound casual, thinking about what she had crammed down inside her bag and the fact that she wasn't the type who usually spent time in a women's prison—her six years at Wellesley aside. "I'll be perfectly fine."

"It's the middle of the night, Miss Chase-Pierpont," Melvin said. "Here, let me help—"

"No!"

He looked at her like she was crazy. Maybe she was. Maybe this was what happened to single, lonely, pornography-stealing women about to turn thirty.

Piper and Melvin remained awkwardly silent on the elevator ride and through the garage, their footsteps echoing in the emptiness.

"Here we are!" she announced, gesturing to her rusty

Honda Civic. She flung open the passenger door and placed the messenger bag on the floor.

"Thank you again, Melvin!" she said, racing around to the other side of the car. "Have a good night!"

Without warning, Melvin smacked his hand on the roof of her Civic. Piper was so startled that she nearly jumped from the pavement. She panted, clutching her car keys to her chest.

Suddenly she pictured her criminal trial in great clarity— her mother in a front-row courtroom seat, her shoulder bones rattling as she sobbed, her father shaking his head in disapproval (if he could even bring himself to witness the public shaming of his only child), and the jury box? That's right—it would be filled to the brim with members of the museum's board of trustees, hearing aids and all.

Now, wouldn't that be something? The first time in thirty years that Piper Chase-Pierpont doesn't play by the rules and she gets sent to the big house.

"Hairspray and baby oil!" Melvin announced, laughing.

Piper blinked. "Uh . . ."

"I've been racking my brain for how my wife got that printer cartridge ink off her fingers a few years back, and that's it! Hairspray and baby oil!"

"Oh." Piper began to breathe normally again, bracing herself against the car door. "That's an excellent idea. I'll try it as soon as I get home. Good night!"

She burned rubber on her way out of the parking lot, another first in a night full of them.

I tightened my arms about his neck and cried out at his entry, my sob of aching satisfaction disappearing into his hot mouth.

No wonder it was taking Piper forever to copy these diaries. Every time she found an efficient rhythm while managing to maintain the rigorous preservation standards the job required, she'd run across another word or sentence or paragraph that would stop her cold.

> *He said, "I will bury my hands in your hair and drive my cock deep, then pull it wet and slippery from your lips, only to do it all again."*

Seriously. Her priority needed to be copying each page, not reading for her own titillation. The heat and humidity of her post-war, no-frills box of an apartment was the worst possible environment for these artifacts, and the window fan she'd strung up from the kitchen pot rack was doing nothing but stir the sticky heat around. Each second she wasted put the fragile paper, leather, and ink in further peril.

Piper suddenly felt evil feline eyes boring into the back of her head. "I *said* I was sorry," she snapped at Miss Meade, dabbing her own forehead with her sleeve, her gloved fingers carefully fisted against contamination. "I told you I can't run the air conditioner and this behemoth at the same time or I'll trip the fuse box again."

In response, the Divine Miss M. raised her overstuffed, gray tabby hind leg and licked daintily at her kitty giblets, her disapproving gaze still focused on Piper.

Back to the task at hand. The original journals had to be returned on Monday to the museum documents room, where they could be stored properly. She'd keep the copy with her at all times, to read, reread, study, make notes on, and use to painstakingly compare to the known historical record.

Clearly, there was no time for diversion. If she stopped to linger over every provocative phrase and erotically tinged word she encountered in Ophelia's elegant and fluid handwriting, she'd be standing at the copy machine for the rest of her natural life.

Piper carefully lifted Volume II from the glass surface and forced herself to concentrate. Though she followed document-handling protocol to mitigate damage, each turn of a page had resulted in some additional injury to the journals, the paper tearing slightly along the hand-sewn spine. It was unavoidable. The pages were brittle with time, pockmarked by insects, and weakened by mold and mildew. Yet it could have been far worse, she knew. The diaries were in surprisingly good condition for their age and had remained mostly legible, thanks to the way they'd been wrapped and stored.

Ophelia Harrington had meant business when she packed these away in the false bottom of her trunk, a task that she accomplished on or after April 16, 1825, the date on the *London Examiner* news sheet used to wrap them. Nearly six layers of newsprint had encased each volume.

In addition, the trunk itself had offered a good deal of protection from humidity and light. Whoever built the travel chest had been a master craftsman, fitting the seams so tightly that the secret compartment and its spring release were invisible even upon close examination. In the three months Piper had been poking around the trunk (along with all of Ophelia Harrington's belongings), she'd never suspected such a feature. And it would have remained a secret—the diaries lost forever—if Piper hadn't knocked the trunk on its side when she tripped.

She cautiously turned the page, lifted the journal, carried it to the glass plate and turned it over for copying. That's when her eye caught the phrase "my masked lover" and her pulse spiked once more.

This stuff was addictive! Mind-numbingly erotic! Historical and sexual C-4! And Piper knew if she lost her focus and started reading the diary entries as a woman instead of a scholar, then she'd be in serious trouble. She'd already seen enough to know that Ophelia Harrington had lived a far juicier life than Piper had. Furthermore, she'd done it in an era of limited rights for women, a strict social construct, and before the girl even turned twenty-five!

Piper, on the other hand, lived in a time where she could

be anything and do anything she wished. And what had she done with thirty years of freedom?

She'd studied. Worked. Read the classics. Traveled when she could. Tried to please her parents. Dated men who weren't quite right for her, and only occasionally.

With the discovery of these journals, Piper had to face the fact that compared to Ophelia Harrington, she was in danger of becoming a dried-up, frustrated, bitter, and *boring* woman.

The most hurtful event of her life flashed through Piper's brain—the way it often did in moments of self-pity—and in her mind's eye, she watched Magnus "Mick" Malloy's strong and straight back as he walked out her door.

God, the thought of Mick Malloy still made Piper's belly clench in shame. She'd followed his superstar career over the years, of course. It would have been hard not to in their line of work. Mick Malloy had become the unofficial cover model for *The Curator, Archaeology Today,* and *Science Magazine.* She'd even heard the rumor that Malloy was getting his own cable reality show. And why not? He was made for TV. Sexy. Sun-bronzed. A real-life Indiana Jones with a brilliant mind, a sharp wit, and a devastatingly fine . . .

Forget it. It doesn't matter anymore.

Piper sighed. The details she wanted to know about Mick weren't to be found in magazines or TV shows, anyway, and she'd never dare come right out and ask someone.

Was he happy? Had he ever married? Had a woman ever captured his mind and heart the way archaeology had? If so, who was she? And in how many ways was she the complete opposite of Piper?

I will not go there.

Piper straightened her shoulders and carefully executed the task at hand, reminding herself that these journals were not about her or Mick or how she'd blown her chance with him a decade ago. The diaries weren't some kind of yardstick with which to compare her own adventures—or lack thereof. These journals were a historical treasure with yet unknown repercussions.

Ophelia's firsthand accounts of her life as a London courtesan would not only add a fascinating complexity to her role in history, but it could improve understanding of early nineteenth-century underground London economy, its social mores, and the indiscretions of the rich and powerful. This was a serious scholarly matter, not a *Cosmo* quiz.

"Mrrraow." Piper turned to the yellow demon stare of Miss M., who had draped herself over the back of the Queen Anne chair in dramatic fashion, her tail swishing in the stuffy air as if she were fanning herself.

"You think I'm enjoying this?" she asked her cat. "I'm exhausted. It's ninety-four degrees outside. My life is about as fun as one of Mom and Dad's dinner parties! And this girl—this *courtesan* chick who ran around calling herself 'the Blackbird' and bending over to light men's cigars so that her mammary glands fell out of her dress—" Piper gestured toward the diary she held above the copier. "My God! What a complete *tart* that girl was!"

Miss Meade blinked, then looked away as if offended by the outburst.

The phone rang, saving Piper from further crazy cat-lady conversation. She eased the journal into its makeshift cradle of organic cotton batting covered by acid-free cloth, and checked the caller ID. Suddenly, chatting with her cat seemed like a perfectly reasonable endeavor. Piper let the call go to automated voice mail, but clicked on the speaker.

"It's your mother," the clipped voice said through the telephone console. "Unless I hear otherwise, I'll assume you're not coming for dinner tomorrow. I am concerned about you. We haven't seen you for going on a month. You haven't returned my calls. Your father thinks you might be back on dairy and are experiencing symptoms of bloat and/or depression. Are you back on dairy? Are you depressed? Are you bloated? Call me, please." *Click.*

This would be as good a time as any to take a break,

Piper decided, heading into her tiny kitchen for some ice cream. The real stuff, too. Häagen-Dazs Vanilla Bean. Five hundred eighty calories and thirty-six grams of fat in a one-cup serving.

As Piper opened the freezer compartment and stuck her head inside for a quick respite, she thought about how she'd like to answer her mother. If she had the nerve. She might say, *"Hell, yes, I'm back on dairy, Mother dearest! And by the way—you seem to have forgotten your only child's thirtieth fucking birthday!"*

A sudden tingle that went through her had nothing to do with the open freezer. She found it immensely satisfying to speak to her mother like that—especially using the f-word—even if only in her head.

She smiled to herself. Oh, if her mother only knew . . .

Just yesterday, Piper had enjoyed a Polish sausage, fries, and a giant vanilla shake. And three days prior to that she'd gotten completely out of control and had a huge slice of New York cheesecake—the chocolate marble swirl kind.

Piper was aware that her bingeing on dairy was a classic case of rebellion, the kind she should have experimented with at seventeen. But she hadn't had the nerve at seventeen. Or eighteen. The truth was, it sucked being the only child of the founders of the Caloric Restriction and Human Longevity Lab at Harvard. They were among the country's most revered biomedical researchers—and two of the most tightly wound, repressed human beings ever to inhabit the earth.

Birthdays weren't celebrated in her family. Her parents said holidays were just an excuse to overdo. For her birthday, Piper could count on a kiss on the cheek and a new book, but never cake and ice cream or a beautifully wrapped gift.

"Will vanilla work for you?" Piper asked Miss Meade, who was rubbing against her ankle and purring, a sure sign of her improving mood.

As she scooped out two bowls of the heavenly substance, it suddenly struck Piper as pathetic. Her idea of debauchery in the twenty-first century was a cup of vanilla ice cream.

Ophelia Harrington had spent part of 1813 studying the erotic arts, under the tutelage of a masked man she knew only as "Sir," who served as her professor of gluttonous depravity for seven days and seven nights.

There was something wrong with this picture.

Two

Thus emboldened, I returned to the witness stand, determined to skewer the hypocrites, all of them.

"I stand accused of a murder I did not commit. And who are my accusers?" I scanned the packed courtroom and pointed to the offenders.

"The prosecutor is a man who has unsuccessfully courted me for more than a decade, a man known to grovel at my doorstep, only to burst into sobs when I sent him away. And the man bringing these charges?"

I took great relish in facing the sullen, vindictive wastrel, wondering how I could have ever found him dashing. "This is the blackguard who tried to sell me into sexual slavery years ago, only to beat me severely when I escaped his control."

The courtroom erupted into gasps and murmurs. Yet I was not done. I stood in the witness box and raised my voice high and clear.

"This trial is naught but a temper tantrum thrown by enraged and undisciplined little boys, all of whom are in dire need of a good spanking!"

The alarm had gone off long ago, but Piper remained propped up on her pillows, in the same daze she'd been in all weekend. There was no other way to look at it—Ophelia

Harrington had balls. The lady didn't take crap off anyone—
not her guardians, not the arbiters of decorum, not the men
who sought out her company and then sought to rule her.

That chick had the courage to live life to its fullest—in
and out of the boudoir.

It was all very inspiring. And exhausting.

After spending forty-eight hours in Ophelia's exotic
world of lust, excess, seduction, intrigue, and betrayal, Piper
felt overwhelmed. The journals had aroused her and piqued
her curiosity in equal measure, but she was far more accustomed to being piqued than being aroused, so, by this time,
she was wiped out. Wasted. Hung over on a Monday morning and running late for work.

The sun sliced through the miniblinds. The window air
conditioner hummed and rattled. Miss Meade was curled
up at the foot of her double bed. This was where Piper was
supposed to rise and dress and pack her brown-bag lunch and
get herself to the museum. She had a 9 A.M. staff meeting.
She had an afternoon monthly budget session. But how was
she supposed to do all that? How was she supposed to drag
her sex-dazed self in there and pretend she was the same girl
who'd come to work on Friday?

She wasn't. And she'd probably never be that girl again,
would she? Piper wiped at the tears suddenly running down
her cheeks, laughing at her own ridiculousness. She'd made
quite the wet mess of herself, hadn't she?

Last night, for the first time in years, Piper had touched
herself.

Last night, for the first time in her life, she'd managed to
bring herself to orgasm. And not just the standard kind of
orgasm. Inspired by the diaries, somehow Piper had charged
headlong into a searing, core-rattling, devastating place
she'd never visited before. She didn't go there once. She went
four times. And the most shocking part of all of it was that
somehow, Mick Malloy had risen from her past and inserted
his man-candy self into her orgasmic fantasies, weaving in

and out of the jumbled historical sex-stew that had temporarily taken over her brain.

So now, as Piper sat there propped up against her pillows, it felt as if a dam had burst in her soul, as if the heat of Ophelia and Sir's two-hundred-year-old sexual liaison had somehow burned down the walls she'd built inside herself.

And all Piper could think was, *Shit.* Because the truth was she needed more. And she needed the real thing. Like Ophelia. She wanted all of it—the intense passion, the devotion, the entire arc of a love story for the ages! Unfortunately, these things required an actual man.

I will not go there.

She laughed again, so loud she disturbed Miss M. The cat raised her head and opened one eye long enough to pass judgment, then went back to sleep.

Piper needed to get a grip. She closed her eyes, breathed deep, and concentrated on removing herself from Ophelia's sensual world. She forced herself to reenter her own mind, her own time and place, her own body.

She took a moment to notice that the sheets tossed over her legs were practical cotton, not the finest satin. She wore a holey Red Sox T-shirt, not some of Lementeur's hand-stitched lingerie. Her muddy brown hair was pulled back in a tight ponytail, not loose and glossy and jet black as it fell over her shoulders and onto her bare back.

Eventually, Piper became aware that her limbs trembled, either from exhaustion or exhilaration, she couldn't be sure. But it was no mystery why her chest felt tight and heavy—it was the burden she now carried. Piper had become the sole executor of Ophelia Harrington's secret legacy—every shocking and succulent morsel of it. In less than three months, Piper would have to unveil the Ophelia Harrington exhibit at the annual BMCS Fall Gala. She'd have to stand before the board of trustees, the cranky Claudia Harrington-Howell, and a lobby full of big-money museum donors and

Boston muckety-mucks and show them what she'd come up with.

And here was Piper's dilemma: would she proceed with her plan and give everyone a technically accurate and thoroughly inoffensive look at Ophelia's home life and abolitionist work, or would she dare tell the whole story, as she now understood it?

Would Piper have the guts to commit professional suicide with an exhibit exposing the *truth* about Ophelia Harrington— that the righteous Yankee matron who demanded the end of American slavery was once a London call girl who gleefully rented herself out for debauchery?

Piper tossed the copied pages of Volume III to the bedspread and groaned with frustration. Who was she kidding? Even if she possessed balls the size of grapefruits, there was no way she could do justice to Ophelia's decadent London world on a nonexistent budget. How could she re-create the courtesan's boudoir, salon, and wardrobe—not to mention the Regency London social scene—without spending a fortune?

She wasn't like her best friend. Piper couldn't go around batting her eyelashes and showing a little cleavage the way Brenna did, getting people to upgrade her to first class or give her the window table.

Piper swung her legs over the side of the bed and staggered toward the bathroom, her mind reeling with every newly discovered fact about Ophelia Harrington and every corresponding missing piece with which she was now obsessed. For herself. Exhibit aside, she felt compelled to understand Ophelia and her choices. Just for herself.

How had that woman ever summoned the courage to live life on her own terms? What had that girl had that Piper didn't?

She stretched, ripped off the T-shirt, and jumped under the spray. She had time for a lightning-quick shower but wouldn't even bother with her hair. Who cared what she looked like, anyway? Piper was a scholar, an academic with her master's in anthropology from Wellesley and a Ph.D. in history from Harvard. She hadn't been asked out on a date in six months. She operated in a world where her mind was all that mattered, all she needed. The fact that she was a woman in possession of hair and a face and a body was immaterial.

Piper toweled herself off roughly and grabbed her toothbrush. She caught sight of her reflection and gasped. Her lips were still a ghostly blue from the ink pen disaster. Her eyes were bloodshot. She was terribly pale. Her wavy hair had frizzed in the heat and humidity, defying the rubber band that imprisoned it. Piper reached for her broken glasses and burst out laughing.

God. No wonder no one had asked her out lately. Her femininity was more than immaterial—it was downright undetectable!

No wonder Mick Malloy had walked out on her.

She dug around in her closet for something cool and roomy to wear and some comfy sandals to slip into. She returned the original diaries to her briefcase and shoved her working copy alongside. Piper set out on her Monday-morning commute into downtown Boston—there was no way she'd take the T with the original journals on her person—and arrived at the museum with a half hour to spare before her meeting. She would have just enough time to safely store the diaries, and once that was done, she would be able to breathe.

Piper swung into the first parking spot she found. She jogged to the rear museum entrance, already sweating, and used her employee card key to gain entrance. She scurried down the back hall toward the employee elevator, her glasses askew, rounded the corner . . .

And was knocked on her rump, the victim of a full-frontal collision with a person she never saw coming.

She watched, horrified, as the diaries ejected from her briefcase and went sliding across the linoleum floor, clearly visible through their Mylar storage sleeves. Without wasting a second, Piper scrambled on her hands and knees to collect them, shoving them one by one into the briefcase, hoping beyond hope that no one had seen anything.

She bolted to a stand, her chest heaving, and glared up into the face of the asshole who'd knocked her over.

She froze.

"Piper? Is that you?" The man's blue eyes widened along with his dazzling white smile. "Hey! I was hoping I'd run into you on my first day here, but not like this!" He laughed. "Are you okay?"

Oh no. Please. Oh God. Oh holy shit. Any day but today.

Magnus "Mick" Malloy wrapped his fingers around Piper's upper arm and leaned in close. He studied her broken glasses and blue lips.

"Rough weekend?" he asked.

Moments later Piper sat across from Mick in the museum café daintily sipping coffee from a Styrofoam cup and trying to appear cheerful while anxiety ripped through her body. Mick had just told her he looked forward to catching up.

Catching up on *what*?

She hadn't seen him in a decade. The last time she'd spoken to him about anything other than her master's thesis, her underwear had been down around her ankles, *Let's Get It On* was playing on her off-campus apartment CD player, and he was striding out her door, taking with him every morsel of bravado she'd scraped together for just that occasion. Mick Malloy had broken her heart. He'd crushed her self-confidence. Much later, he'd invaded her orgasms. But the point was, Mick was just a stranger.

There, she felt like saying. *Now we're caught up, you douche.*

Piper clutched the briefcase to her chest with her free arm, determined to prevent another brush with catastrophe.

"It really is wonderful to see you," Mick said, smiling like he meant it.

He'd arranged himself at a casual angle in the chair

across the café table from her, the museum coffee shop humming with morning activity all around them. His long, denim-clad legs were nonchalantly crossed at the knee and an elbow was hooked over the back of his chair. His face was relaxed and handsome, but Piper would have to say he was more striking-looking now than when he was an assistant lecturer at Wellesley. He'd had a kind of baby-faced charm back then. Now, his face was thinner and more rugged, and his charm had an edge to it—not arrogance exactly. Maybe just an abundance of confidence.

He had the same black eyebrows that contrasted so dramatically with his pure blue eyes. He had the same hair, dark and thick with curls, still a little longer at the collar than the norm. Black Irish, with the sexy accent to match.

But one glance was all it took for Piper to tell that his body had changed dramatically. He was harder and bigger than he'd been at Wellesley, probably because he'd been doing fieldwork for the last decade instead of teaching others how to do it. She could detect the cut of his biceps and the swell of his chest beneath his collared T-shirt, which clung to a superbly flat stomach and tapered down into his belt. Too bad Mick was sitting down, she thought to herself. His best asset was hidden from view.

Piper surprised herself. She rarely allowed herself such base thoughts about a colleague. Reading the diaries must have rewired her neurons.

Oh, but who was she kidding? Mick had never been just a colleague. He'd been her first and only object of lava-hot lust. He'd been the only man she'd ever fantasized about, the only man who'd ever inspired her to touch herself.

She'd been so young and stupid back in grad school. And she'd placed ridiculously naïve hopes and expectations on him, a man far beyond her grasp.

Piper winced at the memory of how she and Brenna had drooled over Mick all those years ago. They set up camp in the front row of Mick's ethnoarchaeology graduate seminar, transfixed by his baritone brogue and stupefied by his looks.

And whenever he'd turn and raise his arm to write on the board, they'd clutch at each other and cease to breathe, waiting for the exact moment his herringbone jacket would rise over the belt of his faded Levi's, exposing the curve of what was then and remained to this day—at least the last time she and Brenna discussed the matter—the single finest male butt either of them had ever encountered.

It was understandable how Piper might still make that claim, since she hadn't exactly gone on to a life of inspecting male posteriors. But for Brenna Nielsen to still rank Mick Malloy at the head of the rear-end list? Now that was saying something, since Piper's best friend not only was a sexologist by profession but dedicated most of her free time to the study of the male form, the male psyche, and the male gender in all its glory. Piper couldn't *wait* to tell Brenna that Mick was visiting Boston.

She shifted uncomfortably in her seat. The way Malloy was staring at her, it was obvious he expected her to engage in conversation. "It's nice to see you, too," she said, avoiding eye contact, afraid the shame she felt would be broadcast in her expression.

Why did she have to meet up with Mick Malloy on the most angst-filled day of the last decade of her life? What had she ever done to deserve this kind of punishment? It wasn't fair! Of course she was no fashionista, but at least she made an effort to look presentable on most workdays. But not today.

Today, she hadn't washed her hair or applied tinted moisturizer. Her lips were blue. She wore Birkenstock sandals and a rather shapeless linen dress in a dusky pink that brought out the bloodshot quality of eyes framed in duct tape. And beneath that disheveled exterior, Piper's mind was in similar turmoil, short-circuiting with flashes of naked flesh sliding on satin sheets, silken ropes tied to bedposts, a perfumed bath drawn for two before the fireplace, and the vexing row of buttons on the front of an English gentleman's breeches . . .

I wanted this. I wanted to experience everything, to feel everything, to live, fully and unrepentantly, to suck the marrow out of every moment of freedom. I wanted to touch and be touched, to love and be loved, to fuck and be fucked.

Across from Piper, Mick raised an eyebrow. "Hello?"

She forced herself to breathe. Holy shit, she was having flashbacks! "Right. Yes. It's been a long time." She added, "Sorry, but I need to be going." Piper stood, still clutching her briefcase. "The staff meeting is about start."

"I am aware of that," Mick said, rising with her, his smile now decidedly devilish. "You know, you haven't even asked me what I'm doing at the BMCS."

Mick was correct. She hadn't asked. For the last fifteen minutes, she'd half listened to him describe his life of adventure while she'd been wrapped up in her own embarrassment—and embarrassingly sex-saturated thoughts—all while watching the clock and knowing she wouldn't have time to get the diaries locked away. What if the stress caused her to develop a tic? That would be perfect. Blue lips. Duct-taped glasses. A facial tic. She'd have to beat the men off with a club.

They began to walk together from the café.

"You're not the least bit curious?" he asked, looking down at her.

Piper rolled her eyes. "Fine. I'm curious. What are you doing here?"

"I'm on loan to the museum," he said in the deep, melodious brogue that had haunted her for a decade. "For the next six months, I'll be on sabbatical working as a consultant to the board of trustees."

Piper stopped walking. *"What did you say?"*

"It's part of the faculty exchange agreement with the university."

Piper felt her blue lips go slack.

"You don't look thrilled," Mick said.

She shook her head, attempting to process the information. "Wow. That's so great. Really." The tears were seconds from spilling down her cheeks. "I have to go."

Mick studied her from across the conference table, perplexed by what he saw.

The last time he'd seen Piper she was the girl with the brown French braid, the huge green eyes, and the heart-shaped chin. In his mind he saw her clomping through campus on her scuffed clogs, usually reading, sometimes bumping into people, sporting a wardrobe of baggy Levi's, turtleneck, and a moth-eaten Fair Isle sweater. She always wore preppy glasses. No earrings. No bracelets. No lipstick. No nothing.

Twenty-year-old Piper Chase-Pierpont was known back then as the best friend of Brenna Nielsen, a Nordic beauty of good Minnesota stock, long-legged, blond, and sporting an attitude. He'd always found it funny that the two of them had glommed onto each other the way they had, giggling from the front row as they stared at his ass.

But from the start he knew that Piper was more than the beauty queen's sidekick. She was brilliant, cute, and shy, but her reticence was punctuated with moments of dry humor and dead-on insight that intrigued Mick.

And through the years, if his mind happened to wander to Piper Chase-Pierpont, he'd imagined she'd grown into her looks, that she'd ditched the drab preppy look and admitted to herself that she was *fine*.

He told himself that if he met up with Piper again, he'd find her sleek and sexy and in full control of her bad-ass female self.

He'd been wrong, apparently.

She sat directly across the conference table as the museum staff meeting dragged on into perpetuity, reminding him why he'd steered clear of desks and offices for so long. Piper had been doing an excellent job of avoiding eye contact, or even acknowledging his presence. According to one of the other curators—a little neddy-boy arse-kisser named Linc Northcutt—an ink pen had exploded in Piper's mouth sometime over the weekend. That explained the blue lips. It didn't explain everything else he was seeing.

She looked hollow-eyed and fatigued, yet her cheeks were in a constant state of blush. She clutched that briefcase so tightly to her belly that you'd think she was carrying around the original Dead Sea Scrolls. She wore beat-up Birkenstocks and some housecoatlike thing she'd probably found at a fancy organic free-trade boutique that managed to convince otherwise intelligent women to spend a fortune on a burlap sack.

She deserved better.

Piper glanced up at him. Mick jolted to attention. But she looked away immediately. He could see the red stain of embarrassment spread down her throat to her chest.

Mick heard his name mentioned, and turned his attention from Piper to the museum's executive director, Louis LaPaglia, who was obviously in the middle of introducing Mick to the staff.

"And no," LaPaglia added, a wry smile on his chubby face. "His salary is not coming out of our operating budget— it's part of the university's faculty exchange and sabbatical program, which is covering his entire six-month assignment."

Mick watched as the suspicion faded from several faces at the table. He couldn't blame them for feeling threatened— the museum had lost close to six million of their endowment value in the last three years, and their exhibit receipts had plummeted forty-two percent in the same time period. Seven positions had been cut, more were likely, and it was a pattern being repeated all over the country throughout the nonprofit universe—museums, symphonies, zoos, libraries, theater companies—and everyone at that conference table knew they'd be substitute teaching or waiting tables if they were let go.

He was here to help turn that trend around at the BMCS.

He'd agreed to help launch a new fund-raising campaign if a portion of the proceeds went toward future archaeological exploration of Boston's earliest urban settlements, one of his pet projects.

He had other reasons for a visit to Boston. He needed to help his brother, Cullen, resuscitate the family pub business. And he needed to negotiate the terms of the Compass Cable Network reality TV project.

Mick let his gaze wander back toward Piper. Suddenly, her bloodshot eyes locked with his. The connection lasted just an instant, but it was an instant longer than she'd managed all day and enough to send out a flash of sharp need. And sharper anger.

But that couldn't be. She was angry at *him*? She was the one who blew him off all those years ago. She wouldn't return his calls. She refused to speak to him except to talk about her feckin' thesis, like the disaster in her apartment had never even happened! She turned away every time he asked for a few moments of her time.

Dear God, the girl had been stubborn. And he'd left Boston after that semester, headed to the Isle of Wight, and shoved the memory of that night to the back of his mind.

But looking at her now, he couldn't help but remember. The sweet, innocent Piper had gone and gotten herself absolutely *langered* at a department wine-and-cheese, then asked him to walk her back to her place, where she pulled him in the door by his lapel and became hell-bent on getting him in bed. Sweet Janey Mack! Like he didn't want what she offered. But he'd never taken advantage of a woman in such a weakened state, and he wouldn't be starting with a brilliant student he suspected was a virgin, especially weeks before he would be leaving Wellesley to start fieldwork. That wasn't his style.

Mick shut his eyes for an instant, trying to block out the details that were coming back to him. It didn't work. He remembered how she'd stumbled toward the CD player and slipped in some Marvin Gaye, then begun a torturously clumsy striptease that, within seconds, revealed that Piper Chase-Pierpont had the mind of a future Ph.D. candidate and the body of pole dancer.

Right before Mick's eyes, his shy, cute prepster had morphed into an extremely fuckable drunk chick within arm's reach, practically begging for it. Mick froze. His eyes got huge. His fingers trembled. The zipper on his jeans nearly busted.

He couldn't do it.

So he'd scooped her turtleneck from the floor, covered her perfect bare breasts, and kissed her forehead. He told her he'd call her the next day. And he headed for the door.

Mick had kept an eye on her career through mutual acquaintances over the years. He heard she'd had a rough go with her last exhibit, something about the contribution of New England's women telephone operators during the first half of the twentieth century. Apparently, it had cost a bundle to stage and was heavily promoted, yet didn't bring in the visitors. Mick even heard rumors that her job was likely the next to go. So when he accepted the temporary BMCS gig as a way to get home to Boston, he thought maybe she'd appreciate a friendly face—the face of a man who only wished the best for her.

"Dr. Malloy?"

LaPaglia was asking Mick to say something. He stood, told everyone a little about what he had in mind, and made a point of pausing to meet the eye of each staff member at the conference table.

Except for Piper, of course, whose eyes were cast down onto her notepad, her left hand orchestrating white-knuckled flourishes of pen against paper. Her collection of doodles featured arrows shooting off in all directions and rockets blasting into space. Mick was no fan of Freud, but he couldn't help but note that all Piper's sketches were . . .

Basically, they were phallic as fuck.

Three

Piper ignored the pounding on her door and pressed the couch pillow to the side of her head, hoping whoever it was would go away. She was finally enjoying a moment of peace, the diaries safely and intentionally miscatalogued into obscurity in the museum. Then she heard Brenna's unhappy voice.

"I saw your car parked on the street. I know you're home, Piper. Open up or I'm calling your mother."

Ugh. Piper shuffled to the door and opened it a crack.

Brenna's eyes went wide. She quickly scanned Piper from head to toe, then glanced beyond to the large Konica digital copier that occupied half her living room.

She narrowed one eye at Piper. "I don't know what you're up to, but you better let me in."

She sighed, gesturing for her friend to cross the threshold into the apartment's small foyer. Miss Meade toddled over to greet Brenna, and Piper's friend picked up the cat and gave her an affectionate scratch behind the ears, even as she frowned at Piper.

"It's Monday. We were going to celebrate your birthday tonight. You haven't returned my calls or texts. You look like Lindsay Lohan after a bender. And your lips—did you finally bite a pen in half? After all these years?"

Piper rubbed her face to try to wake up. She must've

fallen asleep on the couch. Clearly, she'd forgotten all about their weekly girls' night out, and her big birthday blowout.

When Brenna's hand landed softly on her shoulder, Piper looked up. The sympathy she saw in her friend's expression caused tears to well in her eyes. She didn't want to cry anymore. All she'd been doing from the second she got home from work to the moment she fell asleep was cry, read, and then cry some more.

"Oh God, what's happened? What's wrong?" Brenna dumped Miss Meade to the floor, a rude dismissal the cat didn't appreciate, and led Piper to the couch. She cleared a spot for both of them to sit by gathering up all the copied diary pages and dumping the stack on the coffee table. In the process she noticed the duct-taped glasses, picked them up, gave them a quick inspection, then tossed them back to the table.

"Were you in a car accident? When did this happen? Did you get medical attention?" Brenna's pretty face began to twist in concern. "Piper, why didn't you tell me? I swear to God I just don't get you sometimes! You go around thinking you can handle everything by yourself! Why didn't you let me help you? I've been worried *sick*!"

Piper shook her head. "There was no car accident. I'm fine. A couple things happened that left me a little shaken up, that's all."

Brenna slowly exhaled, and began rubbing Piper's back. "Don't bullshit me. You're about as fine as your glasses are. What's going on?"

"It's kind of a long story—"

"And what are you doing with the ginormous copier?"

Before Piper could answer, Brenna's gaze wandered to the papers she'd just cleared aside. She grabbed the top pile, held together with a large paper clip and riddled with penciled-in notes. Piper leaned over enough to see a date and deduced that Brenna was examining a diary entry midway through Volume II, just before the crap hit the fan for

Ophelia. It had been a time in her life when she was between "protectors" and playing the field, living large as the
ultimate catch among London's gentlemen. That time was
spent gallivanting to the opera, the theater, and the finest
dinners and parties. It was also a time when she regularly
held private "salons" with gentlemen in her own home, a
perfectly outrageous activity for a proper lady in that day
and age, but not for the courtesan known as the Blackbird.

Piper smiled as her friend's eyes scanned frantically from
line to line. She'd already decided to share her discovery with
Brenna, which was good, since there'd be no chance of hiding anything now. Besides, she'd always told Brenna everything. Brenna knew she was back on dairy. She knew she'd
struggled to find a theme for the Ophelia Harrington exhibit,
and would surely appreciate the value of the journals.

And her friend knew all about Mick Malloy.

Just then, Brenna's eyeballs popped. She began flipping
from page to page, gasping and clicking her tongue in disbelief. Piper watched her desperately search for the cover
page, written in an elegant, flowing hand.

Volume II
The Life of Ophelia Harrington, Courtesan

Brenna looked sideways at Piper, not moving except to
blink. "What in the name of God *is* this?" she whispered.

Piper shrugged. "It's pretty self-explanatory, don't you
think? The one you're holding is the middle of her three
journals. In my mind, I've been calling it her 'Britney Spears
Years.'"

"But . . ." Brenna stopped, sat up straighter, and cocked
her head. It had been a long time since Piper saw her elo-
quent friend speechless.

"Basically," Piper continued, "Volume One is 'The De-
flowering,' while Volume Three—that's the shortest one and
the one that has all the details of the murder charges and the
trial, not to mention an absolutely mind-blowing twist I

never saw coming—I like to think of that one as 'The Morning After.' "

Brenna's brow knit together in bewilderment. "But this can't possibly . . ." She paused, taking a second to rephrase her words. "Are you sure this is the same Ophelia Harrington?"

Piper nodded. "Oh, I'm sure."

"The abolitionist? The one whose portrait is hanging in every elementary school in Massachusetts?"

She nodded again.

"Claudia handed these over to you?" Brenna shook her head in confusion. "It took that woman three months to agree to let the museum borrow the family candlesticks! Why in the hell would she give you something as . . . as . . . *incendiary* as this?"

Piper chuckled. "Yes, well, there's a story behind—"

Brenna waved her hand through the air, cutting her off. "Wait!"

Piper knew what was happening—her friend's mind was barreling down a single track of inquiry and it wouldn't be slowed or stopped until her relentless curiosity was sated. It's what made Brenna an outstanding scholar and an often annoying conversationalist. (Just ask any of her former boyfriends.)

Brenna scowled. "You told me once that it didn't make sense that the courtesan put on trial in London back in 1825 was *your* Ophelia Harrington. You said there was speculation, but no proof."

"I did say that."

"And you said there was some innuendo about Ophelia Harrington's having a mysterious past, but that nothing could be substantiated."

"And it never was," Piper said. "Not until about seven o'clock Friday evening, when I bit a pen in half, broke my glasses, and tripped over Ophelia Harrington's travel trunk, and out fell diaries that had been stuffed in a false bottom for the last one hundred and eighty-seven years."

Brenna sucked in air. Ever so carefully, she extended her hand and returned the document to the coffee table, almost as if she feared the pages would break. "Where are the originals?" she whispered.

"Locked away in the BMCS climate-controlled document room, buried in Ophelia's household accounts."

Brenna scrunched up her mouth. "Her accounts? You mean with, like, her grocery lists?"

Piper smiled. "Exactly. 'Stop by the butcher. Swing by the greengrocer. Fuck Lord Wellington's brains out after tea.'"

Brenna smiled softly, then nodded while she thought over the situation. "You know you've hit the mother lode, right?"

Piper smiled back. "I'm aware of that."

"Who else have you told?"

"Not a damn soul."

"Probably a wise move."

It went without saying that Brenna was a brilliant woman. Only brilliant women were full professors in Harvard's Department of Sociology by the age of thirty-four. So when her eyes shot over to the copy machine and back to Piper without missing a beat, Piper knew she'd figured everything out.

"You brought the journals home, didn't you? You copied them here in secret instead of at the museum."

Piper nodded, half expecting a reprimand.

But Brenna laughed. Not only did she laugh, she grabbed Piper's ink-stained hands in her own and screeched like a kid. "You broke the rules!" she shouted. "Hot damn! Piper Chase-Pierpont colored outside the lines!"

Piper laughed along but ended up yawning. The exhaustion was impossible to suppress.

Brenna's worried expression returned. "You haven't slept since Friday, I bet."

"Not much, no."

Brenna dropped Piper's hands and snatched Volume One from the coffee table and began leafing through the pages, stopping to read a passage here and there. She tapped a finger at all the handwritten notes along the margins. "You've done about a month's work in three days."

"Yeah, tell me about it. Would you like some iced tea or something?"

Suddenly, Brenna's hand slapped down on Piper's forearm. She dug her fingers into Piper's flesh the way she used to do in the front row of Mick Malloy's ethnoarchaeology class.

"Holy porno, Batman," she mumbled, not removing her eyes from the page. "This shit is flaming hot! It's like a two-hundred-year-old guide to releasing your inner harlot!"

Brenna jumped from the couch and began to pace, Miss Meade eyeing her from her perch on the back of the Queen Anne chair, tail swishing. Piper watched, too, as Brenna quickly skimmed over the document, gasping at one point. She glanced at Piper, her eyes narrowed.

"The Seven Sins of the Courtesan?" she asked, flipping through the pages again. "Lust, Appetite, Idleness, Covetousness, yadda-yadda?" She looked up at Piper, amazement in her expression. "And she does all this with a dude who never takes off his mask and who tells her to call him '*Sir*'?"

Piper giggled.

Brenna's mouth fell open momentarily. Then it snapped shut. When she spoke, it was with the cadence of a sexologist. "What you've got here is a brilliant example of nineteenth-century Western European *kink*."

Piper nodded. "Yeah. It's pretty over the top."

"It's *The Story of O-phelia*!"

Piper smiled. "I guess it is."

"This is like finding out that Susan B. Anthony dropped some acid with Jimi Hendrix at Woodstock."

Piper laughed loudly.

"But I still don't get the name," Brenna said, scowling. Piper could tell her mental engine had just gone from zero to sixty. "How could she be the unmarried Ophelia Harrington on trial in England and the married matron Ophelia Harrington in Boston? Did she keep her name? That was unheard-of then! Impossible!"

"It's complicated," Piper said.

"And does she ever discover her tutor's identity?" Brenna held the copied journal out to the side of her body and glared at it. "Does Sir ever ditch the mask?"

Piper knew her friend well. She knew that among Brenna's most violent pet peeves were people who revealed the ending of a book or movie before she'd had a chance to experience it for herself. In fact, Piper recalled how Brenna had once broken off a perfectly lovely two-year relationship because the man let slip that Dumbledore died at the end of the sixth Harry Potter book.

"Let's do it this way," Piper said, rising from the couch. "You read Volume One in its entirety. When you're done, tell me if you want me to cut to the chase for you or if you'd rather take the ride yourself."

Brenna's eyes flicked toward the coffee table.

"It's a great ride, by the way," Piper added.

"Fine. Don't tell me how it ends." Brenna stared at Piper again. "But what was the second thing? You said a *couple* things happened back-to-back that left you shaken up. I'm assuming the diaries are one thing, so what's the other?"

"Ah," Piper said. She glanced longingly toward her bedroom, knowing it would be hours before she could retreat to the refuge of her cool cotton sheets. She made sure her voice sounded far more perky than she felt. "I ran into somebody interesting today at work, is all. I'm going to make a pot of coffee. Want some?"

Piper headed into the kitchen. Brenna followed on her heels.

"Really? Who?"

She turned to face her friend, remembering how wonderful Brenna had been that night so long ago, after Piper's failure to seduce. Brenna had held her hand as she cried.

She'd even held her head over the commode as she heaved up the remnants of seven glasses of cheap Chardonnay.

Clearly, Brenna deserved to know that the man solely responsible for Piper's decade-long dating drought was suddenly, horrendously, back in her life.

Piper waved Brenna away and stepped into the kitchen. "I ran into Mick Malloy, okay? He's putting together a fundraising campaign for the museum. He'll be in town for six months."

Piper looked over her shoulder in time to see Brenna's mouth fall open. She said nothing.

"You can stop with the lecture," Piper said, taking coffee from the cabinet shelf.

Brenna remained silent.

"Stop making such a big deal of this!" Piper slammed the cabinet shut. "I'm over him! Completely over him! Sure, he destroyed whatever self-esteem I had at the time, but I'm totally over it."

Brenna blinked.

"Frankly, it took me a few minutes to even recognize the man today. Let's just say he hasn't aged well."

Piper poured water into the coffee maker. "Plus, he's probably let his fame go to his head. Another mediocre male intellect hiding behind a bloated ego! Great! Just what this town needs!"

Still, Brenna said nothing.

"And the answer to your question is no, his ass is no longer worthy of your top bottom spot."

Piper heard Brenna inhale sharply. She spun around to see her friend bite her lips closed.

"What?" Piper demanded. "Just say it."

Brenna began to speak but stopped herself.

"I shouldn't have even mentioned this to you," Piper snapped. "You're making way too big a deal of it." Piper grabbed the half-and-half from the refrigerator.

"Piper?" Brenna whispered.

"I know! I know!" Piper threw her hands into the air. "What am I going to do? Look at me! I'm totally *screwed!*"

Mick plopped down at the bar and watched Cullen fill the ice bin, noting that his older brother's hair was as thin as the Monday-night pub crowd. Mick shouted out his order for a pint of Murphy's and then laughed at the way Cullen raised his eyes, primed to deliver one of his cheerful obscenities.

"Get it yerself, you uppity dosser," Cullen said.

Mick laughed again as he got up and made his way down the bar, ducking under the flip-top. He grabbed a pint glass from the shelf and edged the Murphy's tap forward expertly, admiring the surge of liquid gold topped by a layer of foam. How many thousands of times had he seen his father perform this very ritual back in County Kerry, and then here in Boston?

Mick took a long sip of the cold, smooth Irish lager, eyeing his brother over the top of the glass.

"What's up, Magnus?" Cullen asked him, throwing a bar towel over his shoulder. "How was your first day at the Museum of Wealthy Dead Boston Protestants?"

Mick nearly spat out his mouthful of Murphy's.

"That good, eh?" His brother grinned. "Something to eat, man?"

Mick shook his head. "Nah. Thanks. Just wanted to stop by and see if you needed any help tonight."

Cullen let go with a loud guffaw, gesturing grandly at the dim interior of Malloy's Pub. The crowd—all three of them—glanced up nervously, fearing they were about to be tossed into the street by a daft pub owner. "I do believe I can fight back the throng me'self tonight," he said, exaggerating his accent.

Mick drained his pint and put the empty glass into the sink of suds. Despite Cullen's joking, he knew there was nothing funny about the bar's declining daily receipts. Cullen had taken out a second mortgage to pay off the medical bills after Da had passed two years before, but business had been so slow that he'd barely been making enough to cover the payments, let alone send his three kids to the parish Catholic school and keep his own modest household afloat.

Mick had a plan to ease some of his brother's burden, but he couldn't say a word to Cullen about it yet. He couldn't get his brother's hopes up unless the reality show was a done deal.

The agreement currently on the table would give Mick $25,000 an episode, with a promised run of sixteen episodes on the Compass Cable Network. The agent brokering the deal for Mick recommended he hold out for more, but Mick was ready to accept. No, *Digging for the Truth with Mick Malloy* wouldn't make him a billionaire, but it would generate more money than any Malloy on either side of the Atlantic had ever laid eyes on.

And Mick knew that whatever fame and fortune came his way was as much Cullen's doing as his own. Not once in the five years Da was sick did Cullen complain about taking care of him. Never once did Cullen point out that Mick was running all over kingdom come looking for treasures from the past while Cullen stayed put, ran the bar, and handled all the problems of the present—including caring for a demanding old man slowly dying of cancer.

Whenever Mick would try to help out financially, Cullen would tell him to put his money away. Whenever Mick would attempt to confess he felt guilty, Cullen would have none of it.

"Quit your daft tommyrot," Cullen always told him. "You're the only Malloy to ever have all those letters after his name, and you're feckin' going to put them to good use if I have anything to say about it."

The trick would be navigating his big brother's pride. Mick would have to find a way to make sharing his good fortune look like more of a collaboration than a handout. Mick made a mental note to enlist the help of Cullen's wife, Emily, when the time was right.

"So? Did you see her?" Cullen asked. "Your girl? That

piece of college fluff from all that while back. The one you mentioned worked at the museum."

Mick returned to his stool on the other side of the bar, confounded. He had only mentioned Piper to his brother once. Trust Cullen to make a big deal out of the smallest offhand comment.

His older brother leaned his elbows on the shiny mahogany bartop and peered into Mick's eyes. "So?"

Mick nodded. "Yeah, I saw her."

"And?" Cullen reached for a clean pint glass and was about to pour Mick another when he stopped him.

"No. No more for me. I gotta go."

"Bwaah!" Cullen barked. "Hot date?"

"You're insane," Mick told him. "You've got this completely arseways. She was a friend. A student of mine. That's it. Nothing ever happened between us."

"A shame," Cullen said, shaking his head. "Turned out to be a real loosebit, eh?"

Mick ignored that comment. Cullen was fiercely loyal to his wife and family, went to mass every Sunday, and worked like a demon. But when it came to the fairer sex, he'd never been the world's most evolved man. Back when Mick was in primary school and Cullen was preparing for his senior leaving certificate, Mick had already been indoctrinated to his big brother's philosophy on females. In Cullen's mind, there were two kinds of women—saints and *hoors*—without much gray area between.

"She's a brilliant academic and a good person," Mick replied, determined to get his point across without arguing with him.

Cullen gave Mick a sympathetic nod. "A face that could chase rats from a barn, eh?"

"Hear me out on this," Brenna said, her eyes pleading with Piper. She set her cup on Piper's coffee table and leaned forward.

"It's ridiculous," Piper said, shaking her head.

"No, *fate* is what it is," Brenna said. "Would you just think about this for a second? You literally *trip* over these diaries, uncovering what is basically a two-hundred-year-old instruction manual for vixens, and then, *bam*! Out of nowhere, Mick Malloy walks back into your life, the only man you've ever really wanted, the man you've never been able to forget."

"The man who humiliated me," Piper said with mock enthusiasm. "The man who got one look at me naked and ran away like the place had just been gassed."

"But—"

"Mick has nothing to do with the diaries. The two events aren't even remotely connected." Piper stood from the couch and reached for Brenna's coffee cup. "Would you like—"

"No more coffee! No more pretending you don't understand what I'm telling you!" Brenna squeezed Piper's wrist. *"Please,"* she said, her voice softer. "I'm sorry to be obnoxious about this, but I think the universe is trying to tell you something. You need to pay attention."

Piper froze. She stared down into her friend's sincere expression. Maybe finding the diaries and seeing Mick again for the first time in a decade were somehow tied together, but what Brenna was proposing was absolute lunacy.

Ophelia Harrington's journals were not a self-help workbook. They were a valuable firsthand account of a woman's life from another time and place, one that had nothing in common with Piper's.

Ophelia had been a glittering courtesan. Piper was a dumpy curator. Two women couldn't *be* more different!

"Sit. Just sit down and listen. Please." Brenna pulled on Piper's wrist.

Piper groaned in protest as her butt hit the sofa cushions.

"Okay. Let's look at this objectively." Brenna flipped through the first volume again before she locked her eyes on Piper's. "Ophelia was miserable. She was expected to marry a man she didn't love. She was expected to dress in a certain way and think, speak, and behave in a particular manner. She felt trapped. She wanted something more for herself, something larger."

Piper raised an eyebrow. "Are you implying that I'm like Ophelia?"

"Not really," Brenna said, her eyes suddenly quite somber. "Ophelia had limits placed on her by society. They came from outside herself. But you—"

"Me *what*?"

"Granted, your parents have played a role, but for the most part, you limit yourself, Piper. You've always been the one holding yourself back."

Piper felt her jaw unhinge. Brenna had never spoken this way to her before. Sure, she'd hinted along these lines in the many years they'd been friends, but it was as if she'd always been careful not to judge Piper's lifestyle choices. It wouldn't have been fair, after all. Brenna was glamorous. Men threw themselves at her. Piper was . . . *generic*. Men didn't know she existed.

"That's harsh," Piper said, crossing her arms over her chest defensively.

"Sweetie, that's just half of it." Brenna's voice was softer now. She reached out and stroked Piper's shoulder. "I've known you a long time, and here's the real shame—you have no idea what's waiting for you, what you've been missing, because you've been too scared to find out."

Piper felt her face go hot. "Excuse me?"

"You're hiding, Piper. You don't want a man to see how lovely you are. You make no effort to showcase your beauty."

That made Piper laugh. "Showcase? What am I—an ancient Peruvian wedding vase? A Cadillac Seville?"

Brenna shook her head, looking quite serious. "You're hiding behind your incredibly large brain, Piper. You always have. Your intellect is your armor. And frankly, your choice of clothes and shoes seal the deal. You might as well wear a sandwich board that reads, MOVE ALONG—NOTHING TO SEE HERE."

Piper scowled. "There is nothing wrong with my shoes. They support my natural arch."

Brenna didn't take the bait. Instead, she eyed Piper up and down. "And that dress you're wearing looks like it should have the words YUKON GOLD stamped on the front."

"Oh, really?" Piper tightened her crossed arms. "Well, at least I can sleep at night knowing it wasn't manufactured in some Bangladeshi sweatshop by a starving grandmother earning slave wages."

Brenna glared at her. "It's possible to be globally aware and dress well at the same time."

Piper didn't reply. This argument was pointless.

Brenna sighed. "So here's the deal, Piper. From what I can tell from this first volume, it looks like Ophelia had a mentor, a woman she trusted to help her get where she wanted to go."

"The Swan."

"Yes. She was a successful courtesan living the life Ophelia wanted. The Swan was elegant, independent, beautiful, and, from what I've seen of her, damn smart." Brenna patted the stack of copied pages in her lap.

"What are you proposing?"

Brenna tipped her head and smiled softly. "I don't want to be unkind."

"Too late," Piper snapped.

"I just want you to be happy, sweetie," Brenna said. "And you're not."

That was it. Piper had had enough. "Let yourself out," she said, jumping from the sofa. She bolted toward her bedroom and slammed the door behind her.

Four

Piper hurled herself face-first onto the bedspread and growled her rage into the mattress. Who the hell did Brenna think she was? She'd *thought* Brenna was her friend! But what kind of friend intentionally hurts you like that? Brenna had no right to force her to confront the truth about her life. It was *her* life! She could live it however she wished—in denial, in fear, in hiding—or in a potato sack!

Or not at all!

There was a knock at the door.

"Go away!" Piper moaned into the bedspread.

"I just want to read you something."

"No." Piper raised her head. "Leave me alone! I don't want to be some kind of science experiment!"

"It's from Volume Two," Brenna said.

"Whatever it is, I've read it a million times. Now go!"

"But have you ever really listened to it? Do you get what Ophelia is telling you?"

"She's not telling me anything!" Piper yelled. "She's dead!"

"Fine. But when this girl was alive, she was *alive*."

Piper grabbed a tissue from her nightstand and blew her nose. Brenna must have misinterpreted this act of personal hygiene for her cue, because she began to read.

I walked boldly in the new flesh born from Sir's wicked lessons, and my every motion captivated the men around me. I felt sensually naked in my revealing gown, yet the power of my laugh, of my smile, of the way I stroked my fingers artfully down my neck intoxicated me!

Piper shut her eyes. "Oh, for the love of God," she mumbled.

Brenna continued.

I had expanded into every inch of my flesh, inhabiting my entire body, mind and soul. I was now deliciously familiar with every inch of my skin. The walls around my most secret thoughts had been stormed and I knew my own darkness and felt no shame. I answered to no one and nothing but my own dreams and desires and wildest fantasies.

Piper stood up. She sniffed. She took a few steps toward her closed bedroom door.

I could scarcely remember the girl who had locked herself away in fear. I was now the artist of my own fate and I would paint it in blinding colors. The Blackbird had wings. Poor naïve, powerless Ophelia Harrington was no more.
   I did not miss her.

Piper flung open the door. When she spoke, she heard her voice shake with anger. "You want me to enroll in the Ophelia Harrington School for Sluts, where you'll be the Swan to my Blackbird? Is Mick going to be my Sir?"

Brenna pursed her lips. "The advice in these journals is timeless, Piper. The human spirit—not to mention the human sexual response—hasn't changed much in two hundred years. What worked for Ophelia in 1813 will work for you today."

"What are you suggesting?"

"I'm suggesting that you use this volume as a guide to self-discovery, and if you manage to learn a little something about how to seduce Mick Malloy along the way, then hey—great. Though I have no idea where a girl can get a peacock feather in this town." Brenna smiled.

Piper didn't find it amusing.

"We'll take a two-pronged approach," Brenna said, grasping Piper's hand and dragging her back to the sofa. She patted the cushion and got them settled. "The Seven Sins of the Courtesan will become the guidebook for exploring your inner sexuality. I'll handle your outer metamorphosis. You'll find that one will facilitate the other."

Piper laughed bitterly. "What, you're going to give me pop quizzes in the morning and let me borrow your slinky dresses at night? How about your high-heeled boots that do nothing but cut off the blood to your toes?"

Brenna shook her head soberly. "Your feet are too small for my boots and your ta-tas would pop the seams on my dresses."

Piper blinked in surprise. Her feet were daintier than Brenna's? Her body was more voluptuous? But how could that be?

"I can help you if you'll let me. Hair, makeup, fashion— *attitude!*" Brenna smiled. "God, Piper! For ten years now I've been dying to do this, but I never thought the time was right or that you'd be even slightly open to the idea. Until right this second."

Piper sat frozen on the sofa, her chest flooding with heat and her limbs tingling with life. Everything Brenna had said was true. Piper had been in hiding. She'd been afraid of what she might find, how she might be forced to face who she was deep down—a sexual being, a woman who really, really wanted a man. But not just any man. She wanted Mick Malloy. She always had.

And now she was turning thirty.

Fine. Fine. *Fine!* She was open to the idea. She admitted it. Ophelia Harrington's diaries had kicked down the padlocked door to that part of her, and when the door opened, Mick stood waiting. Brenna was merely offering to drag her over the threshold.

"We'll take it slow," her best friend said, smiling. "If anything makes you uncomfortable, we'll adjust the plan."

Piper squinted at her. "You already have a plan? It's barely been an hour."

Brenna laughed. "I've had a plan from the first day I met you."

"I feel cheap."

Both of them burst out laughing, and Brenna brought her forehead to Piper's. They smiled at each other.

"We'll start tomorrow."

"I have to work tomorrow."

"Maybe you've got a horrible case of salmonella."

"Maybe botulism."

"No! Ink poisoning. We don't even have to lie!"

They laughed louder, then Piper felt herself collapse into Brenna's arms, where she began to sniffle.

"It's going to be okay, Pipes," Brenna whispered.

Piper nodded through her tear-damp hiccups.

"But here's the thing." Brenna gently pushed Piper away to gaze seriously into her face. "Once you know what's possible for you, you can never go into hiding again. So you have to be sure."

Piper's spine straightened. Those were the exact words Sir had spoken to the Blackbird, just before he patted her bottom and sent her out into the world.

She took a huge breath and pointed her chin high. She hiccupped just once more. It was the strangest thing, but it felt as if Ophelia herself were whispering the words needed directly into her ear.

"I know what I want," Piper said. "I want to start living."

It took another couple hours to get Brenna out of her

apartment, but the two of them had accomplished quite a bit in that time. First, Piper e-mailed in sick for the rest of the week. Then Brenna began calling in favors from adoring men in a variety of disciplines—hair stylists, dermatologists, personal shoppers, dentists, and ophthalmologists. Before she knew it, Piper had her whole week of vixenification mapped out for her. If what Brenna said were true, she would emerge from her cocoon next week, not a Blackbird, but a butterfly.

Eventually, Piper found herself tucked in between her sheets, Miss Meade curled into a ball at her ankles. As exhausted as she was, she was aware of something tugging at her mind. It was the memory of something Ophelia had written. Piper knew she had to read it once more before she fell asleep.

She wouldn't lie to herself. This had nothing to do with scholarship and everything to do with preparing herself for what lay ahead.

Piper found the passage almost immediately.

I felt the bindings of my life slip away. My body grew light and my pulse quickened. I breathed as if I had never breathed before.

The dizzying expanse of a limitless future stretched before me. The possibilities, the pitfalls, the delights and the dangers. I cannot do it, I thought. I am afraid. I am weak. I will not survive fluttering on the tip of a limb in the midst of a storm.

Then it struck me that although it was possible that I might perish in the wild ride upon the winds of change, it was a dead surety that I would expire sooner in my sheltered cage.

Without having had nearly as much fun.

Five

London, 1813
In the odiously decorated dining room
of my odious relations

I, Ophelia Harrington, am not usually an impulsive person. In fact, I pride myself on my logic and forethought.

All of which made it very difficult to understand why I'd just thrown a platter of beef across the dining room.

Every person present, both those at the table and those serving them, stood frozen in shock at my actions. Every eye followed the brown, oily juices as they dripped down over the patterned wallpaper. One last slice of beef, more stubborn than the rest, finally gave up its grip. It slithered down the wall to join the others now jumbled on the floor amid the shards of blue-patterned china.

That was going to leave a stain.

I bit my lower lip, trying to keep the hysterical laughter hidden deep where it belonged. Then, pair by pair, all eyes turned back to stare at me. The giddy explosion of absurdity faded, leaving me with nothing in my belly but fury and a little nauseous regret.

I lifted my chin and gazed back at my aunt and uncle. Uncle Webster's jowly face was growing redder by the moment. He tossed his napkin down onto his plate in disgust. "Ungrateful girl!" He stood, then turned his glare upon his wife. "She's your responsibility. You talk some sense into her! I'm going to my club, where the food stays on the table and not on the bloody wall!"

With a last growl at the forlorn pile of juicy rare beef on the carpet, Uncle Webster strode from the room.

Aunt Beryl fixed me with a baleful gaze. "Idiot child!"

I folded my shaking hands before me and tried to keep my fair skin from blushing with shame. It was no use, of course, but I refused to give my flaming cheeks any notice.

"Aunt, I am not a child. I am eighteen and I am legally allowed to choose my own husband." *Or not at all,* but best not to say that out loud. Boiled potatoes might not be much of a dinner without the beef, but they would make handy projectiles and I had never seen my aunt so enraged.

Her cold eyes narrowed. "You are our ward. You will do as you are told and you will wed Lord Malcolm Ashford!"

"But I do not know him!"

My aunt waved a hand in dismissal. "Everyone knows him. He's rich and well-born and his holdings will turn your uncle's business prospects around by summer's end!"

The truth was out. My belly chilled at that pragmatic reasoning. There would be no appealing to my guardians' finer feelings, not where Uncle Webster's business was involved. My uncle liked to think of himself as a gentleman, but he had invested every penny of his expectations in trade, hoping to make himself wealthy as well. Aunt Beryl kept a fine and impressive home, at least to the outside observer, but she ran it on a narrow budget. Her industry would have been admirable if not for the fact that it was spent entirely on keeping up appearances in Society. Furthermore, she and Uncle Webster were unkind and exacting employers who paid their staff late if at all.

It was probably a good thing that my own small inheritance was untouchable by anyone but myself.

Unless I wed. In which case it would of course become the property of my husband.

But if this suitor was so very wealthy, what did he need

with my poor little six hundred pounds? That would scarcely run a grand house for a year!

"Aunt, don't you think I should at least meet him first? After all, I am English, not some daughter of India! No one here weds sight unseen!"

Aunt Beryl, who couldn't find India on a map, scowled blackly. She did not appreciate having her ignorance pointed out to her.

I worried. My relatives were not highly educated people, at least not by my standards. They knew nothing of the world past their social ambitions and the acquisition of wealth. There was no philosophy spoken in these halls, nor any intellectual conversation at all! Gossip and trade were the only approved topics, and neither interested me whatsoever.

How could they ever understand that I had dreams of a much larger sort of life?

Later that evening, having locked myself away in my room, I dug out my hidden trove of sweets for my dinner. However, I could scarcely touch them for the roiling in my belly.

Instead, I paced my chamber in fury and the beginnings of serious fear. Could I truly be so helpless? I had never thought of myself so, yet in this new world, my world since the passing of my beloved parents two years past, I was no one. I had a pretty face and a figure somewhat more bountiful than was fashionable. My mind meant nothing in the ranking of my value.

So this was all that I was to them, a commodity in their hands, a mere offering to be sacrificed on the altar of their social greed.

I ached for my parents, for the love and support and respect I had always known.

They were not here. They would never be here again. I was entirely alone.

"A commitment once made cannot be broken, sir!"

The gruff voice from down on the lawn drew me to my window. Bracing my hands upon the sill, I leaned as far out as I could. Below me, on the walk up to the steps of the house, I could see a man, large and looming, facing down my shorter, stouter uncle.

The stranger continued, his tone arch and scathing. Although his hat shielded his features, I hated him quite completely for his voice alone. "I do not understand your difficulty, Harrington. I made careful selection based on appearance and associations. I told you what I wanted. You promised to deliver her, willing and happy, to my hand. I have already spoken to the bishop. I was prepared to post the banns in a matter of weeks!"

My breath left me. Weeks?

"You have to give us more time!" Uncle Webster insisted. "The girl will soon come around. I shall make sure of it!"

That voice again, clipped and scornful: "Can you not keep your own house, sir? I must wonder at your inability to manage such a simple transaction."

I closed my eyes against the blow. *Transaction.*

If I had held any romantic hope that this fellow actually loved me from afar, this cleared up that little misconception quite nicely. I was a purchase. I was a horse added to his stables, a painting added to his gallery. I was a thing, to be bought and sold.

There were more words between them but with their voices lowered in more peaceful consultation, I could not hear them, no matter how I dangled my upper body from the window. Agreeing on the price, perhaps? Asking for the groom to check my teeth? Would I be weighed and measured, placed on the scales opposite a pile of gold?

Helpless fury overwhelmed me. I ought not to be in this position! My parents would be appalled and revolted if they lived. Of course, if they lived, then I would not reside in this house with these people who thought I should behave like an ordinary girl.

I knew what my relations wanted of me, but I had not been brought up to be obedient and unthinking. My mother, an unrepentant bluestocking, had wed quite late to a quiet bookish man, a philosopher and scholar, who found her unconventional notions delightful and stimulating. I was raised on freedom of thought and lively debate. If I wished to refuse my supper and only eat my cake, I might be allowed if I was able to put forth a case convincing enough to either make my parents laugh or even to begin a discussion between them so distracting that they took no notice of my sugar-coated fingertips.

Perhaps it was no mystery that my relatives found me to be foreign and bizarre. Now, alone in my room, alone in my heart, even I wavered. I did not fit in to this world. I did not understand why I should hide behind my fan. I could not conceive of shutting my lips and closing my mind.

Perhaps there was something wrong with me, not with them. I seemed to be the only one who did not wish to play by these rules . . .

Or was I?

There were women in the world, beautiful, elegant creatures who slipped through the rigid stratifications of Society like silk-clad wraiths. They had no husbands, no fathers, no high-handed uncles who sought to twist their lives into restrictive knots.

The first time I ever saw the Swan was at Mrs. H——'s musicale. It was quite an eclectic gathering, daringly including those who were rising in Society as well as those who fell just a bit outside it. To welcome a notorious courtesan to one's home was entirely outré.

I'd wager that half the women there wished they'd thought of it first.

The other half were violently offended. Mrs. H—— is a patroness of the arts and quite influential in certain circles, and so Aunt Beryl dared not offend her by insulting one of her guests. It was only I who was subjected to Aunt Beryl's vitriolic opinions.

"Filthy, abandoned creature" was the mildest of those insults. "Untamed independent" and "ungoverned wanton" only piqued my interest at the time.

Hereby came my conviction that Aunt Beryl was something of an imbecile, for it was quite obvious to me that the Swan was everything that was elegant and gracious. She swept into the room, tall and golden and smiling so sweetly that I could not help but smile back, though she beamed her charm indiscriminately about the room.

The whispers ran about the perimeter of the hall, scurrying like vermin, carried mouth to ear, but the Swan smiled as if she heard none of it and held out her gloved hand to greet the soprano who had so entertained us.

The Swan had beautiful features, of course, but it was more than mere symmetry and hair of gold that fixed everyone's attention so. She moved through the room with the confidence of a duchess, surely knowing that men admired and desired her even as their wives admired and despised her.

And envied her.

But perhaps that was only me.

It simply seemed to my eyes that the Swan had a rather marvelous existence. She was cosseted and spoiled and adored as much as any cherished bride, but if the love grew stale or the man became unbearable—as I was beginning to suspect that many men did, in time—then the Swan was free to sail as grandly out the door as she had sailed in.

The Swan was a woman with *options*.

If only I could be like her.

I wrapped my shawl about my shoulders and sat in my open window, gazing unseeing into the deepening night. It was very late but the chill kept me awake. There was a notion swirling in my mind and I wished to capture it and make it hold still for examination.

No matter how I argued and pleaded, I knew I could not win against my relatives' determination. Their self-interest far outweighed any sense of responsibility to me. In fact, they likely felt they were indeed charting the correct course for my future.

Merely fleeing would serve no purpose. I had no refuge but this one. I had no doubt that I would soon be found and brought back in disgrace, bound for a convent or a sanitarium, a common end for girls who refused to conform. My mother had railed against such practices enough times for me to have a depressingly realistic vision of such a future.

Therefore, my rebellion must be extreme. It must shatter all ties. It must be so scandalous, so entirely and completely unacceptable, that my aunt and uncle would rather touch a hot coal than associate themselves with me.

I lifted my gaze to the sky, though the stars were hidden behind the sooty London clouds. "If I am to be bought and sold," I whispered to the sky, "then I should profit from the *transaction*. I should be the merchant and the banker, as well as the livestock."

I have never been one to dawdle once having made a decision, so I began to put my plan into motion the very next day.

All of Society knew that the Swan wore only the most beautiful gowns. Since it was widely understood that the most beautiful gowns were those crafted by the great Lementeur, I knew that I might find the wearer of such gowns by attending her dressmaker.

Lementeur kept a very exclusive shop on the Strand. It was discreetly announced by a sign containing only a scripted, flowing *L*. It might as well have been heralded by a military brass band, for there was not a woman in London who did not sigh upon passing the mysterious entrance to the most elite arbiter of style in all of England.

That next afternoon, I lingered across the road with my aunt's maid, Sylla. I had been allowed out of the house due to the realistic tenor of my heartfelt and sincere apologies to my relations. Once I had explained my childish qualms at being worthy of such an overwhelming honor and profusely thanked them for their most industrious efforts on my be-half, I was given back my freedom. I was even, as long as I was accompanied, permitted to venture to the Strand in or-der to peruse the shop windows. After all, I had to acquaint myself with the costly accoutrements that would soon be part of my new, glorious existence as Lady Ashford.

I daresay that my aunt and uncle thought I was quite mad, but they were far too interested in their own advance-ment to question my motives in changing my mind. They simply went on planning the wedding that they had never canceled.

For my part, I pled shyness and maidenly nerves and hoped to avoid meeting with Lord Malcolm even once.

This did not prevent him from showering me with costly gifts. The first day was velvet, in the form of a cloak that swept the floor with the length of it but was so fine that it weighed quite perfectly for a summer evening.

I gave it to Sylla.

Aunt Beryl discovered my deed and forced poor Sylla to give it back. How the cloak ended up in the coal chute I'm sure I don't know.

Sylla was scarcely older than I, so I contented her with a lemon ice and the bribe of my pink-trimmed bonnet if she did not convey my doings to Aunt Beryl.

Now Sylla, who bore no personal love for my exacting aunt, accepted the bribe with glee and settled into a door-way with her ice.

I had feared it might take days or even weeks to catch sight of my prey, yet we had scarcely loitered an hour before a very distinctive carriage pulled to a stop before the bou-tique entrance. Who but the notorious Swan would ride about town in a dainty white-lacquered carriage emblazoned with a graceful golden swan upon the door? I was in awe at the flagrant lack of discretion. The Swan was a woman after my own heart.

I fear I followed her directly into the shop, like a hound upon her heels. The elegant fellow who held the door gazed at me curiously but I merely lifted my chin and strode into the establishment as if I had every right to be there. The Swan shot a single startled glance over her shoulder, then pointedly looked away from me.

Another pair of ladies stood in the elegant receiving room. They eyed the Swan with regal disdain, yet they did acknowledge her presence with cool nods. The Swan dipped a gracious but impenitent curtsy back. I copied her motion out of pure instinct and their narrowed gazes shot to me. The Swan stepped away from me and moved to the grand window, leaving me standing quite alone. Disregarding the watching ladies, I scurried after the Swan.

"Madam, I must speak with you," I whispered. "It is a matter of the direst urgency!"

She turned her shoulder to me and pretended to examine the draperies. Unwilling to admit defeat, I presumed to reach my hand to pluck at her sleeve. When I heard a hiss and then an astonished giggle from the elegant pair lingering in the receiving room, I saw the Swan twitch with annoyance.

Then I noted the twin blotches of color staining her elegant cheekbones and realized that I was wreaking some sort of damage to her graceful dignity. I thrust my hands behind my back and clenched them there, but I did not move from her side.

The beautiful boy returned and bowed the other ladies from the chamber and into their ostentatious carriage outside. When he returned, he began to approach us. I glared him away with every ounce of desperation I possessed. I can be quite intimidating when I choose to be, though I stand less than five and one half feet. His eyes widened and his gaze flicked between myself and the Swan. I added a scowl from my arsenal. His eyes narrowed and his suspicion grew very apparent, but he turned to retire into another chamber.

The moment he disappeared, the Swan turned to me with her blue eyes blazing with fury. Beautifully, of course.

"What is the meaning of this?" she hissed. "Who are you?"

I had prepared quite an earnest and poetic plea for this moment. However, in the urgency of my need, I quite forgot it. "I want to be a courtesan!" I blurted.

The Swan drew back in surprise. Despite my desperation, a part of my mind took the time to sigh over the perfect symmetry of her features, even when blank with shock. Admiration aside, however, I was never one to pass up someone else's silence.

"I am being forced to wed a loathsome fellow," I continued, my words firing at her like bullets. "I have no recourse but complete ruination!"

She narrowed her gaze at me. "Then go ruin yourself on some hapless horse groom and leave me out of it." She began to turn away.

I grabbed her hand in desperation. "My relations would only conceal it and sell me off anyway! You have no idea of the power of their ambitions!"

She hesitated. "Sell you?"

I swallowed. "I am naught but a *transaction,*" I said bitterly. Though I was prepared to endow my performance with further theatrics, it turned out to be unnecessary. My voice broke down entirely as my throat closed tight. Hot tears threatened and I thought I might wish to vomit soon.

Until that moment I had hidden my true grief from even myself.

The Swan withdrew her hand gently from my grasp, but she did not turn away again. "This loathsome fellow—who is he?"

I wrapped my arms about my belly. Only with such firm support could I still my trembling enough to speak again. "I am to wed Lord Malcolm Ashford."

"Ah. Malcolm." Her brows rose and her lips pursed. "Loathsome, indeed." Her irony was not lost on me, even in my distracted state.

My chin rose defiantly. "I know he is considered a handsome catch, but he does not love me. He doesn't even know me. He likes my face and my lineage—"

The Swan's gaze roved over me. "I daresay that is not all he likes," she murmured.

I dismissed that notion with a toss of my head. "I do not wish to be some lord's plaything against my will, nor even his lady wife. I wish to live in my own way, to reside where I choose, to eat and drink and sleep where I choose!"

I heard another carriage roll to a stop before the shop. The Swan straightened. The cool distance returned to her expression. "While I might sympathize with your situation, I cannot help you. I should not even be speaking to a girl such as you!"

I shook my head. "I care nothing for my reputation," I cried.

The Swan flicked a glance toward the shop door. "I, however, care a great deal for *mine*. It would not do for the mamas of Society to suspect me of luring their daughters from their virtue."

I looked away, near tears. "I have no mama," I said. "I have only the keepers of the keys to my prison."

The young man, apparently having expected the carriage, strode through the room toward the door. The Swan moved as if to turn away from me before the new customer could enter. I clutched at her hand once more, for I truly had nothing to lose. Flagrant coercion seemed like the tiniest of sins.

"Please! You must help me! I have nowhere else to turn!"

"Let me go!" She tugged at her hand and glanced worriedly at the door.

"No! Let them see!" I was not my mother's daughter for nothing. "What will they think when I fall at your feet and beg at your hem?"

She paled. "You wouldn't!"

I bent my knees, prepared to wail away.

"Very well!" The Swan pulled away violently. "You may come to me tomorrow morning, early. You must come before the rest of Society begins to make calls." She took a calling card from her reticule and handed it to me.

"Thank you! Oh, thank you, Swan!" I wanted to embrace her, but feared alienating her entirely. I settled for smiling and, I confess, jumping up and down a bit.

Her eyes narrowed. "This is not agreement. This is merely permission to begin a discussion." She pressed her lips together. "Although I suspect I shall regret conceding even that much."

I nodded eagerly. "Yes, yes. Thank you!" With that, I let her slip away and allowed the handsome young man to show me from the shop. I left with my chin high, my heart flying.

I had won the first round. Everyone knew that the first round was the most important.

Except, of course, for the last.

Six

The Seven Delights of the Courtesan
The freedom to dance
To make music
To compose poetry
To paint
To contemplate literature
To converse
To perform
To delight oneself with one's own mind and soul.

Were it not for Sylla's discretion and heretofore unbeknownst talent for deceit, I should never have been able to make my way to the Mayfair home of the Swan without my aunt's interference. Aunt Beryl had decided that it was high time for me to begin planning my triumphant wedding celebration. I demurred, but she would not listen. On my prompting, it was Sylla who begged that I should be permitted to accompany her to visit the house of Baroness G——, who kept a cousin of Sylla's as one of her many maids.

Aunt Beryl immediately turned about and insisted that I wear my best day gown and take the carriage for our excursion, and to leave my calling card, though we visited a lowly maid, and most important of all, to be sure to drop the news of my impending marriage in the hearing of the baroness's butler.

I murmured my assent and slipped away before she could offer any further advice. Sylla and I giggled as we jolted away in the glossy but ill-hung carriage, giddy with our brief taste of freedom.

Someday soon, I hoped, that freedom would be a permanent flavor upon my tongue.

When my uncle's sullen driver pulled the carriage to a halt before the baroness's house, we hopped down before he stirred himself to open the door and waved him on his way. "We shall be hours inside," I told him breezily. "I have coin to hire a hack for the way home."

With an indifferent grunt, he nodded and drove away. When we turned, we saw that the baroness's door stood open and that a gaunt, supercilious fellow in livery regarded us suspiciously from the top step. I grabbed Sylla's hand and we fled, laughing like naughty children. The baroness would have to do without my intrusion today! I had no fear of discovery, for Aunt Beryl would never dare question her.

The Swan lived a scant few blocks and a million degrees of Society away. Even I knew that outside the streets and squares of the elite lay the small, intimate corners of the demimonde. Her home was every bit as luxurious as the baroness's and quite a bit more tasteful, I imagined.

The Swan's housekeeper led us to sit in a very pretty parlor done up in the colors of ivory and palest periwinkle. I thought to myself that if I ever had a home of my own, I should like it to be exactly like the Swan's. With a few more cushions and a dash of brighter color, of course.

The Swan met us there in a matter of moments. After greeting us graciously, if coolly, she sent the housekeeper away to prepare a tea tray and directed Sylla to await me in the kitchens if she liked.

Sylla glanced at me and I nodded. When she was gone, the Swan seated herself across from me and regarded me with cynical appreciation. "I did not expect you to come."

I felt as though I had passed some sort of test. "I mean what I say, madam—er, miss . . ."

"I fancy 'Your Grace,' myself," the Swan said dryly.

I raised a brow. "Why not ride full canter? Why not 'Your Highness'?"

Her cool reserve faltered as her lips twitched. I knew then that the relentlessly elegant woman before me possessed that most prized of virtues—a sense of humor.

She sat back then, lounging with feline grace upon her sofa. "I allowed you here to plead your case," she reminded me. "Go on, then. Convince me."

I took a deep breath and recounted every single rationale that had brought me to her parlor. I wished independence, freedom, a life of my choosing, a destiny of my own.

At length, she held up a hand. "You are forgetting something," she told me.

I reconsidered every reason and argument I had prepared for this moment. Yes, I had expressed them all.

The Swan smiled softly at my confusion. "My dear little girl, what of love?"

I frankly gaped, I fear to say. "Love?"

She laughed outright then and the exquisite illusion shattered. I realized at that moment that the Swan was no more than a few short years older than myself.

"You might be missing the point, just a bit," she said, still chuckling. "Or am I mistaken? You do wish to become a courtesan?"

I frowned, blinking at her. "But men pay you for sexual favors. What has love to do with such a cold contract?"

She twinkled at me. "Done properly, there is naught cold about it. In fact, my lover finds me quite warm, indeed."

"But you are a prost—"

Her hand came up as quickly as a slap, but she simply held it before me, palm outward. "That word has nothing to do with me. A courtesan is not a commodity, she is an artist of love."

I lifted my chin. "I do not believe in love."

Relaxing back into her lazy sophistication, the Swan smiled benevolently at me. "Ah, but love believes in you, little girl."

"I am not a child." I bridled. "I am eighteen years of age."

"Ah, you are practically a spinster. Perhaps you had best take that loathsome gentleman up on his offer before you shrivel away."

Her teasing did not upset me for nothing could deter me from my course. "I have every intention of taking a lover as required," I told her. "I simply wish a straightforward business arrangement."

She leaned forward then, completely serious. "You are an ignorant snippet from an ignorant world, so I will not throw you from my house. However, if you call me a prostitute one more time I shall strangle you with your own prissy little bonnet strings! Have I made myself perfectly clear?"

I felt those ice-blue eyes burning me, so I put my cup down and returned the Swan's gaze. "Are you rethinking your decision to help me?"

She didn't smile or avert her intense gaze. I began to feel a bit nervous. I had thought myself becoming inured to her eerie beauty, but sitting in silence before her now, I rather felt as though I were being judged by a Faerie Court. Still, stubbornness might be thought a flaw in Society, but it had always served me well. I raised my chin and held that gaze with my spine straight.

And waited.

I felt a small flash of triumph when she finally broke, looking down to stir her tea with a silvery ringing of the spoon against the china. I had no idea what I had won from her. A modicum of respect, perhaps? At the very least, when she looked back up at me it was with a smile. It was nothing like her regal benevolence of before, but more like the shy smile of a young girl who thinks she might have found a friend.

"You are a most unusual girl, Miss Harrington."

I dared a saucy grin. "You are not but three years my senior, my dear Swan."

Her smile widened. "I certainly strive to make everyone think so." Then she tilted her head as she gazed at me. "Why are you doing this? I know you wish independence, but *why*? You could stay the course you're on and all the world would envy your good fortune."

I had known the question would come but I felt helpless before the pressure of my feelings. "I cannot explain it. It is as . . . as if my skin is too small for my spirit. I feel as though I must be free or I should explode! Or worse, shrivel day by day until I disappear. Both ends terrify me more than notoriety or scandal."

She raised a brow. "Perhaps because you have never experienced such things. You have no idea what it is like to be rejected by your peers."

I gave a short laugh. "I have no idea what it is like to be accepted by my peers. I have ever been the oddity, the ill-fit piece to the puzzle. I wear a red rose in my hair when the other girls wear white ones. I think too much, I say too little . . . except for now, apparently. With you I seem to have no trouble speaking my mind with ease."

"As opposed to?"

I shrugged. "As opposed to speaking my mind and causing chaos."

She gave a secret little smile. "Hmm. Chaos. One of my favorite flavors."

"Really?" I asked faintly. "I prefer mayhem myself."

Her lips quirked. "You would." She lifted her gaze and stared thoughtfully at some point over my shoulder. After a moment, she smiled slightly and shook her head. "I have no doubt whatsoever that I shall live to regret this but . . . it is time for your lessons to begin."

I felt my heart give a leap of fear, yet I was equally thrilled. My pleas were to be granted.

I would be a courtesan.

I watched the Swan stand and move gracefully to the door. "If you will come with me?"

She led me to a room filled with books, a sense of

masculine comfort, and the lingering scent of pipe tobacco. The deep blue of the wallpaper and the subtle glow of dark polished wood turned the Swan's pale beauty into something ethereal. She was a shimmering pearl in the deep blue sea of the room. A man sitting in the wing-back chair, reading a book and smoking his pipe, would surely find his eye and his attention completely arrested by her.

"He cannot help but watch your every move in this room."

The Swan turned to me with a single elegant brow raised high. "Very good. Most people would not notice the purposeful nature of the décor. You get high marks for observation, little bird."

I bowed my head in gratitude, only a little facetiously. "Thank you, O Sage."

She snorted. Yes, the Swan actually snorted. The smile that broke across my face was as wide as the Thames. How delightful to find a playfellow beneath that façade of dreamy perfection.

On impulse, I took her hand in mine.

"Thank you."

She eyed me for a long moment. "I wonder if you will still thank me in five years?"

Then she seemed to shake off that strange melancholy and led me to a side table where a brandy snifter awaited. "First, you must understand a man's taste in fine liquor . . ."

To have a man's hands upon you, his mouth moist and gentle on your skin, the feel and weight and heat of him there for your pleasure, even as you are there for his . . . there is naught so beautiful as skillful, gracious love.

When I appeared at the Swan's house every morning while Society still slept off the excess of the night before, she would greet me with fond resignation.

I quite pestered her with questions about her life and her

world, and the more I learned of the Art of Love, the more I wished to experience it myself. The way she described it was both frank and lyrical. I had never thought of men much beyond admiring the fellows pacing their Thoroughbreds in the park, but each thing I learned about their bodies and their needs inflamed my curiosity further.

And the stories of the physical pleasure I might someday experience! My imagination was afire, along with other portions of my anatomy. Such awareness of my own potential left me restless and susceptible to every sensation. Even the slide of warm water over my skin in the bath seemed new and delicious.

Everything she told me, I committed to memory. I have ever been an excellent student!

On this particular morning, a week into my lessons with the Swan, I informed my relatives of a last-minute fitting at the dressmaker's, so they sent me on my way with only Sylla at my side. We giggled like schoolgirls as we made our escape.

Sylla had taken a fancy to the Swan's young footman, Jessup, so it was not difficult to shoo her from the parlor as the Swan and I sat down to tea.

At first, she spoke of the freedom of her life, of her standing and her responsibilities, of the need to be the setter of fashion, not the slave of it, of how one's wealth should turn to charitable work and the patronage of the arts.

"I should like to encourage writers," I told her. "I fear that all the good literature has already been written!"

She laughed at that. "I believe every generation claims this." Then her gaze turned more serious. "Little Ophelia, I must ask this yet again. Are you certain of this path? You have a safe life, a life that might very well turn out more happily than you believe."

I shook my head. "I wish you would believe me. I shall never be happy until my destiny lies in my own hands. As long as I am ruled by another, I shall shrivel and die." Then I gave her a gamine grin. "And how else am I to sample life's full and varied *men*-u?"

The Swan smiled at me sadly. "How else, indeed?"

She leaned forward to set her tea down and I could not help but notice that even such a mundane movement was laced in elegance. I tried to emulate that ease as I did the same. I was pleased to note that I did a creditable job of it.

"Today we are going to find you a house. It must be not too large, for it will be too costly to manage, yet not too small, for a courtesan must not ever *appear* to economize. Every moment should seem like an exercise in indulgence. Every cushion, every carpet, every silver spoon must announce bounty and comfort, for that is why men come to us."

"I thought they came for sexual favors."

She laughed. "Goodness, no. I spend far more time listening to men than I do fondling them. Sometimes I think a man's favorite feminine organ is her ear!"

By that evening we had settled upon a house for me. It was small but of pleasing proportions. There was a parlor to delight my friends. There was a gracious bedchamber with which to delight my lover.

And best of all, there was a library with which to delight myself!

The Seven Obligations of the Courtesan . . .
The duty to know and understand him
To be his solace and his fire
To take part in his Society
To bolster his endeavors
To bring witty conversation and tender touch
To give comfort to those in need
To give strength to those who are weak.

"I don't think I should like a man too much my elder," I told the Swan as we sat over tea one morning, compiling a list of possible clients. My lovely little house in a pretty square had been secured and furnished, although with a large bite out of my personal inheritance. We'd had quite the amusing time choosing décor. I had settled upon the colors of jewels. Deep sapphire and rich ruby to make my skin glow and to hint to my lovers the preferred colors of their most appreciative gifts!

And let us not forget comfort. As Aunt Beryl blithely planned the wedding without the inconvenience of my opinion, I purchased thick carpets, deep soft chairs, and a single, magnificent bed. Fortunately, the Swan knew every reputable secondhand dealer in the city!

I chewed meditatively on a lemon biscuit and went on. "If he is too much older than I, he might think himself like my uncle and believe he commands me."

The Swan nodded thoughtfully. "Yes, it is best to begin with someone you can manage easily." She grinned. "Although I defy the Prince Regent himself to resist your prodigious bosom!"

I rolled my eyes. "Surely not all men are fixated on bosoms?"

The Swan laughed. "Thank heavens, no, or I should be in the poorhouse!"

We were in her lovely parlor, where the easy elegance was fast becoming necessary to my being. Every day I dreaded that I must leave this pretty house and return to Aunt Beryl's stuffy, ponderous furnishings and dark, closed rooms. Therefore I pushed the seams of my freedom nearly to bursting. Sylla enjoyed our outings too much to leak a whisper to my relations and we had pacified my aunt with a mythical friendship I had struck up with the baroness's companion, an elderly lady I had never met, but whom I imagined to be quite bored with the baroness's staid lifestyle.

I went home every day stocked with tasty but innocuous Society gossip supplied by the Swan, which made my lie most convincing indeed. I am not a liar by nature, but in my mind a war had been declared and I was within my rights to take extreme measures in order to win my freedom.

Soon, however, I would be an independent woman in my

own house! Bouyed by that prospect, I settled down to select my first protector.

The interviewing of potential suitors was much more comical than it ought to have been. The Swan created a list of gentlemen based on my own first requirements and her knowledge of Society. They were all fairly young, enormously rich, and all unwed.

I knew that most people considered a Society marriage to be little more than a business contract, a joining of bloodlines and property, but I still held a naïve ideal of true marriage, much like a child's dream of a magical unicorn. Silly or not, I still had no wish to be someone who might damage such a mythical creature.

Once we began the actual process of selection, I found myself installed in a tiny, dark room outside the parlor. Before me was a small point of light that became a peephole when I lowered my eye to it. I could quite clearly see into the parlor, including a view of the sofa, the fireplace, and the Swan's dainty harp.

I had learned enough from the Swan's tutelage that I could imagine an erotic use for such a room with a view. I have ever had a fertile imagination. Such thoughts brought a tingle of eagerness to my skin.

When Mr. W—— was led into the room to await the Swan, I was encouraged by my first sight of him in person. I had seen him, of course, but only from afar. His Society was somewhat above that of my aunt and uncle. He was a tall man in his thirties, quite well-formed. He was dark of hair but not swarthy. His face was unobjectionable if one liked a hawkish profile. The Swan had warned me not to choose on looks alone, but so far I found no cause to strike Mr. W—— from the list. He was wealthy and connected and supposedly of a certain intelligence. I eagerly awaited his answers to the Swan's questions. She would be joining him soon—

To my horror, at that moment the refined and elegant Mr. W—— thrust one finger into his nose and removed something so disgusting that I was forced to shut my eyes. I frantically rang the bell pull at my side. No sound came to my ears, but I knew that down in the kitchens, Sylla was on the alert.

Within moments, the Swan entered the room. "Mr. W——, I must make my apologies. Something most urgent has arisen and I must take my leave at once." There was no hesitation and no attempt to appease in her tone. She was polite, friendly, and relentless. Mr. W—— found himself upon the stoop in a matter of seconds.

Then the door to my little chamber opened. "Goodness, what happened?" The Swan frowned at me. "I thought him quite promising!"

Without replying, I grabbed her hand and dragged her into her formerly pristine parlor. With the tips of two fingers, I flipped over the silk pillow that lay on the sofa. Her shriek likely penetrated the revolting man's eardrums as he fled the scene.

It took the Swan's staff nearly two days to completely cleanse the room. The entire sofa was relegated to the rubbish bin and replaced by something even finer. "I sent the bill to Mr. W——," the Swan stated with great satisfaction. "He paid without a quibble!"

"Too right!"

The next gentleman was far more genteel. Young Lord T—— was a fine, spindly specimen of British inbreeding. He was as pale as milk and as fair as corn silk. Against my darkness, I thought we might make a rather fetching couple.

This time it was spittle into the fireplace. Not just a small, discreet clearing of one's throat either. The Swan had the hearth sanded and the carpets replaced as well, in case of any possible spattering. Again, the gentleman paid without a single objection.

"Perhaps you should do this more often," I told her laughingly. "You could redecorate your entire house!"

She shuddered. "Sometimes too much knowledge is a dangerous thing. I shall never be able to look either in the eye, ever again!"

"Are they all so revolting?"

She looked thoughtful. "I hadn't thought so."

I, for one, was beginning to despair of finding a man who did not excrete something ghastly the moment a woman turned her back, yet the next suitor who entered the parlor gave me hope.

He was tall and slender, not to mention young and quite beautiful. I found myself mesmerized by his fine, even features and the way the light glinted from his fair hair. He remained standing while waiting for the Swan and nervously adjusted his cravat half a dozen times in the few minutes that it took her to join him. I found his tension charming. He was wealthy and confident enough to think that the Swan might take his suit seriously, yet not so overbearing that he assumed the outcome of this interview would be in his favor.

The Swan entered and smiled at him. He bowed and cleared his throat twice before greeting her. Adorable. Furthermore, when he bowed, the view from where I sat was most appealing. I have never been able to abide an insufficient derriere. This fellow had the buttocks of a horseman. I wondered if he had the roughened hands to match. I leaned forward to listen to his interview with great interest.

After they were seated and exchanged a desultory amount of social talk, the Swan eyed him seriously for a moment. "Mr. P——"

He smiled. "Please call me Robert. Mr. P—— brings to mind my elder brother."

Hmm. A younger son. Socially, that was not necessarily a detriment, for Robert was a P——, an old family so wealthy and socially prominent that even I knew of them. Although not nobility, they had married so many of their relations to the aristocracy that they were included in that world without a quibble.

Robert was looking like quite a catch, indeed.

The Swan was as obviously charmed as I, for she reined in her formidable elegance and gave Robert a real smile.

"Thank you, Robert. I am honored." Then she glanced in the direction of my peephole.

I wished I could signal her. *Yes, yes, I like him!*

The Swan let a teasing glint show in her gaze, then licked her lips and wiggled her eyebrows at me while Robert was busy with his cravat once again. Yes, she found him quite edible, I could tell. When Robert looked up, the serene courtesan again sat before him without the slightest hint of impish humor on her beautiful features.

He cleared his throat again even as his fingers twitched toward his cravat. The first thing I would do would be to hire him a decent valet who would make sure his cravat knot could survive a tropical hurricane without adjustment.

"I am very flattered that you agreed to see me," he told the Swan. "I find myself in need of an individual like you in my life. I am too young to wed, but too old to simply dream of having a lover. In addition, I have political ambitions," he said seriously. "An elegant and accomplished hostess such as you could help me enormously. However, I truly did not think a woman of your stature would be interested in someone like me."

Humble as well. I wanted to lick him off my spoon!

The Swan bowed her head graciously. "I am always interested in making valuable friends," she told him, "but in actuality I asked you here today to discern your suitability for . . . someone else."

Robert frowned, his face drawing in disappointment. "Someone else?"

The Swan smiled. "Yes. A dear friend has recently arrived back in London from a sojourn with her ailing lover in Belgium. While she found the countryside restful, she is now prepared to make England her home once more. She is exceedingly lovely, of course, as well as intelligent and accomplished. She was extremely popular in Brussels. His High—"

She paused just long enough to let her "slip" register with him, then continued as if she hadn't stopped at all. "Gentlemen were simply begging her to stay, but she wished to come home. However, she has been away long enough to lose track of English Society. She finds herself quite at . . . loose ends." Her voice dropped just a husky smidgen right then as she let a smoky, suggestive hint of what a loose woman might find herself doing while at loose ends. Robert came to point like a setter on a quail.

Fantastic. I must practice that.

"Is she—would I—"

The Swan waited politely through another spate of throat clearing until Robert could contain his obvious surge of arousal. "Would she be interested in meeting me?"

Meet him? I wanted to wrap him up in brown paper and have him delivered to my new doorstep that afternoon, but the Swan had cautioned me not to allow my nether regions to make my decision for me. Still, he seemed entirely perfect in all other ways.

I wondered at the Swan's story of my Belgian lover, although I instantly conceived a picture of an older, distinguished fellow, a man of merit and exquisite taste—not to mention a very arousing accent!—who had sadly wasted away from something not too painful or disgusting while I bravely kept up his spirits with my charm and beauty. Stefan, I named him. Stefan Von Dolken, of the Brussels Von Dolkens, of course. I actually felt a moment of real sadness at his loss. Such a lovely man. We'd had such wonderful times together, Stefan and I . . . and the king, of course.

I wondered if the Swan would call me in at once, but she did not. She told Robert that she would speak to me on his behalf and they spent the next ten minutes sipping tea and discussing the upcoming ball at the home of Lady Montrose and reminiscing over last year's event, which had apparently been memorable for the failed performance of a singing donkey. Or perhaps the donkey did sing, but not very well. It was very difficult to tell from my perch in the hunting blind!

The moment Robert took his leave, I sprang from my

hiding place and bolted to the parlor like a child on Christmas morning. "I want him!"

The Swan smiled. "Yes, I rather thought you would. If he were a few years older I daresay I would fight you for him myself."

I narrowed my eyes at her and snarled playfully. "Hands off." Then I broke my fierce pose to spin wildly about the room. "He is perfect! I adore him!"

"You know . . ." The Swan examined the rim of her teacup carefully. "You could probably convince him to court you legitimately. He will marry eventually and you would be an acceptable match, with a bit of judicious sponsorship by a lady of Society."

I stopped spinning and wrinkled my nose. "Marriage? Ew."

My giddiness past, I flung myself down onto the chair Robert had just vacated. It was large and I am small, so my feet dangled ever so slightly. I swung them. "I mean to say, I like him and I find him very attractive, but if I wanted marriage to a rich, handsome man then I might as well simply wed Lord Ashford."

"Hmm." The Swan was being inscrutable.

I hate inscrutable.

I sat up very straight so that she would take me more seriously. "I want my freedom. I like Robert very much for someone I haven't officially met but why would I trade being his lover for being his bride?"

"Oh, I can think of several thousand reasons," the Swan mused. "Thousands and thousands."

I placed my hands on the arms of the chair and leaned back as regally as a queen. "I intend to relieve him of some of those thousands, of course. And then send him off to wed some sweet little creature who dreams of nothing more than running his household and bearing his children."

"What do you dream of, Ophelia?" The Swan put her teacup on the tray. "If you had the wealth and the freedom to do anything you wish, what would it be?"

I gazed at the fresco of naked cherubs gracing the ceiling of the parlor. "My father was a scholar, my mother a firebrand. I am neither of those things. There is only one thing I like. I love to read. I cannot think of anything I should like better than a lifetime of the freedom to read whenever I wish."

The Swan laughed. "I don't think that quite qualifies as a life's work." She poured me a cup of tea and refilled her own. Smiling, she raised her cup high. "Nevertheless, let us toast your future as a very well-read woman."

We clinked china and sipped to the rosy days ahead for me. I had a house and I'd chosen a lover. I was ready.

However, when I uttered as much to the Swan, she shook her head. "Oh no, sweet Ophelia. You are far from prepared to manage a man on your own." Her expression became very solemn. "Before you can take a lover as the experienced courtesan late from Belgium, you have something else to learn."

Her gravity was alarming. I felt a catch in my throat as I leaned forward, enthralled. "What?" I whispered. "What must I learn?"

Setting down her cup, she folded her hands before her. "Before you may take your place in your lover's bed, you must be introduced to . . ."

I waited, my breath caught in my throat.

". . . the Seven Sins of the Courtesan."

Seven

I ran through the rain from the door of the hired hack to the front door of the Swan's house with the hood of my borrowed cloak concealing my face. It was nearly eleven o'clock at night and my relatives thought me safely in my bed, dreaming of my wedding day less than a fortnight away. Instead, I had crept out of the house wearing Sylla's gown and cloak while she curled up in my bed, trying to look properly plump should anyone check on me.

Meeting me at the door, the Swan greeted me with a quick hug and a steaming mug of spiced wine. Then she knelt before me and removed my sodden shoes. Taking my hand, she led me to her chamber and helped me out of my gown and underthings. She left me standing naked and quivering with nerves, gulping at the warmth of the wine. She returned a moment later with something draped over her slender arm. She took the wine from my chill-numbed hands.

"This is just the thing," the Swan said with satisfaction. "Lift your arms."

I obeyed without protest, for the night had already taken on a sheen of the unreal. When the silken garment slithered cool and slippery down over skin already in a heightened state due to my nerves, my entire body shivered convulsively.

My hair was let down and brushed with soothing hands.

Gentle fingers tied the bow of the gown behind my neck. "There." The Swan turned me toward the standing mirror. "You look exquisite."

What I looked like was more than naked.

How a person could look more naked than naked was a mystery, yet somehow the sheerness of the silk, the way my nipples showed through the fabric, dark and rosy, the way the shadow of my pubis beckoned like a dark invitation . . .

"I look like a sin waiting to happen."

The Swan laughed. "Indeed you are."

I tried to swallow but my throat was too dry. I had thought and planned and longed for this night, yet my hands shook as I reached for the cup of wine. However, after only a sip, it was taken away again.

"Ophelia, if you do not wish to feel, then go back to your little world and marry your suitor." The Swan gazed at me with a single arched brow.

I wanted to feel.

I closed my eyes and took a deep breath. "I wish to feel everything, good and bad."

The Swan smiled and placed the wine back on the dressing table. "I daresay it will all be good tonight. The gentleman in question is quite accomplished."

"But who is he? What is his name? Where is he from?"

"He is a friend, someone I have known for years. He is a skilled and careful lover." The Swan shook a finger teasingly. "And I have already told you that those are no longer the rules. A man's name and social standing mean nothing. You are not on a husband-hunt any longer. From now on you will choose your lovers based on your heart and your mind, not on Society's expectations."

A man from the Swan's world. A skillful lover. I had not thought about it, but if wealthy men required courtesans then perhaps wealthy women were no different. I still had a great deal to learn.

"So is this is a test, of sorts? Am I to take this man into my bed whether I like him or not?"

"This is not a test." The Swan shook her head. "We give ourselves for love, for friendship, for mindless passion—but always, always at our own will."

She stroked my hair back from my brow with gentle fingers as she went on. "The gifts, the jewels, the houses and servants—these are not payment. These are necessities, so that we might devote ourselves entirely to the happiness of our chosen lover, plagued by no distracting worries."

Her voice was lilting and sweet, calming to my raw nerves. I closed my eyes and concentrated on the soothing hands at my brow. "My mother used to do that when I could not sleep," I said.

The Swan gave my hair a playful tug. "Do I look like someone's mother?" She placed both hands on my cheeks and gazed into my eyes. "Have you entirely healed from your visit to the midwife last week?"

I nodded even as I blushed, thinking of the day I had had my hymen opened. The Swan had called it "the Blossoming," and had assured me that it would not hurt much and it hadn't, much. "Far less than it would if we let a lover manage it," she'd told me tartly. "Trust me on that one."

Now, stepping back, she tapped a finger on her chin as she surveyed my appearance. "Yes, you'll do."

I turned to the mirror and tried to assess myself without bias. With the sheer gown draped over me like a Grecian toga and my hair falling free and curling black over my bare shoulders, I looked decadent and shameless and just a bit . . . delicious.

I had often longed for slender grace and elegant height, like the Swan's, yet for the first time I realized that being short and plump and curvaceous might have fresh advantages. My full bosom and my round buttocks gleamed through the sheer silk like the bountiful flesh of a pagan goddess.

"I look—"

"You look like every man's dream come to life," the Swan said without envy. "What I could have done with breasts like yours!"

The Swan leaned forward over my shoulder and smiled at me in the mirror. "The gentleman is waiting, pet."

She took my hand and led me down the hall. At the end, there was a door. The brass latch gleamed in the light of the Swan's candle. I stared at it until the shimmer of the metal smeared and ran in my burning vision.

A man is in there. A stranger who wishes to do wicked things to me.

I was nervous and terrified—but there was no denying the telltale heat of excitement flaring between my thighs. I was a healthy young animal, after all. It was time for desire to burn within me.

The fact that the man was a stranger excited me more than I dared admit except in the darkest corner of my thoughts. To give myself so ran contrary to every rule of propriety I had ever learned. It was a wicked, wanton act, a blatant and shameless act.

It was an undeniable act of free will.

"Go in," the Swan whispered. "He awaits you."

I watched as my own trembling hand reached for the gleaming blur of the door latch. My fingers were so numb with fear that the metal did not even seem chill to the touch. I heard the latch click.

No. Wait. I'm not ready—

The door swung open before me.

The chamber glowed with candlelight. I was vaguely aware that the room was furnished in the same sumptuous fashion as the rest of the Swan's elegant house, but that was only a faint thought registering in my mind.

All I could see was him.

The man stood in the center of the room. He turned toward me and for a moment I thought a shadow obscured his features. Then a thrill of alarm ran through me as I realized he wore a mask over the upper part of his face. Only gleaming dark eyes showed through the holes in the black silk. It made him more than a simple stranger. It made him a mysterious, disturbing apparition. It made him unreal.

It made him no one.

I swallowed as a rush of hot blood flooded my body. He was no man. He was any man. I wanted this, I realized. I wanted the anonymity. This night, this lesson, would not be a marriage, nor even a love affair. It would be a secret encounter between strangers, two people who would remain strangers. This was about simple pleasure, pleasure without consequence or meaning beyond the moment.

Oh, I was wicked to want such a thing! And I did want it. I was overwhelmed with the desire to reach out and touch this amazing apparition, this tall, well-built stranger in the mask who would teach me everything I longed to know. I slowly crossed the room to stand before him.

He loomed over me as I neared. Finally, I was close enough to touch him. Gazing up into his shadowed, hidden face as he tilted his head down to gaze back, I could see his thick dark hair and square jaw.

And his mouth. My eyes locked onto that mouth. His lips were perfect, neither too full nor too thin. With nothing else visible, his mouth took on a significance that I'd never realized. Now it was obvious to me that a fine mouth on a man was imperative.

Without thinking, I ran the tip of my tongue over my own lips.

The corner of that fine mouth quirked upward.

"Hello," he said. His voice was low and husky, hardly more than a whisper, yet deep enough to send a tremor through parts of my body I wasn't accustomed to thinking about. I wanted to speak but my tongue wouldn't obey. My throat was so dry that swallowing was out of the question. I was terrified.

And aroused. I could feel the throbbing of my nethers even past the pounding of my pulse. If I wanted to, I could turn and flee at this moment, before we had so much as greeted each other.

I stayed.

It was more than the need to learn to be the most brilliant courtesan who had ever lived—I was ever enterprising—for I already had a contract negotiated with Robert through the Swan. I did not need to prove my abilities to anyone.

"You are very quiet." The man came closer to me.

I managed to choke out something idiotic. "Yes, sir."

He stopped before me, so close that I had to tilt my chin up to see his face.

Heaven help me, the mask excited me more. I had wanted something anonymous, something wicked and deliciously sinful. I very much feared I had found it.

"Well, my silent lady, I must tell you that I don't approve. I wish you to speak."

To say what? My mind scrambled. "Yes, sir." Goodness, watch me wax brilliant.

He brought one hand up to take my chin between his finger and thumb. I jerked slightly when he touched me, for the warmth of his skin was like fire on mine. He gazed down at me for a long moment.

"Say 'cock.'"

If he had asked me a fortnight ago, I would have answered without the slightest embarrassment, for to me it simply meant "cockerel" or "rooster." No longer. The Swan had told me that men used it to describe their male parts.

His touch roughened ever so slightly, giving my head a tiny admonishing shake. "We will not make it through the first Sin tonight if you cannot say such a simple word."

I swallowed dry. "C-cock."

"Try it again."

I firmed my shivering belly. "Cock." I was pleased that it came out so confidently.

"Cunte."

I only blinked at him in confusion. I had never heard the word. He smiled. His lips were perfect. I couldn't take my eyes off them.

"I have a cock. You have a cunte. Say 'cunte.'"

Oh. It was a word for my nethers. A very naughty word, I knew without being told. The twist of his lips gave that away. He wanted to hear me say dirty words.

At last a flare of my customary audacity warmed my shaking innards. I met his gaze, licked my lips and used the Swan's trick of dropping my tone. "Cunte," I said. I practically moaned it.

Now he was the one gazing at my mouth. I was very pleased until he upped the ante.

"Say 'fuck.'"

Oh heavens. Now he was being truly obscene. I took a breath, determined. "F—" I took another breath. "Fu—"

He grunted a short laugh. "Before the night is over, you will say 'Fuck my cunte with your cock.' You will say it over and over again. In fact, you will scream it out loud."

Oh damn. My knees buckled a little, I confess, but I firmed them with nothing but the power of my will and met his gaze. "Then perhaps you had best stop wasting the night, sir, because that might take a while."

His answer was to slide his hand around the back of my neck and tug at the bow tied there. I gasped as the chiffon nightdress slithered off me like a fall of water. I was entirely naked, gleaming and pale before his clothed darkness. I quickly pulled my hair forward to let it flow over my breasts and then clasped my hands before my nethers. My cunte.

He did not move or speak for a long moment, but only gazed at me through the eyes of the mask. Inscrutable.

I hate inscrutable.

However, my total vulnerability left me too unsure and unnerved to be saucy any longer. I was full of horse apples. I was not brave, or daring, or any of the things I'd imagined when I'd concocted this outrageous plan. I was a girl, an almost virgin, too terrified to do anything but stand there while he violated me with his eyes.

The moment stretched on and on. The suspense became too much for me. I am not a patient person. I shifted restlessly from one foot to the other. I twisted my hands in the way that so frustrated my aunt. I fidgeted.

He folded his arms and watched me.

Finally I could take no more. "What are you looking at?"

"When you fidget, your breasts jiggle most enticingly. I was merely enjoying the show."

I looked down to realize with horror that my restlessness had caused the curtain of my dark hair to part over my breasts, displaying them quite thoroughly.

"I especially like the way your nipples thrust forward so impudently." His voice had changed, going from husky whisper to male growl. "They are very pink. They will redden somewhat when I suck them."

Oh. I wanted him to suck them. I wanted him to suck them hard, to pull them into his hot mouth and tug at them until I screamed his name.

I didn't know his name.

" 'Sir' will do for now," he said when I asked. "The Swan told me that your name is Ophelia."

"Yes." Don't think about nipple-sucking. *I can't help it.* Don't. It was too late, however. I felt a rush of dampness between my thighs. I cleared my throat. "Sir—"

"Yes, Ophelia?" He came close enough to brush my hair back over my shoulders, although he never took his eyes off my rigid nipples. His hands hovered just over my breasts, so that I felt the heat of his palms radiating against my chilled skin. So far he had not touched me other than my chin.

I wanted him to. "Sir, w—will you not remove your clothing as well?"

His eyes rose to meet mine. "In a hurry to beg for my cock, Ophelia?"

His eyes were dark as night. Onyx eyes, like an Egyptian god.

Or demon.

I truly didn't care which. Perhaps a demon made for a better companion down a path of sin.

Then his hot hands fell softly onto my bare shoulders and

I gasped. He moved slowly, circling me clockwise, never letting his hands leave my skin, sliding them over me, over my shoulder and neck and breastbone. Down my arm and up my inner arm. Around my waist and down over my hip. His hot palms left trails of fire on my flesh, burning memories of sensation. I almost expected them to glow in the dimness.

No one had ever touched me thus. I had never had a nanny or a governess. My mother had expected independence at a young age, so no one had even seen me in the bath since I was ten. I had washed and dressed and tended myself—so my skin was as virgin as the rest of me.

He despoiled my skin. He raided me as thoroughly as any Viking horde. He touched me everywhere, slipping his palms and fingers down over my belly, circling the globes of my buttocks, lifting and cupping my tight, tingling breasts, ravaging my innocent flesh with his hot, gentle stroking hands. Around and around me he moved, teasing, touching, smoothing. My body, my face, he even ran his fingers through my hair. My skin awoke as it had never before.

And it woke *hungry*. Like a caged creature too long unfed, it wanted more and yet more.

I was merely the prisoner inside the aroused vessel. I trembled, trapped in his web of teasing, taunting pleasure. His hands slipped between my thighs, but didn't reach my dampened nethers.

Cunte. My dampened cunte.

The words mattered, I realized now. I *would* beg him eventually and it was important that my fevered mind find the right words to satisfy my starving flesh.

When his hot hands slid past the undefended parting of my buttocks, I closed my eyes. *Yes. At last.*

He teased at the lips of my cunte. His fingers stroked up and down the slippery parting but did not enter, though I admit I did try to press back into his touch. He found a small, sensitive area just behind that that even I had never explored. The tip of his index finger, slippery from the exploration of the lips of my cunte, dipped swiftly into my

anus, making me gasp and shudder with surprising pleasure, then moved on, up and over me once more.

Nothing was sacred. No inch of me was left pure. His
touch invaded. It invited. It provoked and offended and
aroused. I was dizzy with it, drunk on it, shaking and raw
and stripped more naked than naked by it.

Then it grew less gentle. Not painful, but rougher, more
demanding. He pushed, he squeezed, he pinched, he tweaked.
My nipples grew hard and pointed under his taunting touch,
my buttocks pink, my scalp tingled from his fingers fisting
in my hair as he pulled my head back to thrust his slick
fingers into my mouth, making me taste myself.

Salt. Cream.

I wanted him to thrust his fingers into my cunte in just
that way. I was soaked with desire. He read my thoughts
and ran a rough, hot hand down my belly to cup my cunte
firmly. I quivered and closed my eyes. "Yes," I whispered
through dry lips. *"Please."*

Abruptly, he took my upper arm in his other hand and
spun me to press against him, my back to his front. My tingling skin adored the scratch of his weskit buttons against
my back. My sensitized buttocks recognized the giant bulge
in his trousers as belonging to me and nestled against it
confidently.

"What do you want, sweet Ophelia?"

I gasped and squirmed. His hand rubbed at my cunte
roughly but did not pass the slick gates.

"Say the words, Ophelia."

I moaned and writhed against him, fore and back, but he
was relentless. "Say it."

"Touch me," I begged. "Please touch me."

"I am touching you," he said, hoarse and hot in my ear.

I whimpered in frustration. "No! Touch me inside!"

"That's not what we call it, is it?"

"Fuck me!" I howled. "Fuck my cunte with your fingers!"

When his long, rough fingers slipped between the slippery folds of my cunte, I nearly screamed aloud from the

relief. I bucked and squirmed against him until he had to pin me tight to his body with his other arm around my waist. Despite his earlier roughness, he penetrated me slowly, almost reverently. I could not move. I could only lean my head back against his shoulder and pant as he slid a single long finger deeply into me, all the way to the last knuckle. A long animal moan rose from my throat.

"The First Sin, my delicious Ophelia . . ." His breath was hot and moist against my ear, his voice rasping and deep.

"The First Sin is Lust."

Eight

My entire body was aflame. I had never felt anything like this intense, wicked awakening. I was a mad creature, begging a masked stranger to do things to me that I had never dared imagine only a few short weeks before.

He stood behind me, still fully clothed against my bareness, having done nothing but touch me with his hands. How could such a simple thing as touch bring me to this state of wild abandon?

His long finger slid into me and then withdrew over and over while I quivered and whimpered in his grasp. My knees could scarcely keep me upright. If I fell to the carpet would he fall with me? Would he cover me with his large, warm body? Would he violate me on the floor while I begged for more?

Such dangerous thoughts were mere wisps of consciousness amid the tumult in my mind. For the most part, my awareness consisted of craving, aching, throbbing *need*. His rough horseman's hands set me afire. His slippery finger thrust into me again and again, sliding up and down against the sensitive flesh of that secret little knob I had no name for. I became nothing but that small knob, or perhaps it grew to become me, for nothing existed in the world but that callused finger sweeping over me, thrusting into me, sending tremors through me. I felt a pull toward something

I had never known before. I wanted something . . . something more . . .

That finger slowed, then stopped. I gasped and moaned in protest as it withdrew from my body inch by slippery inch. I felt raw and empty and unfulfilled. What madness was this?

"Not yet, sweet wanton," that dark voice whispered in my ear.

When his enveloping arm released me I staggered, my shaking knees unable to sustain my weight. He carefully propped me against the bedpost, my bare back to the cool, carved wood. I put my hands behind me to hold on and let my head drop, hiding behind the fall of my hair while I tried to cling to that feeling. Where was I trying to go? I didn't know, but I realized that it was not a place I knew how to find on my own. My body felt chilled and alone without his touch, without his solid presence, without his hot breath in my ear.

I needed this stranger, this "Sir."

It should have been an alarming, even terrifying realization. I, who fought for my freedom, gave myself so willingly into the power of this unknown man. Yet I was not afraid. There was power in this discovery. There was freedom in my response to his large, wicked hands. Somehow I knew that if I could last the night, I would learn to fly.

I felt his big hands smooth my hair. He cupped my jaw in his palms and lifted my face. I gazed up at him, panting and shivering and quite unselfconscious in my nakedness.

"Say 'fuck.' "

I drew a breath. "Fuck." The wicked word came easily from my lips, for had I not screamed it a short while before? This obedient murmur was nothing in comparison.

"Naked and profane." Those beautiful lips quirked. "And yet still so ladylike. I applaud you."

It was ridiculous to feel proud of myself, like a child getting good marks, but I did. Yet were these not barriers to my goals that must be surmounted? I should be proud.

I have perhaps mentioned before that I am an exceptional student.

He still gazed down at me, his eyes entirely shadowed by the mask. What did he see? I had been so involved in my own experience that I had no thought of his needs.

That could not be the mark of a great courtesan.

So I lifted my hands and tentatively smoothed them over his chest, sliding my palms over his waistcoat, up under his surcoat and down again over his flat, hard stomach. His body was so firm beneath the fine clothing. I had never touched a man before but I had imagined something softer from a gentleman. Sir had the body of a laborer, the hands of a groom, and the clothing and manners of a lord.

Perhaps that was what was required of a hired lover. The Swan had emphasized that fitness and grace were most important to a courtesan's career. A hired lover would be prized for his strength and power, would he not?

I suddenly longed to see that strength and power for myself.

"Would you not like to remove your clothing now, Sir?"

He had gone quite still under my hesitant exploration. I put a palm over his chest to feel the thud of his heart, like a horse galloping on a hard road. *He wants me.*

My sense of power grew. I stepped closer to him and slid my hands to the front of his waistcoat. I teased at the top button with my fingertips. "I will wait to be asked," I informed him.

"I will not ask," he replied, his whispered tone harsh. He was not angry. He was inflamed. All I had to do was glance down at the front of his trousers to know that. I might be an innocent—although perhaps not so innocent any longer!— but everyone saw animals mating. I knew what would happen, in a general sort of way. The Swan had tried to explain more explicitly, but I had scarcely listened in my excitement. However, my ignorance did not dismay me. I was incredibly willing to learn.

So, without his permission, I began to strip my masked

lover. I began by undoing each waistcoat button slowly to reveal the linen shirt beneath. When the dark brocade vest hung open, I pushed it from his shoulders, taking his surcoat with it. As the softly scratchy wool slid away, I gave it a last caress, for I confess I would miss the feel of it against my sensitized flesh.

More by feel than by sight in the dimness, I began to untie his cravat. This did not go well for several moments. Then I gained the gist of the knot and soon swept the untied length from around his neck and slung it triumphantly around my own.

"A souvenir," I murmured.

"Yes, it may come in handy later." His whisper was nearly a growl.

My knees went just the tiniest bit weak at the images that provoked, but I soldiered on. His shirt now lay open halfway down the front and I found myself fascinated by the triangle of exposed male flesh before my eyes. His chest was as tan as his face and hands, again like a laborer in a field who worked bare to the waist. Would he leave my side in the morning to go plant a cornfield? Or perhaps—and this thought made it very difficult to stand—perhaps he regularly made love outside? I had a brief mental flash of him naked and sweating over a female form splayed in the high grass. This female form had dark hair and a generous bosom, of course.

Then I remembered that I didn't need to fantasize when I had the real thing before me. I pulled his shirt from his trousers and ripped it over his head. Well, I tried but I am rather impaired in the height department, so all I accomplished was to pop a few threads and make him stagger a bit.

"Allow me," he murmured graciously. He bent forward so that I might pull his shirt off.

I was not embarrassed by my gaffe for his half-naked body was far too distractingly beautiful. The linen fell from my fingers as I stared at his magnificent chest and shoulders. And his stomach! I had no idea a man's body could

ripple so! The breadth of his shoulders was even more impressive now that I truly saw the thick muscles roping over
them, winding down his powerful arms, strapping over his
ribs, plating his belly with iron. I reached to touch him
again, following the same path as before. He stood still for
me as I moved around him, almost as he had circled me
earlier. However, I had come to worship, not taunt. I slid my
fingertips up the bones of his spine, then spread my hands
wide over his shoulder blades like wings on his back. So
tall . . . so wide . . .

So perfect.

No wonder he was in great demand by the ladies of Society! I would hire him simply to look at him.

Well, perhaps not *only* to look at him.

It was not until I had smoothed my hands over his entire
upper body, a process that left both of us breathless, that I
dared the untried territory of a man's breeches. I lightly
traced my fingertips over the thick ridge that bulged within
those breeches.

A sound escaped him, something between a growl and a
moan. I could feel the caged power of that beast pulsate
beneath my touch.

Oh dear.

Cowardice won and I knelt before him to remove his
boots. He loomed above me, dark and powerful, as I knelt
naked at his feet. I shuddered with a sudden bolt of desire.
His black boots took the brunt of my tension, for I fairly
ripped them from his feet, taking his stockings off as well.

I licked my lips and gazed at the obstacle bulging before
my eyes. Only the breeches were left. He waited silently but
the air was thick with unexpressed lust, the only signs of it
the throbbing pulse in his neck and the faint sheen of sweat
on his muscled chest. I could feel his black eyes hot upon
me, twin points of dark fire roaming my naked skin.

*Buttons. You can do buttons. You've been managing those
for years.*

Yet my hands shook as I reached up and undid the two

rows of buttons that lay each just inside his hipbones. The heat of his bare skin teased at my knuckles as I fumbled the job. When I inadvertently brushed my hand over the rigid rod swelling beneath the taut fabric, he drew in a breath that did fascinating things to the rippling muscled belly before my eyes.

I did it again, just to see.

His torso tightened and his hands fisted at his sides. "You should not tease the caged beast, sweet Ophelia."

I scowled at my clumsy fingers. "I'm trying to free the damned beast, Sir."

Large swift hands took over briefly. I pulled my own hands away and watched in fascination as he stripped his breeches away and the trapped creature was set free. He wore no drawers. Impatient fellow.

Released, his thick organ—his *cock*—jutted forward. I, who had been shy of the candlelight before, was now glad of it. It was a beautiful thing, his cock. I reached my hand to take it in my fist like a club, for it jutted both fore and aft of my grip. For a moment I feared such size within me, but the Swan had promised his skill and care and in that moment I chose to believe in the coming pleasure. Fear had no place in this night of delicious awakening.

He inhaled as I tightened my fingers slowly, gently, thinking I should like to tug him a bit closer. It thickened in my hand at once, turning from hard flesh to iron. I could see the silken skin of it darken as well. The rounded head of it swelled before my eyes and I saw a tiny shimmering bead appear in the small slit at the tip.

He dampens as well, I thought, and the knowledge made my cunte throb in response.

"Stand." His husky tone was a gravelly command I willingly obeyed.

Fascinating events lay before me and I had no wish to delay. My empty fist closed about the lingering sensation of his silk-and-iron cock in my palm, unwilling to lose the feeling of him. I need not have worried.

Sir stood naked but for his mask. I stood naked but for my hair. I could feel the very heat of him radiating upon my awakened skin. I wanted him to touch me again, to pull me close to his heat, his hardness. My knees trembled with the power of my wanting. I could see by the gleam in his shadowed eyes that he knew it.

I lifted my chin. "I will not ask."

Those beautiful lips twitched in amusement. He stepped closer, moving his large body into mine as if he had never lived anywhere else. His jutting cock dug into my belly for an instant, then he slid his hand down to lift it between us until it pointed upward along the swell of my stomach, as if to lay claim to its right to the inside of me as well.

Then his hard chest pressed into my soft breasts and his rigid thighs aligned with my plump ones. I tipped my head back to meet that onyx gaze. My breath came so fast it dizzied me and my hands came up to rest upon the rounded steel of his biceps. My lust, so new to me, so achingly delicious, spun my mind sideways until I scarcely knew my own name.

"Ask."

I tried to, but my dry throat stopped me.

He dropped his large, hot hands to my waist and pulled me close into him, spreading my softness into every hill and valley of his hardness. *"Ask."*

As I gazed up at him, at his blazing eyes behind the mask, at his magnificent mouth below it, I knew what he wanted me to say. *Fuck my cunte with your cock.*

I licked my dry lips. "Kiss me," I whispered.

His eyes widened in surprise, and then something flared in his gaze, something like wonder or awe. I forgot that notion in the next moment, however, for his wonderful mouth came down upon mine for my very first kiss.

I think he meant it to be somewhat gentle and warm, but the touch of his lips upon mine set the smoldering coal of my lust to instant flame. With a small cry I went up on my toes even as I slid my hands about his neck to pull him closer. My parted lips clung to his as I pressed myself to him with all my might. In response, his arms came about me, one big hand on the small of my back, the other deep in my hair, cupping my head. He groaned into my mouth even as I felt his thick cock pulse against my belly.

Then he lifted me right from my feet and within a few steps had tumbled us both onto the richly appointed bed. The cool silk beneath my hot skin made me gasp, but then his warm weight covered me as he smoothed my wild hair from my face and kissed me again and again. *"Ophelia . . ."*

I had no name for him. "Sir . . ."

He pulled his mouth from mine and dropped his forehead upon my collarbone for a moment. I could feel his breath hot upon my breast as I panted as well. Then he lifted his head. Dark eyes focused on me and I swallowed at the intensity in his gaze.

He took my hand in his and placed it above my head, then did the same with my other hand. I lay willing and passive, waiting for him to cover me again, to penetrate me with his rigid cock, to teach me what it was to be fucked hard and well.

He did none of that. Instead, he lay next to me and slid one large horseman's hand over me, from my throat down between my aching breasts, over my trembling belly, until his hot palm cupped my cunte once more. I closed my eyes and quivered, waiting for him to slip a long finger into me. I felt a single callused fingertip dip inward to slowly caress that most sensitive point. Then I felt his mouth upon my breast, pulling my nipple between his lips, sucking as he teased with his tongue. Bright bolts of pleasure shot between those two points, my nipple and my cunte, lightning rods to my lust.

I began to writhe once more, raising my hips from the bed, straining toward his touch. His mouth moved to my other nipple while his unoccupied hand toyed with the already aroused one. My awareness shrank to those three points of exquisite sensation. I was clay in his big hands, a

moaning, gasping creature of his making. He drove me upward, using his fingers, his lips and teeth, until I fought for
more, crying out in my need for . . . fulfillment.

His hands stilled. His mouth left my nipple. The chill of
the room hardened the sensitized tip to aching fullness. I
protested, opening my eyes, trying to speak, reaching for
him with my hands. "No . . ."

He took my hands and pressed them to the bed over my
head again, keeping them there with the pressure of his own.
When he rolled onto me to lie between my damp, trembling
thighs, I nearly wept with gratitude.

I gazed up at him above me, dazedly admiring the glow
of candlelight upon the rippling, perspiration-glossed perfection of his chest and shoulders. I was more than ready to
receive him. Sighing, I rolled my hips upward, reaching for
the satisfaction I knew his cock would give me. "Please," I
whispered. "Please fuck my cunte with your cock."

His eyes locked with mine. I breathed deeply, my lips
parted, so very ready. He tilted his hips until the bulky weight
of his cock rolled into the slick crevice of my open thighs.
My breath stopped as I waited. A tiny flash of fear in my
mind must have shown in my expression, for his eyes narrowed. I hungered for him more than ever. I wanted this. I
wanted to experience everything, to feel everything, to live,
fully and unrepentantly, to suck the marrow out of every
moment of freedom. I wanted to touch and be touched, to
love and be loved, to fuck and be fucked.

It was only an instant of worry that he might not fit but
that moment cost me greatly.

His jaw tightened. He began to move. Instead of entering
me, his thick cock slid upward along my slit, parting the
wet lips of me and stroking slowly against my swollen, sensitive bud. The pleasure of it made me roll my head on the
coverlet. Then he drew back and the slow, drawing ecstasy
increased as the hard ridge at the head of him tugged at me
as it passed.

I was pinned beneath him like a butterfly, my arms above

my head, my thighs pressed wide by his weight and by my own need. The only touch, the only caress was that long, torturous, wicked slip and pull of his cock sliding against me.

I lost my mind. I cried out, I begged, I bucked and convulsed in his grip, I wept from frustration and arousal. I pleaded against that sweet, endless, aching pleasure that nonetheless held me just short of that unnamable moment I needed so badly.

"Please!" I shouted. "Please fuck my cunte with your cock!"

At that instant, he released my hands and fell upon me. His strong arms enfolded me and he covered my mouth with his own as he at last allowed the large, blunt head of his jutting cock to press into me.

I was no true virgin and I was wet and so very ready, but I could not help but cling weakly to Sir as he entered me. He was careful but implacable. His thickness stretched me to aching. I shuddered in the grip of the pleasure/pain and even whimpered into his mouth but he neither slowed nor increased his merciless pace. I was to be impaled and nothing would stop him now. I fisted my hands in his dark hair and gave myself completely to his rule, melting into his hold, opening to his wicked invasion.

As he drove the last rigid inch of himself deep into me, I wrapped my arms about him and buried my face in his neck and shivered in sweet agony as I was opened nearly beyond bearing.

I felt a shudder go through his big body. Sir was not so in control of himself after all. I knew then that he desired me every bit as much as I wanted him.

He stayed deep inside for a moment longer as my body eased about him. Then he slowly withdrew, leaving behind him a glowing trail of delicious pleasure inside me. I gave a long, slow exhalation of ecstasy and eased my tight-fisted grip on his hair, stroking my hands down his long back. I could feel the flex and draw of his muscles as he began to thrust into me once more. I could feel my cunte grow slick as he filled me again and nearly laughed at my own worries of a few moments before.

Then the pleasure swept me away once more, fully now, a whole-body ecstasy that tingled from my cunte all the way to my fingers and toes, to the roots of my hair. *Oh sweet heaven.*

I wrapped my arms about him. I wrapped my legs about him. I kissed him long and hard and deep as he fucked me. I moaned into his mouth and panted into his neck and begged, oh how I begged for that final moment, that vaporous ambition that he had held back from me. I used all the words he'd taught me. I slid hot, seeking hands down to cup his flexing buttocks, digging needful fingers into his muscled flanks.

There was no need to fear. Sir kissed me back as he drove his cock deep into me, through at last with restraint. Together we climbed, two panting, sighing partners in creation, building something that at that moment we needed more than breath itself.

And then I found it. I at last rose above the peak of the mountain and for an instant glimpsed an eternal ecstasy I had never before imagined. There was nothing in the world but Sir and his magnificent cock and that dazzling, golden moment of pure bliss. The rhythmic detonation of hours of unreleased pleasure rocked my body in waves. I clung to Sir and wept with the strength of my release.

In that moment, he tightened his arms about me and drove deep. I could feel the rumble of a repressed roar in his chest as he held me tight. His thick cock throbbed inside me even as his great heart thudded against mine. I shivered in time with the pulsing of his cock, small shocks of pleasure still coursing through me.

We stayed thus for a long moment. Breathing was all we could do, helpless as we were in the wake of such overwhelming pleasure. Then Sir lifted his head. His masked eyes were a bit glazed, as I expect mine were as well.

He drew in a long breath. "You are . . . more than I expected, sweet Ophelia."

I blinked at him. "The sentiment is most sincerely mutual, Sir."

He smiled then, quickly, merely a flash of white teeth. That almost shy expression, combined with the dark mystery of the mask, sent another heated pulse through my body.

I rather thought I'd like to do it again.

The morning found me sprawled deliciously nude in the giant bed, alone. I hadn't truly thought he would stay, though I had hoped.

A note lay upon a silver tray. It was from the Swan. "Welcome, beloved sister."

I lay there, contemplating the bed hangings, the complex appeal of the male body, and my newly ruined status until the Swan's maid came to rouse me. It was an hour until dawn and time for me to flutter back to my dreary cage.

Flight had ruined me for treading upon the ground.

That afternoon, after a bath and a nap, I managed to make stilted boring small talk with Aunt Beryl's guests at tea. I rather thought that the night before would be shining from my face like a flaming brand, but no one seemed to notice my awkward distance.

Pleasure still shimmered through me every time I shifted my perch on the hard, overstuffed sofa. My body tingled with memory and just a little of last night's swollen sensitivity. I tended to blush at random mental flashes of his mouth, his hands, his hard, muscled body.

His cock.

No one gave my scarlet cheeks a second glance.

Of course they wouldn't. Who noticed the carriage horse's feelings until he actually came up lame? I was nothing more than a means to an end to my guardians.

A small smile crept across my face. I longed to leap up and announce my ruin to all present. My marvelous, wondrous, delicious ruin! Uncle Webster must not be up to snuff, for if Aunt Beryl knew aught of such wicked pleasure, she would never leave her bedroom!

The dull feeling of disconnection faded and I began to enjoy my secret. Gazing around at the visitors seated in the parlor, I wondered what the parson would say if he knew the exquisite pleasure I'd lately experienced at Sir's talented hands? What would old Mrs. Simpkins say if I reenacted my orgasmic screams for everyone's educational benefit?

I am wanton.

The word slipped sensuously across my mind like Sir's fingers on my wet slit. Other words did as well—wonderful words, like "wicked" and "wild" and, my new favorite, "willing."

Willing. Will. *My will. My choices. My decisions.*

My future.

Mine.

Nine

Late that night, as I lay sprawled naked upon Sir's chest, dreamily thinking him such a magnificent beast, I spared a moment to fear that no other man would ever live up to such delicious expectations. Then I bent to worship his body once more.

His taste filled my mouth, the salt of his skin mingling with the flavor of the honey I had drizzled over his chest. I felt him draw a startled breath when I let my teeth graze his nipples every so slightly, but it was only fair. My own nipples had been dusted with sugar and suckled until they stood diamond hard and tingling, jutting forward as if asking for more.

Then he had pinned me down and filled my cunte with raspberries, which he had then extracted one by one with his nimble tongue. I kissed him again, just to taste the lingering flavor of berries on his lips.

Soon, however, the honey infiltrated our entire bodies, making even parting our laced fingers difficult. Laughter overwhelmed our lust and we made for the tub that stood by the fire.

The water in it had chilled but more pails stood in the coals, steaming gently. While Sir poured the hot water into the cold, I found a dish of soft soap that did not waft too greatly of femininity. I settled upon something citrusy,

in the spirit of our exploration into foods. When I turned back
to the tub, I found him lounging within it. He leaned back
with his muscled arms draped along the sides and his
thick erection clearly visible through the clear water.

He still wore his mask. I frowned at him. "In the bath?
Truly?"

His lips twitched. "It will dry."

"Why will you not show me your face? You must know
that I would keep your secret."

"Whom would you keep it from?"

Hmm. It seemed oddly indelicate to discuss our careers
while soaping each other in the bath. I let my gaze wander
to the glowing coals in the hearth. "I would not tell your
patronesses. Is that the right word?"

"My patronesses." His tone was very neutral.

I twitched one shoulder in a discomfited shrug. "I mean
to say, your female . . . protectors. Oh dear, that sounds
odd." I met his gaze with a frown. "Is there a better term?"

He was silent for a moment. "Did the Swan tell you
about my . . . lovers?"

I had been indiscreet. I was only a neophyte but even I
knew that discretion was everything. "She only mentioned
that you did not wish to be known by your true face. She
would not say more, but I know that you have been part of
her world—this world—for years."

His silence began to alarm me. I rushed on. "It is perfectly understandable that ladies might wish a discreet
alliance with an . . . imaginative, talented lover. I would
recommend you most highly—"

He snorted. Then it seemed he could not hold back his
laughter any longer. He threw back his head upon the edge
of the tub and laughed until the water threatened to slosh
over the sides. At first I was relieved that he was not upset
over my blathering, but after a time I folded my arms over
my bare bosom and tapped my fingertips impatiently. "If
you're quite finished?"

Still chuckling, he smiled, a flash of white teeth beneath

the mask that made my knees weak. "Sweet Ophelia, I shall gladly call upon you for references, should it ever be necessary. In the meantime, I would very much like to impale you on my cock whilst I wash all the stickiness from those lovely breasts. And no, I would prefer not to discuss other lovers in our time together. I find it douses the flames."

His flame did not look any too doused to me, but I did not argue. Instead, I clambered eagerly into the tub with him.

He did not impale me straightaway, despite his proposition. First he tenderly soaped my skin from between my toes to my scalp, removing every last bit of honey and berries and—did I forget to mention the chocolate? As he washed my hair, he had me sit within the vee of his open thighs and tilt my head back as he poured warm water over my scalp. He seemed to like the way my hair streamed down my back. I liked the way his big hands stroked gently through it, massaging and combing without ever pulling.

Feeling soothed and cherished, I took the soap and did the same for him. I had touched him everywhere, but using my hands to spread the soap over every inch of him warmed more than just my lust. I liked caring for him. I liked feeling as though I had the right to, even if only for the duration of one bath.

When the water cooled, he added more hot water without comment. I understood. I lay quietly upon his broad chest, my legs entwined with his, as he held me loosely in his arms. Lolling in the warmth, tending each other, basking in the heat of the coals was so decadent and yet so sweetly innocent.

That is, until his hands slowly swept down my thighs to cup my buttocks. Without a word, he slid me up his body, bringing my mouth to his. His kiss began soft but soon I had my fingers tangled in his wet hair as I clung to him. Our tongues battled even as our hearts began to pound. When he pulled my knees wide to straddle him, I opened readily, more than eager to take his thick cock into me. With his big hands wrapped over my hips, he restrained my fervor. I whimpered in protest as he forced me to move slowly over him, letting his cock penetrate me inch by exquisitely agonizing inch. I was forced to feel, forced to wait, forced to take him on and on and deeper than I ever had as he pressed me down while thrusting upward.

I shuddered and moaned but his grip was merciless. He controlled me completely, allowing me only as much movement as he wished. As he raised me upward once more, I threw back my head and wailed as he slowly left me, only to drive torturously into me once more. It was such gorgeous, wicked patience—surely meant to drive me completely mad as I writhed helplessly in his hands.

I fear I went quite wild, crying out and clawing at his shoulders in my frenzy. He would not relent until my body had eased about him completely and my cunte was wetted with more than bathwater.

His hands slid upward then to cup my breasts. "Ride me now, sweet. Ride hard."

Freed at last, I wrapped my hands over his rigid biceps and rose and fell upon him with all the fury of my trapped lust set free. I forced his hard length so deep that it made me gasp in pleasure/pain, but I could not stop myself. Ignoring the cooling water, deaf to the splashes striking the floor, I shut out all the world but for that massive, rock-hard cock I rode with all my might.

My orgasm struck me like a speeding cart, flinging me out of my own mind. I fell. I flew. I spiraled across the sky like a kite lost to the storm. I was scarcely aware of Sir's own deep roar of completion as my cunte convulsed about him. He thrust deep and hard as he came.

I let out a single, final squeak and collapsed upon his heaving chest.

Exhausted and barely conscious, I only dimly recall how Sir lifted me from the tub, wrapped me in a generous swath of toweling, and tucked me into the bed we had never managed to use that night. I think I reached for him, wishing to be clasped in his arms once more, but my hand found only the chill air of the bedchamber as he closed the door behind him as he left.

Our night of fulfilling our appetites had only left me wanting more.

That afternoon, as I attempted to yawn demurely through Aunt Beryl's interminable callers, yet more gifts came from Lord Malcolm Ashford.

"If he truly wished to be generous, he would give me my freedom," I complained to Sir that night as we lay exhausted from our hours exploring the Sin of Indulgence.

I had come to our bower of Sin to find Sir prepared to introduce me to the sensuality of the finer things in life. Expensive scents, fine wine, silken sheets, luxurious naughty lingerie—which now dangled from the chandelier. We had played with everything a very exclusive scarlet woman needs to surround herself with—and use to snare a man's every thought and desire. I had no idea that peacock feathers were not just for bonnets!

I stretched languorously into Sir's side and walked my fingers along the trail of dark hair leading me temptingly down his belly. My body ached from the strenuous pleasure he'd provided me. Even now I could feel the cool silk sliding beneath my heated skin and I shivered against the lingering throb of desire.

Sir grunted in response to my judgment. "Perhaps he is merely generous," he murmured without much interest.

I scowled and began to stroke my fingers back up his body. "He gives me the gift of gold and diamonds, empty gifts, for they would belong to him again once he wedded me. He wants to put me in one of his velvet boxes to be taken out and displayed at his pleasure."

I went up on one elbow to glare down at Sir. He opened one eye behind his mask. "There was a note with the gift," I told him indignantly. "It said, *'I'm looking forward to the world seeing you in my diamonds.'* Can you believe that? I am to be a display stand for his wealth!"

"You'd make a lovely one, with these breasts." He gave my nipple a teasing tweak. "Why, you could hire yourself out to display all sorts of wares. Jewelry, mufflers—"

"Cowbells!" I laughed. "Oxen yokes!"

He gave me that half-grin that always made me melt. "You could have everything you ever dreamed of."

I shrugged. "I could sell my soul for it, yes. Or I could keep my soul, become a courtesan, and have it all anyway."

Shaking his head, he pushed a stray tendril of hair behind my ear. "You never fail to surprise me, sweet Ophelia." His husky murmur never failed to make my toes curl. "Most women want jewels."

"Oh, I like jewels," I said as I snuggled into the dip of his shoulder. "I intend to have boatloads. What I do not like are presumptuous gifts that are not gifts at all, but bait with hooks secreted within, from a man who doesn't know me and who doesn't care to. What of true flattery, based upon true understanding?"

"Hmm. Will you send his diamonds back to him?"

I chuckled. "Heavens, no. I gave them away. The Chelsea Orphanage will have an outstanding year or three, due to Lord Malcolm's generosity. When I left they were thinking of hanging his portrait in the front hall."

Sir was silent for a long moment. Then a low chuckle began as a rumble deep in his chest. "All hail Lord Malcolm!"

Smiling, I twined my arms about his neck and closed my eyes. I hoped he would stay until I woke.

He did not.

The night that followed was a blur of wicked, exquisite pleasure. Under Sir's capable tutelage I studied the Sin of Idleness, which revealed itself to be the art of erotic massage and slow, leisurely joining. Time stretched out our senses as we slipped into another dreamlike world of unhurried pleasure. I was stunned when such delicious, easy sweetness abruptly whirled me into an intense and prolonged orgasm!

I suspect Sir was equally surprised, for his subsequent powerful release left him trembling in my arms for several moments.

The entire session left me with shaky knees and a tendency to giggle.

Sir did not seem to find it so amusing for some reason.

When I appeared the next night, the Swan met me at her door.

"He is not here," she told me.

I'm quite sure my expression fell like that of a child told that Christmas had been canceled. "Where is he?"

The Swan raised a golden brow. "I do not keep him on a leash, Ophelia."

I wanted to, I realized. Appalled at my own lack of maturity, I instantly drew up and gave the Swan a haughty nod. "Of course. Please tell him I shall await his message regarding our next meeting to finish my lessons."

She smirked at me. "Not bad. Very queenly. But you needn't worry. He wishes to see you tomorrow night. He instructs you to get a good night's sleep." She folded her arms and looked wise. "You're going to need it."

Refusing to acknowledge the way my mood rose at the news that he wished to see me soon, I bade the Swan goodbye and stole back to my relatives' house. As I slid between my Sylla-warmed covers, I had to admit that I would be grateful for sleep not stolen in fitful naps.

And the Swan was quite correct. I would need every moment of rest for the night ahead.

Instead of stroking my skin as they should be, Sir's hands were clasped behind his back. He stood clad in his dark dressing gown and breeches, while I remained in the black chambermaid dress in which I had escaped.

I swallowed. "I don't understand. You wish me to make love . . . to myself?"

He seemed taller for some reason, or perhaps larger. He seemed colder as well, more like the first night we spent together. I had grown accustomed to the warm and adventurous lover and had nearly forgotten the darkly wicked taskmaster of before.

In answer, he opened one hand toward the bed. "The Fifth Sin is Covetousness. It is the art of creating desire without a single touch."

I had wondered how the sin of envy might be turned to a courtesan's advantage. Now I frowned. "You are not to touch me?"

He put his hand back behind him. "I will not. I have placed items on the bed. You will use them to perform for me, to make me want you."

I licked my lips and eyed the things on the bed. I saw my old friend, the peacock feather. That was easily understood. Next to it lay a small corked flask of Venetian glass filled with a golden liquid. There was a short, thick ivory rod intricately carved in a rather familiar shape.

Feather. Oil. I stroked one finger down the ivory rod and glanced inquiringly at Sir.

The dark consideration in his eyes made me shiver. "It is an olisbos," he said in his husky murmur.

I had a perfectly excellent education in the classics. "From the Greek verb 'to glide,'" I whispered. Well, that explained things a bit.

I looked again at Sir. He waited with a sardonic glint in his eyes and his lips set beneath his mask. This, then, was a test. Did he think me unimaginative or lacking in initiative? Goodness, that was a mistake.

I turned and walked to the fire, where there sat a wing-back chair. Without a word I began to maneuver the heavy thing across the floor. Although he could have lifted it easily, Sir merely watched me. With a few unladylike grunts and a bit of screeching across the floor, I placed the chair perhaps five feet from the bed, facing the side of it squarely.

"Sit," I commanded him.

After regarding me silently for a long moment, he sat with as much dignity as a king upon his throne. I decided at that moment that I was going to make him leap from that chair with lust.

I had never considered that a chambermaid's costume could be an erotic stimulus, but when I stood before him and dropped the cloak there was no mistaking the flash of heat in his black eyes. I made a note to myself. Sir had chambermaid fancies even as I had horsegroom fancies.

That was the last time I met his gaze. It seemed to me that I should behave as if I were alone. So I lifted my hands to the tiny buttons down the front of the dress and began to slowly undo them. When I slid my arms from the sleeves and let the black gown slip down off my hips to puddle about my feet, I heard the chair creak as Sir shifted his weight slightly.

Emboldened, I stood there in my chemise and underskirt and silently declared war upon Sir's self-restraint. As gracefully as the Swan, I reached up to remove the pins from my hair, allowing it to tumble over my shoulders. Sweeping it off to one side so that he could easily see my face, I then lifted one foot and placed it on the bed. Bending, I removed my kid leather slipper and dropped it to the floor. Then I smoothed both hands up my calf to my knee, rucking up the underskirt as I went so that it crumpled over my thigh, hopefully revealing a flash of bare flesh.

I heard threads pop. I knew without looking that Sir's fingers had tightened on the chair arms. Without showing a shred of my satisfaction, I began to untie the ribbon garter that held my stocking just above my knee. Slowly I rolled the stocking down, over my knee, smoothing it down my calf, revealing my skin inch by leisurely inch. I drew it off entirely and tossed it aside.

It landed on Sir, draping insolently across his thigh.

Oops. Teasing had just become taunting. I tore my gaze from the scrap of white silk on black and began to repeat the process with the other stocking.

My rebellious hand repeated the careless toss. From the corner of my eye I saw Sir carefully remove the second stocking from his shoulder and wad it slowly in his fist. I lifted my chin in defiance, though I did not look directly at him.

It was time to remove the underskirt. The tie at the back of my waist gave me no trouble and it was only a moment before the fluffy muslin piled at my feet. Wearing only a fine batiste chemise, which was mine instead of Sylla's, I brought my hands up to the small ribbon bow that gathered the neckline of the chemise just between my breasts. I slowly pulled the ribbon tie until the neckline began to sag dangerously low. At that moment, I paused to stretch my arms above my head and twist myself a bit to and fro. I was a hardworking chambermaid getting ready for bed, after all. And the movement greatly accentuated the jiggling of my bosom within the thin chemise.

Sir shifted his position again. I thought of his cock swelling in his trousers. Most satisfying.

I reached for the hem of the chemise and pulled it over my head, ready for the next step in my plan.

The oil.

There was a moment when I began to despair of driving Sir to losing control. After all, I had seductively stripped, oiled myself from eyebrows to ankles, tantalized my own flesh with the feather, and finally brought myself to a small but satisfying orgasm with the carved olisbos.

I do believe the arms of the chair might never be the same, yet he did not rise from it until I fell back panting upon the pillows, setting aside the carving with a last shivering gasp.

Then he was upon me. His large hands came down to

wrap about my wrists and he easily pulled me upright to stand next to the bed. I stumbled, my knees still trembling, and sagged against him.

Sir drove one hand deep into my tumbled hair and pulled my head back for a single hot, ravaging kiss that stole the last of the strength from my legs. As he plundered my mouth with his other hand caressing my bottom, I could feel his trapped erection pressing into my bare belly. I clung to the lapels of his dressing gown and kissed him back, grateful to feel his hot hands upon me once more.

Yet after only that mind-altering kiss, he set me away from him, holding my shoulders steady until I found my feet.

Then he dropped his hands and stepped back. He cleared his throat. "I believe you have some natural talent in that direction."

Confused and fully aroused once more, I could only blink at him in astonishment. He turned to stride across the room. He removed some items from a chest there and returned to stand before me. From his hands hung crimson silk cords as thick as ropes.

"The Sixth Sin is Wrath."

Ten

Although I had been an eager student thus far, I must admit to a small shiver of apprehension when Sir began to bind my wrists behind my back. He did it slowly, winding the soft leather strap in a figure eight about one wrist, then the other. I twisted my hands but the straps did not give, though they were neither painful nor numbing.

The pose forced my breasts to jut forward. I felt my nipples crinkle in response. I could see Sir's eyes begin to gleam with appreciation behind the shadow of his mask.

"Your nipples are begging for my mouth," he whispered into my ear. The heat of his breath on my neck made me tremble.

When I opened my mouth to answer him, he quickly slipped a smooth, hard ball into my mouth. I realized it had cords emerging from each side as he deftly tied them behind my head. I could not close my lips, nor speak intelligibly. Muted by his toy, I could only raise my startled gaze to his.

"You are mine to play with tonight, in any way I please," he growled into my hair. "Since I shall not be requiring permission of any kind, there is naught for your mouth to do until my cock needs servicing. Fortunately, you will still be able to moan in ecstasy." He pushed me against the bedpost most firmly and ground his erection into my quivering belly. "And pain," he whispered. "Sweet, torturous pain that will soak your cunte with desire. Like this . . ."

He held me by my shoulders and lowered his mouth to my nipples, sucking them fiercely into rising for him. Then he rolled each between his sharp teeth until I squeaked with dismay. At my protesting sound, he removed one restraining hand and began to twist the opposite nipple with equal force. The pain was not unbearable, but I was used to more tender treatment. I writhed in rebellion, yet I could not escape my bonds, nor spit out my gag. He easily held me pressed to the chill, hard post with his one hand while he continued to torture my sensitive nipples. He was so much stronger than I.

I was completely helpless.

I was his creature now, just as he'd said. His plaything. His power over me was complete. I could neither protest nor escape his hot, wicked mouth and his sharp, teasing teeth. A feeling came over me then, a vulnerable, feminine flash of desire. The powerful male animal who controlled me sounded a chord within the female animal that was buried so deep beneath my civilized layers that I had never known it existed.

Yes. I trembled with the strength of my acquiescence. My cunte moistened instantly and completely, just as he'd promised.

He knew it at once. His pinioning hand left my shoulder and slid down between my thighs, catching the dew of my lust and spreading it over my labia in teasing circles. His fingers dipped and played but did not penetrate me as I would have liked. I tried to press into his touch, moaning, but he would not allow it.

He pulled his mouth from my nipple. "You have not fully succumbed, sweet student." He cupped my pubis in his palm for a long moment, then stepped away.

I let out a sigh, but I need not have worried. He was soon back and this time he had two small devices in his hands. I watched in alarm as he raised one to my right nipple. It was a hoop of gold wire, but it was not a complete circle. A small portion of the diameter had been cut away and gold balls the size of pearls had been soldered on, leaving a slight empty place between. The entire item was no larger than a shilling. I watched as he carefully spread the opening wider with the pressure of his fingers, then pressed my hardened nipple into the space between the balls. When he released the wire, the circle sprang together again, pinching my nipple tightly between.

I let out a small scream, for the pressure was intense. It was sharp, like the feeling of his teeth on me, like a long, continuous bite that did not end! Then I felt the other gold circle close upon my other nipple and I could no longer bear it! I flung myself away from him, only to discover that at some point he'd attached my bound wrists to the bedpost itself.

I became quite wild then, twisting and fighting my bonds, making noises more animal than human. I felt his large, hot hands close over my shoulders again, pressing me still.

"You are not harmed," he murmured. "When I remove the rings, you will be as you were before. See?"

He released me long enough to demonstrate, slipping the gold ring open enough to let my nipple slip out. It was rosy and rigid and the tingling sensation was intense, but he was quite right. I was unharmed.

I calmed then and stood still, my breasts rising and falling as I fought to catch my breath.

When he reattached the ring, I closed my eyes and shuddered against the intensity of the sensation, but I did not protest again.

Unfortunately, it seemed my acquiescence had come too late.

"Now I must punish you for such disobedience." His voice was low and dark, full of wicked threat and promise. I shivered again. I wanted to tell him I would not fight him again, that I would be a dutiful student and bow to his strength, but the gag that muffled my protest also muted my apology. He only shook his head in mock regret. "You are a willful creature," he told me. "Tonight, my will is the only one that matters."

Reaching behind me, he released my tied hands from the bedpost, though I was still bound. He turned me until I faced the side of the bed. Then I felt him untie my hands. Before I could celebrate this freedom, he wrapped his big hands about my wrists and raised them high. I had not realized that there were loops of leather tied to the curtain rail of the bed until I found myself strapped by them. My arms rose straight up and I was bound quite tightly, though not enough to make me rise to my toes.

Sir came close behind me and I realized that he was now as naked as I. His hot, hard palms came about to cup my breasts. He toyed with the rings dangling from my throbbing nipples. I gasped as the pain sharpened, just a little, just enough to remind me.

I am his plaything. I am his creature.

I am his.

My cunte became wet once more. What was this mad reaction? How could I, who had fought so for my independence, be so aroused by a man reducing me to such a state of submission?

Yet, this was Sir. I had trusted him to show me lust and appetite and indolence. He had pleasured and empowered me, teaching me new and astounding things about myself over and over again. I trusted Sir. I could not truly come to harm at his hands. I resolved to ride this strange, outrageous ride to its completion.

He lightly twisted the curious rings and pinched the tips of my wildly sensitive nipples themselves. The sensations shot through me like needles of torturous ecstasy.

I began to see that the pain/pleasure was not the truly arousing thing. The erotic hum throughout my body was not so much because he did these things to me, but because he *could* do these things to me. I was helpless before his power.

In a blinding flash it came to me. I was *helpless*. I was

not responsible for my reaction. When he reached down to slip his fingers between my soaking labia and teased at my swollen clitoris, it was not my doing when I gasped and trembled and pressed closer to his hand. Freed by his dominance, released by his authority, I was without shame, without blame, without any thoughts of modesty or disgrace.

In that moment I traveled to a place I had never known. Transformed by Sir's overwhelming strength into a being without power or responsibility, I slipped beneath the surface of my mind and drowned in the trust I held for him.

When he began to spank my buttocks with his open hand even as he continued to slide the fingers of his other hand up and down my slick, throbbing slit, I took the sweet, hot punishment as well as the teasing, slippery pleasure. The two sensations swirled around me and through me. The hot, sharp slap of his open palm on my reddening flesh. The dip and tease and swirl of his fingers rubbing at the sensitive swollen tip of my clitoris. I whimpered in pain. I moaned in ecstasy. I could not tell the sounds apart.

He smoothed my tingling buttocks with his open hand. "Do you feel it now, sweet rebel? You belong to me tonight. I am your master. I am your air, your water, your sustenance. If you wish to come at my hands, it will be when I decide and only when I decide."

I sighed in agreement. It crossed some faint corner of my mind that if I gave in too soon then the lesson might end, but there was no danger of that. The flat of his hand came down upon my sensitized buttocks again, harder than before. Then, harder still. I was being tested. I remained relaxed and submissive, taking the punishing spanking without protest or even a shiver of withdrawal.

When he brought me to orgasm while the spanking intensified, I went willingly, panting and moaning and, in the end, screaming my release around the ball gag even as the tears of pain rolled down my cheeks.

My submission, strangely, did not seem to satisfy Sir. As I panted, moaning, hanging from my bonds weak from my release, he growled something harsh and ripped my bonds from my wrists. I fell forward onto the mattress, bent at the waist, my hands still above my head as if bound there.

Sir entered me hard from behind, driving his cock into my soaking, slippery cunte in one forceful stroke. The abrupt penetration coincided with one of the trembling aftershocks passing through my body and I cried out in exquisite pleasure. As he thrust hard and fast, my sore nipples dragged back and forth over the coverlet, the golden rings twisting beneath me. I cried out again and again as he fucked me, but my pleasure only seemed to release some dark force within him. He gripped my hips in his hard hands and used his strength to deepen his thrusts. It hurt. The wildness and pain drove me higher.

It was glorious. It was hard and pitiless and animal. I came again, my gasps leaving my open mouth only to be muffled by the coverlet. I filled my two fists with the silken stuff and heard threads pop beneath the strength of my grip.

Sir reached orgasm with a roar. His grip on my hips tightened painfully as he thrust into me hard, once, twice, thrice more. His thick cock throbbed inside me and I gloried in my helplessness, in my power.

I felt his weight on the mattress next to me as he collapsed, pulling my hips with him, keeping himself driven into me. I rolled easily, as limp as a sleeping cat, unwilling to let him leave me.

We panted like horses after a hard gallop, our breaths coming in ragged unison. After a moment, he reached around me to carefully release the gold rings that had so effectively tortured my throbbing nipples. I gasped as the pain slipped away to leave a rich tingling behind. It was then that I realized I could have removed them myself any time after my hands were released. Such was his power over me in that moment that it had not even occurred to me. I let my hands lie limp and obedient, leaving the gag untouched. It was not for me to remove it. Tonight, swept into the Sin of Wrath, I belonged to him.

* * *

After I had dozed for a little while in Sir's arms, still obedi-
ently gagged, I had a single erotic thought drift across my
sated mind.

Your mouth shall service my cock.

I slid from the circle of his sleepy embrace. He grunted
in surprise and sat up as I left the bed to kneel on the carpet
beside it, facing the great bed like an altar. *I wish to worship your cock.*

Sir sat up and gazed at me for a long moment. I dropped
my eyes and sat back on my heels demurely, naked, be-
seeching, my hands loosely upturned on my lap.

"Do you wish me to remove the ball from your mouth?"

I nodded silently.

He stood to walk the necessary half-step toward me.
Even as he reached behind my bowed head to untie the
cords of the gag, I had raised my cupped hands to caress the
weight of his testicles with my palms. I heard him take a
quick breath in surprise. I did not know they were so sensitive. I was intrigued.

The cords loosened and I let the ball slip from my mouth
and fall to the carpet. I was well done with it. My lips had
another purpose now.

Before my eyes, his cock began to rise. I had not seen
this before, this rush of blood to darken the head of him,
this pulsing swelling and thickening. I knelt before him and
observed the power of my merest touch upon his senses. I
softly massaged his testicles, as gently as I would two ripe
fruits, and his stiffening cock throbbed before my eyes.

He caressed my hair, his eyes unreadable behind his
mask. "Open your mouth, Ophelia. Take my cock inside."

I licked my lips and bent to kiss the silken head of him. I
tasted my own salty cream and yet another flavor, sharp and
tangy. His come, the same milky liquid that now slicked
down my own thighs and had every night for nearly a week.
I liked the taste of him. I began to lick at the bulbous head,

to catch every hint of his come on my tongue. He gasped as I lapped at him. One big hand came down to fist in my hair. He pressed my head closer. I opened my mouth and let him enter me that way.

As he slipped between my lips, inch by inch, I stroked him with my tongue, rolling it over and around him to get all of that mysteriously delicious taste from his rigid flesh. Intent upon my feasting upon him, I did not realize until a moment later that his entire body trembled in response.

This gave him so much pleasure, this swirling motion?

Apparently so, for he tightened his grip in my hair and began to enter my mouth so deeply that the thick head of his cock drove far back into my throat. It took a moment of concentration to allow that thick invasion, but when I had the trick of it I could take the entire length of him into my hot mouth.

As he slowly withdrew, I let suction build as I swirled my tongue upon the pulsing vein running beneath his rod. The sound he made, somewhere between harsh and helpless, made me realize that the tables had turned on his game tonight.

Even naked and on my knees, it was I who controlled him.

Remembering how he had held my hips as he fucked me, I raised my hands to his buttocks to pull him more deeply into my throat. He might have intended to dominate me, but in that moment, I took control of his pleasure.

I gained the rhythm quickly, digging my fingers and fingernails into his buttocks to control his speed. He wanted to go faster, I could feel it, but my new power intrigued me. He wished to teach me dominance and control. Well, I wished to learn it well.

I backed off from the length of him, despite his pressing hand in my hair. Licking my lips, which were swollen and puffy from sucking at him, I lifted my head to meet his dark gaze. His expression was unreadable behind the mask, but I knew from the trembling of his body and the pulsing rigidity of his cock that my lover was well at my mercy now.

"Do not touch me," I ordered him. "Grasp the curtain bar above your head and do not release it."

His jaw tightened. I could see him begin to form a protest. My fingernails tightened ever so slightly over his buttocks even as I ran my hot tongue possessively over the smooth, rounded head of him. His hands flew to grasp the curtain bar as his eyes closed and he let his head fall back, so racked with pleasure that he had no will left to argue.

I could not let such obedience go unrewarded. To show my appreciation, I took his cock back into my mouth in one deep, wet plunge, all the way to the hilt.

If I had not heard the animal moan from his lips myself, I would not have thought it to be human.

Left to the joys of my own exploration now, I allowed my world to narrow down to two things. His cock and my mouth. While he strained and writhed above me, I tortured and pleasured him for as long as I cared to. I felt the pulse in his thick vein increase more than once, upon which moment I decreased my suction and my lapping and let half his length fall untended from my lips. Each time the cry he gave became more desperate.

It was cruel. I quite enjoyed that fact. I knew from my own experience that when I finally allowed his orgasm to overwhelm him that it would be tenfold in power, so I felt no guilt at my pitiless play. I had endured much restless aching at his hands this week and I found myself disinclined to ease his longing anytime soon.

It was only when my own jaw and mouth, unaccustomed to such activity, began to protest that I decided to drive this weary stallion home at last. Redoubling my caressing of his testicles, including the hard, throbbing place just behind them, I took his cock deep into my throat. Increasing my pace, I even allowed him to move his hips toward me now, helping to thrust and withdraw as I sucked and swirled and lapped at the underside of his length.

In this moment I raised my gaze to catch the sight of him, powerful and strong, yet helpless in his lust. His naked, muscular body rippled with tension in the light of the single candle, shining with sweat from his long torture, stretched taut and undulating between my sucking mouth and his own white-knuckled grasp on the curtain bar. His dark head dropped back as wordless pleas left his lips, moans so full of deep, hoarse begging that I knew it was time to allow him to break.

I felt his testicles tighten to hard rocks in my hands and instinctively I drove his cock deep into my throat. It swelled to such an enormous proportion I feared it would crack my jaw. He let out a deep, helpless roar even as his cock pulsated violently inside my mouth.

I was too filled with him to breathe. I held on by will alone, letting every drop of his come pour down my throat even as I began to feel dizzy. When his moans decreased to helpless panting, I finally backed away, slowly allowing his still thick cock to slip from my swollen lips. He left a trickle of that sharp, sweet taste on my tongue as he left me.

He released the bar above his head then, only to collapse to his knees before me. We knelt together on the carpet, leaning against each other. Sir wrapped one caressing palm around my sore jaw and dropped his damp forehead to my shoulder. We spent several moments relishing the simple act of breathing normally again.

Then he lifted his head. With both hands, he swept my wild hair back from my face so that he could gaze into my eyes. "What possessed you?" His voice was hoarse from his guttural cries.

I licked my swollen lips. "You deserved nothing less."

A small laugh escaped him. "I deserved the torture, or the pleasure?" His thumb slid to caress my lips, silencing my reply. "Never mind. I don't think I want to know."

I smiled wearily. *Precisely, my darling Sir.*

Eleven

On the seventh night, I traveled to the Swan's house in late afternoon, uncaring that I would be missed by Aunt Beryl that evening. It no longer mattered. I was more than through with my relations and intended to inform them of my victorious ruination on the following day. My little house was fully furnished and Robert had already agreed to everything the Swan had negotiated for on my behalf. Society had already begun to buzz with gossip about the new courtesan in town.

All was ready, but I missed the Swan. I had only seen her once during the week, when she'd informed me of Sir's absence. It seemed whenever I arrived or awoke in her house that she was out or unavailable.

This day was no different. The Swan's footman allowed me in the house without hesitation, but she was not within. At loose ends, I wandered up to "my" room and dawdled there.

The restraining straps had been removed from the bed frame. The room looked as if any respectable guest might occupy it. Mere walls and curtains and carpet told no tales of the wicked pleasure and naked debauchery they had witnessed.

The only evidence that remained lived in my memory.

I sat upon the bed where I had spent so many marvelous, unbelievable hours and stroked my hand down the satin counterpane. Then I lay back upon the pillows and imagined my new lover-to-be, Robert, straining and gasping above me.

The picture did not displease me, especially when I put Robert in a mask.

Warm lips descended upon mine. I opened my eyes to see that the room was dark, with only a single candle lighted upon the mantel.

Sir sat beside me on the bed, a slight smile upon his masked face. He looked thoughtful and a bit . . . sad? It was as if the mask beneath the mask had fallen away.

Yet before me was a man who could be whatever a woman wanted him to be. He was as skilled a player as the Swan, as I myself hoped to be.

If a woman wished to see love in his eyes, she could convince herself it was there. If she wished to see sadness at a parting of the ways, I knew perfectly well that it would gleam from his dark eyes.

So I banked the girlish romantic coal of hope that tried to glow in my heart and smiled easily up at Sir. "Let the lesson begin."

He lifted his chin and the trick of the candlelight was no more. Standing, he took my hand and helped me from the bed. Still with my hand in his, he led me across the room where stood a tall dressing-room mirror.

I was placed to face the mirror, while Sir stood behind me and his gaze met mine in the glass.

"The Seventh Sin," he said in my ear in his husky whisper, "is Pride."

He undressed me then, removing everything from the pins in my hair to my stockings. He would not let me help, but attended me like a servant—a servant whose touch lingered rather inappropriately! I enjoyed the sensuousness of his gentleness. When I was entirely naked with my hair falling riotously over my shoulders and my nipples crinkled from the chill of the room, he stood behind me once more.

With both hands resting warm on my shoulders, he turned my face toward the mirror. "You are magnificent," he told me. "Your beauty is undeniable, but you are so much more than milky skin and flashing eyes. In our few days together, you have shown me the wisdom and joy and effortless courage you hold within you."

His hands slid down my arms. I leaned back into the warmth and solidity of him. He stroked his palms up over my belly, crossing them to embrace my waist. "You are a powerful being, sweet Ophelia, glowing with strength and spirit." He bent his dark head to kiss my neck. I reached a hand up to bury my fingers in his thick hair.

"I beg of you," he murmured into my skin, "let no man wrest that indomitable will from your generous heart."

I turned into him then, intent upon his kiss. I wanted every moment, every taste, every touch of Sir's I could have that night, for I knew that when our time was over he would return to his patronesses and I would move on to Robert.

Our last lesson.

I was proud. I had become someone I had never believed I could be. I was a scarlet woman, an artist of pleasure, a rebel soldier. I was the sword-wielding insurrectionist of my own life.

I was a courtesan.

In the darkest hours of the night, when the coals had burned down to ash and the candle's flame had long ago stuttered out in a pool of melted wax, I let out a long sigh of completion.

A large, masculine hand ran up my naked thigh.

"I have taught you everything I can," he whispered into my ear, his breath hot. "Tomorrow you will choose your first lover." He kissed me, more tenderly than he had in the last seven nights of exquisite pleasure. "Are you certain that this is what you wish? Once you become a courtesan, you may never return to the life you've always known."

I hooked my arm about his neck and kissed him back with all the skill and confidence that he had given me as he'd instructed me in the Seven Sins of the Courtesan. "I know what I want. Only as a courtesan can I be truly free to decide my own destiny."

He bowed, a little sadly, I think. "So be it. I shall leave you, sweet blackbird."

I lay back down in the nest of silken sheets a different woman than when I had first slid between them. I watched him leave with a smile, although I think my heart broke just a little. He had taught me so much, although I had never learned the name of the man I knew only as "Sir."

The next morning I found a gleaming black feather upon my pillow.

It was time to begin my new life.

The Blackbird had taken wing.

VOLUME II

Twelve

Boston, Present Day

It is only one step, I told myself, a single step forward or a single step back. It was up to me to decide which I would take.

My hand hovered over the latch. My heart beat fitfully. My mind whirled. Hadn't I longed for this moment? Hadn't I dreamed of the freedom to determine my own destiny? Of course I had. But in my girlish dreams, I had been unaware that freedom came at a price, and the currency was risk.

So be it. I opened the door and stepped across the threshold, not knowing which world I had entered. Was it the beginning of a life fully lived, or a willful and perilous mistake?

Piper placed Brenna's checklist on the edge of the bed, right next to the outrageously impractical pale pink bra and panty set, the cost of which could cover a day at the Cape, complete with parking, hot dogs, and butterscotch sundaes from Four Seas.

The underwear was just the finishing flourish of a week-long consumer orgy Brenna had called Piper's "Reinvention." The narcissistic bacchanal had included teeth whitening, a new pair of designer eyeglasses (*plus* her first contacts ever), a deep-conditioning hair color and cut, a facial, an exfoliating massage, eyebrow shaping, a bikini wax, and the purchase of tote bags full of expensive makeup (complete with lessons on *how the freaking hell* Piper was supposed to use an eyelash curler without causing a corneal abrasion). Then there was the new wardrobe— fitted blouses, tailored skirts and trousers, and even a few curve-hugging dresses—complemented by five pairs of impractical shoes, an assortment of statement-making bags (never call them "purses," Brenna had explained), and accessories such as earrings, bracelets, and scarves.

Piper now understood that the pursuit of beauty was a full-time job. It was a wonder Brenna had ever managed to earn her doctorate. It was a pricey hobby, too. Piper's makeover required siphoning six figures from Granny Pierpont's trust fund, a reckless decision as that was her only buffer against poverty should she lose her job. And what did she have to show for all the effort and expense? Piper's eyes swept to the new full-length mirror bracketed to her bedroom wall. She stared in fascination at her naked reflection.

She still didn't recognize herself. True, she no longer gasped at the creature looking back at her, but Piper remained cautious of the woman with the killer green eyes, the lustrous skin, and the shiny, bouncy dark brown hair. She was curious as to how long the woman in the mirror had possessed those smooth shoulders and delicate collarbones. She wondered how the woman could have been running around Boston for the last decade with her 36C boobs smushed into a 32B sports bra. She couldn't remember why the woman had been morally opposed to contacts, lipstick, and mascara.

As for everything below the underwire? She was a stranger to herself, really. Brenna claimed Piper had never allowed herself to bask in her own glory. Though her friend might have found a less histrionic way to phrase it, she had to concede Brenna had a point. Piper had never been the type to spin in front of the mirror in the buff, checking out the curve of her buttock or the slope of her thigh. She'd never been the type to enjoy being moisturized, fluffed, coiffed, and generally encouraged to feel connected to all her body parts.

But if Ophelia Harrington could learn to love it, there was no reason Piper couldn't. Right?

She sighed. *This had better work,* she thought. *I had better stroll into the museum tomorrow and see Mick Malloy slip in a puddle of his own drool.* That's what all this was for, after all. She was on a mission of seduction. She was getting her do-over-of-a-lifetime.

Piper was about to reach for her panties when she saw her own sly smile in the mirror. Sir's words to Ophelia floated through her mind.

"You are alive. Your heart beats. Your skin is hot and pliable and responds to my touch. Every one of life's pleasures will come to you through this magnificent body, Ophelia. Don't be afraid to take ownership of this treasure."

Piper shuddered, the goose bumps visible on her own nakedness. *Holy shit,* but Sir had been one astonishingly sexy man. Yet, even after all her careful study of the journals, so much of him remained an enigma to Piper. She longed to hear his thoughts, to get a peek at the secrets of his heart. Too bad he hadn't been the diary-keeping sort himself. At least his words lived on through Ophelia.

Still smiling, Piper turned on her heel to check out her own treasures, the voluptuous curve of her ass and the smooth line of her thigh. Not bad, she had to admit. Not bad at all.

As she slipped into the bra and panty set, she went over the agenda in her mind. Today was to be her trial run. She'd have coffee with Brenna at L'Aroma, followed by a visit to her parents. The coffee had been Piper's idea. The parents had been Brenna's. As she'd fearlessly pointed out to Piper, her parents' home was the one place her transformation would likely meet with resistance, if not outright scorn. If Piper faced her mother and father first, Brenna reasoned, any snickers or stares doled out by her coworkers on Monday would be a snap to handle.

As usual, Brenna probably had a point.

Once Piper had finished dressing in a casual skirt and a stretchy cotton blouse, carefully made up her face, and put the finishing touches on her hair, she left her apartment and waited for the elevator. That's when she discovered that the changes reached beyond her own bedroom mirror. Apparently, there'd been a cataclysmic shift in her world.

When the elevator door opened, three men greeted her. She knew two of them—the retired medical illustrator who lived on the sixth floor and the somnambulant med student who lived on the tenth. When Piper said hello, two sets of eyeballs expanded and two mouths gaped. The men looked too shell-shocked to speak.

The other guy was a thirty-something jock who'd never uttered a word to Piper in the three years he'd lived in the building, not even when the two of them had awkwardly ended up in the tiny basement laundry at the same time. But today, he smiled and raised his eyebrows, coming alive like someone had just plugged him into a generator.

"Hawh ah yah?" he asked, unabashedly letting his eyes roam from her face to her sandals and back up again. "Going down?"

Piper spun around to face the elevator doors, feeling little needles of anxiety prick at her skin. The jock seemed dangerously hungry, like how one of her parents' calorie-restricted friends might look if confronted with a deluxe burger with fries from Mr. Bartley's.

She stared ahead, breathing hard and telling herself to calm down. After all, what was the point of looking hot if you were still scurrying around like a scared mouse? She consciously relaxed her shoulders, softened her stance, and remembered Brenna's instructions: "Let the feminine energy flow through you. Feel the power. Loosen your hips and rock it."

After that uncomfortable interlude on the elevator, the world-shifting moments just kept coming. A teenager got up and gave her his seat on the T. The old man at the fruit stand on Newbury smiled and said good morning, then handed her an orange. A man exiting L'Aroma held the door open for her, even though he had to juggle a to-go box filled with drinks and baked goods to get the job done.

Piper smiled shyly at him and ducked into the air-conditioned coffeehouse, where she was promptly rewarded with the attention of every male in the place. It made her involuntarily gasp and clutch her purse—no, wait, her *bag*—to the front of her body. She walked as fast as possible on three-inch heels to reach Brenna.

Piper fell into the chair and leaned over the small table. "My God, Brenna! Is this what your life's always been like? How do you do it? How do you live this way?"

Brenna slid a hot and foamy café au lait toward Piper and smiled softly. "You simply accept it. You appreciate it. And you go on about your business."

Piper shook her head. "I feel like I'm on exhibit. Like I'm advertising myself."

"Well, *duh*." Brenna's smile widened. "That's what women have always done, from courtesans to curators and everyone in between. When you present yourself in the best possible way, you're telling the world you know you're beautiful and valuable and that you deserve the best. And that's precisely when the best starts to come to you."

"But—" Piper dared take a quick peek around the room to reassure herself that men had stopped staring. No such luck. "Why would I want a man who's only interested in what I look like?"

"We've been over this a thousand times," Brenna said, chuckling. "Mick Malloy is a lot of things—academic, adventurer, owner of one fine ass—but first and foremost, he's a man. Men are visual. They notice the outside package first, so that's where we have to start. Do you want Mick Malloy or not?"

The question jarred Piper. Of course she wanted Mick. She'd always wanted him, whether she'd admitted it to herself or not. Ophelia's journals had given her the courage to face her own desires. They'd also given her the clarity to see that her desires began and ended with Mick Malloy. And now, for the first time, she believed she just might have a shot at getting him.

"Yes," she answered.

"Okay," Brenna said. "Then you can either sit around complaining about nature or you can use it to your benefit. It's your choice."

Piper rolled her eyes. "I understand that."

"Do you?" Brenna leaned closer. "Really?"

Piper took a breath, preparing herself to recite one of the fundamentals of seduction, as distilled by her panel of bi-century teachers—Sir, the Swan, Ophelia, and Professor Brenna Nielsen. "I really do," Piper said, smiling. "Once I have Mick's attention, I can begin to reveal the incredible woman I am inside. But I have to do it slowly and carefully, ever aware that my goal is to heighten anticipation and maintain the mystery."

"Bravo!" Brenna said, clapping softly. "So do you feel different today?"

A little shiver went through Piper's body. "I do," she said. "I feel feminine. I feel sexy."

Brenna let go with a huge grin, and Piper couldn't help but notice how proud she seemed. But the grin quickly faded, and her friend appeared as if she were going to cry.

"I'm fine," Brenna said, raising her hand before Piper could speak. "It's just—" She shook her head. "Piper, it's remarkable. This is the first time I've ever seen your inner and outer beauty match up."

Piper reached out for her friend's hand. "Thank you for helping me with that."

"You're more than welcome."

They stayed quiet for a moment. Brenna looked Piper right in the eye. "Are you ready for tomorrow?"

Piper jerked her hand away. She bit her bottom lip, trying not to let on how nervous she was about seeing Mick again. Sure, she was thrilled about the possibilities of her new life, but the idea of moving from theory to practice was terrifying.

"No more doubt, Piper," Brenna said. "Seriously. You are so hot that Mick Malloy is going to feel like he's been hit by the lust bus."

She giggled. "Okay."

"So." Brenna widened her eyes. "You were about to tell me about tomorrow."

"Right," Piper said. "If Mick asks me about the change in my appearance, I'll answer truthfully but as vaguely as possible. If he asks me to go for lunch or something—"

"*When* he asks you."

"*When* he asks me to go to lunch or coffee, I'll politely demur due to work, but suggest that some other time might be better. Though technically not a rejection, the answer establishes the challenge, heightens anticipation, and sends the mystery level into the stratosphere."

One of Brenna's pale eyebrows arched over a blue eye.

"What?" Piper asked. "You *know* I take excellent notes."

Brenna's eyes had wandered past Piper's shoulder. "Good, because here comes your pop quiz."

"Excuse me, miss." The deep voice came from behind Piper. She spun around in her chair, startled to see a handsome college student holding her purse—*her bag, her bag, dammit*. "This fell off the back of the chair and I . . . uh, you know . . . I didn't want someone to steal it or anything."

"Oh!" Piper accepted the bag with a smile. "I appreciate that."

"No problem," the college kid said. "Hey, um, you know, can I have your number?"

Piper quickly looked to Brenna for help. None was being offered. Her friend simply pasted a pleasant smile on her face, leaned back in the chair, and made a gesture to indicate the ball was in Piper's court.

So she turned back to the kid. "My number's thirty," she said flatly.

He frowned.

"As in, I'm thirty years old." Piper waited, fully expecting to see the young man scurry back to whence he came.

Instead, the kid's lips curled up and he let his eyes roam all over her. *"That's wicked sick hot,"* he said.

"Oh, for crying out loud." Piper huffed. "Let me rephrase this for you, then. The answer is no. I'm not interested. Have a nice day." She turned back to Brenna and said nothing until she sensed that the young man had begun to slink away.

"So, how'd I do?" she asked, sipping her drink.

Brenna chuckled softly. "There's certainly nothing wrong with telling a man you're not interested if it's a true statement."

"I've seen you do it a few thousand times."

"Yes, but you might want to work on your finesse."

"Oh yeah?" Piper folded her hands on the table. "So how would you have handled it?"

Brenna tipped her head thoughtfully. "I suppose I'd have said, 'Thank you. I'm flattered.' Then I'd mention that I don't give out my number as a matter of policy. Then I'd add, 'Please respect that.' "

Piper sat up a bit, impressed at how easily that rolled off Brenna's tongue. "Nice."

"I'm sure you'll have ample opportunities to practice in the near future."

Piper shook her head.

"You don't agree?" Brenna asked.

"No. I mean yes! It's not that."

"Then what?"

Piper laughed nervously. "I was just thinking how great it would be if I could come up with some magic phrase for my parents; you know, just waltz up to them and say, 'Mother and Father, please stop trying to control me. I want to live my own life. Please respect that.' "

Brenna laughed. "That sounds about perfect to me."

"Yeah, well, I'm starting to have second thoughts about letting them see me like this." Piper gestured to herself.

"Maybe I should wait a while longer, ease them into it over time."

"Sure," Brenna offered with an enthusiastic nod. "Why not wait another thirty years? That way, you'll be sixty when you get around to telling your parents to back off, and they'll be in their nineties, but they'll be able to handle it, since they'll still be working full-time and running marathons and shit, right?"

Piper pursed her lips. It was interesting how, as part of the Reinventing Piper Project, Brenna had suddenly decided to say exactly what was on her mind.

"Point taken," she said. "But I'm not looking forward to it."

"Of course you're not." Brenna patted Piper's clenched hands. "But really, what's the worst that could happen?"

Piper pondered that question in great detail during the subway ride back to Cambridge and during the nine-block walk from the Harvard Square T station to her parents' house on Towbridge Street. By the time Piper stood on the sidewalk in front of her childhood home, she'd come up with her answer.

The worst that could happen was nothing. It was possible that she could show up with her dramatically different hair and clothing and attitude and her parents wouldn't notice a thing. They might very well launch into the usual topics— whether she was eating properly, their research funding, maybe even her job—and never detect a single change in their daughter.

Piper took a deep breath and eyed the house warily. The three-story 1920s gray clapboard structure had white trim, black shutters, and strong Yankee bones. A squared-off line of boxwoods squatted below the porch railing, the only bit of decoration in sight. There were no geraniums in the flower boxes. No pretty wreath on the door. No welcoming porch rockers with toss pillows.

It hadn't always been this austere, Piper knew. When Granny Pierpont was still alive, she made sure the house looked cheerful. The window boxes were always overflowing in the summer, and the porch featured wicker furniture with floral cushions.

For a long time now, Piper had wondered how her father had managed to avoid inheriting any of his mother's blithe cheerfulness. Only recently did she consider that she might have been asking the wrong question. Her father could have started out plenty cheery, but a few decades with Piper's mother had sucked it right out of him.

"Come in if you're coming." Her father poked his head out the front door. "Unless you're waiting for the weather to change."

The sharply angled salt-and-pepper pageboy of Piper's mother popped out from under her father's arm. She smiled tightly, paused for a moment, and frowned.

"Heavens!" Piper's mother raised a hand to her mouth as she scanned the sidewalk, almost as if she feared Piper's appearance would frighten the neighbors. "What have you done to yourself? Is this some kind of joke?" Piper's mother began to wave frantically for her to get inside.

It was then that Piper looked down at herself, just to refresh her memory about what she'd decided to wear on that Sunday afternoon in June. A simple, knee-length, light gray linen-blend skirt with a side kick pleat. A pale pink, collared, three-quarter-length-sleeve fitted blouse with the top two buttons open. A wide black leather belt. Delicate silver hoops in her ears. Simple black sandals that showed off her pink manicured toes. A pink and silver bracelet. The slouchy gray leather bag with a big silver buckle. Her hair was down. Her makeup was light with a sweep of liquid eyeliner Brenna said would hint at her sensual side.

She'd done everything she was supposed to do. And this was the reaction she got.

It had to be the eyeliner.

"Piper! Don't just stand there!"

As she raised her gaze to her frowning mother and climbed the porch steps, she took comfort in the fact that at least they'd noticed.

The inquisition began as soon as she'd stepped into the foyer.

"What happened to my sweet and normal Piper?" Her mother fingered the cuff of the new blouse as she pulled her lips tight.

"I decided to change my look."

"And carry a *purse*? Since when do you carry a purse?" Her father scowled at the statement-making accessory.

"It's a bag, Father."

He laughed. "Fair enough," he said, nodding. "I'll play along here. Would you mind telling me just *who* you and your *bag* are trying to be these days?"

Piper stopped walking. Her scalp felt hot. Her chest knotted up. "Myself," she said.

Eventually, her parents allowed her into the dining room, where her mother served the Chase-Pierpont clan's version of a Sunday dinner. The menu consisted of sautéed ginger cabbage, a mint cucumber salad, and raw tofu. Her mother measured out half-cup portions of each item, and placed them onto plates. Then she announced the nutritional makeup of the feast.

"Only five grams of fat per meal," she said, spreading her linen napkin across her lap. "Fewer than one hundred and thirty calories, with ten grams of protein. Plus it's high in fiber, folate, vitamin C, manganese, and calcium." Her mother smiled broadly. "Bon appétit!"

As she began to pick at the tofu, Piper told herself that if she survived this homecoming, she'd stop by the All Star for a patty melt with Swiss and a side of onion rings and snarf the whole greasy mess while walking home.

The conversation took its usual turn, and soon Piper was hearing about the lab's latest grant proposal, who among her parents' friends had died at an early age due to unhealthy practices, and her father's training regimen for the fall senior-division competitive-crewing season.

"I'm down to eight percent body fat," he told Piper.

"Wow," she said.

"My weight this morning was one hundred fifty-four point six and my BMI is hovering right around twenty-one point six, which is well within the bottom ten percent of the population."

Piper nodded silently, concentrating on chewing her mouthful of gooey sawdust.

Her father cleared his throat. "Your mother tells me you're back on dairy. I must say, you do look a bit puffy. Did you bring along your food journal?"

Piper glanced up in time to see disdain flash across her father's face. He quickly covered it with a vacant smile. "Are you? Back on dairy?"

Piper set her fork down. She felt nauseated, though she didn't know if it was from the anxiety or the cuisine.

"You haven't asked me about my work," she said, her voice soft. Underneath the table, out of sight, Piper began violently wringing the cloth napkin in her hands. "But I'll tell you anyway. My work is going well. I'm getting quite excited about the Ophelia Harrington exhibit, even toying with the idea of focusing almost exclusively on her private life."

"That's wonderful," her mother said. "Have you heard anything about possible job cuts at the museum?"

"Nope."

"Is your position still at risk?" her father asked, dabbing at the corner of his mouth with his napkin. "And do you really think now is the right time to be 'toying' with anything? Shouldn't you putting your nose to the grindstone and staying out of the spotlight?"

Piper thought her head would explode. *What is wrong with you people? My God! No wonder I'm so repressed!*

Her mother pursed her lips. "I just read a report that almost three-quarters of U.S. museums are experiencing moderate to severe budget constraints. I know how you love your job, but perhaps you should prepare yourself for the worst."

"Indeed," her father said, sighing heavily. "Thank goodness you haven't touched Granny Pierpont's nest egg."

"So," her mother said. "Tell us what this makeover is all about."

Piper opened her mouth to speak but her father cut her off. "I doubt painting your face will help you keep your position," he said. "The last thing the trustees want is a streetwalker planning their exhibits."

Piper's eyeballs bulged. She bit her tongue. Her hands shook.

"Did Brenna put you up to this?" her mother asked. "She might be able to pull off this kind of borderline-inappropriate look, but it doesn't suit a girl like you."

"Actually, I'm a thirty-year-old woman."

"Yes, and that's exactly my point, dear. Women in academia don't get taken seriously if they dress in a provocative manner."

That was the moment Piper knew with certainty that her parents hadn't even noticed she'd had a birthday. The two of them were so self-involved, so soulless, that they'd paid no mind to the fact that their only child had just, officially, become middle-aged.

In her lap, Piper twisted the heirloom napkin until she felt the elderly linen tear.

"Listen to your mother," her father said.

"Hey, I have an idea!" Piper shouted. "How about the two of you listen to me for a change?"

The air began to saw in and out of Piper's nostrils. It was the only sound in the dining room.

"Listen up, peeps—I just turned thirty, right? I got no card from you. No gift. No nothing. Perhaps it slipped your carbohydrate-starved minds. And the only thing provocative about this outfit is that it reveals the fact that I'm a woman with double-digit-body-fat-covered female parts. You know—hips, thighs, breasts—the whole borderline-inappropriate shebang!"

Piper's father sputtered. Her mother dropped her fork onto her plate, and a wad of sautéed ginger cabbage landed with a splat on the tablecloth.

Oh boy. Oh shit. Piper hadn't meant to say that *out loud*. And note to self: *the word "peeps" has no place in my lexicon.*

She shoved herself to a stand. She threw the damaged napkin to the table, grabbed her bag, and squared her shoulders.

Her parents' faces remained frozen in disbelief. Maybe she should've waited until she was sixty.

"Look, I'm sorry I spoke to you like that." Piper forced back the tears. Her shoulders sagged. Her chest felt hollow. "I'll just go now."

Before she reached the door, Piper heard her father offer a one-word explanation for his daughter's uncharacteristic outburst.

"Dairy," he said.

Later that night, Piper took no joy in preparing for her return to work. She chose her outfit, packed her matching bag, and laid out her cosmetics on the bathroom countertop, but all she could think about was how she'd failed.

Sure, she'd screamed at her parents. Real mature. But then she'd *apologized*! As if it were *her* fault that her parents were emotionally freeze-dried!

Piper leaned her hands on the edge of the countertop. She raised her eyes to the mirror. The new woman in her life glared back, and boy was she pissed.

You're going to explode if you don't find the courage to stand up for yourself. Without apology. The way Ophelia did. Damn the consequences.

As Piper studied the anger and grief in her own eyes, she was suddenly struck by the irony of it all.

She wasn't brave enough to tell the truth about another woman's life, let alone her own.

Thirteen

The instant Mick saw Piper, his knees gave out. The room went dim. His ears clanged like the bells at Holy Cross Cathedral. His body collapsed into a conference room chair. He struggled to catch his breath.

Piper Chase-Pierpont had just kicked the wind out of him.

A few people in the conference room gasped. One fellow dropped his Styrofoam cup of hot coffee. A couple others scrambled to mop it up with paper towels while their jaws hung slack. One guy even took a picture of her with his smartphone.

But Linc Northcutt, the arse-kisser who'd been assigned as Mick's assistant and then spent all of last week annoying the fuck out of him, was the first person to say anything.

"Piper?" Linc's voice got a bit squeaky in the higher decibel range. "Is that really *you*?"

Mick kept his eyes locked on Piper as she strolled through the conference room like a cat, all shiny and glowing and poised and looking like a shot of eighty-proof sex poured into a pair of heels.

Heels. She was wearing feckin' heels. And a real dress.

Mick's palms began to sweat. This apparition couldn't be real. He blinked, but she was still there, still moving like a hot knife through melting butter. He decided to pinch the inside of his left thigh as hard as he could to be sure he wasn't dreaming. It hurt so bad his eyes watered.

Jaysus feckin' H., Piper Chase-Pierpont was one fine woman.

The conference room was in chaos by the time a sweaty-looking Louis LaPaglia shuffled in, juggling a stack of papers, a laptop, and a cup of coffee. He began talking before he'd gotten himself organized or even put his arse in a chair.

"All right, people. Let's get this going. I have an interview with public television at ten-thirty. Oh, and welcome back, Piper," he said, opening his laptop and hitting the power button. He chuckled to himself, then finally raised his eyes to the assembled staff. "So how's the ink poi—"

The room went silent. Piper stood behind her chair and smiled pleasantly. It was then Mick noticed she'd chosen the seat farthest from him. In fact, any farther away and she wouldn't be attending the same meeting.

"A lot better, thanks," she said.

"No shit."

LaPaglia slapped a hand over his mouth. His eyes bulged in embarrassment. Everyone but Mick and Piper began to howl with laughter. Mick imagined only three little words were now dancing around in LaPaglia's tiny brain. *Sexual. Harassment. Complaint.*

"Er . . . ah . . ." LaPaglia shook his head. He'd gone pale. "That's enough, people. Oh God. Damn. I'm really sorry, Piper. Er . . . It's just a shock. But you look so . . ."

Mick filled in the blank in his head: *Lovely. Sexy. Pulled together. Delicious.*

". . . nice," the museum's executive director said. "Now, ah, let's get started, shall we?"

While everyone else had been laughing, Mick continued to study Piper. Truly, she was a feast for the visual cortex. She wore a clingy wrap dress in ivory with tiny brown dots, and though it was a perfectly businesslike dress, it did nothing to hide the potential for sin that lurked beneath.

She'd chosen neutral-colored open-toed high-heeled sandals. Her face seemed cheerful and healthy. Her smile was blinding. Her hair was dark and lustrous and he suddenly couldn't recall how she'd worn it last week and why it seemed so shockingly *there* today. And her eyes—

He heard himself gasp. *Contacts.* Piper was wearing contacts. And her gorgeous green eyes were large and luminous and looking right . . . at . . . him.

His elbow slipped off the table.

She smiled sweetly.

Fuck me.

Piper slipped daintily into her chair, folded her hands on the table in front of her, and continued to smile benevolently. She didn't mind the stares, the gasps, the spilled coffee. She didn't even mind LaPaglia's oafish slip of the tongue. None of it mattered—because Mick Malloy sat limp in his chair, flattened by the steel-belted radials of the lust bus, just as Brenna had promised.

Piper wasn't the only one who noticed this. Linc had looked sideways at Mick and exploded with a combination choke and guffaw that had him reaching for his coffee. "Excuse me," he said to the group, thumping on his chest.

"We need to move along, people," LaPaglia said impatiently. As Piper's boss raced through the agenda items as if his pants were on fire, Piper felt Mick's eyes bore into her. *Bore away,* she thought.

"Any update on the Ophelia Harrington installation, Piper?"

"Of course." She stood, took a breath, and launched into her much-rehearsed statement. "This exhibit promises to be a moving experience for our visitors, both visually and orally—I mean aurally."

Piper wanted to die from shame. Linc snickered. She hated that little ferret. She charged ahead.

"I've contracted with a British female voice-over artist

who'll read excerpts from Ophelia's Harrington's speeches and personal letters. I think it will add a touch of immediacy to the museum experience."

LaPaglia scowled. "I don't remember seeing that in your budget."

Her boss had made a simple statement. And she knew how to respond. But for some reason, Piper had frozen where she stood, her head now echoing with a British woman's words, husky and thick with desire. *"He brought me to orgasm while the spanking intensified. I went willingly, panting and moaning and screaming my release."*

That whisper Piper heard didn't belong to the voice-over artist, and the sentiment sure as hell wouldn't be part of the exhibit. Piper shook her head, trying to shoo the words away. She was losing it. "Yes, it was in the budget."

"Go on."

But she was drawing a blank. What was wrong with her? She'd practiced this update a thousand times at home, and at no time had the Seven Sins of the Courtesan hijacked her frontal lobe. "Uh, the lighting design is well under way."

LaPaglia tilted his head and stared at her. "And?"

The voice came back. This time it was edged with ladylike fury. *"Why have I not been allowed to speak?"* the voice demanded. *"Do you not think that these fine citizens deserve to hear what I have to say?"*

No, no, no, Piper thought. Ophelia said those words in a courtroom in 1825 while on trial for murder. They had nothing to do with Piper, this staff meeting, this exhibit, or the Boston Museum of Culture and Society. Piper absolutely refused to go insane. Not now.

What was the point of being hot if she went batshit-crazy?

"Are you all right, Piper?"

"Fine." She looked over at Mick. He gave her an almost imperceptible nod, as if he were telling her it would all work out.

She truly appreciated that. It was nice to have an ally for once.

Piper smiled. She squared her shoulders. "My initial floor plan calls for a half circle of six partially enclosed chambers fanning out from a central focal point. Each chamber will tell the story of one component of Ophelia Harrington's surprisingly . . . uh—"

LaPaglia waved his hands. "What's so surprising about Ophelia Harrington? Every fourth grader knows her story."

Oh no they don't . . .

"Each chamber will illustrate one aspect of her surprisingly layered life," Piper said, staying on point. "Central to each will be an integrated media display of her thoughts and words, complemented by a contextually appropriate artifact collection—clothing, household items, furniture, treasured personal belongings."

LaPaglia's brows arched in concern. "Is this going to require headsets? I didn't see headsets in your budget."

"I've always planned for five stationary units per chamber."

"And the central introductory element? The focal point?"

"I'm experimenting with several design options, but I haven't locked into that one, single, perfect concept that symbolizes the essence of Ophelia Harrington's story."

Piper paused. That was an understatement. The truth was, her brain hadn't yet wrapped itself around the inherent duality of the woman in question. Would Ophelia Harrington make her BMCS debut as a bonneted matron entreating an assembly of Quakers, or would she welcome patrons to the exhibit in gartered silk stockings, a corset, and morning-after hair?

"My only crime has been to be a woman with a mind of her own," the voice whispered.

"I find that odd," Linc said.

Piper flashed her eyes at him. "Excuse me?"

"The core display sets the tone and overall context of any installation," Linc said to LaPaglia, ignoring Piper's question. "It's the most critical part of any elevation design. How could Piper move forward without it?"

The conference room stilled. Piper swallowed. She looked at LaPaglia. "I thought it prudent to avoid discussing specifics at this stage of design development."

"Well, ah, as long as your initial presentation to the board isn't delayed."

"No problem," she said with a confident smile. "The trustees will see the mock-up in three weeks, as planned."

LaPaglia nodded. "All right. Good work." Then he shot his eyes to Mick. "Dr. Malloy? Anything you'd like to share with us today?"

Piper was relieved to be out of the spotlight. She sank back into her chair and listened to Mick discuss his plan to link the fund-raising campaign to the Fall Gala, always the museum's biggest annual event, and ask for everyone's feedback. Soon after, the meeting was adjourned.

Piper stayed seated while the staff filed out. Mick nodded politely in her direction and offered her a small smile before he left the conference room.

Eventually, Piper was alone, well aware that one piece of unfinished business remained.

She shook her head. "Here's the problem, Ophelia," Piper whispered, gathering up her papers. "There aren't many women in your league, I'm afraid. What makes you think I'm one of them?"

Linc rapped on her door. "Got a minute?"

He watched Piper look up from her computer and squint at him. Apparently, she didn't like drop-in visitors.

"Is there something I can do for you, Linc?" Piper rose from her chair. She hurriedly began collecting papers, and shoved the stack of documents into a drawer. Next, she came around to the front of her desk and leaned back on her hands, arms splayed wide, as if she were hiding something.

Oh please. Like you have anything I'd want to see.

"I came to apologize," Linc said, moving farther into the huge basement storage space she'd managed to commandeer for the Harrington exhibit. The workroom was packed with all the crap Claudia Harrington-Howell had turned over—settees, candelabras, boxes of old letters and photographs, a pianoforte, travel trunks—Linc had no idea what Piper planned to do with all of it, and after today's meeting it was obvious she didn't know, either.

The Harrington installation sounded like a yawn-fest. Linc had been expecting her to choke with this assignment, and it looked as if she'd be living up to his expectations. Obviously, her recent failure had left Piper too afraid to do anything original.

Poor, pitiful Piper and her switchboard girls. Seriously, who did she think would pay money to go look at twenty-five black-and-white photograph enlargements of Boston's telephone operators and a bunch of moldy old equipment, even with audio? The exhibit had been touted as a tribute to the female army at the front lines of American telecommunications. It was so bad, Linc had had to run to the men's room, where he could laugh his ass off.

Immediately following the opening, Linc had overheard the trustees questioning their decision to promote Piper. But all that didn't matter anymore. The nerd princess was about to prove herself spectacularly expendable. How kind of her.

"I only wanted to help," he said earnestly. "I think it came out the wrong way, and I sincerely apologize."

Linc stopped a few feet from Piper and smiled shyly, all the while taking in the details of her sudden transformation. Whoever helped her pull this off—probably that blond sex professor friend of hers—knew what they were doing. Linc had spent the last four years being entertained by this girl's heinously hilarious fashion offenses, and then, *bam!* She suddenly shows up looking like she just stepped out of the pages of *Elle* magazine.

Really?

Linc wasn't stupid. There was more going on here than a

simple makeover. He'd seen the way Piper smiled at Pretty Boy Malloy, and he'd seen Malloy's pathetically Pavlovian response. Obviously, she'd done this to get his attention.

"That was a funny way of helping me," Piper said, lifting her arms from the desk and crossing them tightly over her chest. It looked to Linc like her boobs had grown over the last week. Did she have surgery done to impress Mr. Lost Ark? If that were the case, he'd have to upgrade his opinion of her—from pitiful to downright tragic.

"Let me make it up to you," Linc said, stretching out his palms in a bit of sincere-looking mea culpa choreography. "There has to be some way I can lend a hand with the Ophelia Harrington project."

"I don't think so."

Linc shrugged. "Have it your way, Piper. You always seem to make things harder than they need to be."

Piper smiled. "Forgive me if I find your sudden goodwill a little hard to swallow."

"Your call." Linc shook his head. "Anyway, you look fabulous. Really. Great clothes. And the hair color makes your eyes pop. Unless those contact lenses are of the tinted variety."

"They aren't."

"So why now?" Linc continued. "I'm just curious. Anything we should know about? Thinking of switching jobs? Was there a life-changing birthday recently? Or has the dashing new addition to the BMCS family caught your fancy?"

Piper slowly unwound her arms. She pushed herself to her full height and walked toward Linc. That's when he noticed that, in heels, she was substantially taller than him.

She got very close. She whispered, "Your fangs are showing, little man."

"Funny," he said, not bothering to hide the fact that he enjoyed her comeback.

She continued to glare down at him. Up this close, he got a good look at the subtle sweep of dark eyeliner on her upper lid. It was perfectly executed.

"You know what, Linc?"

He gulped. The sudden change in Piper was more than skin deep. Her vibe was stronger. It was like she had purchased a backbone along with that spectacular Marc Jacobs bag she'd shown off at the staff meeting. "Yes?"

"You don't threaten me," she said, a strange little smile spreading across her perfectly glossed lips. "We both know one of us is probably going to lose their job soon. It's an economic reality. But if you think the board's decision will be based on your superior skills as a curator, you are sadly mistaken."

Linc sniffed. "Really?"

A glint appeared in her eye when she smiled. It made Linc slightly uncomfortable.

"Really. And just so you know—you've picked the exact wrong time to fuck with Piper Chase-Pierpont."

Oookay. Maybe turning thirty had sent the Geek Goddess right over the edge.

As he departed a moment later, he saw Malloy heading down the hallway. Linc nodded deferentially, watched Mick walk through Piper's open door, then slinked his way back, where he plastered his body against the wall so he could eavesdrop.

"Piper," he heard Mick say. "We need to talk."

Fourteen

Saying no to Mick Malloy was proving to be far more difficult than Piper could've imagined.

Thank God she'd memorized the advice the Swan had given Ophelia: *"Remain loving but elusive, affectionate but intangible. A man must never believe his pursuit is complete. Availability is death to Mystery."*

But damn, he was *gorgeous*! He'd just charged into her workroom like he owned the place, propped his delicious man-bottom on the edge of her worktable, and folded his hands in his lap. "We should have taken care of this ten years ago," he said.

Piper was grateful she was seated and her legs were hidden under the old gunmetal-gray basement desk, because her knees were shaking.

"I'm a bit busy right now."

"You never let me explain myself back then."

She did her best to produce a gentle—and mystery-filled—smile. "There was nothing to explain."

When he frowned, those thick, dark eyebrows angled down, and his entire face took on a broodingly sexual intensity. She couldn't help it. She pictured him lying beneath her in the Irish heather, his waistcoat and shirt ripped open and his nankeen breeches undone, her skirts of gathered muslin and eyelet embroidery puddled around them, hiding their heated union.

Keep it together, Piper.

"Have lunch with me."

"Mick, I'd love to. Really." Piper offered what she hoped was a self-effacing laugh. "But as you might have noticed from my presentation this morning, I'm not exactly ahead of schedule."

Mick turned his handsome head on his sun-kissed neck and began studying the floor-to-ceiling catalog of artifacts. When he pivoted at the waist, Piper could see the firm tapering of his midsection beneath his shirt. Suddenly, Mick jumped up. He strode across the room to the far corner, to the towering chestnut headboard that had once held sentry over the marital bed of Ophelia and her husband.

She watched Mick slowly brush his fingertips along the ornate carved pattern of the wood.

He turned around quickly, a thoughtfulness in his expression. "Coffee, then," he said, lowering his arm to his side. He began to walk back toward her. "I'd like to hear more about your plans for the exhibit. She was quite a character, wasn't she? The world had never seen anything like her, had they?"

Piper straightened in her chair, alarmed. It took a moment for her to realize Mick was referring to Ophelia's solo public speaking engagements, an undertaking thought to be scandalously improper for a woman of her time. Of course, he knew nothing of Ophelia's life as a courtesan. He knew nothing about the roots of her infamous daring. No one did. None of the little fourth-grade girls in Massachusetts had any idea what she'd risked to live life on her own terms.

And they never will—unless I tell them.

Just like that, Piper ended the inner turmoil. There would be no more wishing for things to be different—that the exhibit had a bigger budget, or the trustees were more forward-thinking, or the job market was better. If things were ever going to be different, she'd have to make them so.

Telling the truth about Ophelia Harrington's life was the only choice. It was the right thing to do. She was a curator. It was her responsibiilty. Damn the consequences.

Mick had come to a stop in front of her desk. He peered down at her with a frown. "You okay, Piper?"

"What?"

"You got extremely pale all of a sudden. Are you all right?"

"Oh! Sure," she said, taking a deep breath and shaking off the enormity of her decision. "I was just thinking about what you said, and you're right—Ophelia Harrington was something else."

He smiled at her. "You love your work, don't you?"

"Absolutely." She smiled back at him politely, thinking, *I'm really going to lose my job over this,* trying with all her might not to show him how close to tears she suddenly was. "And on that note, I'm afraid I've got to kick you out."

He nodded. "So we'll go for coffee tomorrow." It was not a question.

Piper bit her tongue. In her mind, she was panting, *Yes! Yes! Take me now!*

"Tomorrow's not going to work," is what she said.

"When, then?"

She watched his chest rise and fall, saw the hint of dark curls at the vee of his button-down shirt. The man was far more spectacular than he'd been a decade ago. Or maybe she was far more obsessed with sex than she'd been back then. She began to feel a bit light-headed.

"Fine." Mick reached for a straight-backed chair and pulled it up to the side of Piper's desk. "You want me to grovel? No problem." He crossed one leg over a knee and clasped his hands behind his head, as if he were settling in for a nice long chat.

Piper shook her head. "That's not—"

"I wanted you that night, Piper. Bad." Mick paused for an extended moment before he let his hands slip from behind his head. He leaned forward, wide shoulders rounded, and studied the floor.

Piper had the urge to grab a handful of thick black hair, yank up his head, and maul his lips with her own.

"But I couldn't." He looked up, a sadness in his blue eyes. "Piper, you were polluted, talking crazy and tearing off your underwear. I wasn't even sure you knew who it was you'd decided to drag off to bed. And what kind of man takes advantage of a girl—one of his students, no less—when she's out of her head like that and he's planning to leave the country as soon as the semester's over?"

Piper didn't know what to say.

"I admit I may have left in a hurry, but I didn't trust myself to stick around." Mick ran a hand nervously through his hair, which made Piper's mouth go dry. "I had to get out of there before my lizard brain kicked the shite out of my good judgment."

She couldn't help but chuckle.

"And afterward, you never let me anywhere near you. Never once did you pick up the phone or answer my e-mails or come to the door to talk to me." He shrugged. "I sent you flowers, you know."

Piper let go with a quick gasp. The scene flashed before her eyes—a dozen long-stemmed red roses scattered in the dirty snow. She'd thrown them out of her second-floor window, locked the sash, pulled the shades, and promptly forgotten she'd ever received them. It was less painful that way.

"You turned a cold shoulder to me, colder than Cambridge in February, and before we knew it, the spring semester was history, my teaching assistant job was over, and I left the country."

Piper tried to create one of those mysterious smiles again, but her cheeks hurt from the effort. Everything Mick said was true. She hadn't wanted to talk about any of it, because she didn't want to admit it had happened.

"So, here I am now. I'm explaining."

Piper stared at him, blinking, stinging with the realization that she might not have been the only one hurt by the episode. Suddenly, she wanted nothing more than to open her arms and smother him in her newly freed 36Cs.

She summoned the wisdom of the Swan again: *"Men are hunters. The chase itself is their true ambition. The moment they feel they have won, they will turn to a new pursuit."*

"You're absolutely right," she said. "We left a lot unsaid back then, but now really isn't a good time." She reached out and placed her hand on his forearm. The harmless contact sent heat radiating through her belly and right into the business section of her expensive panties. She snatched her hand away. "Can you check back with me later in the week?"

Mick laughed and shook his head, his eyes moving to the exact spot where her hand had been. "Fine," he said, looking up again. "I'll leave you and Ophelia to your secret plans. But only if you answer me one wee question."

Piper did a combination sigh and giggle, hoping it showed she was only slightly annoyed, yet flattered. The dance of seduction had so many twists and turns it was making her woozy. "Sure, Mick."

"What's with the change in your appearance today?"

"You mean the clothes."

"Yes, and the hair and the shoes and the . . ." Mick's voice trailed off. "Please don't get me wrong. You look truly beautiful. But why now? Why so drastic?"

"Ah." Piper folded her hands in front of her on the desktop. "Well, last Monday, when you ran into me? That was the worst day I'd had in quite some time. You know, bad hair day, bad lip day."

"The duct tape was quite fetching, however."

When Piper and Mick laughed, it reminded her of how it had been with them so long ago. Mick had made her laugh every time they'd talked. Even on that infamous night— somewhere between walking her home and walking out her door—he'd made her laugh. Funny how she'd forgotten about that, too.

"I turned thirty last week," she said, knowing that would

be explanation enough. "I'd been thinking about making some changes. I thought of it as my gift to myself."

He smiled at her, all white teeth and full lips and dimples. "Happy birthday," he said, his voice a deep whisper.

Piper had to shut her eyes and summon the Swan again, due to the fact that she was dangerously close to jumping up and wrapping her thighs around Mick's neck. *"Fully half the art of seduction is the creation of Mystery . . ."* Piper stood suddenly. "Unfortunately, I've got to get to work."

"All right, then," he said, pushing himself from the chair. "I'll check in with you later in the week."

"Wonderful." She watched him walk out the door, fixated on how his dark curls brushed against the back of his shirt collar. Then she allowed herself a brief fixation with the rest of him. If he didn't hurry up and leave, she'd start screaming for him to stay. It seemed they both had a lizard brain to contend with.

She didn't ask for intervention, but the Swan popped into her head anyway: *"A man must never believe his pursuit is complete."*

"Shut the hell up," Piper hissed.

"Did you say something?" Mick spun around so suddenly he nearly caught Piper in mid-fixation.

"What? No." She waved at him awkwardly. "See you later."

"You know . . ." Mick let his eyes do a double take on Piper, then he scratched at his chin as if he were stalling for time. She found it charming. "When I said you looked beautiful, I wasn't being completely honest."

She sucked in air.

"You look strong, Piper. Sexy as hell." When Mick smiled at her this time, she felt her insides drop. "I've always thought you were pretty, but I've got to tell you, there's nothing hotter than a woman who's not ashamed of her beauty—*or* her strength. I'm happy to see that you've found both."

He walked out the door.

As much as she hated to see him leave, Piper was relieved that her first attempt at seduction was over.

She really, truly, had work to do.

Linc studied the two of them at every opportunity that week. The dynamic was fascinating. Mick was smitten with Little Miss Makeover, who had somehow acquired enough master-class flirtation skills to handle him with aplomb. Maybe she'd taken some kind of online course.

True, Linc's position as Mick's errand boy completely sucked, but it had provided a ringside seat to the action. On several occasions, Linc witnessed Piper lure him in only to gently push him away. And Mick Malloy, for all his much-publicized worldliness, had become just plain stupid for Piper.

It was as amusing as it was vomitorious.

The workplace seduce-a-thon took a sudden turn on Friday, when Mick mentioned he'd scored a coffee date with Piper for Sunday afternoon.

That pretty much locked it up, Linc knew. He'd be the only senior curator on staff immediately after the Fall Gala, because there was no way Piper could simultaneously start a hot-'n'-heavy relationship while reaching any modicum of success on the Harrington exhibit.

It wouldn't be long before Linc was back in the men's room, laughing his ass off.

Fifteen

Piper smiled and waved when she saw him, and Mick's heart kicked in his chest. She was seated at a small table in the café section of Beantown Books. From his vantage point, he could tell she was wearing a pair of jeans and a sleeveless silvery top that draped right above the swell of her breasts. At closer range, he noticed that a peek of cleavage was showing—incredibly sexy but ladylike at the same time.

She stood to greet him, and that's when he noticed her choice of a low-slung leather belt, another pair of sexy heels, and silver hooped earrings peeking out from under her shiny hair. She was hot enough to toast bread.

"Hi, Mick."

He grabbed her hand and bent close to kiss her cheek—the first time he'd put his lips anywhere on her body in ten years—and breathed in her essence. Piper Chase-Pierpont smelled as sweet and silky as she felt. The hint of flesh beneath his lips tasted like some kind of exotic confection. He hated to end the contact, but it had to be done.

The last thing Mick wanted to do was scare her off. He'd worked too feckin' hard for this Sunday afternoon sort-of-but-not-quite-date, and he planned to make the most of it.

They sat down across from each other. He watched her cross her legs. He listened to her talk about how this little independent bookstore was her favorite Boston hangout.

That led into a good, long conversation about books, which segued into music and movies and work. By then he was parched.

With the help of the nice young man running the café cash register, Mick managed to rustle up a pot of strong Ceylon tea—from the bags, of course, but what could he do?—and set about giving Piper a short lesson on the Irish and their tea.

He filled both cups about a third of the way with whole milk. "Did you know the Irish are the largest per-capita consumers of tea in the world?" he asked her.

Piper shook her head. "I had no idea."

Next, he poured in the tea. "The Gaelic expression for this delicacy is *cupan tae*." He looked up at Piper to find her studying him, those stupendous green eyes lit up with enjoyment. "That's what our family's always called it, even after we came to the States."

Piper repeated the phrase, slowly and carefully.

"I had no idea you spoke Gaelic!" Mick said, grinning. Clearly, Piper enjoyed his teasing. She looked so very beautiful when she laughed. It came back to him: how lovely she'd seemed all those years ago, how he enjoyed her sense of humor, her headlong passion for knowledge, her kindness—and how horribly it had ended.

Mick began to spoon in the sugar. "What we really need here is a couple thick slices of Irish shortcake. Have you ever had that?"

"No," she said. "But it sounds glorious."

"Oh, it's decadent, all right." Mick wagged an eyebrow as he stirred. "All that rich butter melting on your tongue."

He peeked at Piper, noting how she hung on his every word. "Or a nice slab of chocolate potato cake—ever have that?"

Piper shook her head.

"I'll bake it for you one day." Mick reached over and handed Piper her cup and saucer. "Have you ever prepared your tea this way?"

"Nope." She took a small slurp.

"Do you know I never forgot you, Piper?"

Her cup clattered onto the saucer.

"Did you know that for the last ten years I've regretted that night with all my heart?"

Her eyes bugged.

"I should have walked you home like a gentleman, tucked you into your bed—fully clothed—and called you the next morning to explain my intentions."

Piper gulped. "What intentions?"

"That I was interested in getting to know you, but not while I was your teacher and heading for an overseas dig site as soon as the semester ended. You may think I'm old-fashioned, but that sort of slam-bam sex has never set right with me, and never will."

Mick sat back in his chair, crossed his legs, and took a sip, watching the emotions float across Piper's face. She seemed truly surprised.

He took his time with her. He told her about the women in his life over the last ten years, relationships that went nowhere—the British research assistant, the South African yoga instructor, the poet from Quebec. He told her about his father's death, how his brother had shouldered the burden of caring for him, and why Mick felt he needed to come home and make up for his absence. He told her about the reality show, and how a decent deal could save the pub. He told her that all of these things had helped to pull him back home, but the possibility of seeing her again was part of the lure.

"Did you ever think of me, Piper?"

She tipped her head and ran her fingers through her shiny, deep brown hair. Mick wanted desperately to experience the sensation for himself—thick and soft handfuls slipping between his fingers, brushing against her bare shoulders . . .

"Sure," she said, a wry smile on her lips. "Usually in my moments of self-pity and loneliness, when I'd look around and wonder how other people managed to find love and companionship while I was slowly turning into a brittle, dried-out old hag."

Mick nearly spit out a mouthful of tea. "Say again?"

Piper waved her hand and laughed. "It's not a big deal," she said with a shrug. "I'm starting to see that blaming you for my dry spell allowed me to avoid responsibility for my own choices, my own fears."

Mick was gobsmacked. It made no sense. "Uh, you mean to tell me you've been lonely for ten years? You've been walking around *alone* for all this time?" He studied her carefully. The sorrow in her eyes confirmed this was no joke.

"I didn't exactly advertise that I was available, or even remotely interested," Piper said. "Looking back, I realize the men who did approach me had to be some pretty brave souls, but none of them were right for me."

A shiver went down Mick's spine. "And I did that to you? I made you go into hiding?"

"No. I did it to myself." Piper sat up straighter in her chair. "It was just easier to blame you."

Mick spent the next forty-five minutes in rapt attention as Piper described her life—her controlling parents, her cat, her little Cambridge apartment, the failure of her last exhibit, good ole Brenna, and the complete *nob heads* she'd dated over the years. It all helped him understand her better, but left him holding a raw sadness deep in his gut.

He reached across the table and Piper quickly slipped her hand into his. "I am sorry my actions hurt you," he said.

She tilted her head and smiled at him thoughtfully. "And I'm sorry I pushed you away when you tried to explain. I messed up."

"We both did."

They wandered the bookstore together for another couple of hours. They lingered in the poetry section, taking up residence there, heads together. In the sweetest of whispers, Piper read him selections from Shelley, her blue-blood Boston accent making him smile.

Then Mick reached for a volume of Yeats, and gently backed Piper against the shelves, his mouth close to her ear. He began to read aloud:

> Wine comes in at the mouth
> And love comes in at the eye;
> That's all we shall know for truth
> Before we grow old and die.
> I lift the glass to my mouth,
> I look at you, and I sigh.

Mick replaced the book and cradled Piper's face in both his hands. He lowered his lips to her forehead and the tip of her adorable nose before he set about kissing her properly.

It was a long, hot, luxurious tangle of lips and heat and tongue that paid no mind to the busy bookstore, the spinning of the earth, or the passing of time.

It was a kiss potent enough to make up for lost opportunities and heal the sting of regret.

It was a kiss for the ages.

Brenna circled the bed, a slight frown forming between her eyes. The reaction surprised Piper, because she really thought she'd done a bang-up job turning her apartment into Scheherazade City. She only had five days until the sinning was scheduled to start, so if Piper needed to do more shopping, Brenna had better let her know now.

"Why are you frowning? Am I missing something?" Piper checked her notes again. "I got everything from the list—the corsets, the stockings, the peacock feather, the velvet ropes, the blindfold, the lace-up high-heeled boots, the heavy cream, the—"

Brenna placed a hand on her forearm. Piper stopped talking and glanced up.

"None of it will matter if you're twitchy. There's nothing even remotely sexy about twitchy."

She narrowed an eye at her friend. "Which volume was that in?"

"It's in *my* volume!" Brenna laughed as she put an arm around Piper. "You've done an amazing job with the place. Relax! It's a pleasure palace!"

Though Piper heard Brenna's reassuring words, she couldn't help but scan the bedroom, still concerned something might be lacking. The last thing she wanted to do was be smack in the middle of the Fourth Sin and not be able to get her hands on the massage oil.

"Take a deep breath," Brenna said.

She did as directed, gazing at her handiwork with pride. She'd bundled a dozen harem-inspired white sheers into a fluffy rosette, then tacked it to the ceiling over the bed. The sheers were loosely tied at each corner, leaving enough room for other things that might need to be attached to the bedposts—which would begin on night five, if all went according to the calendar.

Piper had piled her bed with ivory silk sheets, pillow-cases, and accent pillows. She'd arranged scented candles in the bedroom and bath. The nightstand held a book of erotic poetry and a few DVDs Brenna said were clinically proven to increase arousal, though if that kiss in the bookstore was any indication, Piper doubted they'd need it. She'd also topped the bed with a fluffy satin comforter. She'd purchased a fluffy white flokati throw rug that felt like mink under her bare feet. She'd folded fluffy new towels and washcloths in the bathroom. Piper suddenly panicked—was it too much? Had she reached a fluffiness critical mass in here?

"What's on Friday's menu?" Brenna asked.

Piper shook her head in an effort to stay focused. She followed Brenna into the living room, also newly jazzed up with colorful scarf throws, jewel-toned toss pillows, two new lamps, and a fireplace filled with four tiers of tea lights to provide that romantic glow in the middle of a heat wave.

"Champagne, of course," Piper said. "We'll start with an

avocado, tomato, and basil salad, then move on to linguine with scallops, followed by juicy sliced papaya and mango and a dark chocolate mousse with fresh whipped cream."

One of Brenna's brows arched. "That oughta do it," she said. "What's the schedule leading up to the big night?"

Piper consulted her smartphone. "We're having tea after the staff meeting tomorrow. Tuesday and Wednesday we're doing lunch. Thursday I've begged off—too much work. And that brings us to Friday, and the first sin. Of course, all Mick knows is that he's agreed to put himself in my hands for seven nights in a row, but he's probably thinking more along the lines of movies and quaint restaurants and walks in the park."

Brenna emitted a soft *hmm*. "Too bad you can't take the week off from work—you know, use the daytime to recuperate from your nights of debauchery."

Piper collapsed into the armchair and laughed. "I wasn't kidding about having too much work to do!" She looked up at Brenna, a bit sheepishly. "I think I've gotten myself in a bit of a *situation,* actually."

Her friend gathered up the purring Miss Meade and stroked the cat behind her ears, raising her eyebrows at Piper. "What kind of situation?"

Piper tossed her smartphone and notebook to the coffee table. "I'm going for it, Brenna. I'm telling Ophelia's story. All of it. I can't be worried about whether I'll lose my job or scandalize the trustees."

Brenna's eyes widened.

"I couldn't live with myself if I created an installation that merrily skipped over my discovery. The facts are the facts." Piper sighed. "Besides, I owe her one."

Brenna reached back and caught herself as she fell onto the couch, a move that was not to Miss Meade's liking. The cat wiggled her way free, hit the floor, and ran off. "How?" Brenna asked breathlessly. "They'll never go for it."

"I know they won't, and my mock-up is supposed to be in their hands in ten days."

"So how—"

"The proposal will be a dummy, similar in design and interactive elements but with completely different content than the real exhibit."

Brenna's mouth fell open.

"Something like this is way too radical for the trustees, and LaPaglia would have a coronary at the mere suggestion. So I have no choice but to sneak it in behind their backs."

"Holy shit, Piper."

"I know," she said, shaking her head. "I surprise myself more every day."

Sixteen

"Come in," she breathed.

Mick stepped inside the apartment. Piper—magnificent in a short, clingy black halter dress and heels—reached for his hand. She tugged him closer, tangled her fingers in his hair, and kissed him sweetly.

Jaysus H.—he nearly dumped the chocolate potato cake on the floor.

"Here. I'll put this on the counter." When Piper relieved him of the pretty, doily-lined cake plate, Mick suddenly appreciated Emily's assistance in the kitchen. Cullen's wife had been horrified to learn he planned to bake a cake for a girl and deliver it in a square metal pan.

"It's so pretty!" Piper said, carrying it off to the kitchen. Mick licked his lips and stared at her mostly bare back, the dress scooped tight and low across her hips, her legs long and shapely. He began to salivate, and it had nothing to do with the savory aroma of a home-cooked meal.

"This is thoughtful of you," she said from the kitchen.

He was about to reply when he felt someone giving him the stink eye. He turned to see a rotund gray tabby cat perched on the back of a wing chair, tail swirling.

"Oh, that's Miss Meade," Piper said, returning to the living room. "Ignore her. She's a she-devil."

Mick raised an eyebrow, suddenly aware of the nature of

the trap he'd just entered. It was a vixen's lair if ever he saw one—silky and colorful and strewn with candles, a gleaming table set for two, the bedroom door left ajar and hinting at a bed worthy of a harem girl.

His curious gaze moved to Piper and her glossy lips, succulent cleavage, and round hips. That look in her eye told him she knew exactly what she was doing.

She was an enchantress, and Mick was falling under her spell. Happily. Enthusiastically. The only thing that bothered him was how different Piper seemed from the girl with the duct-taped eyeglasses and ink-stained lips from just a couple weeks before. Where had she gone?

"Would you like something to drink?" She gestured to the pillow-strewn sofa and the coffee table set with champagne flutes, an ice bucket, and a bottle of what looked like good stuff.

"Are you trying to seduce me, Piper Chase-Pierpont?"

She laughed, throwing back her head. Her shiny hair went cascading down her nearly bare back, her eyes sparkled, and she dragged her fingertips down the length of her own neck.

Fuck me.

Aside from that silent declaration, Mick's mind had gone blank.

She fed Mick another slice of mango, slipping her fingers just beyond his lips and into his hot mouth, the fruit's juices dripping down her arm. She watched him chew, his blue eyes incandescent with lust.

That's when Mick grabbed her wrist and licked the inside of her forearm, from the crook of her elbow to her wrist.

Piper knew it was time. His belly was full. His head was buzzing with champagne. He'd been touching her every opportunity he got. Things were moving at a perfect pace.

She leaned toward him, aware that her bosom was about

to spill from her dress. *I've become such a tart!* "Do you want me, Mick?" she whispered.

His lips twitched but he said nothing, and a sharp panic raced through her. She'd never even considered he might say no. What would she do with all the whipped cream?

"I've wanted you for a long, long time," he finally answered, which sent relief flooding through her.

"Good." Piper stood, her belly directly in his line of sight, showcased nicely in tight black knit. "Why don't you pick out some music for us? I'll be just a minute."

Piper strutted on her heels toward her bedroom, knowing his eyes were glued to her behind, then shut the door without a backward glance. Once inside, her knees buckled and she began to slide down the inside of the door.

This was no fantasy. She was really going to do this. In moments, Mick Malloy's hands and mouth would be all over her and she'd be returning the favor. Piper would finally be getting what she'd been denied for too long. How in the world was she going to keep her head screwed on straight?

Focus, she told herself. *She* was the one who had to set the pace and direct the passion. It was up to *her* to establish the rules for the rest of the week.

With a deep breath, Piper pulled herself to her feet and went to the closet. As she took off her dress and put on the evening's costume selection, her hands began to shake. What was it that the Swan had said to Ophelia? Oh yes . . .

"Don't think of it as nerves. Think of it as the hot fuse that lights the fireworks—flame to gunpowder."

The candles were lit. The lights were dimmed. The bed was turned down. She heard Marvin Gaye (*oh God, no*) floating from the living room speakers.

Forget the nerves—Piper was scared to death.

Lust, she reminded herself. The First Sin of the Courtesan was lust, so lust was to be the theme of the evening. Her goals would be simple: drive Mick mad with desire, break down his barriers with visual teasing, wild dirty talk and mad skills, tease him until he begged for release, then, finally, give it to him.

She'd stashed a cheat sheet in the bedside table, just in case.

Piper took one last glance at herself in the new bedroom mirror, making sure the contraption was laced tight enough to accentuate her waist but remained loose enough to draw air. If she passed out, she wanted the cause to be an overabundance of orgasms, not a lack of oxygen.

She ran her hands down her hips and studied herself. This was one of seven lingerie combinations Brenna had helped her select, one for each theme night. She'd advised Piper to start off soft and feminine so she'd have some room to branch out as she approached the latter—and wilder—sins. Piper had to admit that Brenna possessed an expert eye for these things.

Tonight's selection, a pink jacquard corset with white satin trim, was chosen for its sweet and dainty quality. But the attached garters, matching thong, sheer white thigh-highs, and the extreme low-cut boobalicious design of the ensemble were anything but. Piper turned her head to examine the sparkle of her dangly gold filigree earrings. She fluffed her long, loose hair. She slipped into her white, three-inch-high kitten slippers topped with little dollops of snowy feathers.

Piper crawled onto the bed. She situated herself in the middle of the gauzy paradise. Bent one knee. Spread her hair out on the pillows. Tossed an arm over her head.

"Mick?" she called, hoping her carefully planned summons would be audible through the closed door and over Mr. Gaye's familiar lament that he was hot just like an oven. "Could you come in and help me with something?"

She waited. One second. Two. Three.

Where *was* the man?

Then the door opened.

Seventeen

My darling Robert left England, sailing away to his new diplomatic post in Copenhagen. After our five years together, I shed more than a few tears at his going but that did not sway my decision to stay behind.

Poor Robert. He begged so prettily to wed me. He was such a fine young man, gentle and sweet and intelligent. He would go far in the world and no doubt do great things. He had dreams of high rank and courtly glory and I believed him more than capable of achieving them.

Yet, no matter how I had enjoyed the process of building his career and playing hostess to some of the most powerful political names in England, those were his dreams, not mine. I had not established myself so securely in this marvelously liberated world merely to shackle myself into marriage in the end!

So, once I had waved my handkerchief most sincerely at his parting ship and spent my tears into it after, I returned to my house and sent a message to the Swan.

She joined me promptly, sweeping elegantly into my comfortable parlor followed by her maid, Elise, who carried a hamper. "I bear claret and chocolates," the Swan announced with playful grandeur, "to help you through this trying time."

We indulged ourselves quite shamelessly with wine, con-fections, and confessions. This ritual dissection of the affair was sometimes my favorite part!

She sent me a considering glance. "You do not seem heartbroken."

"Should I be?"

The Swan shrugged gracefully. "I had thought you quite enamored of him. Your devotion never wavered, despite all those lucrative offers."

I smiled. "I adored Robert. Yet our days—and glorious nights!—were never meant to last forever. We both knew that." I did not tell the Swan everything. I did not tell her how the last year had been tainted by Robert's injured feel-ings. I had refused his offer of marriage then as well and had begged him to speak no more of it. Robert pretended to be a man of the world, but that injury to his romantic heart had never entirely disappeared. There had been silences and, sometimes, hard words.

The entire affair had, in my mind, become rather too much like a marriage. He resented my refusal and I re-sented the inclination to feel guilty, simply for being pre-cisely as advertised.

We had parted with tears and protestations of deep feel-ing, but deep down, I believe we were both relieved. I wanted no part of such emotional exploitation. I wanted only the freedom to live as I chose, and to love whom and when I chose.

The very notion of such ownership left me feeling quite violently allergic.

Then the Swan announced that it was time to assess the jewels. I rather unsteadily fetched my jewel case and spilled its bounty into her waiting lap. After tossing back the rest of her glass of wine, the Swan fished a jeweler's loupe from deep within her bodice and held it to her eye. "Hmm."

I sprawled on a cushion and watched with great amuse-ment. Her pithy commentary was more entertaining than any theater performance.

"Aren't you pretty?" she cooed to an emerald ring. "You ought to keep that one." She rummaged further. "Oh heavens, how dreary." It was a necklace of jet. "Did he peel this off his grandmother's dead throat, do you think? I forbid you to wear it until you are at least eighty! Better still, sell it at once. Aha, a sapphire bracelet!" She waved it drunkenly at me. "You don't look nearly as good in blue stones as I do. Shall I trade you a ruby for it? It's quite rosy, a perfect match for your nipples. Yes? Excellent. Sweet heaven, what is *this*?"

She held up the last gift dear Robert had given me. It was a necklace simply crusted in diamonds. I suspect he'd thought it would change my mind and then he'd not had the nerve to ask for it back when it didn't achieve the desired effect.

I sighed. "Isn't it vulgar? Wherever shall I wear it?"

The Swan blinked at me for a long moment until she realized that my indifferent tone was entirely in jest. Then she kicked me right off my cushion in revenge.

"Oh, this is magnificent! How could you keep it until last? It's glorious! It's positively *royal*!"

I clapped my hands. "I know! I shall be the envy of every woman in London! I'm going to wear it absolutely everywhere! Balls, soirees, walking in Hyde Park!" I took it from her and clasped it about my neck. "Do you think it's too formal to sleep in?"

She giggled at my silliness and we poured ourselves more wine. We were deep into a discussion over whether or not to call for another bottle from my cellar when she sat up straight and gasped. "Oh, I nearly forgot! I have something for you!"

I sat up and blinked blearily at her while she felt about her for her reticule. "It was waiting for me this morning when I awoke." Then she practically dove into her little bag, frowning most severely as she searched. "Ah! At last!" Triumphantly, she pulled her hand from her bag and held an envelope high.

It was thick and expensive and heavy in my hands, yet not embossed with any sort of identification. I opened it. Something slipped out into my waiting palm.

It was the darkly gleaming wing feather of a blackbird.

My heart thudded in my chest at the sight of it, then slowed to a wicked, sensual beat that resonated through my entire being.

Sir would be coming to my bed tonight.

I smiled gaily at the man who handed me another glass of champagne and then dropped my head back and downed the entire contents, to the cheers of the circle of gentlemen surrounding me. Several began to vie for the honor of fetching my next one.

The Blackbird was officially available and the competition was growing playfully fierce. This was the third event I had visited this evening and the third time this scene had been played out. I was having the time of my life, for I had no one to please but myself.

I had not intended to make such a circuit of the night's balls and soirees, but it seemed I quickly lost interest in each event. Once I had greeted the host and danced with a few of the most promising bachelors and tossed back varying quantities of champagne, the sameness of the society made me long for the next adventure.

After all, I was not yet in need of a new lover. Prolonging their anticipation would only increase their interest. Why not revel in my popularity for a time?

So I flirted, I teased, I frankly taunted, but gave preference to no one. And all the while, in the back of my mind, I relished the thought of my coming night with Sir.

My little house was warm and welcoming as I shed my wrap. Sylla shook out the velvet cloak with practiced hands and draped it over her arm. "Did ye meet anyone nice, miss?"

I stripped off my gloves. "Of course. All men are at their nicest, Sylla, when they want you."

"Well, then, ye must've drowned in it, miss," Sylla said stoutly, "for a man would have to be mad not to want ye."

I gave her a quick hug. My loyal Sylla, who had followed me into my life of sin without hesitation.

"Such nonsense." Sylla stepped back with a smile. "Off to bed w' ye, miss."

I glanced toward the parlor but the open doorway was dark. Disappointment swelled within me. He had not come.

Up the stairs and down the hall, my bedchamber awaited. I knew Sylla would have the fire lighted and the bed turned down, so I bid her good night. I was perfectly capable of undressing myself.

As I entered my carefully decorated chamber of seduction, draped in crimson velvet and creamy ivory silk, I sighed that it would go to waste tonight.

"You are more beautiful than ever."

His husky whisper came from behind me. I did not turn. Instead, I closed my eyes, letting the delicious awareness of him radiate upon my skin like sunlight.

Sir.

When I felt the heat of his big body close behind me, and his big, warm hands slid down my bare arms, I let my head fall back upon his shoulder.

Our fingers twined as he wrapped our arms about my waist and pulled me closer into his warmth. I felt his breath on my neck as he pressed his cheek to my hair.

We stood thus for a long moment, simply breathing each other in. My body melted into his like warmed wax. I felt something swell and bloom within me, a part of my heart left dormant for five years.

My friend. My teacher. My Sir.

Each breath of him was a rediscovery, at once familiar and yet new. He was not there to be a teacher at that moment, he was there to be my lover.

The sweet warmth began to transmute to heat. I felt his

hands tighten on mine even as I let out a sigh and shifted my backside against him. His erection swelled instantly, pressing into my bottom. I felt a low rumble in his chest, like faraway thunder. His powerful lust was an oncoming storm. I could feel the darkness gather above my head. It would soon envelop me, overwhelm me, devastate me.

I smiled and turned my face up to the rain.

As always, Sir was gone when I awoke.

I had little time to contemplate this, however, for the very next day, calamity struck the Swan.

Her lover, the wealthy but capricious Mr. D——, betrayed the Swan's deepest confidence, then when gossip began to fly, he most publicly discarded her. I had never cared for the man, but the Swan had been serenely confident in her ability to renovate his character.

The tattle sheets went mad, of course.

Her lover's quick dismissal of her only fueled the gossips. She went from being universally adored and admired to instantly reviled and rejected. In short, the Swan became a not very amusing joke overnight.

She did not alert me to this misfortune herself, the idiot. Instead, I discovered the melodrama already entirely unfolded along with my morning news sheet next to my breakfast custard and toast. I froze there, reading in horror, my breath arrested in my lungs and my toast arrested halfway to my lips. I read the entire thing through—I shan't repeat the gleefully merciless taunts regarding "the Goose"—then I rang for Sylla and flung myself into action.

First, I thought to throw on some old gown and take a hack to the Swan's house instead of waiting for my carriage to be brought round. Then it struck me that in the public eye, everything is meaningful. I decided to make a terrific procession of it all. If all eyes were upon us, then let them see me rally in support of my friend!

I told Sylla to round up all the extra footmen that I kept

on register for my large parties and have them kit themselves out in full Blackbird livery. I told my groom to be sure the horses were shining and spotless and at the last moment even went so far as to order the black feather bridle head-dresses that I usually reserved for the most formal outings. "Full bells and brasses," I told him sternly.

Now for myself. I needed to sweep from my carriage in full sight of Society, or at least as might be out and about on a Tuesday afternoon. Driving by way of Hyde Park would do for starters. Then, back through Mayfair to light upon the Swan's doorstep with full fanfare.

And then what? What could I do to help her?

I had no idea, truly. She had always guided me before. Perhaps now she could help me help her.

The Swan was, in short, a revolting mess. Reddened eyes, raw, swollen nose, and so pale that she looked nauseatingly cadaverous. I had not realized before how truly clever she was with her cosmetics, for it was clear now that she possessed no real eyebrows at all. Her golden hair was tangled and dry and her cheekbones quite sunken from lack of nourishment.

I stripped off my gloves and tossed them atop my reticule on a side table. "You need breakfast," I told her sternly. "And a bath."

"Go away," she mumbled into her pillow. "You can gloat from your own boudoir."

I put my fists on my hips. "Oh, shut it, you lunatic. Now which will it be first, soap or kippers?"

I swiftly formed a plan, though the Swan held out little hope. "Sir must escort you about!" I proclaimed, sitting across from the freshly bathed Swan in her dressing gown, watching her grudgingly nibble on a piece of toast. I leaned back in my dainty gilded chair and folded my arms. "In his *mask*."

She chewed slowly, then swallowed. "He will not partici-
pate."

"He will," I declared, although in truth I was none too
sure. "You have been friends for many years, after all."

The Swan tilted her head. "Yes, but I believe he is quite
fond of you. It would not surprise me if you could persuade
him to do what I could not."

I reached for a piece of her toast and munched it, thinking. "Then again, wouldn't his lady protectors recognize
him?"

The Swan blinked at me. "Ah. Well, if they did, they
surely would not admit it."

"True!" I lifted my toast triumphantly. "Then that is
what we shall do. The *haut ton* will be abuzz, wondering
who your masked lover is! I think I shall even spread it
about that he is royalty from another kingdom, hiding from
assassination."

The Swan rolled her eyes, but I noticed that she reached
for a slice of fruit without prompting.

Unfortunately, although Sir would have been the perfect
escort, he refused. Although the Swan had warned me, I
could not believe it.

I gaped at him from across my bedchamber, where he
had awaited my arrival home from the Swan's. "But why
not? She needs your help!"

He was retying his cravat with swift movements. I folded
my arms and watched with narrowed eyes. Served him right
for being half undressed already, the presumptuous lout!

"I need not explain myself." His voice was low as always
but there was a bite to his tone I had not heard before. "It is
enough that I have said no."

"It is enough when I am satisfied with your explanation,"
I retorted. "An explanation you are not about to provide me,
I take it." I threw out my hands. "Why do you come to me if
you refuse to share yourself with me? I thought we were
friends. Or am I naught but a bed warmer after all?"

He dropped his hands from his cravat and glared at me. I could see his frustration, even behind the mask. "You are—"

I waited, my eyes narrowed. "What am I?"

"Exasperating." He took a step toward me. "Exciting." The tension about his lips eased and his black eyes began to heat. "Entirely delicious."

I bit my lips but could not stop the smile. "And you, Sir, are also all of the above."

When he came close enough to take me into his arms, I spread both hands over his chest and looked up into his masked eyes. "Are you quite certain you cannot help her?"

His eyes searched mine. "I am. Will you someday forgive me?"

I reached up to trace a fingertip over his lower lip. "I don't know," I murmured. "I am not the forgiving sort." It was the truth. I always told Sir the truth.

As he nodded in resignation and dropped a quick kiss on my forehead before he left, I thought what a pity it was he did not have the same trust in me.

Sir would have made the perfect escort. However, the plan was still a good one. Furthermore, if there were ever two women in the world who did not need a man's permission, it was myself and the Swan!

On the evening of her resurrection, the Swan was glorious in sapphire silk. Her recent despair had made her thinner, but now that she was once again glossy and polished, her slenderness only emphasized her extraordinary bone structure and grace. She seemed a being from another world, a fairy creature who only deigned to walk the earth through some moonlit magic.

For a brief moment, I felt a bit dark and just a bit . . . round. Then I banished my envy to take joy in her rise from the ashes. I took both her hands and spun her eagerly in a circle. She laughed at my silliness but I could see the worry still shadowing her eyes.

"Stop that," I ordered. "This will work. You will be London's premier courtesan once again, desired by many, envied by all."

She shook her head at my ferocity. "What manner of creature are you, tiny Ophelia? Any other woman in your position would have been happy to watch me burn to the ground in order to claim my spotlight as her own. Yet here you are, going to such lengths to return me to my former status." Her perfect brows gathered. "I fear you are not a normal woman."

I tilted my head. "It took you five years to determine that? Goodness, most people realize it in the first ten seconds."

She gave me a shy smile. "I realized it in five. I simply didn't know how much that mad girl in the dressmaker's shop would come to mean to me in time."

I gave her a fey smile and a hug. Then I stepped back. "Wait! You have not yet seen my costume for this evening's rout!" I flung off my cape with a flourish and a flutter of black silk, then cocked a knee and gave her a jester's bow. "My lady, may I be your escort this evening?"

Her surprise was everything I could have hoped for. I laughed aloud at the shock upon her lovely face, then gave a quick pirouette. "What do you think? Do I not make a most delicious fellow?"

Her eyes traveled up my body, blinking at the way the stockings revealed the shape of my legs up to the knee, where the pegged breeches continued to outline every inch of thigh. Perhaps they were a bit shamefully snug across the buttocks, but in for a penny, in for a pound! Besides, I doubted that anyone observing the fact that I wore a deep-cut weskit with nothing beneath it but the sheerest lawn chemise would spend much thought on the tightness of my trousers. I tugged at my cravat knot, for it was tied about my bare throat, emphasizing my lack of shirt and creating a most singular focus on my bare cleavage. My scarlet silk surcoat was a dandy's extravagance for an event where true gentlemen would be clad all in black, but I adored the color. After all, I was going to stand out no matter what the color of my tails!

The Swan exhaled at last. Then a slow, wicked grin lit her faerie features. "You will cause chaos in every corner of the room. How delicious!"

I bowed again. "Why, thank you, milady. And may I return the compliment? Although I do think you might let your hair down your back. Then you will look entirely escaped from some wild place of magic."

She raised a hand to her perfect chignon. "Really? Loose and free?"

I gave her a teasing leer. "As if you had just rolled out of bed."

"Out of bed with you?" She bit her lip. "Oh, they'll simply die." Before she could think better of the idea, she yanked the pins from her hair and tossed them aside. Leaning her head back, she shook free the rippling river of gold.

I took two narrow strands from either temple and quickly braided them back from her face, binding them off with a trailing blue ribbon. A white rosebud plucked from the arrangement on the table and tucked into the knot completed the illusion. "There," I said with great satisfaction. "You look like a gift from the gods." I narrowed my eyes. "Or perhaps a gift to the gods."

She grimaced. "Sacrificed upon the altar of Ophelia's madness."

I gave her a remonstrative pinch. "Shut it. Nerves are not permitted. This will work."

She nodded, then flashed a devil-may-care smile. "Or if it doesn't, we shall at least be gossip fodder for eternity."

"Precisely. All or nothing." I reclaimed my cloak from where it dangled from the dressing table mirror and grabbed up her silk and ermine cape. "Shall we?"

However, when we reached the bottom of her front steps,

we found a gleaming black carriage parked before us. The rich ebony sides bore no mark or emblem, but this was no hired hack. As we stared at it, the door opened, pushed by a gloved hand from within.

"Ladies, if I might offer conveyance?"

I gazed up into the familiar masked face and felt my face split into a wide smile.

Sir.

Eighteen

The Swan's return was an outrageous triumph. Even I could not have predicted how successfully Sir's dark enigma would capture the imaginations of all, *haut ton* and demi-monde alike. Trailing behind them both, content to play third wheel, I settled for playing the clown, as well. I flirted with all the women present, even the stuffy dowagers. I begged them to dance with me, but none dared, though I am vain enough to think that some were tempted.

The gentlemen would not dance, either, though I bowed low and kept my voice deep as I asked for their hands. I openly mocked them, after all. Still, I enjoyed my evening mightily, circling the ballroom as I looked for some mischief and all the while keeping my eye upon Sir and the Swan. They did look most handsome together, she so tall and graceful to his height and strength. I felt a twinge of envy at how well matched they were.

Well, it was perhaps a tad more than simple admiring envy. My easy joy in the Swan's success slowly faded as I watched them pass the evening together. It was more than a superficial suitability.

When a man and a woman hardly know each other, there is a distance between them. It is not much of one, but I could always tell. It always took time to warm the air between a couple, requiring often and repeated exposure to pull aside the countless tiny social barriers and gender mis-communications.

The Swan and Sir had no such distance.

I could not help but watch Sir slip his hand into the curve of her waist as they waltzed, nor could I miss the blazing fact that he did so with a familiarity only the bedchamber could give a man.

I had never before had the thought that they might have been lovers.

And still might be?

Disturbed by the notion and entirely bewildered by my reaction to it, I turned my full attention to creating some distracting chaos of my own. The sting of jealousy could not be borne, so I refused to feel such a ridiculous sensation. Sir was a lover of many women. It was his role, even as the Blackbird was mine. The Swan was an irresistible beauty, indeed. They had been friends before I had ever entered their lives.

Furthermore, I refused to think on it any longer.

At all.

A dark gentleman across the ballroom caught my eye. I watched him from behind as he threw his head back and laughed at something said. He was tall and well built, perhaps thirty years of age. I liked the width of his shoulders and the way his expensively cut surcoat hugged his trim waist. His curling black hair was rebelliously long.

When he turned, I recognized him. Lord B——. We had never been introduced but he was a popular guest at the sort of events where I was also welcomed. He was, by all accounts, a very bad influence.

How intriguing.

He was a writer of some recent note and he played the value of his connections and his notoriety to the hilt. I admired the dash and disregard with which he traversed Society. He knew all the proper forms and phrases, yet did not hesitate to twist them to suit his dark sense of humor.

In my years with earnest, pure-hearted Robert, I had come to long for a man who could make me laugh.

Lord B—— looked up just then and noted my regard. A wicked, inviting smile played upon his handsome lips as he boldly met my gaze. I lifted my chin and let my eyelids drop slowly as I rudely eyed him tip to toe. A flash of white teeth and a deep laugh answered my wordless sally. He held out his hands from his sides and turned slowly and obviously in place, offering himself for my view.

I had to admit, he was a very fine figure of a man.

I watched his approach with narrowed eyes and satisfaction singing in my veins. He was most definitely on the hook.

Lord B——'s eyes gleamed at me as he handed me a fresh glass of champagne. "You are without a doubt the most desirable woman in the room," he said without preamble or pretense that either of us required introduction. "Why did you waste so much time with that stuffed arse, P——?"

I smiled archly. "Perhaps it was the incredible enormity of his . . . brain."

Lord B—— laughed easily.

Then he bowed to me and extended his hand. I smirked and set aside my champagne, then bowed back like a gentleman. He laughed aloud and straightened. Taking my hand, he pulled me into his arms and swept me out onto the ballroom floor, holding me much too tight and dancing much too broadly. We barreled through the dancers like bowling pins, howling with laughter, parading ourselves madly before the crowd. Just to make him laugh more, I fought to lead. He retaliated by lifting me entirely off my feet and whirling me madly. My giggles rose carefree as my tightly bound hair broke its bonds and tumbled down my back.

When he returned me to my feet, we grinned at each other like naughty schoolchildren.

I felt pleased to make him respond so. He was known to be cynical and dry of wit. When he dropped his bored façade and warmed to me, I felt special. When he leaned in close to whisper in my ear, I felt his charm envelop me entirely. He caught me up in a sense of intimacy between us, as if we were alone in the crowded room.

"You look like a schoolboy's sticky fancy come to life in that rig. I imagine you would look quite astonishing naked and perspiring in the candlelight, impaled upon my enormous . . . brain." His breath was warm and damp on my ear and I did not bother to fight a shiver of arousal. How delicious to be seduced! I felt the danger of him; I knew his reputation as an outlaw and a rogue, yet it only excited me more.

I was not a woman like others were. I was not looking for a husband. I was not seeking a good provider or a steady master. I did not even currently require a protector. Robert's generosity had left me quite able to choose a man simply because I wanted him.

I was a woman free to be extraordinarily unwise.

What a delightful notion.

However, though I made no effort to hide my attraction, it would not do for him to be too sure of me. The Swan had taught me well.

I pulled my head away in order to smile up at him. "You are quite correct. I do look extraordinary naked and perspiring in the candlelight." Then with a careless shrug of my scarlet-clad shoulder, I turned easily away from Lord B—— and sauntered away.

I could feel him watching my bottom in the snug breeches. I tossed him an extra bit of sway, just to make his mouth dry. Smiling my triumph in my latest conquest, I almost didn't see Sir until his broad chest rose before me, blocking my way.

Cocking my head at him, I grinned. "You have outdone yourself, Sir. The Swan will be more popular than ever as the world strives to learn your identity."

He said nothing, but only continued to gaze down at me from behind his mask. I was too full of myself and Lord B——'s flattering attentions to care. I merely rolled my eyes and began to push past him.

His large hand closed about my arm. His touch always aroused a shiver in me and this time was no exception. For once, this annoyed me more than pleased me. I turned my head to snap something rude at him.

He spoke first. "Do not toy with that man."

I blinked. "Lord B——?"

"Yes, Lord B——. He cannot afford you."

That was true enough, but I disliked being told my own business. I lifted my chin. "I am not toying with him. I find him most entertaining company."

Sir gazed down at me. For the first time, I realized that his eyes were not black-brown at all, but a deep hazel that reminded me of a forest so thick it never sees the sun. Startled, I realized that I had never seen Sir out of the dim candlelight of our lover's bower. We had never stepped from that room.

We had never waltzed.

I found myself overpowered with the desire to dance in his arms. I looked away from his gaze. "Would you—" I felt absurdly shy. "Would you care to waltz, Sir?"

He did not reply. I looked back up to meet his eyes, but he was looking past me. I glanced over my shoulder to see the Swan, surrounded by eager men once more, holding court as of old.

"I cannot play the fool with you as B—— did," Sir said, his voice a growl. "Do you care nothing for preserving the victory you fought so hard to bring about?"

My gut went cold and I cursed my costume. For the first time that evening, I felt ridiculous instead of alluring and outrageous. I tugged my arm from his grasp and turned my back on him. I wanted nothing more than to run from the ballroom and strip my silly male clothes from my body. I could not leave, however, for I had arrived in the company of Sir.

Hot humiliation tempted me to walk home rather than submit to riding back with him and the Swan, but the London streets were not safe, not even for a man alone. Anyway, I looked nothing like a man. I looked like a plump prostitute stuffed into male clothing like a sausage about to split its skin.

I strode away, my eyes hot. I did not cry, for weeping in public was something I could not do. Instead, I forced my way through the crowd, snarling at any man stupid enough to utter a sally in my direction. When I arrived at the front door of Lady Montrose's house, I had made my decision.

Sir's gleaming black conveyance stood waiting with all the others, lined up across the street, the horses bored and the drivers snoozing on their seats or gaming on the cobbles with dice. I slammed my hand upon the shining ebony door to wake Sir's driver. "Oy!"

He sat up abruptly and glared down at me. "What ye want, there?" Then, "Oh, it's you, miss."

"Take me to my house at once."

He blinked at me uncertainly. "Er . . . is Himself ready to depart?"

I snarled. "Himself is busy with Herself. I, on the other hand, have a splitting headache and no desire to stay and watch the nauseating conclusion to the evening. Either you drive me home or I walk. Do you think your employer wants me walking the streets alone tonight?"

Straightening, he hopped down from his perch to open the door for me. "If yer sure, miss."

I bared my teeth. "Never have I been more so."

I collapsed in the back of the carriage and pressed the heels of my hands to my hot eyes. I knew how ridiculous I was being but I seemed to have no control over my behavior at the moment. Too much champagne and too little Sir.

I would not be this silly girl. I was the Blackbird, seductress extraordinaire! Leaning back in my seat, I turned my mind from Sir's callousness to Lord B——'s flattering admiration. His blue eyes flashed in my memory, his interest evident, his desire present in the heat of his hands on my waist when he'd lifted me.

He was very strong. I had the certain impression that he liked using his strength in bed. I thought of him above me, driving his cock into me powerfully, his large hands pinning my wrists down on either side as he took me again and again. My cunte dampened instantly.

Yes, I could take a man like that to my bed, simply for my own amusement. I had never done such a thing before, but why not? It would do my reputation no harm to break my own patterns of behavior.

Mystery, after all, was everything.

The next morning, Sylla brought me a sparing breakfast of dry toast and boiling hot tea to wash the night's drinking from my throat. My eyes still burned, I knew not why. I had put Sir and the Swan entirely from my mind and focused all my thoughts on my latest seduction.

I was not surprised to see a letter from Lord B——. He did not seem the sort to waste time and I was right. His note was bold and insultingly erotic. It left me breathless.

> *Where did you go last eve? I would have taken you away in my carriage and stripped you naked before we'd driven a block. I wanted to bind you with your own cravat and keep you for my pleasure. I thought about you all the way home and imagined myself on my knees before your lush beauty, my face buried between your thighs as you writhed above me, your skin ivory in the darkness, your cries rising above the rattle of the carriage wheels, your hot, salty nectar sliding down my tongue . . .*

Oh yes. This was a man I could spend a few wicked hours exploring.

Or days.

Perhaps even weeks.

The letter closed with, "You know you want me as well. I could smell your desire, like a hound after a fox. Just like that hunting beast, I will not leave the trail. Surrender now

and spare yourself the distress of trying to make up lies
why you won't see me."

His joke made me smile, until the thought slid through
my mind that I did not know him well enough to know if he
were jesting.

Do not toy with that man.

My chin lifted with a jerk and I determined to reply to
Lord B——'s invitation as soon as I had bathed and dressed.

Then I opened the next envelope on the tray. There was
nothing inside but a blackbird feather.

He wants to see me.

Me.

I closed my hot eyes and trailed the cool feather across
my flushed cheeks. Perhaps . . . perhaps my reply to Lord
B—— could wait until the morrow.

That evening's display of the Swan was a simple visit to the
opera. Sir had managed to procure the very best box in the
house through his mysterious connections. The Swan wore
silver brocade, a rich, lush gown with more than a hint of
Renaissance styling. Once more her gleaming hair rippled
loose down her back, this time crowned with a wreath of
tiny white flowers. She seemed more elaborately costumed
than the performers and was certainly more closely observed by the audience.

I wore a revealing silk gown of deep rose that was all
bosom and no mistake. My curves set off the Swan's slenderness. We both provided a feast for the eyes, no matter
one's preference. Sir brooded darkly between us, his evident lack of interest in the substandard performance only
adding to his arrogant appeal. Indeed, the man with the
square jaw framed by the mysterious mask was all that was
required to distract the ladies. I doubt that anyone present
could recall a full minute of the evening's entertainment.

Mission accomplished. Thank goodness nothing was required of me but to provide visual fodder, for my mind was

in tumult. I wanted nothing more than to get Sir alone, but whether to speak to him or to strip him naked and make him pay? I wanted his apology. I longed for his touch. I needed to feel him next to me, above me, inside me. I needed him to tell me he was sorry.

The ride home from the opera was slow, for the streets were full of carriages leaving their various diversions offered by the city. Sir sat opposite the Swan and me, facing backward as gentlemen did, so I could not speak to him privately at all. The Swan seemed relaxed and weary and entirely unaware that her reintroduction to the *haut ton* had any personal repercussions for me. She made a little desultory conversation about the packed audience and I managed to reply sensibly, after which she faded away, a satisfied little smile on her lovely face.

My jealousy repelled me. How could I let such darkness come between me and the best friend I knew? How could I allow Sir to do this to my emotions?

It isn't Sir. It is you.

I knew I was being selfish and entirely absurd. I had lovers. We all three had lovers. Our friendship was what made this mad threesome better than merely sexual. I would not allow my strange possessiveness to interfere with that magical circle.

I want him.

Honestly, I despair of myself sometimes.

Nineteen

Although the carriage dropped me off first, I did not fear I was being left out. I knew he would come as soon as he'd seen the Swan home, and I wished for every possible moment to prepare. I tossed red roses into my bath by the handful and rubbed them into my steaming skin. I massaged myself with sweet almond oil until my body gleamed like satin. I brushed my long curling hair down my back and forward over my breasts and tied it up high, finally growing weary of my indecision and letting it fall naturally where it might. Gown myself in something sheer or await him naked and eager? I tossed through my wardrobe of wicked attire but everything seemed too studied, too much the arsenal of the professional. I finally donned a simple, short chemise that clung to my already aroused nipples and showed off my bottom with clinging emphasis.

Bare and natural, I awaited him as myself.

I knew Sylla would let him enter unannounced, so I lay down across my bed on my belly and tried to busy myself arranging the rest of the rose petals upon the coverlet. The tick of the clock seemed like a painfully slow heartbeat as the long minutes passed. With all the traffic on the streets, it might take another hour for him to make it back to me.

Or perhaps he dallies with her.

I dropped my face into my hands. "Really, really stop doing that."

"Stop doing what?"

With a gasp I flipped over to see Sir looming dark in the doorway of my bedchamber. What should have been sinister was instead so welcome that I felt my eyes dampen ridiculously. I hid my reaction with a wicked smile and climbed to my knees to kneel on the mattress.

"You're still dressed," I said.

I saw his lips twitch. "It is a curable condition." He gazed at me for a long moment. "You are delicious. I think I like you this way best. No ball gowns and definitely no breeches."

His frank, unadorned admiration warmed me much more deeply than did the wicked flirtation of Lord B———. I gave him a real smile, then bounced from the mattress and ran to him. He caught me in his arms and buried his hands in my hair.

"You smell like a garden."

"I swam in roses." I twined my arms about his neck and pulled him down for a long kiss. The taste of him soothed my restless imagination. The heat of his big, solid body reminded me of all the hours he had spent with me in the past. Whatever the past held for him with the Swan, whatever the future held for him with me, he was here now and I was happy to see him.

I felt his cock harden against me as we kissed. I never let my mouth leave his as I slid my hands down his hard chest and rigid belly to reach the fastening of his trousers. When I released his thick length into my hands, he groaned into my mouth, deep enough to send tremors through my belly and cunte.

Our kiss turned abruptly hard and hot. I lost my grip on his cock to clutch at his shoulders as he wrapped his big hands around my waist and lifted me. Turning, he pressed my back into the closed door. I wrapped my thighs hard about his hips, never allowing his mouth to leave mine. He entered me swiftly, easily, for I had lain longing for him until my body throbbed in readiness. I tightened my arms about his neck and cried out at his entry, my sob of aching satisfaction disappearing into his hot mouth. He took me there, hard, one arm about my waist, the other hand bracing his weight upon the door, my chemise rucked up over my hips, his breeches about his knees.

I clung to him as he thrust deeply into me, my hands buried in his thick hair, my feet crossed behind his back, the hard oak of the door behind mine. It was fierce and relentless and wild, without a smidgen of control or seduction. I lost myself in his pounding rhythm, feeling nothing but the hot, wet slide of his thickness in and out of me and his groans, rumbling warm and deep down my own throat. When I began to orgasm, his pace increased, until he fucked me wildly. I could no longer breathe. I tossed my head back and wailed aloud as his cock pounded into me again and again. I thought he might come as well, but when I began to lose my ability to cling to him, he held me tightly and fell to his knees, rolling me to the floor without losing an inch of penetration. He rose above me on his hands as I panted weakly on the carpet, my legs barely with the strength to grip his hips with my knees.

He thrust pitilessly, gazing down at me, his eyes enigmatic behind his mask. I tossed my head in protest as my body responded yet again. How did he do this to me? How could I want him again so soon? Yet my body slickened and heated for his thick cock yet again, just at the sight of him above me, still in evening clothes as he fucked me on the floor.

I stretched my hands above my head and let him, sighing my way into yet another orgasm as he drove hard into me. I would be sore tomorrow with an ache so deep I could not soak it away. I relished the notion and drove my heels into his rigid buttocks, taking him deeper still.

My voice rose in panting, wordless begging as I came and this time he came with me, driving into me with a final groan so guttural it was almost a roar. I enfolded him in my arms as he fell upon me, gasping at the power of his release.

I slept a little, I think, despite the hardness of the floor. His weight upon me was warm and comforting, his pounding heart beating alongside mine. When he rolled from me I roused. My skin chilled rapidly, for the fire had long burned low. I shivered and protested sleepily. Sir lifted me in his arms and put me into bed. I snuggled beneath the coverlet, barely aware that he was quickly stripping off his clothing. I simply opened my arms and thighs when he slid between the covers. He pulled me close and tugged one thigh up onto his hip. I let my head rest upon his broad chest and slipped away to someplace safe and warm, a place I had not found with Robert, despite his earnest sweetness. Sir offered me a shelter and freedom from judgment that no other man could understand.

In the early morning hours, we lay in each other's arms and talked.

"Sir, I have been thinking . . ."

"Hmm. I'm frightened now."

I tugged vengefully at his chest hair. "Listen to me. Robert left me very well set, at least for a time. I've been considering that I need not find another protector for a while. I could use a bit of time to myself, and . . ." I trailed off. How to ask what I wanted to ask? Could he even afford to devote himself solely to me for a time? Would I be willing to share him with his female companions?

Exclusivity. Love given freely. These were dangerous thoughts for a courtesan. I might never regain my popularity if I rendered myself invisible now.

I might never want to.

"And?"

"I wondered . . . I thought . . . perhaps I might take a lover without recompense."

His body stiffened. "Stay away from B——," he ordered sharply.

I blinked. "What?"

Reaching across us both, he threw the covers off and swung his feet to the floor. I sat up chilled and naked to watch him stride across the room to the pile of his clothing. "W—wait—" I scrambled to find my chemise in the covers. "I was talking about—"

"You were talking about going against my counsel and dallying with that wastrel," he snapped out, his voice a rasp. He was half dressed already. He turned on me with his lips tight with fury beneath his mask. "For once in your life, Ophelia, would you just do as you're bloody told?"

My belly turned to ice at the anger I saw in him, but my spine snapped straight in response to his manner. "No man orders me." Was that my voice, low and even and spiked with fury?

He finished pulling his shirt over his head and threw his hands wide. "No man or woman! You do not even care to restrain yourself! You can be as foolish and thoughtless as you like, for you care for no one but Ophelia!"

My heart was spinning and crying out against how matters were going so very wrong. My head, I fear, was as stubborn as always. Better to be entirely misunderstood than to give in, even once! I folded my arms and coldly watched him dress. "Don't forget your cravat," I reminded him. "I've no need of it, for I've one of my own."

He slung the length of linen over his neck and stared at me for a long moment. "Is this it, then?"

I pretended not to understand.

His shoulders fell slightly. "Is this how we end, you and I? Over a scum-eater like B——?"

End? My heart gibbered in panic, running in tiny circles in my chest. My mind would not falter, not even to keep Sir by my side. If I gave in to his demands, what would be next? Would he begin to decide my friends, my wardrobe, the length of my hair? I had given up every expectation of a normal life in order to ride the winds of freedom. To clip my wings now would mean that I had been wrong all along.

So I gave nothing, said nothing, let him leave my house with naught but stony silence from me. I remained behind, still free.

However, those cherished winds now blew colder than they had before.

The next morning, I listlessly poked at my breakfast, breaking the dry toast into ever smaller squares while my tea grew cold. From the corner of my eye, I could see the always substantial pile of invitations. On the top lay a distinctive blue-tinted envelope. Another missive from Lord B——.

Why did I hesitate? Had I not ruined a treasured friendship in order to have this man?

Well, not precisely, but that had been the end result. If I did not pursue a liaison with him now, would I not be admitting to myself that I was wrong?

Heaven forfend. Wrong I dared not be. If I were wrong about this, I would be wrong about everything.

Besides, he was handsome and exciting. Indebted to his eyeballs as well, but what did that have to do with me? I was rich enough to entertain us both for months. Even then, if I ran short of funds, there were a dozen men who would sign away their inheritances for a single night with me. I might take one up on his offer, as some of the other courtesans were wont to do.

The Swan's voice rang in my mind. *"We are not prostitutes. We are artists of love."*

The Swan might not know everything. An affair could last for months or years.

So why not hours, if that was how I wished it?

Rebellion is a heady mix and I was drunk on it. I angrily pushed my breakfast tray from me and scrambled over my vast bed to the other side. My writing desk was in my bedchamber sitting room. Sitting down in the chair, nearly naked in my chemise, I removed paper and ink. Sharpening my quill took too long, for the strokes of my knife were too fierce by half. Finally, I dipped my quill and began.

> *My Dear Lord B——,*
>   *I have considered your offer of a carriage ride*
> *and find I am without distraction this evening.*
> *Perhaps an outing of this nature would suit. Call for*
> *me at sunset.*

I had the note posted at once. It was rude and unromantic in the extreme. I knew he would not care, for tonight he would have me as he wished, naked and writhing above him in the carriage. Dark arousal made me slippery even as I wondered if I would regret my hastiness. It was too late now—the note was on its way and our liaison was already in progress.

As I rose, I felt a twinge of soreness from last night's episode against the door. My thoughts turned to Sir but I did not allow them to linger there with him. I would not let Lord B—— fuck me quite yet, I decided. It would do him good to earn what he could not afford to buy.

It was odd that, for all I was giving myself freely, I had never felt more for sale.

Twenty

Boston

The promise of discovery had always kept Mick going. It was his reward. When an object would finally peek from its ancient tomb of sediment and rubble, all of time and space would fall away, only to be replaced with wonder.

Life at a dig site was often exhausting, filthy, and monotonous. His back and legs would ache. Progress could come painfully slow if at all. If the site was in the desert, his skin might start looking like beef jerky. In high-altitude temperatures he could get frostbite. The tropics might leave him waterlogged and covered in insect bites. Wherever the location, the days of frustration sometimes piled up into a mountain of doubt.

All of it was forgotten at the moment of discovery, however. The tiniest bone fragment. A coin. A primitive weapon once held in another human being's hand. Whatever the find, it became Mick's job to unravel its deepest mysteries. He lived for these moments, and the challenge they delivered to his door.

But this? Nothing had ever come close.

Piper was shockingly beautiful. Unexpected. She looked like a hot piece of cotton candy. A wet dream in little poofy fuck-me slippers. And the decadent display of flesh and sex had Mick sprouting a near-fatal hard-on before he'd had time to enter the room.

His throat went bone-dry. *"Piper,"* he managed to croak. "What are you doing?"

Ah, yes—it was the stupidest comment ever made by a man in the course of human history. But that was the best Mick could do under the circumstances, since all of his available blood supply had just relocated to his cock.

She gave him a sly little smile and wiggled her delicious hips against what looked like satin sheets. He stared at her in awe, waiting for all the visual data to click in his brain.

"I'm seducing you, Dr. Malloy," she said, her voice huskier than it had been all evening. "Haven't you ever had a woman display herself like this for you?"

Crickets. Mick's brain echoed with the sound of crickets. Then he couldn't remember what she'd asked him but was pretty sure the answer was no. All he could focus on was the delicate vee of thong peeking out from between her juicy thighs.

"Mick?"

"I'm here," he rasped.

Piper laughed. He liked what happened with her breasts when she did that—all the fascinatingly soft swells of female flesh began to rise and fall, popping their way out of the top of her . . .

Mick suddenly couldn't recall the name for the thing she was wearing. A teddy? No. A camisole? No. Oh, Janey Mack, who gave a feckin' rat's arse what it was?

Then it suddenly dawned on him. *This is for me. Whatever she's wearing and everything she's packing into it is for me. She's doing this for me!*

"Why don't you come over here and get comfortable?" She patted the bed next to her.

Mick moved fast. If he dawdled, she might change her mind.

Piper brought her arm down from over her head and reached out for him. He dove right into her embrace. Immediately, he was struck by the heat of her skin, the heady scent of her girl flesh and hair.

"You relax," she whispered. "I'll get the champagne. Then I have a little surprise for you."

Mick nearly choked. "You mean this isn't the surprise?"

She giggled, slipped out of the bed, and walked on her fuck-me slippers right out the door. Okay. Her ass was completely bare. Nothing but gorgeous globes of pink perfection framed in thigh-highs and garter belt. Like it needed framing! Like he wouldn't have noticed her ass unless it had been brought to his attention.

"Damn," Mick sighed, falling back against the satin pillows and gazing up into the swags of silky gauze. So Piper wanted to seduce him into her trap? She wanted to fuck with his head? Grind his nose into the fact that she was the finest piece of female he'd ever be lucky enough to know, past, present, or future?

That worked for him.

"Are you ready?"

Mick shot up to a sitting position. She'd returned with a fresh and frosty bottle of bubbly and their glasses. He watched her place everything on top of the dresser, then turn her back to him, spreading her legs apart, locking her knees, and whipping her head around to smile at him over her shoulder.

Then, with Marvin Gaye being kind enough to provide the soundtrack for his second chance, Piper began to strip for him.

Mick swallowed hard. He grabbed the first little foo-foo satin pillow he could get his hands on—this one, ironically, was shaped like a giant breakfast sausage—and pressed it to his loins.

Piper's hair went swinging across her bare back. She slowly twirled around, her pretty slim fingers working to loosen the laces on the thing she was wearing, all while her hips languidly swayed and circled. Unless Mick was hallucinating, the garment had opened enough that he could spy the barest hint of rosy pink nipple, hardening as it popped out into the air.

Suddenly, Piper stopped. "Would you prefer that I leave the stockings on?" she asked him.

Oh, she was a wayward minx, this one. Mick laughed. If he said, *"No, take the feckin' things off so I can run my tongue up and down your shins,"* she'd think he was an animal. But if he said, *"Hell, yes, leave 'em on!"*—she might think he was a little twisted.

"You decide for now," he said, his eyes locked on hers. "If I want something off, it'll come off. Trust me."

She thought that was funny, did she now? Piper tipped her head back and laughed, her nipples getting full access to the air-conditioning with the movement. Then she straightened, walked to the end of the bed, and leaned forward on her hands. It offered him a fascinating view down the front of her . . . whatever it was . . . and a closer look at her tight and flat lower belly, the tiny triangle of the thong, the pinch of the garter belt into her blushing thighs.

He hugged the giant breakfast sausage to his lap.

"I have a proposition for you," she said, those deep green eyes looking up at him through thick black lashes.

"I can see that," he said.

One corner of her lips twitched. "Here's the deal—I'd like to be in charge. There are some things I want to experiment with, and I think I'd be less inhibited if I set the pace."

"Less inhibited? What's that gonna look like?"

Her smile spread. "Stay tuned, Dr. Malloy." She straightened again, bringing her fingers back to the laces on her . . .

"Piper," he said, sighing. "What the hell is that thing you're wearing?"

Her face fell. "You don't like it?"

"Oh, Jaysus and Mary, yes, I like it! I feckin' *love* it! I just can't remember the name for it—my mind has gone completely blank because of how sexy you are."

She giggled. "It's a corset."

"Ah! Of course!" Mick settled back down into the pillows, the sausage still strategically placed. He didn't want to frighten the girl, after all. "So, uh, are you feeling uninhibited enough to take off the corset?"

"I believe I am," she said, and she launched into the agonizingly sensual striptease that Mick knew would serve as the Continental Divide of his life—separating everything that had come before it from all that would come after.

She'd made him suffer terribly, and she felt a little guilty about it. For hours now she'd laved him with her tongue and stroked him with her hands and held him close and kissed him until he couldn't breathe.

Piper looked at the poor man now, on the edge of coming again, and she sensed the basic unfairness of the whole proposition—she'd had four orgasms, and he'd had zero. Almost certain she'd met all the requirements of the First Sin, Piper decided it was time to move on.

She pulled her wet lips from his cock, so hot and swollen for so long now, and sat up on her haunches on the bed. The sudden movement caused one of her garters to snap loose. She noticed there was a run in the left leg of her stocking. Her breasts were decorated with hickeys.

Piper reached around her for a condom. The sound of the foil being unwrapped caused Mick to open one eye.

"Please, woman, this better not be another way to tease me. I'm not sure how much strength I have left."

"No more teasing," she said, handing Mick the condom and watching as he hoisted himself up from the bed on his muscled arms, his dark curls in disarray, his blue eyes glazed over.

He was such a beautiful man. She'd been studying his beauty for hours now, but the sight of him still took her breath away. His face had softened in arousal, contrasting with the hard contours of his flesh, bones, and tendons, the masculine tapering of his torso, and the dusting of springy black hair around his magnificent man parts.

"Actually," Piper whispered, "I think it's time for fucking."

His eyes popped wide.

"Do you want to fuck me, Mick?"

Apparently, he did, because Piper was tossed toward the end of the bed and in seconds Mick was all over her, his fingers laced in hers, his hips pressing her thighs wide apart, his lips smothering hers, all while he kept mumbling, *"Yes, yes, yes."*

The moment was upon her. The tip of his cock pushed into her. Since her body had been warmed up with Mick's fingers and tongue for what had felt like *days* of foreplay, she was soaking wet for him. He slid into her with a moan of relief.

But was it his moan or hers?

It didn't matter. Nothing mattered to Piper. Nothing but the sensation of his hard cock and his lips and the tingling she felt beginning yet again, this time from deeper within her body, flooding her, erasing all thought, all sense of order, normalcy, limits, lifting her higher . . .

She jolted, sharp pleasure striking into the core of her.

"That's it, Piper," Mick encouraged her, dragging his lips down her throat, over her collarbones, as she arched into him.

"Squeeze me. Come all over me. Bloody scream if you want to."

So she did. And she felt Mick switch into overdrive, grabbing her ass in his hands and focusing all his body's energy on getting deeper into her, faster, harder. She felt Mick's big body shudder, clench tight as he called out her name, then slowly unwind.

Many long moments later, Mick chuckled into her ear. "There's only one she-devil around here, and it's you," he said.

Even in her postsex stupor, Piper found the energy to smile.

Mick dragged his sorry arse into the museum Monday morning, arriving a good half hour late, floating in a Zen-like zone of sexual contentment, his bones liquified, his flesh slightly sore, and his mind stuck on one thing:

What the hell did Piper have planned for tonight?

He wasn't complaining. On the contrary—he'd never had such a wild three-day sensual bonanza in his life, and he was already signed up for four additional installments. He just thanked God he was young, healthy, and in the best physical shape of his life, because anything less and he'd already be a dead man.

It started with Friday's over-the-top seduction, which culminated in an all-night marathon of fiery sex. By the crack of dawn, Mick realized that Piper was a woman with a heretofore unexplored subterranean sexual landscape chock-full of surprises. It was going to be an interesting week.

Saturday brought an edible sexual orgy—cream and honey and chocolate-covered strawberries—dear God, there was sweet juice of every description running everywhere! Piper told him she simply wanted to give him an opportunity to take a big bite out of life, which was right about the time he sank his teeth into her arse and they fell off the bed laughing. He didn't go hungry that day, that was certain. Thankfully, Piper had plenty of towels about the place.

And then yesterday, Sunday, Piper treated Mick to what she called his day of indulgence. She drew him a bubble bath and scrubbed his back and washed his hair. She wrapped him in a fancy silk robe she'd bought for him, and insisted on giving him a pedicure while he watched the Sox game on TV. He'd said no, of course. To the pedicure, not the game. Any normal man would've done the same. But after she pouted and sat on his lap, he gave in, and it wasn't long before he was moaning out in pleasure, Piper's strong fingers kneading the soles of his feet. It turned out his feet shared a direct neurological pathway with his crotch! Who knew?

And so now it was Monday morning, and though the staff meeting was set to start, all Mick wanted to do was cross his arms on his desk and collapse face-first.

There was a rapid tap-tapping on his open door, and Linc Northcutt appeared, in possession of a steaming cup of coffee and a smirk.

"Another long night planning the fund-raising campaign?" he asked, sitting down in the chair across the desk without being invited.

"Yeah," Mick answered. "Ben Affleck has signed on to do the public service announcements for the Fall Gala."

Linc snorted. "Right."

Mick enjoyed this exchange. Linc was a jaded lad—a sad state of affairs for someone barely out of his twenties—and Mick almost felt it was his duty to shake him up a bit.

"Which reminds me." Mick pretended to rifle through papers on his desk, though what he needed was right at his fingertips. "Would you call Affleck's assistant and tell her we've had to change the studio taping time?" Mick held out a computer printout. "Her number and all the info is right here."

Linc narrowed his eyes and slowly reached for the document, like the paper would bite him. Mick watched his gaze light up and his fingers begin to tremble. Then Linc's eyes got huge. "Absolutely!" he said. "No problem. Right away." As he ran from the office, Mick reminded him to shut the door on the way out.

Ten minutes later, Linc was back, shaking Mick from a dead sleep and inquiring whether he planned to attend the staff meeting. Mick got up. He went to the conference room. He sat down. And it wasn't five minutes into the meeting that Mick glanced across the table to see Piper staring off into the distance, a half smile on her face, and a nice-sized love bite on her neck. He sent her a text message. Almost immediately, she adjusted her collar and smiled his way.

Later, Mick thought about how funny it was that he and Piper had already fallen into a routine at work. Round about half past three every afternoon, he'd stop by her workroom to see if she'd like to grab a cup of tea in the museum café. Today was no different. He took the elevator to the basement and knocked on her door. No answer. He opened it a crack. "Piper?"

Nothing.

And then he remembered—she'd mentioned having an outside meeting until at least six P.M., something to do with additional artifacts for the Ophelia Harrington exhibit, though based on the overflowing contents of the workroom, Mick couldn't imagine what she might still need.

He decided to leave her a note. He'd make it sweet and just a little suggestive, something that would make her smile and think of him.

He sat down at her desk. He reached for a pen. Something caught his eye. A stack of paper stuck out from the center desk drawer, and a fluorescent yellow Post-it had been slapped to the top page. On it was scrawled this sentence: *"Does Mick like it standing up?"*

"What the—"

He pulled the drawer fully open and removed a hefty stack of what looked like photocopied historical documents.

It took him a few seconds to adjust to the fainter, highly stylized cursive. But when he did, these were the first words he read: *"I clung to him as he thrust deeply into me, my hands buried in his thick hair, my feet crossed behind his back, the hard oak of the door behind mine."*

Mick's whole body began to buzz. He flipped through the pages madly, attempting to reason, understand, land on some kind of alternate explanation for what he was seeing. But there was none.

Diaries? Sexually explicit diaries? Ophelia Harrington's sexually explicit diaries? And Ophelia was a—

Mick jolted upright.

No feckin' way.

He read more. Then more.

He began to perspire. He checked the clock on the workroom wall. It was four P.M. He'd been sitting there a half hour. He had two hours before Piper got back, but he couldn't risk cutting it that close. He had to have everything back in her desk drawer by five. Obviously, there was no way he could risk copying the documents on site—no one knew about this for a reason, and he planned to keep it that way.

He clutched the papers to his chest. As he waited for the elevator, it started to sink in. Ophelia Harrington was a courtesan, and her diaries included details of her own erotic awakening, which, obviously, Piper had been using to seduce *him*.

He took the elevator up to the lobby, thinking that there was nothing wrong with that. Not really. Not *technically*. So what if Piper had been inspired by a two-hundred-year-old pornographic diary? Clearly, she thought she needed a gimmick to attract his attention.

Ah, Piper. Baby.

He arrived at his destination two blocks from the museum. He tossed his credit card on the Sir Speedy counter, unclipped the pages, and began the self-serve copier's autofeed feature. With the heartbeatlike pace of the copy machine in the background, Mick rubbed his face with his hands. He shook his head.

Piper was using another woman's adventure to create her own. She'd become a fearless seductress because she thought that's what it would take to get his attention, and it had worked. The thought of that nearly broke his heart.

Suddenly, Mick felt a chill. The hairs on his arms rose in alarm. He spun around but saw no one paying him any mind. Then the copier ground to a halt. It beeped. It was jammed.

"Excuse me," Mick said to the kid behind the counter. "I could use a hand." Nearly five minutes later, the nice young man had fixed the copier, tossed the problem page into the trash, and got Mick running again. "Thanks," Mick said, handing him a couple bucks.

As Mick watched page after page stack up, he realized these diaries weren't just a guide to inspired sex. Piper was installing an exhibit about this woman, yet she was hiding the punch line in her desk drawer. What the hell was she up to? What was she thinking?

When he left the copy shop, Mick looked both ways along the sidewalk, spooked again. Ridiculous, he told himself.

He got the diaries back in Piper's drawer by four-fifty P.M. He left work early, taking his contraband with him. He'd be awaiting Piper's call that evening, and in the meantime, he'd stop by the pub for a pint and a little light reading.

The instant Mick disappeared into the flow of pedestrians, Linc Northcutt popped out from his hiding place and slipped into the Sir Speedy. He pretended to browse the wall display of supplies until all the salespeople were occupied. Then he bent casually at the waist—as if he were stretching—and snatched the discarded sheet of paper from the trash.

Linc smoothed out the wrinkles as best he could, dismayed that some of the writing was left unintelligible by the paper jam. He scanned the archaic script and knew immediately it was from a historic document of some kind, perhaps even a journal. A few words into the first sentence, his eyes bugged out.

> *My dear Robert has never been interested in pursuing the deliciously wicked practices I'd come to enjoy during my nights with Sir, and I intend to find a new lover who is vastly more adventurous.*

Linc stopped. He glanced over his shoulder to make sure no one was nearby. Whatever the fuck this was he was holding in his hand had to be some sort of secret or Malloy wouldn't have come here to copy it. He continued to read.

> *I have fully embraced my wantonness as the Courtesan the Blackbird, after all, and am no longer living in the world as Miss Ophelia Harrington. That tame*

*and predictable life is dead to me. I care nothing for
the so-called virtue of respectability.*

Linc folded the paper into fourths, shoved it in his pants
pocket, and chuckled to himself all the way back to the museum.

Twenty-one

Mick forgot about the city heat the moment he ducked into Malloy's Pub. As always, the narrow establishment was bathed in cool dimness, punctuated by the squeaky-clean mirror behind the bar, the sparkling brass of the taps, and the much-polished mahogany of the bar itself.

Mick inhaled, and it was almost as if he could draw in his family's story along with his breath. Suddenly, he stopped. Something was wrong.

No one had greeted him.

Glancing around, he saw a couple sitting at the tiny table by the front window, lost in each other, their pints hardly touched. A lone old fellow Mick had never seen before sat hunched on a stool. His clothes were well to the other side of fresh.

And nobody was tending bar.

Mick tossed his Sir Speedy's package onto a pub table and ducked under the flip-top. He was donning an apron when Emily burst through the kitchen's swinging door.

"Hullo, Em. Where's—"

"I told him to bugger off," she said, delivering a plate of crisps and a fried egg to the tattered-looking fellow. "You enjoy, now," she said to the man.

Mick watched the old guy attack his food like he hadn't

eaten in a week. Right then, it occurred to him that he probably hadn't.

Emily turned to Mick with her hands balled on her hips
and her mouth set tight. "Can I pour you a pint?"

"No. Nothing, thanks," he said, aware that she still
hadn't revealed the whereabouts of his brother. Sure, Emily
was known to feed the homeless and take in stray cats, but
by this point, Mick needed to be reassured that his brother
hadn't been chopped to bits and stuffed in the walk-in
freezer.

"He's out in the alley," Em said with a sigh. "I locked the
delivery door on him, so if he's comin' back I suspect it'll
be through the front."

"What happened?"

Her face saddened, and Mick thought she was about to
cry, which was unheard of for Emily.

"Ah, *psshh*." She turned on her short, sturdy legs and
waved her hand dismissively, grabbed a rag, then began to
wipe down the bar with strokes hard enough to strip the finish. "Nothing we can't get through, I suppose."

Em and Cullen were known to get snippy with each other
on occasion, but Mick's sister-in-law seemed truly down today, and that was not her style. He slowly approached her
and put a hand on her moving shoulder.

"Emily? What's going on?"

She spun around, the rag clutched in the hand she'd chosen to gesture with. "The gobshite has put the pub up for
sale! He's called a real estate agent!"

Mick felt his jaw open in shock. "Wha . . . when did he
do this?"

"Today. I caught him on the office phone." Em raised
both hands over her head, the rag now her flag of surrender.
"We hadn't even made a final decision about it, and he takes
it upon himself to—"

The front door flew open, and there was Cullen, his chest
heaving and everything above the collar red with fury. Without a word, he ducked under the flip-top and put on a clean

apron. Em glared at her husband like he was Satan himself, and headed back into the kitchen.

Right about then, Mick knew his plans for the evening were shot.

In truth, Piper didn't mind that Mick got sidetracked at the family pub. She was so exhausted she could barely stand, let alone concentrate on the Night of Sin at hand, even if it were all about relaxation and slow lovemaking. That would be too conducive to nodding off at an inopportune moment.

Never in her life had she had so much sex. Literally— Piper had experienced more sex over the weekend than in all her thirty years combined. And the quality of the sex?

Not even comparable. Off the charts. The stuff she thought existed only in paperbacks with half-naked men gracing their covers. All that pleasure had been a shock to her system.

So Piper came home Monday evening and took a hot soak in the tub, put on an old, worn-out nightgown, and crawled under some threadbare cotton sheets.

Almost immediately, her phone rang. It was Brenna.

"Hello."

"Why are you answering your phone?" she asked. "Right about now you should be breaking out the body oil."

Piper chuckled, too tired to even laugh properly. "We had to skip tonight. Mick's brother had an emergency at the pub. We'll pick up where we left off tomorrow night."

"Hmm. But everything's going well?"

"Ooh, yeah."

"No morning-after awkwardness at work?"

Miss Meade began rubbing against Piper's arm, demanding attention. She scratched the cat behind her ears, suddenly feeling guilty—only one pussy had been getting attention around here, and it wasn't the one with four legs.

"No weirdness, unless you count the fact that I showed up at the staff meeting with a giant hickey on the side of my neck."

Brenna sucked in air.

"Concealer covered it right up."

"And how was the meeting with Baz? Is he going to be able to help you out?"

"Oh, Brenna—he was incredible! He might just save the day."

Basil Tate was Brenna's former graduate assistant, now working as an associate professor at Amherst. His area of expertise happened to be the historical context of promiscuity, and he had dozens of contacts he said could help provide artifacts for an exhibit on the life of an early nineteenth-century British courtesan. Most were in London and Paris, unfortunately, but Baz gave Piper the name of a private collector near Philadelphia and a friend on staff at the Museum of Sexuality in New York City.

"When I think about how much work I've got to do I start to hyperventilate," Piper said.

Brenna laughed. "You can do it. Like I've told you a thousand times, I'm here to help."

Piper smiled, realizing that she'd never responded to Brenna the way she was about to. "I'll take you up on it," she said, meaning it.

After hanging up, Piper reached for her copies of Ophelia's journals, which she'd grabbed from her workroom office just before heading home. Selecting a dozen or so excerpts to enlarge and mat for display would be one of her first challenges. Piper was reviewing the now-familiar words and thoughts when she noticed a few pages were out of order. That struck her as odd, since she couldn't recall removing the document clips and working with loose pages.

But then again, Piper was so out sorts these days that she could hardly recall what century it was.

Malloy's was hit by an unexpected happy-hour rush, and Mick helped Cullen at the bar until about eight, while Emily whipped up pub food and dinner entrees. When Cullen had things well in hand, Mick retreated to a booth and enjoyed a plate of Emily's delicious beef pie with potato mash and a side of spinach, all washed down by two pints of Murphy's. Only then, when his belly was full and he was assured that his brother and sister-in-law would soon be discussing their problems like adults, Mick turned on the pub lamp and reached for the Ophelia Harrington diaries.

What a fascinating read! Ophelia was only a girl when she told the aunt and uncle to bugger off and set off on her own. The Swan was over-the-top. And how about this "Sir" character? Mick laughed his ass off. What a racket, going around wearing a mask and relieving girls of their innocence, all the while insisting they call him "Sir"!

A few moments later, Mick's laughter subsided. He had to admit the masked fellow had some valid insight. Mick also deduced that if he and Piper had been following the Seven Sins of the Courtesan in order—and it sure looked that way—tonight was supposed to be about slow and sensual lovemaking.

He put the documents aside for a moment and sighed. Ironically enough, his first instinct was to share this with Piper. He missed his lover. Mick had half a mind to call her, just to hear her voice.

With renewed curiosity, he scanned the first volume to discover what sins awaited him, and found they were Wrath, Covetousness, and Pride. It didn't take a genius to figure out how those goodies might transfer into the twenty-first century, and he broke out in a sweat.

Mick suddenly sat up in the booth, a shock of awareness going through him. As exciting as all this was, it was just the pretty wrapping for what he'd been experiencing with Piper. He wasn't missing the sin of the day—he was missing *her*. He missed Piper's laugh and her softness and that mix of innocence and wildness that he found intoxicating.

A twinge of anxiety shot through him. What the hell was he doing falling for a woman when he was hoping—planning, really—to start traveling the world for a TV show?

Cullen suddenly stood over him. "What ya readin'?" He bent down and shoved his nose where it didn't belong.

Mick slapped the pages closed.

Cullen roared with laughter. "Relax the cacks, Magnus! What—you got some nudie pics in there or something?"

Mick shoved the diaries into the Sir Speedy bag, knowing there was no way on God's earth he would be sharing two-hundred-year-old English porno with his brother—he'd never hear the end of it. Besides, this wasn't his secret to divulge—he wasn't even supposed to know the diaries existed.

"Just research," Mick said.

"Yeah? Well, we're winding down. You said you wanted to talk."

Mick nodded, following Cullen and bringing along his dirty dishes. The three of them met up in the kitchen office. Mick and Cullen were in chairs and Emily leaned on the doorjamb, keeping one eye on the bar and another on the security monitor aimed at the front door and dining room.

"I hear you want to sell the place." Mick decided he'd just get to it.

"Who said that?" Cullen's eyes flashed to Emily. "That phone call was just for some of the preliminary, you know, information gathering."

Emily lowered her chin to her chest and gave her husband a look that needed no words.

"Don't do it." Mick leaned forward on the desk. "Let me invest in the pub. I can get you out of whatever temporary spot you're in and we'll move forward together. I . . ." Mick paused before he went any further, knowing that if he mentioned the reality-show money he'd damned well better deliver. "I might be in a position where you won't have to worry about money anymore."

Cullen and Emily glanced at each other in shock.

"You win the Mega Millions?" Cullen asked.

Mick shook his head.

Cullen folded his arms over his chest. "Don't be daft,

Magnus. You're already part owner. Da left the pub to both of us. This place is as much yours as it is mine."

"Then what are you doing trying to sell the feckin' place behind my back?"

Cullen's eyes went wide. "Ha! I'm the one who's in here bustin' my bollocks every day trying to squeeze out a livin' in a recession!"

Mick smiled. "Exactly my point, old man," he said, reaching over to put a hand on his brother's arm. "Isn't it about time I did my bit?"

While they'd argued, Em had been studying Mick and Cullen, nervously fiddling with her ponytail. "That's enough," she said, her voice so soft it alarmed both the men. She looked at her husband. "Now, would you kindly explain what kind of spot we are in? I'm well aware we're not making money hand over fist here, and I know we've been a few weeks late on bills, but is there something yer not telling me?"

Cullen swallowed. "We're . . . ah . . . about three months behind on the mortgage," he said.

She blinked. "Which one—the house or the pub?"

"Both."

"*What?*"

"Ah, shit." Cullen wiped a hand over his face. "I was hoping I could get us square before you found out. I didn't want you to worry. But the receipts just kept getting less and less . . ." Cullen tried to smile. "But tonight might be a sign things are turning around!"

"Oh, for feck's sake, Malloy," Em said, shaking her head in disbelief. "You hid all this from me? Why? I have a right to know if we're headed to hell in a handcart! Anyway, I thought we did everything as a team."

Cullen lowered his head, chastised. "I just didn't want . . . *this,*" he said. "I couldn't face you finding out I'd failed you, failed the children."

"Look," Mick said to both of them. "You have a lot to sort out, but there's still an offer on the table. I have about fifteen thousand saved and it's yours. Catch up on the mortgages, get ahead on your bills."

Cullen shook his head. "We couldn't. We'd be wiping you out."

"You wouldn't." Mick laughed to himself before he elaborated, knowing his brother might very well assume he was joking. "I'll be getting my own reality show soon."

There were two beats of silence before Cullen exploded. *"Bwaa-haa-haa!"*

Emily smacked him on the top of his head.

"Why did you go and do that?" Cullen glanced back and forth between Emily and Mick. "He's coddlin' us, Em!" He paused. "Right?"

Mick shook his head. "It'll be on the Compass Cable Network. I didn't plan to tell you until it was a done deal and I'd signed on the line, but when this business with selling the pub came up . . ."

They both stared at Mick in silence.

"All I'm sayin' is, please don't worry about money. Don't sell the pub."

Cullen jumped up from his desk chair and nearly knocked Emily over on his rush back to the bar. "Drinks are on me!" he called out to anyone who might still be in the place. "My baby brother's a famous TV star!"

Twenty-two

That next evening, Piper pulled into the drive of the Georgian-style brick mansion with its Ionic columns and steep entrance stairs, still unsure why, exactly, she was there. Mick had slipped a cryptic note under her workroom door sometime that afternoon, asking her to meet him that evening at Towne Gate Historic Guest House about a half hour south of Boston.

Being a good girl—and a constantly aroused one—Piper had gone home to feed Miss Meade, grab a few overnight things, and do as she'd been asked.

She knocked on the glossy black door, noting with interest the low fanlight above the entrance, patterned with a typical teardrop design of the period.

"Well, hello!" A pleasant older woman opened the door to the bed-and-breakfast, ushering Piper into a magical world. Her eyes widened at the sight of the historically accurate splendor of the foyer, with its deep burgundy Regency striped wallpaper, the cantilevered iron staircase that curved graciously upward, and the ornate Indochinese-style light fixture over her head.

"Yes, Dr. Malloy said you'd be interested in the history of the house," the woman said with a smile. She held out her hand. "Nanette Benson, innkeeper."

"Piper Chase-Pierpont."

Nanette laughed merrily. "Please come in." As she gave a quick tour of the downstairs public rooms, Piper had to resist the urge to gasp and pant. She couldn't help herself—there was classic Palladian plaster detailing. She saw tall, narrow windows and a columned fireplace inset with marble. Then there were the Sheraton sitting-room chairs against the wall, the mahogany and red velvet armchairs with sabre legs, and the glazed yellow chintz draperies. Even the small ornamental touches such as the blown-glass peacock on the mantelpiece, the framed floral paintings, and the silver plate . . . Piper could almost picture the Blackbird sweeping through with the gored hemline of her long skirt trailing behind.

"I'm sure you don't want to spend your evening looking at knickknacks," Nanette said, wiggling an eyebrow. "But here, take my card." She slipped an elegant white business card into Piper's hand, along with a room key. "It's the second door on the left at the top of the stairs. You two are my only guests this evening, being a weeknight and all, so feel free to roam about." She patted Piper's hand. "Enjoy your stay."

Slightly confused—and still reeling from the beauty of her museum-ready environment—Piper pocketed the card, held on to the key, and climbed the stairs. She opened the lock, turned the brass knob, and swung the door open to . . . the Blackbird's boudoir?

Her overnight bag fell to the floor. She heard the beat of her own heart. *What in the world was Mick up to?*

Piper stepped into a small sitting room, its rich yellow walls glowing in the candlelight. Her eyes were immediately drawn to the decadent giltwood chaise longue in the room's center, with its scrolled arms and blue-and-gold striped silk upholstery. Next to it was a sizable circular table of mahogany, adorned with fresh flowers and a tray of fruit, cheeses, and sliced bread. And next to that sat a bottle of red wine, opened and breathing. She noted the two wine goblets. Two plates.

Her head swiveled around.

And one man.

She nearly passed out at the sight of him. Lust and alarm in equal measure rushed through her.

He leaned against the doorway to the adjoining bed-chamber, dark loose curls around his head, a devilish smile on his lips. From the waist down he wore a pair of tight nankeen breeches and black Hessian boots. On top, he was decked out in an unbuttoned waistcoat, a billowing white linen shirt open all the way down to his rippled abdomen, and a cravat that fell loose from his neck.

But what startled Piper most was the black satin mask that covered his face from brow to nostril.

Sir?

The masked man took three steps toward her. Piper watched the hard muscles of his thighs undulate and the ridges of his stomach move as he came closer. She was mes-merized by his male beauty, but baffled. Clinging to the knowledge that she had not, in fact, become batshit-crazy and that this gorgeous man was, in fact, Mick Malloy, her only question was, how did he know? Was that why the pages were out of order? Should she be angry that he'd snooped around her office?

Oh God, no—he'd seen all my notes!

On fire with shame, Piper backed away.

"Oh no, you don't." A hand gripped her arm. Piper stared into the cobalt-blue eyes that burned from behind the mask. "Tonight you're all mine."

Piper let go with a bark of bitter laughter and tried to pull away. He only yanked her tight against his bare chest.

"Don't be angry," he said, his voice low and husky as he dragged his lips upon her cheek, down the side of her neck. "This is all for you, Piper. If you don't enjoy yourself, we'll stop, but tonight is all about your pleasure, your fantasy."

She leaned away, staring up into his eyes. Piper saw no teasing there, though she had to admit it was difficult to read a man in a mask. Plus she was thoroughly distracted by his mouth—erotic and delicious—the only exposed fea-ture of his face.

"I—" Piper stopped herself, suddenly overwhelmed. "I'm embarrassed."

"No! Don't be!" Mick cupped her chin, encouraging her to look at him. "I sat down at your desk to leave you a note yesterday, and saw my name on a Post-it stuck to a stack of papers. I was curious. I shouldn't have looked. It was none of my business. Forgive me. But once I started reading, I was hooked . . . shocked, even. As a scholar I was fascinated by her story, but I admit, I just got plain turned on as fuck."

"Did anyone see you reading it?"

"Piper," Mick said, holding her by the shoulders. "I figured you had good reason for never mentioning the diaries as part of your exhibit, and I kept your secret for you. I went to the copy shop and had your copy back in your drawer in twenty minutes. My copy has been in my possession every minute since. It's here tonight. I thought we could have fun with it. Or, we can burn the damn thing if you like."

Piper let her eyes feast on the living, breathing girl fantasy that stood before her. It was ironic that Mick had gone to these lengths for her, because the basic Mick Malloy was almost more than Piper could handle. And "Sir" Mick Malloy? With that familiar velvet brogue now distilled into a husky bedroom whisper? Those twinkling eyes? That man-package all gift-wrapped in a too-tight pair of riding breeches?

That should be illegal.

"It'll be okay, Piper." Mick pulled her close and held her tight, his large hands rubbing up and down her back as she melted into him. "I want to give you something special tonight—that's all," he whispered. "I want to feed you and play with you and watch the expression in your eyes as all your wildest fantasies come true."

Piper hid her smile.

"Brace yourself, woman, for I plan to force you to say the word 'cunt'—and with an *e*, no less—and watch you morph into a wild, wanton slut."

She closed her eyes and buried her laugh in his hard, down-covered chest. He smelled warm and masculine. She wanted to sink her teeth into him.

"And after tonight we can continue on our merry way with the sins exactly as written, maybe even find a few new ones as we go. Does that sound doable?"

"I suppose." He had to have felt her smile widen against his chest.

"All right, then." Mick stood her up straight. He softly patted her on the bottom. "Be a sport then and head to the bedroom. Freshen up if you like. I've laid out a little something for you to wear."

Piper raised an eyebrow at him. "I thought tonight was about *my* fantasy."

Mick tipped his head back and laughed, the rich and husky sound thrilling her to the core. "It is. Now do as I say and wear what I've laid out for you and then get your pretty little arse out here as fast as you can."

Piper obeyed, retreating to the bedroom, smiling and thinking. She took a quick but hot shower, telling herself that she was fine with Mick knowing about the diaries. She had planned on telling him anyway, because she was going to need his help to pull off the exhibit. Piper brushed her hair, reapplied a sweep of eyeliner, and picked up the "little something" Mick had selected for her to wear.

It took her about a half second to figure out where he'd found his inspiration. The first night the Swan had sent the virginal Ophelia into Sir's arms she'd worn something quite similar—a perfectly sheer gown, tied loose at the neck, revealing every contour and swell of her body.

More than naked, indeed.

Piper padded out on bare feet but stopped almost as soon as she entered the sitting room. She had to catch her breath. The still-masked Mick was sprawled out on the chaise longue, skin gilded in the candlelight, long legs wide, shirt still open, smirk still visible. He tapped a thigh to indicate where she was supposed to sit. She did as she was told and walked toward him, the wisp of fabric floating behind her in the breeze, all of her charms exposed to his gaze.

He teased her as he fed her, inserting a strawberry between her lips, then taking it out with his teeth, all while his hands caressed her body. He fed her wine, enough to relax her but not dull her senses, he said. His fingertips stroked her inner thigh, tweaked her nipples. At one point Mick dipped his fingertips into the wine glass and pushed the gown to the side so that he could watch the droplets fall on her erect nipple. Then he licked them off.

"You are so beautiful tonight." Mick nuzzled her cheek and the side of her neck, sending electric shivers through her body. "I hate to tell you this, but your nipples are hard as little pebbles."

She laughed. "I can't say I'm shocked."

"You have very responsive nipples. Anyone ever tell you that?"

"Just you."

"Stand up for me, Piper." His voice got deeper. Raspier. She stood.

Mick stood as well, looking down into her face with those mysterious, half-hidden blue eyes.

"Mick?"

"Yes?"

"Are you ever going to take off the mask?"

He laughed. His laugh sounded slightly devious. Then he slid his warm hands all over her shoulders, cupped her elbows, and pulled her toward him. "You don't like the mask?"

Piper giggled, even as his hands tightened on her arms. "I do."

"Good, because it's going to stay on for a while. Do you know why?"

She shook her head, the heat and need gathering deep in her belly. She realized she liked him taking charge like this, teasing her, playing with her—arranging a surprise like this for her. "Why?" she asked.

"Because I'm going to wear this mask while I fuck you senseless. Haven't you wondered how it would feel to be ravished by a masked man?"

"You mean like the Lone Ranger?"

"You little wench."

He grabbed her up in his arms and supported her under her back and legs. He carried her into the boudoir, where he gently laid her on the spectacularly spired canopy bed, then hovered over her, her dark stranger, the man with the perfect mouth, the generous sense of humor, her dream lover made flesh.

Mick kissed her then. He claimed her with his lips and tongue and before she knew it she was arching toward him, raising her hips into the hard front of his English breeches.

"Get this off," he commanded, pulling on her barely there gown until her arms were free. He tossed the frothy fabric onto the floor. "I want you completely nude underneath me," he said, his hot touch exploring her breasts, her ribs, her belly. He cupped her buttocks in his hands and pressed her even harder to the front of his body.

"Do you feel this? This is for you, Piper. My cock and my lust, this night—it's all for you." His mouth covered hers again, hot and sweet and so very wet. "But I do have a request."

"Anything," she said, vaguely aware of how he toyed with her, surprised by the desperation she heard in her own voice.

He laughed again, the same devilish sound. "I'd like to mix and match the sins tonight. I plan to make love to you in front of that mirror, there, and have you watch me take my pleasure from you. I plan to break out a few toys tonight and make you beg for what you need most. And I want to tie you down. That will be about trust. Do you trust me?"

Piper felt light-headed, dizzy, lost in the candlelight and the sensation of his taut masculine body pressed against hers. Did she trust him? Of course she did. She was here with him, nude and defenseless, wasn't she? He knew all her secrets.

"I trust you," she said, gazing up at him, big, male, and beautiful. She watched as he took both of her hands and placed them high and wide above her head. That's when she felt the silky restraints encircle her wrists.

"Oh," she breathed.

Next, Mick took the flat of his palm and gently pressed down on her tummy. Piper felt the silky, cool bedclothes against her bottom and back. Then his hands moved to her thighs. He spread them wide. He pressed the heel of his hand into each inner thigh, making her shudder with delight, heat moving through her and settling between her legs.

That's when he attached the restraints to her ankles.

"Oh wow," she breathed.

Mick chuckled as he moved down her body, his breath now hot against her opening. She could feel herself getting slick with need. He kissed the tender flesh just outside her swollen lips, began to nibble on her tight curls, bite gently at her mound, all while avoiding what she wanted most—the sensation of his lips and tongue and teeth on her clit and inside the lips of her sex.

She cried out in frustration.

"Do you want more?"

"God, yes."

Mercifully, Mick's fingers began to dance along her slit, seeking out her juice and spreading it all over her opening. "Like this, love?"

As she nodded, she felt his fingers gently pry her open. She felt completely exposed and at his mercy, her arms tied, her legs tied, her back flat against the bed.

"I'm going to eat you up, spread you open and then have my way with you, all tied down and helpless like you are, all mine to do with as I please."

Piper moaned, delirious with the knowledge that she must look like a wanton offering, spread open and pinned down. Never before had she felt this devoured—this owned. It felt as if they played on the edge of something dangerous and dark, precisely what made it so exciting, so intoxicating.

Mick attached his lips to her clitoris while he slid a finger up inside her, hooking it until it pressed against the most tender, alive part of her sex, and she almost immediately began to come.

"Oh no, you don't." He removed his finger and gave her a single long lick up to her clitoris, sending her back arching off the bed in exquisite torture.

"You don't get to come until I give you permission." He smiled up at her, and she could see the fire in the eyes behind the mask. "You are all mine tonight. Did I forget to tell you this?"

From her pinned-down, sexually frustrated position, Piper laughed. She realized that turnabout was fair play and on their first night together she'd done much the same to him, but without the restraints.

"Tell me you're mine," he said, all the humor gone from his voice.

"I'm yours, Mick," she said immediately.

"Good. Then there's one thing I must insist you do tonight."

Piper looked at him through heavy lids. "Anything."

His lips curled in a wicked smile. "Tonight, you may call me 'Sir.'"

He lost track of time. The candlelight spilled over their bodies, casting their skin in gold. Kisses melted into hours and hours melted into ecstasy. He'd ravished her too many times to count, turned her this way and that, tied her down, let her up, enflamed her with peacock feathers, and allowed her to use the bathroom only to attack her on her way out, lift her, and take her against the wall like a Viking on a rampage.

When he caught his breath, he whispered into her sweaty

ear, "Oh, and by the way, the answer is yes—Mick does like it standing up."

Many hours later, they'd finished off the wine and eaten every crumb of cheese.

At some point they lay exhausted, weak, damp, and Mick reached for the mask, pulled it up and off, and tossed it aside. They looked at each other in silence a moment, then began to laugh. But Mick watched as Piper's eyes filled with tears and her laughter came out as a sob.

"What is it?" He stroked her face.

"It's a miracle," she said, wiping the tears from her cheeks. "I never thought I'd get another chance with you, but here you are, and you've brought me so much unexpected joy and sometimes it's hard to believe it's real."

He shook his head, feeling his own eyes well up. God, but he was falling in love with her. "You're the miracle, sweet Piper—a beautiful, brilliant, lusty creature who's only begun to spread her wings." He pressed his lips to her forehead. "I'm the man lucky enough to watch you take flight."

Piper sat up in bed, sweat pooling between her breasts and her heart thundering in her ears. After she gulped in as much air as she could, she reached over and flipped on the bedside lamp.

She nearly screamed. She was in a strange bedroom, beautifully appointed with Georgian furniture and brass candlesticks. She was in a huge bed, looking up at a gracefully arched canopy of white lace.

"Oh!" She stared at the naked man lying next to her, his black satin mask tossed aside on the pillow. No, this was not part of her dream. The handsome dark-haired man was real. And he was blinking and frowning.

"What's wrong?" he mumbled.

"Invisible chains," Piper said, immediately shaking her head at the strangeness of her reply. Where had that come from?

"Come again?"

Piper flung the satin sheet from her nude body and went stumbling toward the adjoining bathroom, dream and reality crashing around in her head, mixing and swirling and rolling until she didn't know one from the other.

She and Mick were at a bed-and-breakfast south of Boston, where he'd created a night of fantasy and passion for her. Okay. As hard as it was to believe, that was the real part—a night filled with sweetness, intensity, and discovery. And Mick knew all about Ophelia's diaries. He was going to help her with the exhibit. All real.

She'd fallen asleep in his arms, sated, warm, loved, happier than she'd ever been in her life.

Then came the dream.

Piper flipped on the bathroom light to examine her wrists. In the dream, the tender skin had been rubbed until it bled. Her throat had been sore from screaming. Chains, ropes—no! Whatever had her tethered down had been invisible, which had enraged her even more.

In the dream she'd cried out, *"How can this be?"* She was naked, on display before a crowd, a strange and ugly man's dirty fingers touching her everywhere. His nasty laugh echoed in her head. She'd nearly swooned as the crowd of men—Lord B——'s dandy gentlemen friends?—taunted her.

Then her surroundings changed. She was part of a crowd, among the mob of men at the Charleston Slave Mart, the feral pack pressing closer, their shouts growing louder, the smell of fear in the fetid air.

But who was she in these dream settings? Was she the young Ophelia, put on the auction block at a country estate filled with sadistic Englishmen? Or was she the Ophelia of thirty years later, standing in the sweltering heat of the slave auction in Charleston, nauseous from the inhumane horror she witnessed, so furious that she ran to the auction master's offices above the stables, holding up her skirts as she splashed through the muck.

Or maybe it was simpler than that.

Piper turned on the bathroom faucet and doused her face with cool water. She hung over the sink, catching her breath, letting the water drip from her forehead and cheeks.

What if the dream had been about her—just Piper Chase-Pierpont—a woman who'd been held down by invisible chains of her own making?

She closed her eyes. She breathed. She felt the water roll from her face to her bare breasts. And she swore to herself: *never again will I pretend to be less than everything I am.*

Piper gasped at the touch of a man's warm, callused hand on her bare shoulder.

Mick stared back at her in the mirror, his mouth tight and his eyes worried. "Are you okay?"

Piper laughed, embarrassed. She reached for a hand towel and rubbed her face dry. "I've finally figured it out, Mick," she said, smiling.

Mick shook his head, waiting for her to provide a few more details—like what the hell she was talking about.

"Sorry. The exhibit. The primary visual for Ophelia's story." Piper turned around to face him. She slipped her arms around his neck as he grabbed her bottom and lifted her to the edge of the sink. As if it were the most natural thing in the world now, Piper opened her thighs and welcomed him closer, clasping her ankles around his firm butt.

"I had a dream. It was so real," she said. "And I know what to do with Ophelia's exhibit now. I realize I'm running out of time and I've got, like, no budget, but I don't think I have a choice about this—"

"Slow down. You've lost me."

"I have to go to Charleston, Mick. South Carolina. I have to see it with my own eyes."

Mick brushed a wet lock of hair from her face and smiled kindly at her. "I'm still lost, love."

She nodded. "It's the narrative thread of Ophelia Harrington's story, her fight against human bondage, in any guise. She refused to be sold off as chattel to a man she didn't love, right?"

A crooked smile appeared on his face. "And her refusal led to her life as a courtesan."

"Yes, and the sex slave auction—I think it changed her forever." Piper kissed him quickly. "But it wasn't until 1856 that Ophelia began her crusade to end slavery. Her first public speech came after she returned from the Charleston slave auction. The site is a museum now. I need to see it."

"Then we'll go."

Piper let go with a surprised laugh.

He leaned toward her, and that's when Piper felt his erection poke against the open center of her body. "Why don't you allow me to give you the trip as your birthday present, since I seem to have missed it by only days?"

Piper's first instinct was to say no, but she stopped herself. She liked the way it felt to have a man be so generous with her. It made her feel special.

"You'd really go with me?"

"Of course I would. We could make a weekend getaway of it." He smiled down at her, puzzled. "I plan to be with you every step of the way on this, Piper."

Mick's words seemed so heartfelt and tender that her chest filled with heat. *He's going to be there for me. He made a promise.*

For an instant, Piper stared at him in wonder. Her lips opened. She was on the edge of asking him what she wanted to know more than anything in the world: *Why? Why are you willing to stick around for all this craziness? Are you falling in love with me?*

But she didn't ask. She wasn't Ophelia. She was Piper. The new-and-improved version, sure, but Piper all the same.

She looked up at him and smiled. "Thank you, Mick. That makes me happy."

"Good. I like making you happy."

With a sly smile, Mick slid inside her body, his mouth

covering hers as she cried out from surprise and pleasure. Before Piper realized what was happening, Mick picked her up—still embedded inside her body—and carried her to their disheveled bed.

Twenty-three

The pilot had just announced their descent into Charleston, and Piper still had her face buried in her laptop. She'd been working nearly the entire trip, even during their layover in Washington. From what Mick could tell, she'd been leaving notes to herself, making lists, and tweaking (and retweaking) the design elevations.

He'd given her the space she'd needed—and took the time to catch up with his own work—but he noticed that as each day passed, she became more focused on the exhibit and less focused on him. It was part of the package, he knew. He was a big boy. He'd survive.

But on more than one occasion, Mick thought about good old Mr. Harrington, Ophelia's saintly husband. As Piper had explained, the fellow always supported his wife's efforts for abolition and women's rights, even when she became a target for derision, his business was threatened, his manhood brought into question, and his family received death threats. Piper had said that Ophelia once wrote in a letter to a friend that she'd gone to her husband and offered to stop if he wished. His answer was to kiss her and say that he might as well command her to stop breathing.

Mick had to hand it to the guy—he was way ahead of his time. And he'd set the bar quite high for every man who would ever find himself involved with a driven woman.

Mick leaned over and kissed Piper's cheek. Her eyes flashed at him at first, then she sighed and closed her computer. She let her head fall back against the airline seat.

"Tell me," he said.

"I'm going to lose my job, you know. Probably right there on the spot." Her words were flat. "And there won't be a lot of choices for me afterward. The museum world isn't exactly clamoring for over-budget, renegade feminist curators these days."

Mick slipped an arm around her shoulders. "But the world is always in need of women brave enough to fight the establishment."

She looked up at him sideways, a small smile touching her lips.

"Besides, I was hoping you might consider working with me on the reality show."

Piper sat up straighter and pulled away from his embrace. Her expression became quite serious. "Do you have news to tell me?"

Mick shook his head. "I wish," he said.

As he'd already explained to Piper, Mick's agent and producers now seemed to be at an impasse. The cable network claimed it was because of temporary production schedule conflicts and budget approval delays, but Mick was feeling more jacked around with every hour. "We still haven't gotten the green light. It's maddening."

"I don't think I could work for you, anyway," she said.

Mick laughed. "I didn't say work *for* me, Piper, I said *with* me."

She shrugged. "I'm a museum curator, Mick. It's the only job I've ever wanted. It's what I love. I'm not sure working for you on an archaeology reality show would be the best use of my education and skills."

"*With* me."

"Right." She sighed. "Anyway, thank you for the offer, but I can handle my own career."

Mick didn't say anything right away. He had to make

sure his next move was a good one. "There are a lot of similarities between your profession and this reality show," he said, taking one of her hands. "Think about it. What is the purpose of a museum exhibit?"

Piper chuckled at the rudimentary question. "That depends on the specialized curatorial mission of the museum, of course."

"Fine. So how about at the BMCS?"

Piper pursed her lips. "Installations at the Boston Museum of Culture and Society must educate, entertain, and ignite a curiosity for how the city's history is connected to its present and future."

"Aha," Mick said, smiling.

"Aha?"

"Same for *Digging for the Truth with Mick Malloy*. We want to educate, entertain, and inspire an interest in the past."

Piper shrugged again and looked out the window. "I'm sure you'll do a wonderful job of that without me tagging along."

Mick let it drop. But he heard loud and clear what Piper left unsaid: she didn't want him leaving Boston, but she wasn't about to go chasing after him.

Mick had experienced his share of oppressive heat before— the summer he spent at the Bronze Age dig site in northeastern Thailand quickly came to mind—but the six-block walk from their downtown hotel to the city's infamous indoor slave market had him dripping with sweat.

He and Piper walked down a slate sidewalk along the cobblestones of Chalmers Street, part of Charleston's celebrated historic district. Lovely row houses in brick, stone, and clapboard lined the narrow lane, flower boxes bursting with welcoming color and Southern gentility.

"The scenery is as charming as the history is ugly," Piper commented. It was just what Mick had been thinking.

They arrived at the brick façade of what was once part of

Ryan's Slave Mart, which had opened for business on July 1, 1856, shortly before Ophelia had made her journey there from Boston. Not coincidentally, the four-building compound opened on the day outdoor slave auctions were outlawed in Charleston. It seemed street auctions attracted abolitionists, and citizens were concerned the constant ruckus took away from their reputation as a "genteel city."

The instant Mick and Piper walked inside, the air-conditioning slammed into them. And so did the heavy sadness of the building itself.

It didn't take long for Mick to realize that touring a museum with a curator was a whole new experience. Piper missed nothing. She commented on every aspect of the design and display of information. She listened to every audio segment, including the powerful Depression-era recordings of former slaves' firsthand accounts of the auction block. She paused to consider and analyze everything she saw. She took notes and drew sketches.

On more than one occasion, Piper sat quietly in whatever chair or bench was nearby. She stared at the ceiling of what was called the "showroom," where slaves were told to strut and dance and hop on one foot, where their teeth and eyes were examined, and where an auctioneer skilled in salesmanship would get the highest price possible for their flesh.

Piper studied the door leading to the "barracoon," a jail that housed slaves ragged from their journeys, where their chains would be removed so their wounds could heal, where they were examined by a doctor, and clothed, fattened up, and exercised to tone their muscles, where young girls' hair was oiled and old men's beards were dyed.

Piper cocked her head and gazed at the auction block, as if it were speaking to her. It was then that Mick saw the moisture in her eyes, the hard set of her jaw. He approached her, not speaking, not touching her. He only wanted her to know he was there.

Piper returned several times to one particular display, a British journalist's account of a young woman being sold by one plantation owner to another, a man infamous for his brutal treatment of slaves. The girl had stood on the auction block, looked the owner right in the eye, and said, simply, "I will cut my own throat from ear to ear before I'd be owned by you."

Though the museum was small—just two floors and probably a fifth the size of the Boston Museum for Culture and Society—they spent three hours inside its walls, and another half hour conferring with the museum's executive director.

Back on the roiling hot street, Piper was silent at first. When they reached the manicured city oasis of Washington Park a few blocks away, Piper collapsed onto a wrought-iron bench in the shade of towering live oaks draped in Spanish moss.

He sat down next to her.

Eventually, Piper spoke. "Did you know Ophelia forced her way into that miserable place, though women were forbidden? She insisted her husband see for himself. She wanted him to end all business dealings even remotely connected to slave labor—rice, cotton, tobacco."

Mick's eyebrows went up. "I just bet he did, too."

"As soon as they returned to Boston," Piper said. "And it cost him half his fortune."

Piper looked up into the tangled canopy of leaves above their heads and when her lovely green eyes met his once again, they were alive with a sudden fierceness.

"What are you thinking?" he whispered.

Piper chuckled to herself. "The truth?" she asked shyly.

"Lay it on me. I can handle it."

She nodded. "This exhibit is going to kick some serious ass, Mick."

"It most certainly is."

Piper stood in the middle of the museum's south gallery, leaning over a makeshift plywood table as she reviewed elevations with the exhibit's lead carpenter. She had to yell to be heard over the buzzing saws and pounding nail guns.

"Are you hungry?"

Piper looked up, and laughed in surprise. In the glare of the stark lighting stood Mick, Brenna, Basil Tate, and bed-and-breakfast owner Nanette Benson. Piper hadn't expected them until much later in the day.

Mick held up two huge paper sacks, imprinted with the logo of Piper's favorite Indian take-out. She gestured with her hands for them to meet her in the museum café.

"Be right there. Let me wash up!"

Brenna veered off and followed Piper into the ladies' room.

"How did you guys get here so fast?" Piper asked, rinsing soap from her hands.

"Mrs. Benson had a whole team of movers, so everything was loaded in less than a half hour. And Baz had everything in shipping crates, ready to go. And it didn't hurt that Mick drives like Stevie Wonder on speed."

Piper was feeling too nervous to joke around. She dried her hands and tossed the paper towels in the trash. "But what about—"

"It's all under control," Brenna said. "Everything for the A exhibit is in the museum loading dock as we speak. Everything for the B exhibit is safely tucked away in the rented storage facility. Here's the key, by the way." Brenna dropped it into Piper's palm. "And I labeled and double-checked every item personally, Pipes. There were no mistakes. Please don't worry."

Piper sighed. "I just don't want LaPaglia picking up a two-hundred-year-old dildo instead of Mr. Harrington's pipe stand."

Brenna laughed. "He wouldn't know the difference. Everything going okay here?"

Piper nodded, then ran her fingers through her hair. She was trying to keep a lid on the panic she was feeling, and thought she had done a good job—until right that moment.

"Speaking of LaPaglia, do you think he suspects anything?"

"God, no," Piper said. "He's too worried about what font I'm using on the display boards and the color scheme to notice I'm a lying, scheming double agent."

"This is no time to doubt yourself," Brenna said, her voice kind.

"Ha! The funniest part is that we've got four weeks now until the gala, and even if I were only putting together one exhibit, I'd be a wreck, but no—I'm a crazy person putting two installations together at the same time, and one in secret!"

"Shh," Brenna reminded her. "It's not going to stay that way if you don't keep your voice down. Have you reached Claudia Harrington-Howell yet?"

"No," Piper said. "She's still in the ashram in India and doesn't want to be disturbed. Her assistant said she has complete faith in my abilities and I should carry on as planned."

Brenna laughed and held open the restroom door for Piper. "Hey, well, she can't say she wasn't consulted!" The two women walked down the main center hallway of the museum. "What do you plan to wear to the opening?"

Piper stopped in mid-stride and stared at Brenna. "Oh my God, I don't have a dress for the gala! With everything going on, I totally forgot. I guess I'll wear a nice suit."

Brenna clutched at Piper's forearm. "No," she said.

"Fine. I'll go online and—"

"Let me take care of this for you," Brenna jumped in. "You don't have time and I'd be honored. All I ask is you be available for a fitting so we'll have time to get it altered if need be."

"A fitting?" Piper snorted. "It's not my wedding, for crying out loud."

Brenna grinned. "No, but in a way it'll be your 'coming out.'"

"Out of work, you mean." Just then, Linc Northcutt came strutting down the hall behind Brenna. He nodded at Piper, then turned away, and she swore he shook his head as if he knew what she was up to.

What a little prick.

They continued on to the café. Mick already had the food containers arranged on a large table, and paper plates set out. Piper could smell the rich spices from across the room.

He kissed her sweetly and pulled out a chair for her. The two of them didn't bother to hide their relationship any-more—it had been written on their faces since that night at the bed-and-breakfast, anyway.

Everyone served themselves tandoori chicken and tikka masala and enjoyed lunch, and since it was nearly two o'clock, they had the place to themselves. Piper was fasci-nated by Baz and Brenna's discussion of sex toys in ancient Mesopotamia, though the conversation had Nanette Benson blushing. As she looked around the table, Piper knew the exhibit would not have been possible without their help and friendship. Baz Tate's connections had come through with a variety of artifacts—lingerie and underclothing, shoes, jew-elry, hair combs, and even examples of Regency England pornography. Nanette had been extremely generous in loan-ing antique furnishings and décor similar to what would have existed in Ophelia's opulent world.

When she stopped to think about it, Piper was astounded at what was possible when she asked for—and accepted— the help of others.

"Looks like the construction is coming along," Baz said, a smile in his brown eyes.

"We're right on schedule," Piper said, wiping her mouth with a napkin. "The hard fixtures for each chamber will be in place by tomorrow, and then we can focus on wall and floor coverings, lighting and signage, and the acrylic shields and cases."

"Did those wallpaper samples help?" Nanette asked.

"Oh yes! Perfect. I was able to get small-scale facsimiles made for what will become the parlor and the boudoir. It's going to be lovely."

"How about the voice-over artist? Did that go well?" Brenna asked.

Piper nodded. "Fabulous," she said, then lowered her voice to a whisper. "And she gave me a price break on the additional diary readings, since I'm paying for that myself."

"Jeesh, Piper," Brenna hissed. "How much of Granny Pierpont's money are you spending on this?"

She shrugged, a little uncomfortable with the answer—almost four thousand dollars. "Most of it's going to the artist I hired to construct the main visual installation. If he can make my idea come alive, it's going to blow everyone's minds."

Mick made a quick survey of the cafeteria to make sure no one was in earshot. "Have you had a chance to talk to Melvin?" he asked Piper.

She shook her head. That was going to be a bit tricky. The night before the gala, the museum always held a soft opening of the new exhibit for museum staff and the board of trustees. Only after that was over and everyone had gone home could Piper and her accomplices switch out the exhibit. It would be an all-night process, and would require Melvin turning his head to the tomfoolery.

"I'll talk to him soon," she said. When she noted Mick's worried expression, she added, "Melvin's a good guy. He won't give us any trouble."

Twenty-four

London

Lord B—— picked me up in his carriage mere moments after the setting of the sun. I did not invite him inside, but met him at the door clad in a full-length cloak of forest-green velvet. The evening was misty and chill, but that was not the reason for my concealment. When I sat across from him and the carriage jolted into motion, I gazed silently at him as I unclasped the frog at my shoulder. The cloak fell open to reveal that I wore nothing but stockings and high-heeled shoes beneath it.

It was rewarding to see his eyes widen and his jaw drop. Handsome and self-assured men look very appealing when flabbergasted. I ran my hands down my bare thighs to my knees, then pressed them slowly apart, spreading them wide.

His large hands came down over my own and moved them aside, replacing them to push my knees wide. I leaned back against the cushions and ran my fingertips up over my body, pausing a moment to tease my nipples even harder in the chill. His eyes darkened at that, his jaw clenching tight. I lingered a bit longer, just to watch him watch me, then stretched my hands high over my head. I looked as if I were bound, just as he'd fantasized.

"Well?" I breathed the word. "Will you not keep your side of the bargain?"

In an instant he was on his knees before me. His big body

parted me wider, until my feet were stretched almost to the opposite walls of the carriage. I found a parcel hook far above my head and clung to it as he leaned close into my cunte and kissed it. His warm fingers stroked me up and down lightly, then disappeared into his mouth.

"You are wicked honey and wanton salt," he murmured, his breath hot on my spread labia. "I want to feast on you for hours."

He began to lap at me, his tongue slipping up and down and in and out to circle my clitoris. I closed my eyes and gave myself over to lust, pure and simple. Just as he'd said, my cries were drowned by the clatter of the carriage wheels upon the cobbles. I made no attempt to be quiet, but moaned and cursed and cried obscenities until he finally thrust two fingers deep into me and sent me over the edge into a hot and shameless orgasm.

I shouted then, loud and long, aware that we drove through Covent Garden at that moment, that the crowds swarming the square would surely hear me. I relished the wickedness of it and cried out all the louder, reveling in my own wildness.

I caught a glimpse of Lord B——'s face in the light of a street lamp as we passed and saw a like enjoyment in his eyes. He wanted the world to hear and envy us both.

Robert would have been appalled at the very thought of such an act. Even Sir would frown.

At last I had found a playmate I could not offend. I knew that no matter how low I might care to explore, Lord B—— had already gone beyond me and would not judge. Moreover, I found I did not care if he did. I wanted the danger and the darkness and the wickedness I felt rising inside of me. It was beautiful and animal and it wanted out of its cage, damn Sir and even damn the Swan and her Seven Obligations.

No one owned me.

No one.

* * *

Lord B—— wished me to go away with him to a house party the next week. After some urging, I finally consented. I had not yet allowed him to penetrate me and I knew he was eager to do so at last. I did not truly understand my own reasons for this restriction, for I am normally most generous in bed. I told myself I was simply exploring the power of taunting and suspense to increase arousal. Lord B—— seemed to enjoy the game for the most part. After all, I made sure he reached satisfaction in other ways. He had a great fondness for fellatio, in fact. We had devoured each other like animals for the past ten days and I found myself a bit edgy and overheated from it all. A good rogering would set me right, I told myself.

Once I had given tentative agreement for the excursion, Lord B—— informed me with a smile that it was a particular kind of party. "It is a bacchanal," he said languidly as he teased my nipples. We lay entangled in my great copper bath and I had just given him a quick release with my soap-slicked hands. I still tingled with unfulfilled arousal and his relentless tweaking of my nipples was making it worse by the moment.

Then his words penetrated, though nothing else had. I raised my head from his damp chest and looked into his gleaming blue eyes. It could be difficult to ascertain his seriousness sometimes. Or his sincerity. He was a slippery fellow, bathing or clothed.

"An orgy?" I had never attended an orgy. That wasn't Robert's style of entertainment. I imagined piles of sweating, gleaming bodies, men and women touching and kissing and sucking and fucking in a great heaving mass of lust and wickedness. Men with men, women with women, watching and being watched.

I wanted to be bad. This would be bad, indeed.

"You like that, do you, you dirty thing?" Lord B——'s fingertips tightened harshly on my nipples. I took the pain, writhing against him, riding the pulse of fear I felt when his darkness rose thus in him. It excited and alarmed me at

once, flooding my body with sensation, stilling those un-
wanted thoughts in my mind, thoughts of friends lost and
pledges broken.

"Yes," I breathed. "I like it."

"What do you like?" His voice went deep and harsh.
"Tell me."

This was something I had learned from this man. Sir had
taught me to use all the words without shame. Lord B——
had taught me to use the words for arousal itself. Speaking
them and hearing them added a wicked layer to our pleasure that I had not known before. I took a breath to speak.
Before I could say anything, I felt him slide his soap-slicked
fingers down between my buttocks. When he pressed the
tips of two fingers to my anus, I shivered. Lord B——
wanted to take me there most of all. He told me that often as
I sucked him, that one day he would soap his cock and
spread my buttocks and let the tightness of my anus wring
the cream from his cock.

At first the idea had appalled me, but as he slowly circled
my sensitive anus with his slippery fingertips, I felt my
arousal increase. He pressed a single finger deeper.

"Tell me," he urged. He twisted that fingertip.

I gasped and began. "I want to watch," I confessed. "I
want to be watched."

He laughed, a deep rumble against my cheek. "You enjoy making a spectacle of yourself, I know that much. Shall
I fuck you in the center of the ballroom, take you on the
floor like a bitch in heat, while all eyes watch you whimper
and cry as you come?"

The image made me shiver. "Would that really happen?
Is it truly that sort of party?"

He probed me more deeply, using his fingertip like a
small cock, thrusting in and out. "You tell me, wicked Ophelia. Tell me how it will be."

I closed my eyes and clung to him, hiding my hot face
against his chest. I could not shock this man. I could not
repel him. I opened up the darkest chamber of my rather

extensive imagination and said the words aloud. "You will bind me," I whispered. "You will tie my hands and then lead me to the center of the crowd."

With his other hand he continued to twist at my nipples. The sensations from both directions drove me more deeply into the picture in my mind. "You will rip my clothes from my body and display me for everyone's eyes."

I felt his cock rising again, pressing hard to my belly, though I had recently wrung him dry. He liked the image I painted, and that knowledge made me braver still. "While they watch, you will press me down to my knees and remove your rigid cock from your trousers."

He tilted his pelvis, pressing his erection against me, sliding it against my soapy skin. "You will open your mouth, before all their eyes, and take my cock deep into your throat." His hand left my nipples and moved lower.

I wrapped my arms about his neck and pulled myself higher against him, until his questing fingers could find my cunte. All the while, his slippery penetration of my anus had never halted. Now his finger was thrusting up to the second knuckle, fucking in and out slowly and relentlessly. When his other hand began the same process to my cunte, I gasped and shuddered, pressing my body hard against his.

"You will be my little harem slave," he went on, sounding a bit breathless himself. "You will service me while they all watch. I will bury my hands in your hair and drive my cock deep, then pull it wet and slippery from your lips, only to do it all again. Your hands will be bound behind you and your beautiful breasts will bounce from the force of my thrusts."

I could see it, just as he described it. "You will be huge in my mouth. So big I will not be able to take it all."

His fingers quickened. Two long fingers now fucked my cunte and I felt another slippery finger ease its way into my anus. He had never penetrated me so, but he had told me that he wanted to train my anus to take his cock someday. I knew what he was doing.

I made no protest.

Instead, I lost myself in the story. "I need to be fucked," I moaned. "In front of the crowd. Pull your wet, slippery cock from my mouth and push me to the floor."

"On your back or on your face?" he gasped, sliding his cock faster and faster against my soapy belly.

I shuddered. "Facedown," I whispered. "Facedown with my bare breasts on the cold marble and my buttocks high in the air, my hands bound behind my back."

"Yes," he breathed. "Your hair is loose and wild and it hides your face. All gazes are riveted to your beautiful bottom, bare and inviting. I want to spank that bottom, to leave the shape of my hand pink and angry on your ivory skin."

"Yes!" I panted. "Oh yes!" I was impaled now, two fingers deep before, two fingers deep behind. I had never felt such a thing before. He began to thrust them in unison now, harder and faster until the force of it slid me up and down his big body, the pressure of my slippery body satisfying his rigid cock at the same time.

"I will fuck you there, my hot little bitch, in front of everyone! I will take you hard and fast until you come, quivering and begging and weeping in your release. The world will see you come for me!"

I came for him, then and there, my cunte contracting tightly against his invading fingers, my mouth gasping my release into his neck even as his cock spurted hot and throbbing against my belly. I clung to him, shivering at the power of those dark and disturbing words to bring me to such pleasure.

That and his hands—his relentless hands, with daring fingers and shameless invasion tactics—sweet heaven, how I responded to those clever, wicked hands!

After those hands, perhaps I feared that I might not survive an intimate encounter with his cock.

When our breathing had eased, I remained where I was, my face hidden against his neck. Though the water was chilling rapidly, I had no wish to open my eyes. I held very still as he slid his fingers from my cunte and then, more slowly, from my anus.

"I believe," he said meditatively, "that we shall be needing another bath."

Oh God. Hot embarrassment flooded my face. My confession and my response had shocked me, never mind him!

"Ophelia, my little harem girl, why do you cling like a limpet from the sea?"

I clenched my eyes tight but allowed my death grip to ease from about his neck. My body slid back down into the bathwater and I shivered.

"Tell me that you are not discomfited by our little fiction?" He laughed outright. "You are! Why, I had no idea you were so sweet!" He made it sound like a ludicrous fault.

I pinched the skin just above his navel. "I am not sweet," I muttered.

"You are! Sweet little Ophelia, still a virgin—at least in places."

I turned my face away and he relented, pulling me into the warmth of his arms. "Don't be ashamed of a few dirty words, my pet. They are just words, meant to add to our pleasure. When we are done, the words wash away in the bath, just like the other results."

He was right. They were only words. "I must confess, I needed that," I told him. "Your tongue is most talented, but it did me good to be fucked, even a little."

He tipped my face up and caught my gaze with his blue eyes. "I will fuck you at the orgy," he promised, or perhaps threatened. It was difficult to tell with him. "I will take you so hard you will wince when you sit."

I met his gaze boldly. "I shall return the favor, my lord. Right down to the wincing part."

This bargain struck, I began to look forward to the orgy with great anticipation.

* * *

Our destination was a country house outside of the
C—— estate in Surrey. The carriage ride might have
tedious but for Lord B——'s imaginative use of time. I a
rived breathless and exhausted and my knickers had disappeared entirely, though I searched the interior of the
carriage well. Anticipation alone would have kept me in a
state of semiarousal. Lord B——'s clever hands turned anticipation into torturous denial.

I loved every moment of it.

I scarcely cared about the details of our host's home, but
the grandeur eventually penetrated the fog of my sexual
heat. Grand foyer, grand staircase, grand guest chamber.
Our host for this event, Lord C——, had once offered a
fortune for a mere week of my time, but the man's flat, icy
gaze left me feeling as though I ought to check on my loved
ones. The thought of his hard hands on my body made me
shiver and not in a pleasing way.

But I was not here to sleep in Lord C——'s bed. I had my
lover and he had me. We had come to watch and be watched.
If Lord C——'s reptilian gaze was one of those in the crowd,
I scarcely cared. Let him see what he was missing.

Lord B—— and I took a moment to retreat to our chamber and refresh ourselves. I decided against seeking out another set of pantaloons from my baggage, for my lack of
them tended to make Lord B——'s eyes darken in hunger
whenever I reminded him. He pulled me close before we
left our room.

"Sit on my hand at dinner," he demanded. "I will service
you until the last napkin hits the table."

I licked the outer edge of his ear. "I will rub you beneath
the tablecloth until your rigid cock tilts the table. Everyone
will wonder why the apples keep rolling away."

We ran hand in hand down the hallway, eager to begin
our wicked, wild adventure.

Twenty-five

After an amusing feast of food presented in the shapes of various body parts, downed with copious amounts of rather good wine and accompanied by a very ribald minstrel fellow who composed filthy ditties about the various guests on the spot, our group retired to the main event.

The ballroom of the great house was festooned in black drapery. Fainting couches and cushioned settees occupied the not-very-private nooks created by these hangings. At intervals throughout the room, strange exotic objects sat on lacquered pedestals. Some I recognized. There were several olisbos, a few of them of outrageous proportions. I saw marble carvings shaped like elongated eggs, which Lord B—— promised to demonstrate for me as he passed a possessive hand over my bottom. There were black silken ropes, gags with balls, riding crops, and even some silver spurs.

I had dressed for the evening in a deceptively demure gown of pale blue silk. The bodice exposed a great deal of pale flesh and, if tugged just so, would reveal two rosy semicircles of aureola. In addition, if I stood in the right light, the skirts of my new dress became quite translucent, revealing that I wore nothing underneath.

A burly footman announced the next entertainment. A dancer from a faraway land, he told us, a recent acquisition of our host's. The minstrel put down his lute and began to beat a rhythm from a small hide-covered drum.

As we watched, Lord B—— stood behind me with his arms about my waist. I leaned back against him. The girl before us was quite beautiful, in a dark, earthy way. Like me, she was small. Unlike me, she was slender and delicate. Her face was sharply featured, almost boyish. Her body was somewhat boyish as well, very lean and even a bit muscled. I thought of a ballerina, honed and strong.

When she began to move to the drumbeat, I understood her lithe figure. She leaped high, like a cat, then whirled like a dervish until her skirts flared about her flashing ankles and calves. Her exposed midriff undulated in a way I had never seen. Her raised arms beckoned even as she whirled away from us. She seduced us with the erotic motions of her body and then defied us with her angry dark eyes.

Try to tame me, she dared the crowd. *I cannot be caged.*

My heart quickened at her teeth-bared defiance. She was a free and wild creature, brought here against her will, imprisoned like an animal, displayed like a possession. Her black eyes promised retribution, yet she danced on command.

Survival, I thought. She is merely biding her time. The man who thinks her conquered might just wake up dead one morning.

Good for her.

She must have caught something of my empathy in my gaze, for she circled the room in a wide circle, growing ever closer to me, her eyes never leaving mine. Even as she whirled, her head snapped back around to fix me with her feral gaze. My breath quickened as she neared me, for she was lovely in her ferocity. I had admired the Swan's beauty and noticed the lush bodies of the other courtesans at the bacchanal, but I had never been stirred by another woman.

Until now. I wanted her to draw closer. I wanted to reach my hand out to stroke her gleaming golden skin. I wanted to feel the rippling strength of her dancing thighs beneath my palms. I wanted to press my pink lips to her cocoa-tinted ones, to taste her wildness, to sample her defiance.

What was this strange excitement? How could I desire a woman when all I had ever thought about were men?

Then a wave of dizziness struck me. My heart began to pound. I think I must have sagged a bit in Lord B——'s grasp, for his hands tightened about me.

"It's all right," he murmured in my ear. "It is only the Spanish fly."

I gasped. I could not have lived among the demimonde for five years without knowing of Spanish fly. Used as an aphrodisiac, the powder was ground from dried blister beetles. However, I had never experimented with it for it was known to be a dangerous poison if misused.

Lord B—— must have felt my fright, for he laughed reassuringly in my ear. "Do not fret, my wanton. Lord C—— knows his methods well. There would not be enough in the food to harm, only to titillate. You'll like what it does to you. Or at least, if you don't, I will."

He laughed again, sounding hollow and strange in my drugged hearing. I did not understand the jest.

Yet, I could not deny the heat rising within me. The room spun a bit and the candle flames seemed to swell in my vision. I blinked several times to clear my sight, only to realize that the dancer had stopped before me. She stood proudly, shoulders back, one gleaming thigh cocked to show through her slitted skirts. Her chest rose and fell, displaying a sheen of sweat across her shoulders and bosom.

So outrageous. So exotic. My mouth went dry. I licked my lips.

"She likes you," Lord B—— murmured. "Do you like her as well?"

I did not know. I felt a dreamy curiosity mingled with the itch to taste her skin. Which feelings were caused by the drug and which by the girl?

Apparently weary of waiting, the dancer reached out a sure hand to release the tie of my neckline. With a flick of her wrist I was bared nearly to the nipples. The thin silk hung there from my rigid tips as I gazed at the girl in shock. She flashed her white teeth at me, less of a smile than a dare.

I never could refuse a dare. I reached out quickly to snatch at the closest wafting scarf attached to the belt around her waist. It came away in my hand, revealing a swell of golden hip and more of that tantalizing thigh. Lord B—— laughed low.

The dancer bent to take the scarf from my tingling fingers. Then she straightened and stepped closer still. Then another step, until I could feel the heat of her skin against mine. I waited breathless, unsure of what I wanted to happen next.

The dancer came one more step and then brought her lips to mine. My own lips parted in surprise. At the last moment, she did not kiss me but leaned to one side, the side away from Lord B——. I could not honestly say if I was disappointed or relieved.

She whispered in my ear.

"Run away," she told me in a husky, accented voice, with her breath sweet and hot against my cheek. Then she whirled away once more, moving to the drumbeat, the reclaimed scarf trailing high from her raised hands.

My heart thudded as I watched her entertain us all with her flashing limbs and hot defiance. Did anyone else even see her fury? Their eyes were glazed with their own importance. No, they only saw a half-naked woman gyrating before them. Only I had understood her.

Run away. From what? From her? From this house? From Lord B——?

It turned out that she meant all of the above.

After the dancing ended, the guests began to pair off, or in some cases separate into groups of three and even four. We watched. Lord B—— moved us from place to place, enjoying the show with an easy smile. I felt very strange.

I was drunk on the sights around me and fevered from the drug-induced heat in my blood. When Lord B—— stroked his hands over my shoulders and then down to cup my nearly bared breasts, I shuddered. It seemed as if every inch of my skin were on fire. His touch was unbearable. I needed it. Only my release would ease the intolerable tension within me, I thought.

"I'm going to do just as you told me," he murmured.

I was scarcely listening. Lord C—— held the tawny dancer astride him on the fainting couch. She rode him hard as he twisted her small brown nipples. Did he even realize that the foreign words she shouted in her orgasm were obscenities? I could hear them echo black with hatred in my mind.

Lord B—— slid his hands down my arms to take my hands into his. I let him, dazed at the sight of a man suckling at the large breasts of a courtesan while another naked woman caned his bared bottom. His pasty buttocks were striped with angry red marks and bristling black hair. I was nauseated. Fascinated.

When my hands were tugged behind my back, I hesitated a split second too long to pull away. In mere seconds, Lord B—— had twisted a thick cord about my wrists and pulled it tight, binding me securely.

"Wh—what?" I tried to jerk away from him, but he pulled me back against him.

"Is this not just as you described to me?" His hot hands covered my breasts again and squeezed. I gasped and twisted in his embrace, but he only rolled my nipples between his thumbs and fingers.

"I was to bind you and strip you," he growled in my ear. "Then I was to lead you to the center of the room and fuck you before all their eyes. My bitch in heat."

Hot, yes. My body did not feel like it belonged to me at all. I was nearly swooning from the fever in my blood and the burning of his torturous fingers on my sensitized nipples. My heart pounded. My cunte throbbed and moistened.

I found myself grinding my buttocks back against him, seeking the rocklike rod of his erection. I found it.

Yet my heart wasn't partaking of the lust. My mind was fogged and slow, but my spirit wanted to pull away. Part of me longed to flee these bonds and this room and this steaming midden heap drenched in power, submission, and the drugged, heartless drive to satiation.

Who were these panting monsters, these dull-eyed bulls, these shrieking, jiggling cows? What was this soulless place?

My mind fought to make sense of it all. *I am in the country house of Lord C——. I am here because I wanted to come. I am here because Lord B—— wished me to come. He wants to take me like these women are being taken . . . like an animal . . . like a grunting farm beast . . .*

I felt hot. I felt ill. I felt lust that had nothing to do with what *I* wanted. It was infused in my blood, a poison in my veins. My mouth was so dry I could not speak a protest. My feet seemed very far away from my mind's control. I stumbled as Lord B—— led me to the center of the room. The chandeliers dazzled my vision as if they were made of suns, not mere candles. There was a buzzing in my ears.

I am sick. Help me. Take care of me.

Take me away from here.

I don't know if I managed to whisper the words or not. I know that Lord B—— did not listen if he heard me. I was led to the dais where the dancer had begun her first leap. I was lifted. The room changed and spun yet more from my changed perspective.

Then I felt the first sharp tug. My bodice tore, exposing my right breast. I staggered but I was held upright as more tugs turned my gown to shreds that gaped open nearly to my waist and slit high upon my thighs. The humid air of the room was like the slime of a slug against my exposed skin. Naked, or nearly so. Bound.

Helpless.

"I do not wish this." Yes, I had managed to speak aloud that time. I heard my own voice quite clearly. Heartened, I pulled at my bonds. I needed merely to ask to be released. Lord B—— cared for me. He would help me if he understood. "Untie me, darling. I've changed my mind."

He moved before me and simply stood there, his arms crossed over his chest and a sneer upon his handsome face. "So sorry, *darling,* but you made your own wicked little bed. Time to lie down in it."

He jumped up upon the dais beside me and turned to the ogling crowd. "Gather round, ye wicked throng, and place your pennies on the barrel!"

His words sounded almost like those used in the beast market. With horror clogging my throat, I realized that I was the item up for auction!

He went on. "I've a great bloody debt to pay off, so I want you depraved lot to bid high and long!" Like a carnival barker, he smiled, he charmed, he cajoled and entertained as the bids began to roll in.

It soon became clear that one bidder was more serious than the rest. Icy malevolent eyes gazed at me hungrily and I knew that Lord C—— had arranged the entire depraved ruse.

Horror flooded me. I wanted to vomit. My fevered mind fled back to another night when I'd been naked and bound and helpless. I'd been so filled with unbridled arousal that night, that hot, dark, beautiful night with Sir.

How could I have known that it was not the act that aroused me? How could I, in my inexperience, have realized that it was not the binding, but the man who bound me? It was not the helplessness I enjoyed, but the trust?

"Sold!" The fat man slapped his meaty hand down upon his improvised auctioneer's bench, his companion's jiggling buttocks. "To Lord C——, for the price of two thousand pounds!"

The last of the false heat drained from my blood as I stood there, chilled by Lord C——'s flat, cold gaze. His gray eyes were empty of emotion, but I saw him clench one fist in triumph. Or preparation.

Laughter and applause filled the room. I was not admired here. I was envied and resented.

"It is the most fervent admirers who enjoy my fall the most."

The Swan had understood this. In my blithe, willful ignorance, I had chosen to disbelieve it. As I looked around me at the gloating gazes and sneers, my final faint hope of rescue died in my soul, leaving a black, gaping hole. I would not escape this.

As I looked into the deadened gaze of the man who claimed to own me, I was not even sure I would survive it.

As Lord C—— triumphantly dragged me away toward his bedchamber, all the orgy participants gathered around in a sort of grotesque shivaree to see me off to my doom.

The dancer, dark and bold and savage, stepped out of the crowd that surrounded them. She stalked directly to me and raised her hand. I thought she moved to strike. Oddly, this notion hurt more than all the derisive enjoyment of the crowd. However, her hand slowed just before it reached my face. Her fingertips trailed down my temple and cheek, passing lightly down my throat and over my chest. Her palm, hot and callused, came to rest over my exposed breast.

"Pretty whore." Her accented voice was husky, her black eyes unreadable.

Lord C——'s gaze flicked back and forth between us as the onlookers grinned and jeered. "Kiri, do you want her?"

Kiri did not respond to him at all. Instead, she tilted her head and let her eyes follow her other hand up to push back the lock of my hair that had fallen over my face in my struggle. Her fingers lingered in my hair, combing slowly down. Then she stepped closer. I could feel the avid spectators hold their breath. I, on the other hand, cared nothing at all. This creature's inoffensive exploration was nothing compared to the threat of my looming violation by Lord C——.

Her kiss was dry and brief, although more than a peck. Her lips were full and soft. I remained still and simply waited for her to finish. I imagined an abrupt decrease in the mental facilities of every man in the room as their imaginations stiffened their cocks and deprived their brains.

When she pulled away, I saw Lord C—— narrow his eyes in consideration. He tugged at my bonds, urging me into the bedchamber. Kiri followed, though I saw no sign of invitation from her master. When the door closed behind the three of us, I felt no relief from the avid eyes of the guests. There was nothing in me but a numb horror and a powerful need to flee.

My captor pushed me hard and I fell onto the bed, unable to catch myself with my hands tied behind me. In seconds, Kiri was on me. She lay half atop me, pressed bosom to bosom. Her small quick hands played over me like fluttering bird wings as she buried her face in my neck and began to moan with desire.

My own interest in her had been quite squelched by the minor matter of being sold at auction to a sadist, so I daresay my response was somewhat less than she'd hoped for. All I could feel was Lord C——'s icy gaze running over me as he moved closer to the bed.

Then Kiri muttered a foreign word in my ear that had the unmistakable ring of "Idiot!" She also managed to give me a solid blow to my thigh with her knee. Her message became clear an instant later when I felt her roving hands at my bound wrists. She was counterfeiting every second of her lust in order to distract his lordship from his intended ravishing.

I am not the cleverest of women but I am not a fool, at least not usually. I immediately began to writhe and sigh against her. "Oh yes . . . ooh . . . um, ooh . . ."

I have ever been a heartfelt lover, so the moment became extremely odd—two women, ludicrously caressing and tangling limbs, with no intent beyond escape. In some corner of my mind, I laughed even as I silently screamed in panic.

My wrists parted, the ropes gone slack between them. I

remained lying half atop my hands, while Kiri turned from me to beckon to Lord C———. "Tear the dress off."

Apparently the notion of watching Kiri spread herself fully upon me naked was more than he could bear to pass up, for he obeyed her instantly. As he bent to grasp the remaining shreds of my gown in both hands, Kiri moved out of his way. My view of her was blocked by him, but I caught a glimpse of something swift and menacing bearing down upon his skull. He fell upon me with a wheezing grunt.

Kiri stood over us with an ebony bookend in her white-knuckled grip and a look of maniacal triumph in her wild eyes.

Mad, I thought. Then, when Lord C——— stirred upon me, not entirely lost to consciousness, I found myself go a bit uneven in the mind as well. Taking my bonds into my hands, I wrapped the silken ropes around his throat before I could even imagine myself doing so. He gagged and tried to grapple with me, but Kiri's weapon descended again.

He went still upon me. I remained where I was, the ropes pulled tight, fearing a trick. He did not move. I felt Kiri's hands on mine, pulling the ropes away from my numb fingers.

"Stop. Dead is bad."

Yes. Of course, dead was bad. I blinked and shook off my surprisingly homicidal surge. Dead was very bad indeed, especially when in reference to a member of the aristocracy found in a room with two battered prostitutes at an orgy.

I shoved at Lord C———'s limp body with my hands, scrambling out from under him with a damp and desperate giggle. Kiri and I stood on either side of the bed, gazing down in mingled horror and relief at our handiwork. I bent to check him gingerly. Though his head was bloody, he still breathed.

Pulling my torn dress up in an attempt to set something

to rights on this very wrong sort of day, I straightened and gazed at my cocaptive. "We need to get out of this house," I said firmly.

We started for the door as one. I was about to fling it open and race into the hallway but Kiri stopped me with a hand over mine. She pressed her ear to the oak panels and frowned. In alarm, I knelt before the keyhole and peered out.

Shadows in the hall. Voices.

"Which d'you think he'll do first?"

"He's already done the foreign bit o' slag a dozen times. He'll take the Blackbird."

"Not before he's made her pay, he won't!"

Laughter, drunken and dirty.

"Fetch me a drink. I don't want to miss a single scream."

I pulled away from the keyhole and frowned up at Kiri. She gazed back at me stolidly. I stood, brushing at my hands.

"Right," I whispered. "You've more than done your part. I'll handle this." Turning, I strode to the bed. With a brutal yank worthy of Lord B—— himself, I stripped Lord C——'s trousers down to his knees. I turned to choose my implement from the display wall. My fingers hovered over the cat-o'-nine-tails, but moved on to the milder riding crop. Kiri had no such compunction. Her golden hand hefted the great whip with ease.

With a fearsome crack, she brought the whip down on Lord C——'s virgin buttocks. His unconscious body bounced on the bed. I'm sure Kiri's only regret was that the man was not awake to feel it. No matter. The memory would linger, I was sure.

I let out a wild shriek of pain. We heard a thump and a muffled guffaw from outside the door.

Crack! "Oh please, my lord, oh, have mercy!"

Snap! "No, stop, I beg you!"

Crack! "Help me, someone, please!"

Snap! "Oh, my lord, I beg forgiveness!"

My arm grew tired. It had been a very long day after all. I sagged back and watched Kiri wreak just a bit more vengeance before I stopped her. She had been at Lord C——'s mercy longer and I knew her rage was black and bottomless. However, I heard the wits outside the door grow bored and move away. It was time to leave.

When I opened the door a wee crack and peered through, I saw no one in the hall. Kiri and I wrapped segments of torn sheeting about our near nakedness and crept out, looking like Bedouins on a raid, no doubt. By avoiding the ballroom, we managed to make our way outside seen by no one but a weary, incurious maid.

Once outside, I realized to my horror that we had no transport and would be forced to walk to succor in our strange and suspicious state. We would never get out of range of Lord C——'s scurrilous company by morning!

A rattle of carriage wheels on the gravel drive prompted a quick dive into the shrubbery. Kiri and I pressed together beneath the boxwood and watched a familiar vehicle roll to a stop virtually before our noses. Lord B—— had apparently achieved his goal of enriching himself at my expense and was now ready to make his way back to London. His driver jumped to the ground with a grunt and ambled off to alert his master that the carriage was ready.

I smirked at Kiri in the darkness. "Little dancer, our ride is here." We ran giggling through the darkness to steal the carriage.

Hours later, when I entered my house at last, I shut the door behind me and leaned against it in utter weariness. How long since I had slept? It felt like weeks. Sylla stumbled down the hallway in her nightdress, carrying a candle in one hand and rubbing her eyes with the other. I took the candle and sent the girl off to her bed. I wanted nothing more than to fall into my own covers and sleep for days.

Kiri had driven the carriage, for I had no ability there at

all. It took much less time to return to the city because Kiri drove like a drunken blind man. Once back in London, we'd made our way to the Swan's house first for it was closer. I left Kiri there, sleeping on the Swan's velvet settee, too weary to speak more than a brief word before dropping off. The Swan wanted the entire story, of course, and after my ridiculous distance lately I felt I owed her that.

Finally, when the words would scarcely stumble past my weary tongue, she woke her driver to take me home. She begged me to stay but all I wished in the world was my own bed.

So close now. Never had the stairs seemed so steep nor the hall so long. When at last my own pillow beckoned, I nearly wept with relief. The nightmare was over. I fell to bed and knew no more.

It must have been near morning when I woke to a heavy hand on my shoulder.

"Wake, you scheming slag."

So recent was my fear that I knew I was in danger before my eyes could fully open. I jerked away with all my strength and scrambled across the bed. My legs tangled in the covers and I fell over the side, landing on the carpet with a thud. I fought free of the clinging sheets but a vicious kick to my side knocked me down again. Bright agony exploded within me. With the breath wheezing in my lungs, I clawed at the carpet, crawling away as best I could. I cast one look over my shoulder at the twisted, furious visage of Lord B—— and cursed my own carelessness.

I should have stayed at the Swan's. I should have known he would pursue me.

Poor sleepy Sylla was too far away to hear anything in her attic chamber. The other staff lived out of house, for I cherished my privacy. There was no one to help me.

Lord B—— bent over me and took a hard grip on my

arm, pulling me upright. I cried out but my voice was cut off by the next backhanded blow to my face. I saw red and green flashes in my vision as my head snapped back under the force of it. He dragged me all the way to my feet and shook me, his big hands cruel on my upper arms. "Who do you think you are? I had to beg conveyance from Lord C——. He doubled my debt because of you!" Another strike to my face. His hands seemed to be made of stone. "No one makes me out to be the fool!"

I sagged in his grip, stunned and unresisting. I had no wit to fight him off. There was no thought in my head of flight or succor. I was a mindless thing, in too much pain to think at all. My face exploded with agony every time my heart beat. My ribs creaked with every breath, while vicious pain enveloped my chest. Through swollen eyes I saw his fist rise in the air once more. Something small and pointed glittered in the predawn light. The knife I used to sharpen my quill.

"Pretty whore no more," he said through gritted teeth. I despaired at the sadistic exhilaration in his gaze. "No one will want you when I have done with your face."

It was the height of a night full of horrors. I had been so willfully blind to his true nature, when all the while he was worse than the corrupt Lord C—— could ever be. Now I would carry the scars of my stupidity forever.

I had scarcely the breath left in me to care.

In my blurred vision, I saw a large shadow move behind my tormentor. Abruptly, Lord B—— flew away from me to impact the opposite wall with a wrenching thud. That wall, it crossed my mind dully, was brick. Lord B—— slid down to his knees, shaking his head. The shadow moved between us. It was big and wide and powerful.

I had no fear left. I sank down to the carpet, without the strength to even lift my pounding head. From my lowly vantage, I saw the looming shadow stretch his large, menacing hand toward Lord B——. Before I lost consciousness, I noted with great satisfaction that Lord B——'s eyes widened in fear. He scrambled to his feet and fled the room. I saw the shadow hesitate before pursuit. It turned toward me. Then darkness took me away.

Twenty-six

My dreams were filled with black desolation. When I slid from terror to wakefulness, the pain in my face and body led me to believe the nightmare continued. I made a sound, a senseless noise of despair. Something moved near me. I shrank back, lost in the confusing tangle of dream and reality.

Like a dream, I could see nothing. Yet I could smell sandalwood and brandy and the faintest scent of horse.

Sir.

With a wordless cry, I opened my arms. He came to me and wrapped me gently in his embrace. I clung to him, trembling, only then feeling completely safe for the first time in weeks. After a long moment, I eased my grasp, lying weakly back upon my pillow.

I whimpered. "Cannot see." My words were muffled. Confusion whirled inside my battered brain.

I felt the breath of his short laugh on my cheek. "You cannot see because your face is bandaged."

"My face?" My hands flew to my cheeks, only to encounter the layers of muslin strips. They covered my face from my top lip to my crown, with a few more beneath my chin holding my jaw shut. I could only manage a squeak of dismay that did nothing to convey the sickening horror that choked me. "Cut!"

Large warm hands tenderly encased mine and pulled

them away from the bandages. "He did not cut you. However, your nose is broken, your jaw is sprained, and you've discovered new varieties of black and blue. You've some broken ribs as well. The physician said you'll mend in time. Your nose may never be the same, but it was always a bit too snub. I foresee a patrician arch. Most authoritative."

My ribs creaked painfully at my short laugh. "Don't. Hurts." I relaxed back against the pillows once more, too tired to worry about anything short of true deformity. Needing reassurance, I ran my hands up his arms to his shoulders, then up to caress his face.

He wore no mask. "Not fair!" My protest was a weak one, however. I felt sleep tow me under once more and I went gratefully. In the darkness, I did not have to relive my abysmal mistakes.

For several days, I "saw" no one but Sir. I heard Sylla's voice a time or two and once I heard the Swan outside my bedchamber door, but Sir would allow no one to care for me but him. No bite of food passed my lips that he did not spoon up for me. No sip of broth went down my throat that he did not hold the bowl to my lips. He bathed my battered body with warm water and a touch so tender that it nearly made me weep. Never in my life had I been so looked after.

When I thanked him for his treatment of me, his voice turned harsh. "Show me no gratitude. I could have prevented all this, had I not been too proud to speak openly."

I shook my head, wishing I could see his face, read his dark eyes, measure his unease by the way he clenched his jaw. "I am responsible for my own folly, Sir."

I felt him take my hands in his. Heated skin pressed to my knuckles. He rested his brow on our tangled fingers. "If I had lost you . . ."

Warmth bloomed inside me. Unaccustomed shyness stole my voice. I tightened my fingers on his and listened to his breath hitch in his throat. My sweet defender. My conscience and my reason. If he had lost me, I would be lost, indeed.

In my private darkness, I allowed the tears to leak from my eyes. How close I had come to throwing everything away in a childish fit of pique and rebellion. How foolish, to willfully lose before I even realized that I might win.

That night, I pulled him into my bed so that I might sleep in his arms. Sir protested but I would not be swayed. There was no pain too great to keep me from his embrace. Carefully propped and cushioned, we slept the night through together as we never had before. Waking safe and warm and surrounded by him was the greatest pleasure he had ever given me.

In the early morning quiet, we clung to each other.

"I have to leave soon," he told me.

I tangled my fingers in his. "Why?" The word came out small and breathy.

I felt him inhale deeply. "I am not what you need, sweet one. I want too much from you."

My belly went cold. "I am interfering in your work? You are not able to perform with other women?"

He gave a small, rumbling, regretful laugh. "I cannot even imagine performing with other women."

"You could stay with me," I offered tentatively. "I have a little money saved. I would not have to find a new protector for some time."

He was quiet for a long time. "Do you want a new protector?"

I did not answer for a long moment. The same question had been plaguing me for weeks. I had seen my rebellion through and I was done with it. Yet to give up my life entirely? To put the Blackbird to rest forever? I loved the Blackbird. She was so brave, so liberated.

"I must be free," I said slowly.

He sighed. "I do not want you to be free. I want you to be mine."

Sadness coiled within me as I raised my hand to stroke

his beautiful, unmasked face that I had never seen. "Yet I cannot be yours, for I must be mine."

He held me tightly for a long time in silence. We spoke no more of it that day. A tender, silent good-bye stretched through those daylight hours, making each smile and casual touch ache with poignancy.

The next morning when I awoke, the bandages that had covered my face for seven days had been removed.

And I was alone.

A few mornings later, the Swan, who had taken over my nursing, wandered into my bedchamber as I breakfasted at the small table by the window. I sat in my wrapper with my hair braided down my back, gazing dreamily at the garden outside. I was up and about at last and although my face was still swollen and my nose still tender, I could see the distortion diminish every day.

I looked up to see the Swan gazing at the news sheet in her hand with a bemused frown. "Who is scandalizing the nation today?" I asked with a smile. "You and I are keeping quiet. We've left quite a hole in London's spectacle, I fear."

The Swan lifted her gaze to meet mine. "Lord B——."

I took the news sheet gingerly, as though it might bite. Indeed, upon the first page ran a tale of a notorious rake set upon by a mysterious masked attacker. He was quite soundly and publicly thrashed. Although there were many amused onlookers, when the watch was called they found no witnesses.

I put the paper down next to my plate. For a long moment, I gazed at my hands and said nothing. The Swan moved close and laid a gentle hand on my shoulder. "Ophelia, are you all right?"

I turned to her with a smile so wide it made my healing face ache. "I hope he made him weep for mercy!"

She bit her lip but a smile leaked out anyway. "It was wrong of Sir to attack him like that."

"Oh yes. Entirely reprehensible."

"Do you think he is very badly injured?"

"I think he is precisely and accurately injured," I said with great satisfaction. "It says here that he has a broken nose, a sprained jaw, and several cracked ribs."

The Swan stroked a hand over my hair. "Well, then, that's acceptable."

I looked up at my dear friend. "I know I disappointed you."

She tweaked my ear with her fingertips. "Shut it, you idiot. We all falter a step now and then. You just happened to do it in the vicinity of a violent lunatic."

I sighed. "I do have astonishing aim, do I not?"

My further recovery began to gain speed and I was at last able to receive callers. One of my first was a gentleman who had left his card a number of times over the past few weeks. Mr. Eamon Wainwright turned out to be a distinguished fellow of perhaps fifty years. He cut quite a handsome figure in his fine clothes. His face was lean and hawkish, defined by the silver hair at his temples. I liked him immediately.

I seated myself slowly, for my body still tended to twinge now and then. He followed suit, watching me closely.

I smiled. "What might I do for you, Mr. Wainwright?"

He gazed at me thoughtfully. "I had rather hoped I could do something for you, Miss . . . Blackbird."

I blinked at him, puzzled.

He went on. "Though she is but sixteen, my daughter Alice had her heart set on wedding a certain fellow. I despised the man, but Alice wouldn't hear a word I said. I feared he would convince her to elope. In an attempt to outwit the gold digger's suit, I told him that I would consent to give my daughter's hand only if his debts were paid in their entirety."

I drew back. "Ah. Lord B———."

Mr. Wainwright gazed down at his large, capable-looking

hands. "It was I who set events in motion that ended in your . . . unfortunate encounter."

I frowned. "That 'unfortunate encounter' nearly cost me my life."

He swallowed. I saw the shame and regret in his eyes. "I had no idea what lengths to which he would go," he said slowly. "I confess, I did not even wonder."

Pity stung me. "Mr. Wainwright, you are no more responsible for another's evil actions than are the men who hold his debts. He might have gotten the money any number of ways, starting with not gambling it away in the first place. *He* lifted his hand to me, not you."

"That he lifted his hand at all is a crime," Mr. Wainwright said grimly. "I do not know why you do not press charges, and I'm sure you have your reasons, but he has already paid in the loss of my daughter's hand. Though she still refuses to believe in his brutality, she will not wed him while I live." Then Mr. Wainwright straightened in his seat and smiled at me. "In any event, I have come to offer you any assistance I might render. I am not without influence and resources. Perhaps I might aid you in some way?"

I tilted my head and smiled at him. "You are a good man, Mr. Wainwright, to place your daughter's well-being above all else. Many men would sell their daughters for such favorable connections. I know my relations tried to."

"I spoil her, I think." He shrugged. "My dear wife passed on three years ago. It is a sad thing for a girl to lose her mother just when she is becoming a woman."

I looked down at my clasped hands. "Indeed it is." Then I lifted my chin and flashed him a smile I hoped shone through my mottled, uneven features. "Yet I somehow know that your wife was a very lucky woman."

He actually blushed. Adorable. "It was a mutual feeling, I think."

I realized that this man, this rich, handsome, good, kind man who loved his daughter, was absolutely throbbing with loneliness.

Sir was gone. I knew he would not return. We had broken our own rules. Our friendship had changed into something that would ruin us both if we let it.

In the meantime, I had realized that although I was not ready to say good-bye to the Blackbird, neither did I wish to return to my former heights of popularity and notoriety. I was replete with scandal and danger.

Now Mr. Eamon Wainwright sat before me, suddenly as awkward as a boy unable to ask a girl to dance.

A man like this would not set me aflame. He would not caper madly with me in public simply to shock the crowd. He would not twist lovemaking into something addictive and damaging.

He would not hurt me. Ever.

I leaned forward and let my smile warm. "Dear Mr. Wainwright, I think perhaps you should stay for dinner."

He stayed for breakfast.

VOLUME III

Twenty-seven

Boston

Piper's eyes opened slowly. The palest morning light danced in the sheer canopy gathered over her bed. She felt Miss Meade snuggled up to her left hip and Mick at her right. In fact, growing more awake by the moment, she realized that Mick also was pressed against her right arm, breast, side, thigh, and ankle. His arm was thrown protectively over her torso. His deep, steady breathing was hot against the side of her neck.

She smiled. This must be the kind of supreme comfort and safety Ophelia experienced that first time she'd awoken tangled up in Sir. Though Piper had been waking up with Mick for many weeks now, each morning felt like a sweet surprise. A lucky twist of fate. It felt like eating dessert before breakfast.

They needed to get up and get going soon, but Piper lingered there, letting her mind wander and her body luxuriate in Mick's solid warmth.

The Fall Gala was three weeks away. She'd committed herself on a path that was proving more challenging every day. But she wasn't alone, and that had made all the difference.

And she was in love. It was that simple and that sudden. Of course she hadn't told Mick. She felt a little embarrassed about how her love for him had swooped in the way it had, but Mick hadn't seemed to mind. In fact, there were a few times she'd been almost certain that Mick was in love with her, too. But what did Piper know? She might have earned her advanced degree in the erotic arts, thanks to Ophelia, but she was still a novice when it came to love. She'd never experienced it before, and up until recently, she doubted it would ever bless her life.

"Morning, love."

Piper shivered in pleasure, feeling Mick's greeting as much as she heard it. His deep whisper had vibrated into her neck. His big erection was now prodding into her hip.

Miss M. somehow sensed it was her time to vacate the premises and skittered off the bed and into the living room.

Piper felt Mick's hot and firm hand rub her belly. "Mmm. I love waking up with you." He threw his thigh over Piper's sheet-covered legs. "Do we really have to go to work today?"

"I'm afraid so," Piper said, burying her fingers in Mick's thick curls and pressing his head in the direction of her breast. Being a man renowned for his ability to unearth lost secrets from the past, Mick had no trouble locating her nipple beneath the sheet. He trapped it tenderly between his teeth just as his hand slid across her belly, yanked down the sheet, and insinuated itself between her legs. His fingers slid up through the wet seam of her pussy.

"Looks like another hot and humid day," he said, tossing the sheet up and away from both of them. He pulled himself on top of her, one hand still buried in her slit, the other hand used to balance the weight of his body.

Piper sighed, overwhelmed by the beauty of her lover, his upper body muscles working in the morning light. When Mick's finger grazed her clitoris, she jerked with intense pleasure.

"We really shouldn't be doing this," Mick said, using his knees to splay her legs further.

"I have a lot to do today," Piper said, raising her pelvis into the air, hungry and empty and fairly crazed with the heat of his skin on hers, the sight of her lover's deepest blue eyes.

"I'm feckin' swamped, m'self," Mick said as he pushed the rounded end of his cock inside her and slowly pressed his case.

"Do you want the shower first?" Piper asked, her head arching back from the sheer glory of it.

"Ladies first." Mick moaned.

"I'm going to come."

"Like I said, ladies first."

Piper laughed even as she felt the tide of an orgasm gathering at her core. She reached up and grabbed Mick by the neck and kissed him with everything she had in her. And she came—hard—bucking beneath him, a tide of fire sweeping through her, her toes and fingers momentarily made numb with the power of it. She screamed her ecstasy into Mick's hot mouth, surprised at how hard and fast the pleasure had hit her.

Mick suddenly began to thrust into her with speed and force, his kiss never easing, his arms now wrapped under her back, cradling her with tenderness even as he ravished her. He stiffened. He roared when he came. By the sound of it, Mick had been as surprised as Piper.

They eased down together, slowly, the kiss continuing in lazy, sensual touches of lips and tongue. Eventually they lay in each other's arms, breathing, eyes open to the bright morning light, lips smiling.

"Jaysus H.," Mick whispered after a few moments. "You attacked me, woman. Now I'm going to be late for work."

"I'll write you a note," she said.

" 'Dear Mr. LaPaglia . . .' " Mick had to stop laughing before he could continue. " 'Please excuse Dr. Malloy for his tardiness. He was busy layin' the pipe to your senior curator.' "

They laughed lazily, hanging on to each other. When the hilarity faded, Mick pressed Piper's head to his chest and stroked her hair.

"Anything on your mind today, love?" he asked.

"Oh, I don't know. A lot of things, I guess." Though she hadn't planned to, she punctuated her answer with a drawn-out sigh.

"Want to tell me one?"

Piper pushed up onto her elbow and looked down into Mick's face. He looked disheveled and happy. He looked like a satisfied man.

"It's about the exhibit," Piper admitted.

"Well, that's certainly understandable."

She watched her fingers play in his chest hair as she spoke. "Lately I've been wishing that there was more to her story, you know? Ophelia produced a prodigious collection of letters, speeches, and essays once she got to Boston, but there were no more journals—at least that we know of—and I . . ." Piper raised her eyes to Mick. "I want to know her secret heart after she was married and had kids and began her work. I want to know her most intimate moments during those years. The sad thing is, I'll never know."

Mick stroked her cheek. "A lady is entitled to some privacy, don't you think?" he offered.

Piper smiled. "I suppose. It's not that I'm nosy, I just want to make sure everything turned out well for her and her husband. That the love lasted. That it was real."

"You want a guaranteed happy ending," he said, nodding. "You're a hopeless romantic."

Piper exhaled in disbelief. "I am?"

"Oh, most definitely."

"Huh." Piper thought about that for a minute, then smiled. "If I am, it's all Ophelia's fault."

Mick chuckled softly. "Come now, Piper," he said. "You were always who you are now, even back at Wellesley, even before you found those diaries and decided to snare me in your tender trap of seduction."

She giggled. "Yeah, I guess." She sighed again. "Besides, we really aren't very much alike, Ophelia and me. She was a normal girl trying to be outrageous, and I'm just a nerdy girl trying to be normal."

Mick hoisted himself up and gently placed his hands on Piper's shoulders. "Why the feck's sake would you want to be normal?" Mick asked, suddenly very serious. "You are extraordinary, Piper, meaning that you are not an ordinary woman. You've got more brains than most, more beauty, more wit, more drive, more courage. Don't waste another second comparing yourself to or modeling yourself after someone else." He stopped. "Please."

She was taken aback by the passion in his voice.

"You know . . ." Mick brushed his fingertips down the side of her cheek. "I haven't spent all this time falling in love with the Blackbird. I'm falling in love with my Piper."

Mick gave Piper's hand another tight squeeze as they reached the front door. "You're gonna do great," he said, leaning down and kissing her cheek. "And I'll be right next to you the whole time."

Piper nodded, steeling herself. "I've never brought a man to dinner at my parents'."

Mick chuckled. "I'm honored to be the lab rat. Are little green pellets on the menu?"

She didn't crack a smile. "It's a distinct possibility."

"Jaysus and Janey Mack," he mumbled.

Piper glanced up at him and smiled. Mick's easy manner always seemed to balance out her anxiety. Sometimes, she couldn't recall what it was like to go through her days without him.

The heavy oak door flew open, catching them by surprise.

"Ah!" Piper's mother said, beaming. "I thought I heard voices out here. Well, come on in! We've been waiting for you two!"

With Mick's strong hand at the base of her spine, Piper entered her parents' house. Aside from a series of unanswered phone messages and Piper's call to confirm that she and Mick would attend Sunday dinner, this would mark the only contact she'd had with her parents since the night she screamed at them and ran out the door, under the influence of dairy.

Piper's mother hugged her stiffly, shook Mick's hand, and led them into the parlor. That's when Piper's heart fell into her shoes.

"You know Wallace Forsythe, of course, and his wife, Paulette."

"Oh!" The fury rose in Piper so fast she was seeing spots. "Of course! Mr. and Mrs. Forsythe. What . . . ? Uh, what a surprise to see you here."

Bless Mick for being such a social butterfly, Piper thought, because she was on the edge of disintegration. The hand she'd just offered to the museum's chairman of the board of trustees was slick with sweat and her greeting was an embarrassment.

As Mick chatted up Piper's father and the Forsythes, she flashed her eyes to her mother, who seemed enthralled with her role as hostess. Piper tried to pull herself together—her mother had no idea that Piper was in the process of deceiving the museum trustees. She'd probably invited good ole Frosty Forsythe over as a way to grease the social skids for her and Mick. Her mother surely meant well.

"Piper? Would you mind helping me in the kitchen?"

Noting that Mick seemed at ease serving up tumblers of seltzer water and lime, she excused herself and followed her mother. Once the kitchen door swung shut her mother smiled at her and giggled.

"I thought it would be nice for you to spend some leisure time with the chairman," she explained, opening the refrigerator and pulling out a platter of one of her standard hors d'oeuvres—thinly sliced cucumbers spread with a nearly translucent sweep of hummus and dotted with a single caper. (As a kid, Piper had called the creations "cucumbers with baby poop and dead flies." *Bam!*)

Her mother placed sprigs of parsley and mint on the platter along with a scant number of sliced grape tomatoes. "To brighten things up," she said to Piper. "And anyway, your father and I thought it would make it more difficult for Wallace to sack you—should that be a decision he's faced with in the near future—being that he'd recently socialized with you."

Piper nearly laughed. The near future? No shit—the Fall Gala was a week away, which could very well coincide with her getting sacked.

"That was nice of you, Mother," she said.

After returning to the parlor and enduring another half hour of chatting, the group adjourned to the dining room. Under the table, Mick reached for her knee, and heat spread through Piper's entire being. His hand felt so big and warm and real—so completely out of place in this house with these people.

She glanced up at him and tried to smile.

Things went relatively smoothly for most of the meal. Everyone complimented her mother on the presentation of the food—raw cranberry and orange relish, asparagus juice, and sautéed tempeh and green beans sprinkled with sesame seeds. Piper winced as her mother dished out precise half-cup measurements of food onto the Forsythes' dinner plates.

"Of course, you are welcome to have as much as you like," she explained. "We always offer a precise serving size for accurate data gathering."

Wallace Forsythe glanced down at his plate and back up to Piper's father, bewilderment on his face.

Piper heard Mick stifle a snicker. She kicked him under the table—if he started laughing, they were both doomed.

Conversation wound its way to Mick's coup in snagging Ben Affleck for the public service announcements. Forsythe commended Mick for bringing in new corporate and individual accounts. "I have a feeling the gala is going to be something else this year," he said, raising his asparagus juice.

"I'll drink to that," Piper said. This time Mick kicked her under the table.

Forsythe continued in that vein, asking Piper for more details about the Ophelia Harrington exhibit. "Our hope is that it has some real zing to it, you know, something flashy that will grab the attention of the press and patrons."

Piper raised an eyebrow, thinking that Frosty would be getting some zing, all right.

Her father cleared his throat. "I think what Wallace is getting at is that everyone hopes this exhibit will be more interesting—more compelling, shall we say—than last year's switchboard operators."

Piper blinked. *No,* she thought. Her father did *not* just bring that up. Why would he, unless he wanted to cut her down?

Her mother smiled at her sweetly. "We're only hoping you've saved some energy for the exhibit and not squandered it all on your *makeover.*"

It was so quiet in the dining room that Piper figured everyone could hear the pounding of her heart.

"I think you look fabulous," Paulette said. "Your hair is gorgeous." She lowered her voice to a whisper. "I love your bag."

Piper gently put her fork on her plate. Mick started to say something to her but she lightly touched his forearm. "I've got this," she said, standing.

"Oh, now, don't be so sensitive," her father said, laughing uncomfortably. "We're just teasing you."

Piper shook her head. "No. No, you're not. This is not about teasing. It's about being threatened by me."

Her mother leaned back in her dining chair, as if suddenly hit with gale-force winds.

"You can't stand it that I'm coming into my own, can you?" Piper paused, noting the frozen shock on everyone's face—everyone but Mick, anyway. Mick was suppressing a smile. "You're threatened by my appearance. It just screams lust, doesn't it? A lust for food, for sex, for being fully alive."

Paulette gasped.

"Don't worry, Mrs. Forsythe," Piper said. "I have no plans to get profane. I just needed to make a point."

Her father stood up. "That's enough—"

"I'm not even warmed up, Father." Piper motioned for him to return to his seat, and in doing so, knocked over her tumbler of asparagus juice. The green stain spread through the white linen tablecloth, and Piper suddenly had the mental image of roast beef sliding down the wallpaper of a London dining room so long ago. She laughed out loud.

Thank you for showing me how to do it, Ophelia.

"Mother and Father, I am not an extension of you," she said, her voice much softer now. "I appreciate all you've done for me as my parents—provided me with a home and a superb education and exposure to music and art and culture. But I don't owe you my soul. Do you understand that?"

Forsythe cleared his throat. "Perhaps we should be going."

"Don't bother. We'll be leaving soon," Piper said. At that point, Mick stood next to her and reached for her hand.

"Please listen to what I am saying to you." She glanced from her mother's blanched face to her father's angry eyes. "Finally, at the age of thirty, I am becoming my own person. My own *woman.* I am blossoming on all levels—professionally, emotionally, and sexually. I am exploring everything I am and everything I'm destined to be."

"What in the world has gotten into you?" That little squeaky complaint came from her mother's direction.

Piper chuckled. "I think I've sprouted balls the size of grapefruits," she said. "Courage, Mother. That's what's gotten into me. I'm finally brave enough to live my own life and tell my own story, and you know what? It looks nothing like yours. It's full of passionate kisses and whipped cream and silk scarves and . . ."

Forsythe's chair scraped loudly across the wood floor as he jumped up from his seat. Paulette was not far behind.

"No. Really—stay. Enjoy your evening. We're going."

With that, Piper grabbed her bag and started to exit the dining room, Mick's warm and solid hand wrapped firmly around hers. But she stopped.

"Mother and Father, stop trying to control me. It won't work anymore. Please respect that."

Piper couldn't remember walking through the foyer and out the door, but at some point she found herself on the front sidewalk, Mick's arms snug around her, her feet spinning off into the air as he twirled her around.

"I am so proud of you," he said into her ear, his breath hot and his voice sweet. "You are something else, woman."

He put her down. "Whadya say we get us some real food?"

She stepped into the dim and cool pub and heard a chorus of voices welcome her. Piper could tell immediately that the man behind the bar was Mick's brother, because he was an older, chubbier, balder—and much louder—version of Mick. The short woman at his side had to be Mick's sister-in-law, Emily.

Mick introduced her, and Piper felt like a long-lost relative, there was so much hugging and kissing going on. It was like she'd fallen into a rabbit hole outside her parents' house on Towbridge Street and popped up in another world entirely. Cullen and Emily's two children, Maeve and Will, ran out of the office where they'd been doing their homework to get a look at their uncle's new girlfriend.

She and Mick grabbed a couple of barstools, and that's when she was bombarded with questions about beverages— stout or lager? How about a shot of Jameson? Powers? A mixed drink?

"I can make a Cosmo if that's more your style," Cullen assured her.

She felt besieged, which Mick picked up on right away. "Mind if I order for you?" he asked her.

"Please do," she said.

Not long after, Piper was on her second glass of Murphy's

and was diving face-first into a basket of delicious fish and chips, courtesy of Emily. She sprinkled everything with malt vinegar and salt and was taking a big bite of fish, juice running down her arm, when Cullen leaned on the bar and laughed.

"The poor waif is starving, Magnus! When's the last time you bought her a decent meal?"

Piper stopped chewing, her eyes growing big in embarrassment, but Mick leaned over and put his arm around her shoulder.

"Piper's been a bit deprived," he said, squeezing her tight. "She's got some catching up to do."

Full, happy, and glad to have met his family, Piper left the pub with Mick about an hour later. As they walked to the T station, Mick's cell phone buzzed.

"Yes?" he said. Piper watched his face go rigid. His eyes flashed to her momentarily, then he nodded as he listened, holding up a finger to indicate he needed to stop a moment and take the call.

Piper waited. She heard a woman's voice emanating from the phone.

"But why now?" he asked. "They've been jacking me around for months, and now it's suddenly an emergency?" He paused again. "Los Angeles? Why all the way out there? I thought they were based out of New York. Can't we do this first bit over the phone? Some kind of conference call?"

Piper watched him nod a few more times and say, "I understand. All right. Let me know when they pick a date." He said good-bye and slipped the phone into his pants pocket.

"That was my agent," he said, though Piper had figured it out by then. "The Compass Cable people want to meet with me soon. Apparently, the show is a go."

Suddenly, she wished she hadn't eaten the fish and chips.

Twenty-eight

London

As I look back over the last seven years, I believe the greatest difference must be the sweet peace of my contentment. I do not miss the spotlight, although the Swan still reigns supreme. I think she may still own the demimonde when her golden hair turns to silver, for her elegance is ageless and her vivacity is tireless. I, on the other hand, enjoy my quiet evenings curled up with Eamon, at last with the time to read. Most would find us boring. I find us delightful.

Eamon is my lover and dearest friend, but I have never forgotten my beautiful Sir. I carry my longing for him in my most secret heart. Though I have not seen him since I woke alone that morning, I feel him with me every night as I lie in the dark and remember.

I opened my eyes in the night, suddenly and violently awake. My heart pounded, yet I knew not why. The room was utterly silent, with no danger in sight or hearing. Had I been dreaming? I found no trace of nightmare in my thoughts. I lifted my head from my pillow and slid up a little, listening carefully.

The room was utterly silent.

With a start I realized what was missing—what had been

there every night of the last seven years. I could not hear Eamon's gentle snore.

He lay with his back to me, his head on the pillow only inches from mine. With an awful sense of foreboding, I reached my hand out to stroke his big shoulder. For an end-less moment it hung in the air, unable to travel that last inch. As long as I did not finish the gesture, I could hold the hope in my heart a few seconds longer.

Wake.

Turn to me in sleepy good humor.

Take me in your arms and warm my chilled feet.

Please, my darling companion.

Wake.

But Eamon would never wake again. His big heart, that generous and constant heart, had stopped in the night. I would never lay my head against his chest and hear its steady thud again. Worse than the thought that I was alone again was the notion that Eamon no longer existed. How could so much warmth and unassuming gentleness be subtracted from the world by the simple misbeat of an organ?

Those next days passed in a fog. Sadness turned the min-utes to hours, and sometimes hours to minutes. The very earth seemed tilted without his strength and integrity to hold it upright. Not since my parents had died had I been dealt such a blow. In some ways I took this all the harder, for I was a woman of the world. I knew that no amount of wishing would turn back the clock, would declare it all a terrible mistake, would bring back his booming laugh to make me shake my head and smile.

Then, just when I was at last becoming accustomed to the silence, I was called to the office of Eamon's solicitor. There was a will, it seemed. I must dress and make an ap-pearance that afternoon.

Though it would be a presumption to wear black as if I were family, I could bear to wear nothing brighter than a pale dove gray. As I walked into the office of the solicitor, I was surprised to see pretty young Alice Wainwright waiting there as well.

I had not wished to intrude upon the mourning of Eamon's beloved daughter by attending the funeral in full disreputable person, but I had been called here today on business. Should I leave? I backed away a step, about to slip out the door. At that moment Alice raised her head and saw me. Her green eyes were reddened with crying and her red-blond hair was pulled back tightly from her face. Clad in full mourning of the blackest black, she looked painfully pale and vulnerable. My heart went out to her at once, but any motion I might have made to comfort her was halted by the flash of pure hatred that suddenly enlivened her sad eyes.

Yes. Of course. Alice's response was only natural.

As I stood there, wondering if I might yet manage to escape without confrontation, a tall figure in black stepped between us.

I blinked at the sneering rage in the blue eyes of Lord B——. Shock reverberated through me. I had not seen a glimpse of him since he'd beaten me nearly to death. My heart pounded. *Run.*

"Whores should not invade the presence of respectable women." His tone was arch, his words righteous, yet I saw his gaze travel knowingly over my body. With his back turned to Alice, he licked his lips and smiled as a wolf might, showing all his teeth.

I backed away a step. "I——" Time to leave.

The door across from me opened and a small, neat man in spectacles blinked at us all in surprise. "Here already? Goodness, I must wind my watch!"

Alice jumped to her feet and scurried into his office. Lord B—— followed Alice, for after all, she had the purse strings all tied up. Relieved, I turned to flee. I had one hand on the door when the solicitor stopped me.

"No, Miss Blackbird. Your presence is required for the reading of the will."

I turned and blinked at him. Why? I'd thought Eamon might have left me a token, a silver jewel case or perhaps a favorite painting. I shook my head. "I'm sorry. I shall have to come back later."

The little man gazed at me with understanding but no mercy. "No, Miss Blackbird. Your presence is *required*. I shall not be allowed to read the last will and testament of Eamon Wainwright unless both you and Miss Wainwright are in the room."

He bowed crisply and beckoned with one sweeping hand. I walked slowly into the office. *Oh, Eamon, what have you done to me?*

Once Alice and I had been seated, the solicitor scuttled around to his own chair, then blinked up at Lord B——. "My lord, might I ask in what capacity you are attending this reading?"

Lord B——, who loomed behind Alice's chair like a prison guard, folded his arms. "In the capacity of Miss Wainwright's fiancé."

"Oh, Alice," I breathed. "You didn't!"

Alice shot me one guilty, defiant glance. She then pointedly shifted in her seat, turning her back to me. The solicitor's gaze flicked back and forth between the three of us and I knew that Eamon had kept this gentleman informed of all our doings.

I had nothing to hide. Of the many names people might call me, "liar" was not one of them. Alice surely had no secrets worth keeping, for she was but twenty-three. With a start I realized that by the time I had turned twenty-three I had been a courtesan for five long years. I shot another look at Alice. Hmm. It would not do to underestimate the daughter of Eamon Wainwright.

Lord B——, on the other hand, could be called every name in the book and they would still not encompass the extent of his evil.

"Very well." The solicitor shuffled his papers about on the desk and began to read. "Hereby stands the last will and testament of Eamon Wainwright of Bannerfield Hall. I, Eamon Wainwright, being of sound mind, do state that . . ."

The man droned just a little and I was still trying to conceive of what Alice's life might be like in the hands of Lord B——, so I did not closely attend the next several paragraphs pertaining to the dispensation of the estate (to Alice, of course, since it was not entailed) and the fine horses that his wife had so devotedly bred (to his wife's brother, who shared her passion for them) and his personal wealth, which would obviously go to Alice again—

". . . unless my daughter Alice should be so idiotic as to wed that malignant wastrel, Lord B——, in which case half my wealth, some fifteen thousand pounds, will go at once into the hands of my devoted Blackbird, Miss Ophelia Harrington—"

"What?" Lord B—— let out a roar of rage that completely drowned out Alice's gasp of shock.

I sat stunned. *Oh, Eamon, how could you involve me in this, knowing what you know?* And then, in a startled flash, I realized that Eamon had revealed my true identity, which I hadn't even known that he'd known. I wondered how much involvement this capable little solicitor had in tracking down the old Ophelia. He shot me a sharp glance. Oh, quite a bit, I imagined.

Lord B—— was shouting now, his fury unleashed on the bearer of bad tidings, who sat through it all with a quiet lack of intimidation. People must lose their tempers in his office quite often.

Then Alice stood and placed one trembling hand on Lord B——'s arm. He whirled on her, but quieted at once. "Take me home," she said in a trembling voice. "I don't care about the money. I only want to get away from *her.*"

All eyes fixed on me, the apparent cause of all distress. Had I only so much power in the world! Unfortunately, since Lord B—— had already revealed the engagement there was no concealing it now. If the two of them wed, Alice would lose half her substantial fortune.

I only hoped Eamon's last attempt to bring her to her senses would work. I, myself, had no interest in the money. Eamon had taught me a great deal about investments. I was secure, if not actually wealthy. I need not even find another protector if I did not wish it, although if I gave up the life of a courtesan, what life would I live?

When they left, I turned to the solicitor. "Eamon should not have done this."

He spread his hands. "And yet he did. A man's fortune is his to dispense as he wishes."

I looked after Alice worriedly. "I hope she opens her eyes. If the girl has an ounce of self-preservation . . ."

The solicitor shot me a look. "Then you would get nothing."

Oh, Eamon. I gazed at the floor. "What I wanted I lost ten days ago."

Clasping his hands behind his back, the little man rocked back on his heels. "Mr. Wainwright talked about you a great deal. You made him happy, although to be truthful, I thought he was a man in the grip of a middle-aged folly. I am very pleased to see that I was entirely wrong."

I met his even gaze without shame. "I'm glad I pleased him. He deserved whatever happiness I could provide." I thought of poor, deluded Alice. "I only wish I could convince his daughter to look elsewhere for hers."

Twenty-nine

Boston

"I can't thank you enough," Linc told Melvin Tostel. "I'll just be a few minutes."

The security guard hooked his key ring to his belt and looked him up and down like he didn't trust him.

Linc made a rectangular shape with his hands. "It's a day planner, about six by nine, black leather. I must have left it in here this afternoon and I've been completely lost without it—I couldn't even sleep!"

Melvin narrowed his eyes at him. "I'll let you go about your business, Mr. Northcutt. I'll be up at the security desk to sign you out. Soon."

Linc nodded, pretending not to notice that Tostel had warned him to be quick. He began to search frantically for what was already shoved down into the front of his shirt, nicely hidden by a button-down shirt and navy blue blazer that was hot as hell.

"I'll be up in a jiffy!" he said, watching the security guard disappear from the doorway. Linc listened for the elevator to ding and the doors to close. Silence. He had to work fast. He didn't want to raise Melvin's suspicions enough that he would tell Piper about Linc's little midnight visit.

The workroom was a disaster. He spun around, his mind racing. What he needed was something that would shed light on the Sir Speedy mystery page. He needed to confirm that the words on that page were exactly what he thought they were, and that they absolutely had found their way into the exhibit.

The possibility made him shiver with pleasure every time he thought of it.

But what, exactly, was Piper up to? It was driving him *insane* that he couldn't figure out what she was doing. The exhibit taking shape upstairs was exactly as she'd described to the trustees. Yet those erotic sentences Linc had found were written by Ophelia Harrington's hand! Piper and Mick knew that! They had uncovered some kind of seriously juicy scandal, and there was no way they'd hide the truth to avoid causing a stir. They were too honorable for that.

Linc rifled through all the desk drawers, seeing nothing that struck him as noteworthy. He quickly perused the shelves and the boxes near the worktable. Nothing. He scanned a stack of exhibit design sketches, and that's when he saw something quite puzzling.

The physical dimensions on these pages were almost identical to the exhibit proposal Piper had submitted to the board. But that's where all similarity ended.

Linc pulled up a chair, crossed his legs, and tore through the papers as fast as he could. The installation in his hand was entitled "Harrington 2," and the central exhibit was a . . . a . . .

Linc's eyes bugged out. *No fucking way.*

As he pored over the plans for the individual exhibit chambers and an itemized checklist of artifacts, his shoulders began to shake with silent laughter. This was better than anything he could have whipped up in his dreams—Piper was planning a completely and totally different exhibit than what was expected for the Fall Gala.

Oh, this is rich, he thought. Piper fancied herself as some sort of vanguard feminist curator, when in reality, anyone who would rock their career boat at a time like this was a stone-cold twit.

Her office had a bigger window, didn't it? He could probably start moving in next week.

Linc bundled the sketches together as quickly as he could and returned them exactly where he'd found them. On the way up the elevator, he had to force himself to stop giggling. His first duty was to double-check that *everyone* in Piper's life had received their gala invites.

Linc yanked the day planner from inside his shirt just before the elevator door opened on the main floor.

He jogged toward Melvin, seated at the main security desk. "Got it!" he said brightly, waving the book in the air before he signed out. "Have a nice night!"

Thirty

London

Breakfast was once again interrupted by the Swan and her news sheet, but this time she rushed into my chamber, her lovely face as pale as marble. "Ophelia! You must flee London!"

I halted with my toast halfway to my lips. "Before or after I've had my tea?"

"I'm quite serious!" She flung her paper down before me. "Read this!"

The headline declared quite loudly, "Blackbird or Black Widow?", and then beneath that, "London Ladybird to be Charged With Murder!"

My toast fell to my plate, forgotten. I grabbed the newssheet up and read quickly. "Notorious woman of pleasure known as the Blackbird is to be formally charged with the ruthless murder of Mr. Eamon Wainwright, who died a fortnight ago under suspicious circumstances. Mr. Wainwright was found in the bed of Ophelia Harrington without a mark on him. The City Coroner suspects poison."

I looked up at the Swan. "At the inquest, they said heart failure. How can this be?"

"Bribery," the Swan said bitterly. "Or prejudice. There is no law in London for the likes of us."

I gazed back down at the paper in my shaking hands. "Survived by his grieving daughter, Miss Alice Wainwright,

and her devoted fiancé, well-regarded author, Lord B——,
Mr. Eamon Wainwright was a respected citizen of London. Lord B——, in posing the charges on behalf of Miss
Wainwright, claims that Ophelia Harrington seduced the
unsuspecting Mr. Wainwright into leaving half of Miss
Wainwright's rightful inheritance to the woman he knew
only as the Blackbird. 'She is a conniving harlot,' says
Lord B——. 'No man is safe from her grasping claws.' "

" 'On behalf of Miss Wainwright,' " I murmured. "Oh,
Alice." I bit my lip. "She's a lamb in the grip of the wolf."

"She's a twit," the Swan said sharply. "She isn't a child.
There is no excuse for her stupidity."

I traced a finger over the drawing of the Blackbird, a
sketch of a sloe-eyed seductress with long, clawlike fingernails. "I was that stupid once."

The Swan snorted. "Yes, for about a week. Alice Wainwright has been stupid for years."

"It says the trial is scheduled for two weeks from today."

"Which is why you must pack a bag and sail at once. I
hear Barcelona is most diverting." She grabbed my hand and
pulled me to my feet. "You are fortunate that the news sheet
arrived before the magistrate's men."

I was not fortunate for long. Scarcely had I dressed and
thrown a few belongings into a valise than a hearty pounding came upon the door of my house.

"Quick!" the Swan urged. "You must flee through the
back garden!"

However, when she towed me to the rear of the house, we
saw a burly fellow lurking outside. I backed away from the
window. "I will not be dragged screeching from my own
house!"

The Swan followed me as I strode to the front door and
flung it open. "Gentlemen, I've been expecting you," I said
with dignity.

The expressions upon the faces of the three watchmen
was priceless. I doubt they had ever been in the presence of

a woman as beautiful as the Swan and I followed a close second. I smiled regally at them. In less than a second, their hats were in their hands and their feet shuffled on my front step like those of bashful schoolboys. I handed one fellow my valise and took the arm of another. "Won't you delicious fellows show me the way to Newgate Prison?"

"Ophelia!" The Swan's whisper was urgent.

I turned to my dear friend and lifted my chin. "Could you contact Sir on my behalf?" I had never asked it of her before.

She bit her lip. "I shall try."

I turned back and cast a blinding smile upon my captors. "Shall we go?"

As I left my home with dignity, I feared I might never see it again.

The Blackbird had been caged at last. I sat on a bench in the ward reserved for female felons in Newgate Prison. The low arched ceiling of stone made me feel as though I were seated in a sewer tunnel, albeit a dry one. A few small high windows opened to the inner courtyard of the women's quadrangle. These provided enough light to gain a view of my fellow prisoners. All around me, women sat or lay upon pallets that looked to be stuffed with straw. Some of them were grouped together, some sat alone. Some of them had their children with them, sunken-eyed and wary creatures that they were. Was it better to stay with their mothers than to be cast into the streets or warehoused in an overcrowded orphanage? I honestly could not say.

A woman approached me. She was tall and thickly proportioned, but her broad face had once been pretty. Now she sported only a few teeth as she smiled cynically at me. "Fine lady," she rasped, then cackled. "What did ye do to get in 'ere? Did ye drown yer brats like old Bertha over there?" She pointed at a woman who crouched in a corner and scratched mindlessly at her tangled gray head.

I gazed at the woman without fear. "I am Ophelia," I told her. "What is your name?"

The woman's bravado faltered. "Me?"

I smiled. "You."

"I be Hettie."

I held out my hand. "It is very nice to meet you, Hettie."

Forced to either shake my hand or leave me with my arm thrust into the air, Hettie gave my hand a quick fumble. Then she backed warily away.

I kept smiling. "In answer to your question, Hettie, I am here because I managed to upset a man enough to make him want to destroy me."

Hettie grunted, "That ain't hard."

"Indeed," I said regretfully.

Hettie lifted her chin. "Don't ye want to know what I done?"

I tilted my head. "Only if you wish to tell me."

"I kilt my husband. With a butcher knife. Cut his throat, I did."

I took this horrifying news calmly. "I don't know much about husbands," I told her. "I have never married. But I hear they can be a handful sometimes."

Hettie stared at me for a long moment. Then a harsh bark of laughter broke from her lips. "That be the truth, milady!" She turned away, chuckling. "A handful! Ha!"

After Hettie left, I noticed another woman eyeing me warily from a nearby pallet. I smiled at her in a friendly way. She edged closer.

"I never heard Hettie laugh afore," she said with wonder. "And she didn't beat you or nothin'."

I folded my hands in my lap. "I found Miss Hettie to be a scintillating conversationalist."

The woman frowned. "Who did ye piss on what got ye in irons?"

I translated. *Whom did you anger enough to be put in prison?* I have always been clever with languages.

I let out a sigh. "He is known as Lord B——. We were

once friends, but he betrayed my trust. Now he feels he must destroy me in order to gain great wealth." She gazed at me without much comprehension, but I went on. "I am accused of killing my lover. If I am hanged, then I will not inherit the money he bestowed upon me. Lord B—— will be free to marry my lover's daughter and gain all the wealth for himself."

The woman blinked. "That sounds a mess, all right."

"A mess indeed." I rubbed at my aching head. "The ironic thing is that I have recently come to see that the life I have chosen has become unrewarding. I was beginning to form a plan to change it. A shallow existence, based on sex and money and fame, is a thin sheet of ice on which to skate. Everything that is happening now had its beginnings in the past. I have made choices, you see. These choices had insured that I have no powerful friends on which to depend. I have no iron-clad reputation with which to armor myself. The very freedom I have always cherished is the very thing that now makes me vulnerable."

I gazed through the filthy windows at the fading sky. "My chickens, I fear, have truly come home to roost." Then I let out a breath and turned to more practical matters. "I can see by the sky outside that night is coming. How does one obtain a pallet?"

The woman frowned. "Ye take it."

"Oh." I gazed about the room but it looked as if all the pallets were occupied. "Are there spare ones?"

The woman shook her head. "Ye could sneak Bertha's away from 'er, for she's right crazy and won't notice for hours." She scratched meditatively at her dirt-creased neck. "She might kill ye in the wee hours for it, though."

I inhaled. "Perhaps I shall simply lie on this bench. I have my valise as a pillow."

The woman's fingers twitched. "What ye got in there?"

I smiled at her. "These are my things. They belong to me. Bertha's not the only one who can sneak up on someone in the wee hours." I allowed my smile to turn a tiny bit sinister.

The woman drew back. "Aye, that's true enough." She scuttled back to her pallet and sat there, eyeing me with surprised respect. As well she ought. One does not climb to the top of the demimonde without tending toward the competitive. I might be in prison, but I could still rise to the top.

The top of the dungheap.

I wanted my own bed. I wanted my freedom.

I wanted Sir to come and tell me everything was going to be all right.

He did not come.

Thirty-one

Boston

The knock was so soft that Piper almost didn't hear it.

"What?" she barked, struggling with the ankle strap of her left shoe and hopping around on her right foot, looking at the workroom clock. She had exactly five minutes to get upstairs to greet the board of directors. Her navy blazer was covered in lint. She couldn't find her earrings.

The knock came again.

"Come in! *God!*"

The door opened just a crack and Mick poked his head inside. Suddenly, Piper's irritation melted away.

"Is this a bad time?" He gave her a tentative smile.

"I'm so glad it's you. Sorry I snapped at you. Hurry. Close the door." Piper rifled through her large bag again, almost certain that she'd thrown the earrings in there that morning, along with her shoes, a value-sized Excedrin, and a bottle of pinot grigio. She didn't find the earrings, but she did recover the little gift she'd planned to give Mick later that night. She might as well give it to him now.

"Here," she said, holding it out with one hand while ratting around in her purse for her earrings with the other. Maybe she should forget them. Tonight was just a walk-through of the exhibit for the staff and board members. Who cared if she sported earrings? "I wanted you to have this." Piper looked up at him and smiled.

Mick had moved into the workroom and around the desk. "Why, thank you," he said. "Should I open it now?"

"Maybe later tonight. I want to see your face when you get a look at it, but I'm running so late."

Mick laughed. "No problem." He tucked the playing card–sized box in a trouser pocket.

Piper took a swig from the wine bottle. "Want some?"

"Maybe later."

Mick came up behind her. He flipped her hair off to the side and gently rolled one of her earlobes in his fingers. Piper then felt his warm breath tickle the nape of her neck as he slipped the gold post through her pierced ear. "I'm assuming this was what you were looking for?"

She giggled and automatically straightened to lean against him, eyes closed. She took a second to sense him solid against her back.

"Where did you find them, Mick?"

"Right here on your desktop," he said, flipping her hair to the other side and slipping the other earring in place.

"Thank you so much. I'm a mess." She spun around to face him, and although he had a pleasant smile on his face and looked drop-dead handsome in his open-necked dress shirt and dress slacks, she sensed something was off-kilter. His lovely blue eyes were clouded.

"Mick?"

"I know you're running late. I just wanted to tell you good luck with the walk-through." He ran his hands along the slope of her hips, but Piper wasn't buying it.

"What's wrong?"

"Ah, Jaysus H.," he said, rubbing his chin and looking away. "I heard from the Compass people again, love."

She gasped. "You didn't get the show?"

"Here. Sit with me just a moment."

Mick situated himself in Piper's desk chair and pulled her down into his lap. He tilted his head back and gazed up into her face. He looked exhausted. With reason, she knew— she'd run the poor man ragged the last two weeks. Right then Piper told herself she'd make it up to him. Spoil him a bit. Or a lot. God knows she'd have plenty of time on her hands once she was fired.

"I need to go to L.A. right away."

It was almost like Piper's brain refused to accept what he was saying. "You mean, like in a few days? Next week?"

He shook his head. "Tomorrow afternoon."

Piper tried to stand up but he held her firm in his grip. "I tried to get them to wait, but they're being bastards about it—tomorrow or never, they said. But my agent—"

"I have to go." Piper used all her strength to get free. Her head suddenly felt like it weighed a ton. Like it was going to explode. She walked toward the door, knowing she was forgetting something but not caring anymore.

"Piper, please let me explain."

She spun around. She had no idea where all this drama was coming from. Maybe it was the stress. Or the wine. But she felt on the verge of screaming and stomping her feet because Mick had just told her he wouldn't be at the gala tomorrow night.

How could he do this? How could he choose a reality show over her? She needed him! She needed him here with her tomorrow for the big reveal!

He promised me.

Piper felt her gut drop with the weight of the sadness. Here we go again, she told herself. *He's going to walk out on me. He's going to break my heart.*

"Piper, listen." Mick moved toward her slowly, his hands out in front as if he were approaching a skittish wild animal. "I'll be here all tonight and tomorrow morning. I'll do whatever needs to be done to get the exhibit ready, just as I promised. I'm on a ten A.M. flight with a stop in Chicago, but I found a nonstop red-eye back to Boston. I won't even have to spend the night out there."

"It's okay," she heard herself say. Piper raised her chin and brushed lint from her blazer. "I understand. I've got to get upstairs."

He started to touch her but she backed away. "Look, I'm upset. I know I shouldn't be. You have your thing, Mick. This is my thing. They're separate. I shouldn't have dragged you into my mess like I have. It wasn't fair."

"Piper, that's not—"

"We'll talk later. I need to go."

She left Mick in the workroom. Her brain had already been packed with millions of little details she would need to successfully navigate the long night that lay ahead, and now there were giant, swelling waves of emotion crashing into her that she didn't have time for.

Damn you, Mick Malloy, she thought, hitting the elevator button.

Once inside, Piper leaned her forehead against the cool metal wall of the elevator. Ophelia's words ran through her head, from a letter she'd written to a friend soon after her son, William, died at the battle of Antietam. Ophelia had spoken from a place of utter despair in that letter.

There are times we are asked to bear the unbearable, to reach down within and discover a solid core of strength we didn't know we possessed. In the end, courage is a lonely pursuit of the soul. Another person can never be brave for us.

Piper squared her shoulders. Surely, if Ophelia had found the courage to go on living after losing her son, Piper could face tomorrow night's Fall Gala crowd without falling apart.

The elevator opened onto the lobby. She headed toward the south gallery, noting the small knot of museum employees and the trustees gathered around the closed double doors. Frosty Forsythe was there, but he could barely look at her, and his wife, Paulette, offered only a wan smile.

"Thank you, everyone, for stopping by this evening," she told the crowd. "I do hope you enjoy the exhibit."

Piper opened the doors. There were a few "hmms" and

murmurs of approval as people began to gather in a circle around the five-foot-wide pedestal display. They stared up at the scrim held in place with chains from the ceiling, and Piper watched as many began to frown. The scrim featured projected scenes of prosperous mid-nineteenth-century Boston life, superimposed with images of slaves in the field, on the auction block, and lynched bodies hanging from trees.

Once the shocked whispers began, Piper reached behind her and hit the wall switch and the scrim vanished up into the ceiling, uncovering a revolving mannequin display. As it slowly turned, people gasped in appreciation. A few even laughed in surprise. It was two human forms back-to-back, one a female slave in chains and one of the matronly Ophelia Harrington, fist raised and mouth open as if in mid-oration. The audio portion kicked in as designed, and a strong female voice proclaimed, *"To 'own' a human being is to annihilate a human life."*

Piper flipped another switch and a lighted walkway directed staff and board members into the display. LaPaglia stayed behind.

"Quite a statement, Piper," he said. He fiddled with his necktie. "Er, ah, I have to say this is a little more elaborate than I'd been led to believe. Far more politically charged."

Piper smiled at him, thinking, *You have no idea just how elaborate and charged things are going to get.* "I didn't spend one penny of museum money that wasn't budgeted."

"Fine. Fine. Anyway, I'll head into the installation and we'll talk later." He patted her on her bare arm. "Oh, by the way—love the type font."

The second LaPaglia strolled away, Linc sidled up to Piper. He gave her a sideways glance. "Looking forward to tomorrow night?" he asked.

She tipped her head and stared at him. "Absolutely."

"I know *I* am."

Piper gestured toward the exhibit. "Why don't you mosey on in?"

"No, thanks," Linc said, clasping his hands behind his back and tipping on his heels. "I think I'll wait to be surprised tomorrow evening along with everyone else. Best of luck to you."

As she watched him walk away, Piper had no doubt—Linc knew her plan. He'd probably known for a while, though she had no idea how he'd figured it out or what he planned to do with the information.

The funny thing was, it didn't even matter. Any attempt by Linc to sabotage her career would pale in comparison to what she was already doing to herself. So what if Linc ended up with Piper's job? If she were no longer employed here, it would be none of her affair.

About two hours later, Piper took cold comfort from feedback about the exhibit—it was going to be a smash, everyone said. Even Frosty Forsythe came up to shake Piper's hand and compliment her on her attention to detail and the creative use of documentation. "That Ophelia was a multifaceted lady—ahead of her time, I'd say, connecting the fight for women's rights and an end to slavery." He lowered his voice a bit. "If this doesn't steer Claudia Harrington-Howell—and her money—to the board of trustees, I don't know what would."

"Uh, thank you," Piper said. "So we'll see you both tomorrow night?"

"Wouldn't miss it," Paulette said.

At long last, Piper ushered everyone out and began to shut down the lighting and audio. It was 10 P.M. They had nine hours to redo the exhibit and lock up before the morning security guards began their shift. She took a moment to stand before the facsimile of the Harringtons' Bowdoin Street parlor. She stared at the pianoforte, Ophelia's cherry writing desk where she composed many of her speeches, her favorite quill pen, the framed silhouettes of their three children that adorned the walls.

And Piper wanted to kick herself. She'd desired what Ophelia had—an abiding love, a family, a story that her descendants could tell with a mix of fascination and pride. But she'd tied that dream to Mick Malloy—the man of her fantasies. Had that been a mistake?

She blinked back the tears. Crying was pointless. Feeling sorry for herself was a waste of time. This wasn't 1825. Piper could carve out a perfectly wonderful life for herself as a single woman. On her own terms. With her own skills.

She didn't need Mick for that. And she certainly didn't need him here tomorrow night. After all, what could he do when the shit hit the fan except hold her hand?

Not that there was anything in the world better than the feel of her hand in his . . .

"Miss Piper?"

Melvin Tostel had poked his head around the entrance to the exhibit. "I thought you might still be in here. Mr. LaPaglia's gone. Your friends are here. I just waved the truck into the loading dock."

Piper nodded. "Thanks, Melvin. Thank you for everything."

"You sure you know what you're doing, Miss Piper?"

For some reason, that question struck her as insanely funny. She laughed all the way down to her basement workroom, where she'd change clothes and begin the real work of the night.

She'd been perfectly pleasant. Mick was sure that in everyone else's eyes, Piper was simply focused on the job at hand, and if the two of them weren't as affectionate as they usually were, it was easily explained.

But he knew better.

And as Mick leaned up against a partition and watched Piper talking to Baz and Brenna, his chest felt full and heavily weighted.

"I honestly didn't know the English were so feckin' randy," Cullen said, wiping the sweat off his forehead. "I'm telling ya, the only thing that 'bood-war' over there is missing is a trapeze and a pommel horse."

Mick laughed and slapped his brother on his back. "You've been a real help tonight. We're almost done—you can head on home if you need to."

"Trying to kick my arse out?"

Mick shook his head. "Of course not. I just thought you'd—"

"Please don't tell me you've bollixed this thing up with your girl."

"Shh, would ya?" Mick shot him a sideways glance. "She's a little pissed at me at the moment, but she'll—"

"Feck no, Magnus! You didn't! You did *not* decide to go to Los Angeles instead of stay here with Piper! It's a big night for her!"

Mick was suddenly quite angry at Cullen. He pulled on his brother's shirtsleeve and yanked him out into the south gallery lobby, away from everyone. He was breathing hard with the effort it took for him to keep his voice, and his temper, at a polite level.

"The network's not playing around, Cullen. I need to sign that contract if I'm going to help you with the pub. I promised you—"

His brother just stood there, his arms crossed over his barrel chest, shaking his head slowly and deliberately.

"What?" Mick hissed.

"Magnus," Cullen said, laughing softly. "You're standing in the river dying of thirst, boyo."

"What the feck's that supposed to mean?"

"It means you're not seeing what's important here."

"I gave my word to you and Em. I'll lose the series if I don't show up tomorrow afternoon—shite, it's already *today*!—and then I'll have broken my word to your family . . . my family! I think that's pretty feckin' important."

Cullen nodded. "You're an eejit, Magnus. You don't understand women."

He had to laugh—things had gotten mighty desperate if he was accepting romance advice from Cullen.

"You probably gave your word to Piper, too," Cullen went on. "And even if you didn't say it flat out, you know she assumed you'd be here for her. That's how women think. So if you're in Los Angeles and not here with her at this feckin' unveiling or whatever it is, she'll think you don't love her."

"But I do love her!"

Cullen waited a beat before he grinned. "I knew it!" He reached up and draped an arm over Mick's shoulders and steered him down the hall. "See, here's the thing," he said, clearly enjoying his role as adviser. "Do you know why you could even offer to help me and Em and the kids?"

Mick frowned at him.

"Because there *is* a me and Em and our kids."

Mick stopped walking.

"Fine, I admit it," Cullen said with a laugh. "Sometimes I can be a stubborn pain in the arse. But I always put Emily first, followed very closely by the kids. That's the way it has to be, Magnus, because my love for Emily is where it all begins and ends. Everything else—and I mean money and illness and the pub and whatever else gets thrown at us—it has to take a backseat to my girl."

Mick didn't know what to say. Never in his life had he ever heard his brother bare his heart like this.

"Ah, shite," Cullen said, wiping his eyes. "I'm gonna make myself cry. I gotta get home. Just remember what I said." He started toward the exit but turned around to give Mick a quick tight hug. "I love you, you fool. You're a good man."

By 6:30 A.M., they were done. Brenna and the others had taken off. Piper had just gone through the exhibit one last time with her eternal checklist, making sure nothing had been left out. And Mick was running the vacuum, picking up all telltale dust and packing peanuts that had littered the carpet during the switch-out process.

Ten minutes later he and Piper were out in the parking garage. He walked her to her car and made sure she got in safely. He leaned in to kiss her, and it shocked him when she grabbed him by the back of the head and laid a big, juicy, full-mouthed smack on him.

She let him go, then immediately turned the key in her ignition. "Thank you for everything, Mick." She smiled at him, but Mick could tell her outer shell was about to crack.

"Piper—"

She put the car in reverse. "Good luck tomorrow with the network. Have a safe trip. I'll keep my fingers crossed for you."

As he watched her little rusted-out Honda round the corner of the garage, Mick realized he'd never felt more adrift in his life.

Thirty-two

London

The morning after my first night in Newgate Prison, the Swan came to see me.

"I had to bribe the turnkey," she said with a mystified frown. "He wanted to see my bare feet."

I raised a brow. "Goodness, you wanton creature! Go away. We don't want your kind here."

She wrinkled her nose. "I can scarcely blame him. I do have lovely feet."

But my amusement was short-lived. I was exhausted from my wary night on the hard bench. "I do not know if I can last a fortnight here," I whispered.

She reached out to brush a strand of my hair back from my face. "You must keep your spirits, dearest. I called on the solicitor who handled Eamon's will. He is trying to arrange a private cell for you. He can bribe the guards to bring you better food and drink, he told me."

I blinked. "Such kindness. Now I feel terrible that I can never remember his name."

The Swan smiled. "He is kind, but he is also a man. He is coming over to dine with me this evening."

My jaw dropped. "A night with the Swan? I will have a cell made of silver and gold."

She shrugged. "He is unobjectionable. And he was most complimentary about you. I think he envied Eamon his happiness. I have asked him to seek a very good barrister to speak in your defense. He seems to think it will be difficult to convince anyone to take your case."

I crumpled just a little. "No law in London for the likes of us." I sighed. "What of the news sheets? I must be selling like ice in summer. Are they profiting from my misfortune?"

The Swan's lips went thin. "I brought one for you to see because I felt you should prepare yourself." She took a folded article out of her reticule and handed it to me.

I read it in silence, then handed it back to her. "So I am already convicted in the public eye."

"Lord B—— has been very busy." Her voice was tight.

I looked away from her for a long moment. "Have you heard anything from Sir?"

She hesitated. I turned to stare at her. Her blue eyes shifted away from mine. My dearest friend in the world was contemplating telling me a lie.

"What is it?"

She looked extremely unhappy. "Ophelia, you must realize that he cannot come here." She waved a hand. "Can you picture the turnkeys' response to a man in a mask?"

I clenched my jaw. "You have spoken to him. He does not wish to come."

"The newsmongers are all around the prison. He would surely be exposed."

"He went out in public for you."

She practically writhed with discomfort. I was forcing her to choose between two friends. I had no mercy in me. I grasped her hand and made her face me. "He has abandoned me forever, then."

She raised her miserable blue gaze to meet mine. "He *cannot.*"

"You mean he will not."

She shook her head. "I cannot explain it any better than that."

I relented and released her. "At least I have you on my side. And little what's-his-name."

She leaned her head onto mine. "There, see? Your case is practically won already."

"Of course it is." I allowed her to comfort me, although I was beginning to doubt.

The first day of the trial dawned bright and clear. I should have preferred rain, I think. Or at least some sign that the world cared about this act of injustice!

The turnkeys escorted me from Newgate to the Old Bailey, where my trial was to be held. There were curiosity seekers outside the Bailey in throngs. A barker was doing a brisk business in figs. Another offered pork pies from a steaming cart.

"How lovely," I murmured. "A grand day out."

Once inside the Old Bailey, however, an expectant silence fell. The courtroom was a large space, almost like a theater. I stood in the raised "dock," facing the witness stand. Beyond the stand sat two rows of benches for the judges and barristers. Those concerned with the case could sit in another low box on the floor. I assumed it was for the party of the accused and the party of the accuser. This was borne out by the presence of Miss Wainwright and Lord B—— seated on one side.

On the other was seated the Swan and the little solicitor, what's-his-name. There was no tall, dark man with them, of course. I was led to the stagelike stand, to be stood there on display. Stage or cage, it amounted to the same thing.

On the advice of the solicitor, I had assumed the character of a respectable woman wrongly accused. The Swan had obtained a dowdy brown dress that fit me in a fashion. I wore no cosmetics and my infamous hair was wound tightly into a style most grandmothers would be pleased to sport. I kept my eyes downcast but for a few curious glances around the court. They would find no fault with me. I was no courtesan. I was a gently born woman with an undeserved reputation. At least, that was what I kept reminding myself.

The first hours of the trial were an exercise in patience. First one, and then the other barrister would stand and debate the tiniest points of law for the judge. It took an hour to establish the fact that I was, in fact, Ophelia Harrington, otherwise known as the Blackbird. I tried to look more like the Pigeon. The awful dress did its part.

It took another hour to establish the fact that the deceased was indeed Mr. Eamon Wainwright of Bannerfield Hall and not some other poor bastard found dead in a whore's bed.

My barrister objected to the term and the two of them were off again. In the meantime, my legs were trembling from weariness. Despite the fact that the little solicitor had indeed managed to procure a private cell for me, I had not yet learned to sleep through the riotous nights of Newgate.

Surely a slight sagging of my posture would only serve to further the Pigeon's disguise? I let myself lean wearily on the railing of my pen.

A bailiff strode up to me and struck his billy club sharply on the railing, narrowly missing my hands. I snatched my hands back and straightened.

It did not look well for me that day. Every reference to my "profession" incited nasty giggles from the gallery. There was not a dry eye in the house when Alice's barrister movingly described her overwhelming grief at the loss of her beloved father. I cried along with everyone else.

Lord B—— managed to have a chance to speak. He spent a good while affirming everyone's opinion that I was a gold-digging villain of the highest magnitude. I can only imagine that he used himself as an example to follow. He confessed before the entire world that we had once been involved, or, as he put it, that he had once fallen beneath the evil thrall of the Black Bird (emphasis was everything, it seemed) and had only narrowly escaped with his morals still intact.

How nice for him.

The long day drew to a close without my having the opportunity to defend myself with a single word. The judge banged his gavel and declared a continuance until the next day, when more witnesses would be called.

I could not imagine who. The Swan? She looked as puzzled as I. The solicitor? Well, he did rather like me, so his character reference might help a bit.

Then I spotted a man in the nearest gallery to me. He was positioned a few rows back, where the gallery was half cast in shadow, so I could not see him clearly. All I knew for sure was that he was tall and broad-shouldered and dark.

Was it Sir at last?

Before I was led back to Newgate, I was allowed a few moments to confer with my solicitor and his companion. The Swan immediately pulled me into a trembling hug. The solicitor looked very grave, indeed. I knew then that the dire leanings of the proceedings were not in my imagination. I pulled away from the Swan's embrace and glanced back up in the gallery. The man was gone.

"Did you see him?" I asked the Swan. "The tall, dark man, standing up there."

She frowned and blinked at me. "I saw a man such as you describe, but I thought you despised Lord Malcolm Ashford."

Oh. I sagged a bit. "I thought—"

The Swan raised a brow in comprehension. "You thought you saw Sir."

"I feel ridiculous." Then I frowned. "Whatever is Ashford doing here?"

She shrugged. "Curiosity? You are, after all, the one that got away."

I snorted. "More like gloating over his near-miss with disaster." I closed my eyes wearily for a moment. The room seemed to tilt behind my lids.

The turnkey approached. "Time to go, miss."

I wanted to flee, to run screaming down the halls of the Old Bailey like a bedlamite, to scratch and claw and froth at the mouth, anything rather than to return to the cold stone cell. To the iron bars.

On the walk back, we passed the gallows. We had passed them that morning, but that morning I had believed in the power of simple innocence to sway a court. Now it struck me that I might actually be hanged.

Hanged by the neck until dead, dead, dead.

The wooden gallows creaked in the wind. For a second I imagined a body hanging from the rope noose—a plump, dark-haired body with really excellent breasts.

I don't want to die.

Yet it was becoming very clear to me that there was a strong possibility that I would be convicted of Eamon's murder and become yet another public attraction, like Vauxhall Gardens or the swans in Hyde Park.

Dizzy with the grimness of my own probable fate, I allowed myself to be pushed into my dimly lit cell. I slumped on my cot, too horrified to weep. Was I sorry I'd lived my life to the fullest? Was I sorry I hadn't been an obedient female and wed the odious Ashford on command?

A month ago I would have laughed at the very idea.

I was not laughing now.

Thirty-three

Boston

The roar of the Boeing 737 had lulled him into a dull trance. Mick paid no attention to the other passengers on the Southwest flight, busy with their laptops and gadgets, looking successful and important and serious about the travel required to get wherever it is that successful people must go. As he stared out at the blue sky at thirty-two thousand feet, he couldn't shake the feeling that he was going the wrong way.

The plane may have been on its way to Chicago, but his head and heart were looking back over his shoulder toward Boston.

He couldn't use his cell phone on the plane, which made him fairly insane because he had no way of finding out if Piper had returned any of his texts or calls. Just for the comfort of it, he reached in to retrieve his phone from his pants pocket, and instead pulled out the little box Piper had given him the evening before.

He smiled sadly. He'd forgotten all about it in the mad rush to prepare the exhibit. Oh, who was he kidding? He'd forgotten everything and anything last night, including the gift, and not because he was busy. It was because the bitter wind blowing off Piper's cold shoulder had frozen him solid. He hadn't been able to think about anything last night except for the way the oxygen had been sucked from Piper's workroom the instant she pursed her lips and calmly said, "I need to go."

Just like that, the open, lusty, vibrant Piper he'd come to love was gone. Back in her cave. And it was because of him.

His fingers trembled as he tore off the little bit of wrapping paper around his gift. Underneath was a plain white box, the kind a department store might give you with your new tie clasp.

He took off the lid.

His felt his stomach free-fall every one of those thirty-two thousand feet.

She'd given him the key to her apartment.

Mick swallowed hard and looked out the window, overcome with sadness and the weight of his own stupidity.

Piper had just gathered the courage to offer it all to him and he'd thrown it right back in her face. He knew Piper. He knew that to her, the whole exchange must have had a familiar, decade-old stink to it.

And this time she'd bared more than her perfect breasts—she'd opened her perfect heart.

Mick swung his head around and tapped the shoulder of the busy man sitting next to him. The man looked up from his computer and removed an earbud. "Yes?"

"Where are we?" Mick asked.

The guy became instantly wary. "Uh. On a plane."

Mick laughed like a man coming unglued. "I mean, how long till Chicago?"

He shrugged and replaced his earbud. Mick began to poke at the flight attendant button with impatience.

She arrived momentarily, looking a bit perturbed. "Is there a problem, sir?"

"How long till we're on the ground?"

She checked her watch. "Another hour or so. Are you experiencing a medical emergency of some kind?"

Mick ran his hand through his hair and closed his eyes. He groaned in frustration, then laughed. "No. I've just made the worst mistake of my feckin' life, is all. Thanks for asking."

She turned on her heels and headed back up the aisle. "Off his meds!" she chirped.

Mick began making a mental list of what had to happen as soon as he hit the ground—he'd change his airline ticket, have his agent call the Compass people and tell them to feck off if they couldn't wait a few goddamned days, and get Cullen to bring his tux to Logan and drive him into the city.

He was coming home.

Piper could not believe what she was seeing in the mirror. She looked like an early nineteenth-century Englishwoman of scandalous celebrity, not some twenty-first-century soon-to-be-unemployed chick.

She sighed and smoothed down the scarlet satin of the bodice, just a little too formfitting for polite society. "I can't thank you enough for this dress, Brenna. It's so perfect. It's modeled after the one Ophelia wore at the trial, isn't it?"

"Absolutely. I thought it was the perfect statement for you to make tonight."

Brenna stood behind her, beaming with pride. "You're going to take everyone's breath away, Pipes. You're absolutely stunning."

She turned a bit to the side to check her hair and the dramatic scooped back and the fiercely low-cut front. It only made her harrumph. "I wanted to take *Mick's* breath away."

Brenna leaned in close. "You already have, sweetie. I know you're upset that he isn't here tonight. It really sucks."

Piper nodded, seeing her face begin to bunch up with emotion.

"How many calls of his have you ignored today?" Brenna asked, sounding thoroughly disgusted with her.

"A few. I can't deal with him right now. Please just let me get through tonight and then I'll face my demons, okay?"

Brenna shrugged. "I'm just saying—"

"I'll ruin my makeup if I cry any more."

Brenna patted her shoulder. "There's no reason to cry. He's a decent guy who is trying to do what's right, and he'll eventually figure out he fucked up."

"I know, I know. I understand all that intellectually, but I swear, Brenna—all I see is his back walking out of my apartment."

Brenna took Piper by the shoulders and spun her around. "Which apartment are we talking about?"

"My apartment back in grad school."

"When was that?"

"What? What do you mean—it was back when I was in grad school, like I just said."

"Uh-huh. How many years ago?"

Piper laughed. "Okay. I see where you're going—it happened a decade ago, not today, and Mick's not being here tonight is not the same."

"See?" Brenna kissed her cheek, then wiped away any sign of her lipstick. "My work here is done."

"Yeah, well, I'm still angry at him." Piper grabbed her small drawstring reticule from the bed and turned out her bedroom light. "We better go—don't want to be late for my own execution."

Four long hours after the plane landed at O'Hare, the TSA officers and FBI agents finally gave Mick the green light to get back on a flight to Boston. Apparently, any sudden change in travel plans that meant skipping the second leg of a ticketed journey didn't sit well with security officials. Plus, his "odd" conversation with the flight attendant had earned him an escort the instant he'd deplaned.

The first thing he did after he was released was call Cullen. He explained his change of heart, his encounter with airport security, and where and when Cullen should meet him.

"Don't forget my shirt studs," he said.

"For feck's sake, Magnus! What are you going to do,

change into your tux while I'm driving through the Ted Williams tunnel or something?"

"That was my plan."

The second thing Mick did was call his agent. She was bewildered, but agreed to call Compass and give them his message, verbatim.

"I think you've just shot yourself in the foot," she advised him.

Thirty-four

London

The second day of the trial dawned much like the first, gray and dank, just like my cell. My every movement echoed in the small chamber. I felt cut off from the entire world, walled in by what seemed like miles of stone. With something nearing nostalgia, I wondered what Hettie and Bertha were up to.

I washed gratefully. The little solicitor had made sure that I was kept stocked with soap and water and relatively clean toweling. I dressed in the same horrid gown I had worn the day before, although my belief in its power had much diminished. It had not protected me. Instead, I had felt more naked and vulnerable than ever. A courtesan without her bosom on display is a sad creature, indeed!

It seemed I had risen much too early from my lumpy pallet. I sat for hours, simply panting for some distraction from my thoughts. Then I heard footsteps outside my cell and the jingling of the jailer's keys. I stood, feeling ice at the pit of my stomach.

Would I emerge from this day with my feet on the ground or dangling in the air?

The door opened and a man ducked through the low lintel, but it was not one of the turnkeys. My heart fluttered at the sight of the dark head of hair, but when he straightened I saw that it was only the man from the gallery, my one-time fiancé, Lord Malcolm Ashford.

"Good morning, Miss Harrington."

I turned my back on him. "Leave," I ordered over my shoulder. What was the point of good manners now? "You may gloat over my hanged corpse if you must, but I will not waste a minute of *my* life on your petty triumph!"

"I cannot imagine a prettier corpse," he retorted. His voice was deep but his tone was clipped and supercilious. "However, the breathing version is preferable, even to me."

I had to look at him then. "Even now?"

He nodded. "I bear you no ill will, Miss Harrington. In fact, I came here today to offer you absolution from your acts against me twelve years ago."

"How odd." I pressed a palm to my forehead as I sifted through what might possibly have been the most pompous statement I had ever heard. *Is this my final unction?* I felt a bubble of mad laughter rising within me. "Perhaps I should have wed you after all. How appealing the gallows would be about now."

He cleared his throat and went on. "You are in a grave situation, Miss Harrington."

"Did you really just use the word 'grave'?" I let out a breath. "There you go again, being unbearable." I folded my arms and gazed at him in resignation. "You obviously have things to say to me. I, obviously, cannot flee the room screaming." I waved a careless hand. "Have at it."

"I am not the insufferable twit you think me, Miss Harrington."

I gazed at him with no attempt to hide my doubt. He lifted his chin. I had to admit, he was a handsome fellow. I could not see his eyes very clearly in the shadows of the cell, but he looked as though he had all his orifices in the right places.

"When you agreed to wed me—"

"When I was forced to agree to wed you, you mean."

He was silent for a moment. "That was wrong of me, I admit. I apologize."

I drew back, surprised. For some reason, my inability to

fit this man into some little box in my thoughts was very disturbing. Even his voice was less offensive to me now than it had been so long ago. "I accept your apology."

"However, you did lie."

I began to protest. He held up a hand. "I beg of you, let me finish a sentence."

One of my few flaws is my tendency to interrupt. I folded my hands and nodded silently. He went on. "Since you are known to be a forthright sort of woman, I only thought that this old falsehood might still be bearing on your mind."

I opened my mouth to assure him that I hadn't the tiniest of regrets, but I realized that I did. Life had taught me that even good people sometimes made poor first impressions. I had judged and convicted this man on the basis of a single overheard conversation, however damning. Then I had misled several perfectly innocent people that a wedding would soon take place. "Well, I do feel terrible about the florist."

His lips quirked. "The florist was paid handsomely for his efforts."

Not by my relatives, I was sure. "By you?"

He spread his hands. I drew my brows together. "Very well. Perhaps 'insufferable twit' does not apply."

With his hand pressed to his chest, he bowed slightly in thanks.

"But that does not explain what you are doing here, my lord. The turnkey will come any moment to lead me to the Bailey." My last private conversation of my life might be with the man I had jilted. "My existence is becoming increasingly bizarre," I breathed to myself.

He straightened. "Yes. Time is of the essence." He tapped on the door in a manner akin to a signal. The door opened and an object was handed through. Lord Malcolm Ashford turned to me and handed me the large brown paper-wrapped parcel. "This is for you."

I stared at him. "Am I supposed to say, 'Oh, you shouldn't have!'?"

His expression was extremely saturnine. "Open the package, Miss Harrington."

"Bizarre" was really not the right word. I sat upon the cot and untied the string wrapped about the package. The paper fell away to reveal a pile of rich ruby silk. I blinked. "What is this?"

I looked up to see that he had withdrawn into the shadows once more. "That," he said, "is what you should have worn yesterday."

I let my fingers trail over the gown, caressing the fine silk like an old friend I had dearly missed. I stood and held the dress up to me. It was deliciously daring and ruthlessly fashionable. I smiled then, a wild, wicked grin of old.

The Blackbird was back.

Thirty-five

Well, that hadn't taken long.

The scrim had gone up. A young, nearly naked Ophelia Harrington appeared, her hair in disarray, the tendons of her neck pulled taut as she struggled to escape the silk ropes that tied her to the auction block. The audio kicked in, and an Englishwoman's voice cried out in surround-sound glory, *"I had to fight to remember my humanity when all others saw me as something less!"*

Front and center, in strikingly designed lighting, hung the exhibit's new title:

THE COURTESAN CRUSADER: THE LIFE, LUST, AND LIBERATION OF OPHELIA HARRINGTON.

Piper heard the sound of shattering glass, and figured someone had dropped their highball. Claudia Harrington-Howell's face turned the color of half-dried cement. LaPaglia cried out like a man being pulled to pieces on the rack.

Piper flipped the switch that illuminated the six chambers of the exhibit, beckoning them in. No one moved. No one breathed.

She sighed and folded her hands upon the silk of her gown as she watched Claudia flee from the exhibit hall, holding a hand over her head as if she were at a loss for words at what she'd just seen, then parting the crowd with wide swings of her long arms.

Thirty-six

London

I took the stand in that daring crimson gown. My hair rippled loose down my back, a declaration as obvious as a pirate flag. I licked my lips and smiled at every man attending, daring them to deny that they wanted me. I even wiggled my fingers in greeting to a few blokes in the gallery, making their jaws drop as their friends punched their shoulders in congratulations.

The judge reddened beneath his powdered wig. Lord B—— glowered. Next to him, to my surprise, sat the man who'd come closest to caging the Blackbird. Lord C——. Ah. That explained a great deal. I had wondered where a wastrel like Lord B—— had gained the ear of the court. Lord C—— had power and wealth to spare for this act of vengeance. He glared at me malevolently.

Now I wished he'd been awake for Kiri's whipping. I thought of his reddened buttocks and smiled knowingly at him. His sneer faded slightly and his gaze shifted away.

As the trial continued, the London coroner stood to give his statement. I watched him with wide eyes and a sultry fingertip in my mouth. Barely able to tear his gaze from my bosom, he stammered over the lie about the suspicion of poison, turning such a furious shade of red that his testimony became entirely unbelievable.

My barrister, thrilled at the first chink in the prosecution's armor, leaped to his feet and began to rip the rest of the testimony to shreds. Unfortunately, he could only progress as far as turning "foul play" into "undetermined causes" before the judge shut him down with a glower and a blow of his gavel.

Next, I smiled through several gentlemen standing up and claiming that they had sometimes felt ill after dining or drinking in my presence. Since every one of them was an over-imbibing glutton, this fell somewhat flat upon the ears of those in the gallery, especially after the doubtfulness of the poison theory.

Wisely, the prosecution dropped that tactic and decided to concentrate upon the fact that I would inherit giant piles of gold from my alleged felony. I did my best to portray a woman who didn't need money, but the notion cost me a great deal of sympathy with the crowd. Neither a rich woman nor a gold digger was appreciated by the masses.

As the afternoon wore on, I struggled to maintain the Blackbird's saucy insouciance but my fury was growing. I no longer delighted in playing the coquette. I didn't want to disturb and manipulate. I wanted to be *believed*. Yet how could I ever be heard if I were not allowed to speak?

The prosecution's final statement was more twaddle about how I had seduced and manipulated an upstanding man, then poisoned him for profit. My barrister shuffled his papers for a moment, then shot me a hopeless glance.

That, I realized, was the last straw. Even my own defender did not think the fight worth fighting. In that moment I realized that the fight was *always* worth fighting. I glared at my barrister. "You're sacked." Then I stood. "I shall be making my own statement in my defense."

The judge shot a nervous glance in the direction of the seething Lord C——, then pounded his gavel. "You have not been asked to testify, Miss Harrington!"

I folded my arms, which incidentally displayed my bosom to perfection, and faced him down. "Why is that, my lord? Why have I not been allowed to speak? Do you not think that these fine citizens . . ."—I waved a graceful hand to the crowd in the gallery—"deserve to hear what I have to say?"

A grumbling began above us. The judge eyed Lord C—— and raised his gavel once more. Then his gaze was caught by, of all people, Lord Malcolm Ashford, now sitting in the area reserved for my supporters. I saw Lord Malcolm shake his head ever so slightly. The judge slowly lowered his gavel.

"Miss Harrington shall be allowed to speak," he said grudgingly.

I tilted my head. "Thank you, my lord." Not even the snoozing bailiff missed my ironic tone. "How nice to see that you are able to put the past behind you. I recall the first time I turned down your suit . . . and the second . . . and the third . . ."

Snickering began in the gallery, and in truth, on the bench itself. The judge flushed and shot his recorders each a quelling glare. "That is not pertinent to this trial, Miss Harrington!"

I smiled widely. "Isn't it? When we strip away all the lies, isn't that precisely what's behind this trial? You pledged your entire fortune for one night between my thighs. If I remember correctly, you even offered to clap your lady wife into an asylum so that I might take up residence in the Lord Recorder's House. How are your knees, my lord? As I recall, you spent a great deal of time on them, begging."

The judge's upper lip twitched and his knuckles whitened on the gavel, but he only shot a single livid glance at Lord Malcolm before he sank back warily.

Thus emboldened, I straightened in my box, determined to skewer the hypocrites, all of them. "My only crime has been to be a woman with a mind of my own. Because of that I stand accused of a murder I did not commit. And who are my accusers?"

I scanned the packed courtroom and pointed to the offenders.

"The judge, a man who has unsuccessfully courted me for more than a decade, a man known to grovel at my doorstep, only to burst into sobs when I sent him away. And the men bringing these charges . . ."

I pointed at the two men seated on the prosecution's side. "Here again we have two men whom I refused. Lord C—— paid Lord B—— to deliver me bound and bartered to his bed, so desperate was his obsession with me. Yet not even betrayal, silk ropes, and a guard outside the door could induce me to allow him to lay a finger upon me!"

The crowd loved it. I leaned my hands on the railing and leaned far forward, giving half the courtroom an instant erection. "How did you like being whipped, C——? You must have had to sit on a cushion for a month!"

Lord C—— paled at the roaring of the crowd, his face set in wrinkles of helpless fury. I turned my gaze upon Lord B——. "This is the wastrel who tried to sell me into sexual slavery years ago, only to beat me severely when I escaped his control."

The courtroom erupted into gasps and murmurs. Yet I was not done. I stood in the witness box and raised my voice high and clear. "Enlighten us, Lord B——. How did you explain your absence to your betrothed the day you drove me out to Lord C——'s orgy to sell me to the highest bidder?" Oh, I was so very finished with keeping all their dirty little secrets! "And that night, on the sixteenth of May, seven years ago, when you beat me nigh unto death? How did you explain away the bruises on your knuckles the next day?"

Alice's eyes widened and she turned to gaze at Lord B—— in alarm. He glared at me even as he patted her hand reassuringly.

I sneered at the bench and the prosecutor alike. "This trial is naught but a temper tantrum thrown by enraged and undisciplined little boys, all of whom are in dire need of a good spanking!"

I smirked at Lord C——. "Or in your case, my lord, *another* spanking!"

The gallery exploded with glee. I was aware of glares directed at me by several of the aforementioned gentlemen, but none were so malevolent as Lord B——'s blue gaze. He waited out the snickers and guffaws, never taking his eyes off me. Standing, he bowed unctuously to the judge. "My lord," he begged in his most earnest tones, "I beg to be allowed to refute such obvious lies."

The judge waved a hand. "Of course, boy. You have the right to speak on your own behalf."

Odd. Where was that right for me during the last two days?

Lord B—— nodded graciously. "I can prove that all this is nothing but the last desperate fabrication of a murderess about to be condemned. On the seventeenth of May seven years ago, I spent the entire afternoon with the woman who is now my affianced bride."

All eyes shot to Alice, whose pale face and vulnerable beauty made every man in the room bridle in her defense. Alice gazed back with horror at being made part of the spectacle. Lord B—— bent solicitously toward her.

"Do you not recall, my dear? That was the day I rescued that kitten from the thornbush. You bandaged my hand afterward."

Alice blinked and nodded. "I remember the kitten, of course. I still have that cat."

Her statement, uttered in her high, childish voice, brought an indulgent laugh from the crowd. I wanted to roll my eyes. What was it about spineless women that was so appealing? I would never understand.

Lord B—— straightened with a smile. "She bandaged my hand, my lord, so she could not have missed such bruising as Miss Harrington describes. It is all a lie."

The judge seized upon the notion eagerly. "Well, I have had enough of listening to this woman's mad falsehoods!" He raised his gavel. "I sentence thee—"

"Stop!"

Silence fell as all eyes turned. Lord Malcolm Ashford rose to stand before the bench.

Thirty-seven

Boston

Mick almost crashed into Claudia Harrington-Howell. She was hurrying from the museum's main lobby as he was racing in. The rigid set of the woman's jaw—and the echoing silence coming from the exhibit itself—told Mick all he needed to know.

He couldn't get to Piper fast enough. His heart felt as if it were ready to burst from his ribs. He loved her. He'd made the wrong decision. He hoped she'd forgive him.

Cullen had been right. For an educated man, Mick was a slow learner when it came to matters of the heart.

Mick weaved through the crowd of frozen, silent gala guests, most with their mouths hanging open, some holding cocktails in midair. Everyone had gone so still Mick felt as if he were navigating a maze of formal-wear mannequins. At last, he reached Piper's side.

She gave him an almost imperceptible shake of her head but didn't meet his gaze.

"I love you, Piper," Mick whispered directly into her ear. "I got off the plane in Chicago and turned around because I love you. I canceled the meeting in L.A. I was wrong to go."

Piper adjusted her stance, giving him the back of her elegant neck and magnificently bared shoulders. It might not have been the best time to get sidetracked like this, but Mick couldn't help but notice Piper's dress. It had a low, square neckline, a high waist, tight short sleeves, and yards of shimmering red satin with hints of black lace, and all of it hugged every curve of her bust before cascading loosely to the floor. He was no fashion historian, but to him it looked like something Ophelia Harrington might have worn in her courtesan days.

As he stared, Mick wanted desperately to stroke her right between her shoulder blades. Her skin looked as soft and juicy as a pale summer peach. Her dark hair was gently gathered up, tendrils falling soft at the nape of her neck.

She was so lovely. He felt like a complete shitehawk.

Mick noticed the crowd had begun to defrost. Murmuring started, followed by a few chuckles, then a wave of whispers. Suddenly, all hell broke loose, and Louis LaPaglia released a gurgling sound of fury as he pushed his way to the front, shouting for someone to turn off the exhibit lighting. Linc Northcutt volunteered so quickly and with such glee that Mick was worried he might wet himself with the excitement of it all.

"Piper," Mick whispered into her ear.

"I can handle this on my own," she said, speaking over her shoulder and over the noise of the crowd.

"I know there's nothing you can't handle on your own." Mick sighed. "But you don't have to, Piper. Not tonight. Not ever." He reached for her, brushing his fingers against her cool hand.

She spun around. Her expressive green eyes were on fire and her color was high. Mick knew with certainty that he'd never seen a woman as fiercely beautiful—or pissed—in all his life.

"Ladies and gentlemen! Please!" LaPaglia stood in front of the now-dim installation entrance and shouted over the crowd, waving his arms. "I apologize for the inconvenience, but *please*!" He tugged at his tuxedo collar as the panic raced across his mottled face. The guests only got louder.

"Everyone!" he shouted. "I must ask you to move into the lobby area!" LaPaglia gestured with both hands. "This way! Your cooperation is appreciated!"

Some of the guests—Piper's parents among them—turned and headed for the exit. Suddenly, an anonymous female voice rose above the din.

"Nobody's going anywhere!" It was Claudia Harrington-Howell. The crowd parted for her. She marched back into the exhibit hall, chiffon billowing out behind her.

LaPaglia's eyes bulged. "Er . . . ah . . . Claudia—"

"What idiot turned off the lights?"

"Please accept my sincerest apologies to your family and—"

"Oh, just shut the hell up and let's get on with the show." As Claudia adjusted her wire-rimmed eyeglasses, she accomplished what LaPaglia couldn't—the crowd went silent.

Claudia glanced around the hall and waved her hands. "What is wrong with you people? I ran to the limo to get my spectacles—can't see a damn thing without them."

She peered at the guests until she found Piper off to the side, near the wall. "Come on up here, Miss Chase-Pierpont, and somebody, for God's sake, turn on the damn lights!"

With a barely audible squeak, Piper stepped forward and went to stand near Claudia. Mick watched the two women square off, the high-heeled and elegant Piper nearly as tall as the statuesque silver-haired Claudia. Their eyes locked on to one another.

"I will tour the exhibit momentarily," Claudia said, her eyes unflinching. "But right now, you are going to explain to me how you can possibly make such a claim about my ancestor."

LaPaglia couldn't keep quiet. "Ms. Harrington-Howell, on behalf of the museum trustees, staff, and donors, I want to express to you how profoundly sorry I am for—"

"Eee-nough!" She snapped her head toward LaPaglia.

Mick was afraid for the man—Claudia Harrington-Howell looked like she could kick his arse to kingdom come as an afterthought.

LaPaglia must have reached the same conclusion. "Of course," he muttered, shuffling backward until he bumped into someone.

"How?" Claudia asked Piper.

"Uh," Piper croaked, then cleared her throat and started over. "I found Ophelia Harrington's diaries from the years she spent as a courtesan in London," Piper said matter-of-factly. "They were hidden in a false bottom of a trunk."

A collective gasp went up from the attendees.

Oddly enough, Claudia did not seem shocked. Mick detected the beginning of a smile at her lips. "Where are the diaries now?"

Piper gestured toward the exhibit entrance. "Under Plexiglas within the exhibit. I made a copy of the diaries for you as well."

"What the hell is she talking about?" LaPaglia didn't even bother to keep his voice down. "What diaries?"

Claudia nodded sharply. "What do the diaries reveal? Tell me. A snapshot will do for now."

Piper chuckled nervously. Mick figured she was thinking the same thing he was—that distilling Ophelia's story into a "snapshot" was damn near impossible. It had been hard enough to pare it down to a single museum installation.

He watched Piper search the crowd for her parents. She found them holding each other up near the exhibit hall exit, their faces ashen.

"The diaries tell the story of a young woman unwilling to stifle her spirit, her intellect, or her sexuality simply because it was expected of her." Piper smiled sadly at her parents as she finished the sentence. Then she continued.

"Ophelia became a highly prized courtesan living outside the social norms of her time, and though it was a life of pleasure and adventure, it grew stale eventually. She longed for what many of us long for—meaningful work, a family of her own, and a life partnership based on love and mutual respect."

No one breathed.

"And this?" Claudia gestured behind her to the life-sized image of Ophelia in chains. The older woman's eyebrows arched dramatically on her forehead. "Explain this."

Piper nodded. "My central question—and probably yours as well—was how did a London courtesan become a Boston abolitionist? And the answer is twofold."

Piper reached for Claudia's forearm and pulled her to the side so that she, and the rest of the assembled guests, could see the central display in all its glory.

She went on, looking at Claudia as she spoke. "Your great-great-grandmother possessed the courage to battle American slavery because her life as a courtesan gave her a taste of personal freedom. She came to believe that freedom was a God-given right that should be available to all human beings, including women and the enslaved."

Piper paused, noting that several attendees had begun to nod in appreciation. "But that wasn't the only reason," she said. "There was a single defining moment in Ophelia's life, a moment so horrifying, it changed her forever. And a seed of outrage was planted inside her that allowed her to blossom from courtesan to crusader."

Claudia's eyes shot to the image of Ophelia. "What happened to her?"

Piper nodded, and it looked to Mick as if she were steeling herself for the last bit. "Though it was only the barest taste of human bondage, Ophelia Harrington had been placed on the auction block herself, treated as an animal, or worse—a commodity—and sold to the highest bidder. It happened when she was taken to an orgy and sold as a sex slave."

Piper's mother fainted. A woman cried out. The murmurs grew into exclamations of shock and shouts of disbelief.

Piper craned her neck to make sure her mother got back

on her feet. "Does anyone have a Three Musketeers bar?" she asked the crowd. "A Snickers?"

"I've got a Butterfinger, but it's only Fun Size!" A man toward the back held up the telltale yellow wrapper.

"Thank you," Piper said. "That's just what we need right now—more fun."

Thirty-eight

London

My gaze locked on Lord Malcolm's even as my heart stumbled in its beating. He held my eyes with his as he continued.

"Lord B—— blamed Miss Harrington for his inability to pay his debts with the money he was to get for selling her. I saw him enter Miss Harrington's house well past midnight. I—I did not follow him inside until I heard her scream. Then I entered to find Lord B—— standing above Miss Harrington with a knife in his hand. She lay insensible on the floor, having been most severely beaten."

"Not unconscious," I added. "Not quite yet."

His eyes darkened. "It all happened so quickly," he said softly.

"You could not have known," I said. I turned to the judge. "Lord B—— was preparing to slice my face to ribbons, my lord. I did not see who it was that pulled him away from me." I let my eyes rest on Lord B——. "But I definitely recall that Lord B—— ran from the room like the filthy coward he is, only brave enough to brutalize those weaker than himself."

A growl began in the gallery, a sign that public opinion was about to turn against Lord B—— forever.

From my place on the stand, I watched the bewildered green eyes of Miss Alice Wainwright as she heard her fiancé accused. *Don't be a fool, Alice!*

When I saw her confusion turn to stubborn denial, I had

to speak. "My lords, whether or not I am declared innocent, I must do this."

I turned to Alice. "*Run*. Run for your life from this man." She drew back from my intensity. I gripped the railing until my knuckles paled. "Don't you realize that you're free? No matter the splitting of the inheritance, you are a wealthy woman in your own right."

She bit her lip. I softened my voice. "I know you're frightened. I know it's terrifying to be alone. But please believe me, you are better off alone than with this man. Leave him. Take your father's fortune. And *run*."

I could not be sure that she heard me, but there was nothing else I could say to persuade her. I turned back to the judge. "You may continue with your sentencing now."

His eyes narrowed. "Why, thank you, Miss Harrington."

We all waited. I could scarcely breathe. The judge raised his gavel.

"Stop!"

Thirty-nine

Boston

Though LaPaglia seemed dangerously close to a nervous breakdown while waiting for Piper and Claudia to complete their private tour, Mick noticed that not a single gala guest left the museum, not even Piper's parents. They chatted excitedly, drained the bar dry, and consumed every single cheese puff and bacon-wrapped shrimp in the joint.

The break gave Mick a chance to get some air and think things through. He sat on the brick edging of a raised garden in the museum's courtyard, watching the night clouds obscure the moon, and thought about Piper, how beautiful she looked that night, and how he'd mucked things up something awful.

"Mind if I join you?"

Mick looked up to find Brenna standing behind him, cool and ethereal in a silvery cocktail dress, her blond hair pulled back from her face. "Sure," Mick said. "Grab a brick."

Brenna did, settling down with a sigh. "Good of you to join us."

Mick snorted. "Yes, I was a complete tool for going to L.A. I'm aware of that."

Brenna smiled at him pleasantly and folded her hands in her lap. She was as cool a slice as ever, Mick decided, but she was a devoted friend to Piper, and for that he was grateful.

"Do you love her?"

Mick nearly choked at the bluntness of the question, but he supposed it was fair, considering his actions. "I do. I love that woman."

"Good, because she deserves nothing less. She's waited a long time for you."

Mick sighed, letting that sink in. After a moment, he chuckled.

"Something funny?" she asked, looking at him sideways.

"You know, ever since I got on that damned plane I've been thinking how I don't want to lose her. I can't imagine my life without her now. I'm not even sure I want that stupid cable show if she isn't in my life to share it with me."

Brenna nodded.

"I want to marry her," Mick said. It didn't even surprise him to hear the words come from his mouth. They'd been forming in his brain since his talk with Cullen that morning. "I want all those things Piper just talked about—the love and mutual respect, the family, the meaningful work—and I know in my heart that I'm supposed to have them with her."

Brenna raised an eyebrow. "I'm not the one who should be hearing this."

Mick nodded. Brenna was right. "Do you think she'd say yes?"

She shrugged.

"I have half a mind to charge right in there and ask her in front of everybody."

"Hmm," Brenna said, looking him over from tip to toe. "I'm not sure you have what it takes for that."

Mick laughed in surprise. "So you don't think I have the balls, eh?"

"No," she said. "I don't think you have the *ring.*"

Mick had no response for that.

"Here. If you're serious, you can borrow this for the occasion." Brenna tugged at her right hand, then dropped a delicate gold ring into his palm, its cluster of diamonds sparkling in the dark. Mick looked at her in shock.

"Are you sure?" he asked.

Brenna laughed. "I'm sure you can borrow it for the occasion, yes, but are you sure this is what you want to do?"

Mick stood up. He pocketed the ring and offered his arm to Brenna. "I'm sure," he said. "Shall we?"

Forty

"Oh, for pity's sake!" I murmured at yet another interruption. We all turned to stare at the latest savior.

Miss Alice Wainwright stood slowly. From my vantage point I could see that she was shaking with nerves.

Lord B—— looked wary. "My love—"

Alice took a single decisive step to the left, away from him, and lifted her chin. "I drop all charges!" She shot a look of loathing at Lord B——. "I just recalled that I was given that kitten in March, not May," she snarled. "In May, you told me you hurt your hand when you were thrown from a horse." Her eyes narrowed. "One of my *mother's* horses, who are the most perfectly trained beasts in all of England!"

With that she turned her back on Lord B—— and addressed the judge in a quavering voice that grew stronger with every word. "My father was a good and wise man. He believed Miss Harrington to be a trustworthy person. I intend to abide by his good opinion and withdraw the charges—which I didn't truly wish to press, anyway. Without my charges, there is no case." Another scathing glance at Lord B——. "And if my father was right about Miss Harrington, then it follows that he was right about Lord B——. I am officially breaking our engagement, my lord."

Relief made me smile. Alice was going to be all right. I

gazed at my attacker. "It looks like you'll have to find another girl to believe your lies, my lord."

Lord Malcolm Ashford folded his arms. "Actually, you'll find that difficult to do in debtor's prison, B——."

Lord B——'s eyes widened. "But I—"

Lord Malcolm's smile did not reach his eyes. "It seems that the man who bought up all your notes demands immediate payment of them. If you don't have three thousand, two hundred and eighteen pounds in your pocket at this very moment, I'm afraid you'll be accompanying these nice bailiffs across the street to Newgate in a few minutes."

Lord B—— backed away from the approaching bailiffs. "Who—"

"Who holds your vowels?" Malcolm casually straightened his cuffs. "Why, as of six o'clock this morning, that would be me."

As Lord B—— was led out of the Bailey, I called out to him. "Just grab the first pallet you see. No one will mind."

The judge, being quite satisfied that he'd backed the right horse after all, smiled benevolently as he banged the gavel one last time.

"Case dismissed!"

Forty-one

Piper felt giddy by the time she and Claudia finished their walk-through. She'd asked Piper dozens of questions and admitted that she was secretly thrilled that the whispers passed down in her family about Ophelia's wild past had been true after all.

"If it weren't for her, I'm afraid the Harringtons would go down in history as a bunch of insufferable bores," Claudia had said with a wink.

Before the two of them returned to the exhibit entrance and the gala crowd, Claudia pulled her aside. "How did you manage it?" she asked, real wonder in her eyes. "I know the old farts on your board would never let you do this sort of thing, and LaPaglia looked like he'd been hit by a bus at the unveiling, so how did you do it?"

Piper gave that question some thought. "Friends . . . and luck," she said. "But I had a lot of help and encouragement from my friends."

Claudia smiled. "I just bet your dark-haired Irishman was a great source of encouragement. I don't think I've seen a man look finer in a tuxedo in all my life, and believe me when I tell you that I've seen plenty of men in tuxedos in my seventy-eight years."

Piper giggled, then automatically began searching for Mick in the crowd. She saw him making his way through the lobby with Brenna at his side, marching purposefully her way. His eyes briefly caught hers before she looked away.

"He nearly knocked me over running in here, you know. He looked worried that he was too late."

Piper chewed her lip. Oddly enough, she'd not been the least bit nervous leading up to the big moment, probably because she'd been too busy. But now that it had passed, she felt unsettled—likely because she now had time to worry about Mick.

The exhibit entrance began to fill with people again, and Claudia asked them all to be quiet.

"I daresay this was quite a surprise." Claudia paused to dab at her eyes. "But I believe that all of us need a little surprise in our lives. It keeps you young."

Piper tried her best to focus on Claudia's off-the-cuff commentary, but she sensed Mick's eyes on her, hot and intense. She allowed herself a quick peek.

Oh God, he came back to me. He got off the plane. He gave up everything to be here. I can't be angry with him. Why would I even want to be angry with him? I love him. And why is Brenna smiling at me like that?

Piper refocused just as Claudia reached the apex of her speech. ". . . further proof that women are rarely the paper dolls they're made out to be in the history books. Ophelia Harrington was a dignified and brilliant woman with a true lust for life. She should be an inspiration to all of us. I know I'm terribly proud to be her descendant. And I would like to personally thank Piper Chase-Pierpont for having the courage to tell Ophelia's full story to the world. Piper?"

Suddenly, applause broke out. A few people even whistled. Piper was shocked, and for a moment she felt lost.

"Go on and say something." Claudia nudged her forward. "This is your night as much as it is Ophelia's."

Forty-two

I stepped down from the defendant's box and slowly crossed the courtroom of the Old Bailey. All around me, people whispered and some even smiled congratulations my way, but my gaze was riveted on the tall, dark figure still standing by the judge's bench.

Lord Malcolm Ashford, the man I'd fled twelve years before, waited for me—with Sir's smile on his magnificent lips.

I stopped before him and tilted my head. Images of the two men, one arrogant stranger and one tender lover, flashed back and forth in my mind before resolving into a single, inconceivable whole.

My breath left me in a long sigh. "I am going to kill the Swan."

Lord Malcolm's smile flashed white. "She only did as I asked. I had no choice, you see. From the moment I looked across a ballroom and spotted a black-haired beauty with a red rose in her hair, I belonged to her. It simply took some time to understand that she would never belong to me."

Regret swam through me. "I judged you harshly."

He shook his head. "You judged me most perceptively. I was an ass. I convinced myself that my longing for you was nothing more than desire for another acquisition. I had the Swan arrange matters, hoping that your adventure with Sir would satisfy your curiosity and you would decide to wed me after all."

Frowning, I fought to iron out these new wrinkles in the past. "My training was a lie."

He snorted. "You've been the Blackbird for a decade. I'd say your training was most legitimate."

I blinked. "But the Seven Sins?"

He glanced away with an abashed twist to his lips. "Ah, well . . . some of it I learned through extensive reading. Some I fabricated on the spot."

Outrage flared within me at his deception, then just as quickly burned away. Whatever we had done, we had simply been trying to find our way to this moment. I was not the reckless girl of twelve years past. He was not the arrogant cad.

I held out my hand to him. "Hello, Lord Malcolm. I am Ophelia."

He took my hand in his large, warm one and smiled. "Hello, Ophelia. I am in love with you."

Somewhere deep inside I had always known this, yet to hear it aloud made my eyes dampen. "The sentiment is most sincerely mutual, my lord."

His dark hazel eyes, so nearly black, flashed at this. "Then I have something I wish to ask." He reached into the small pocket sewn into his weskit. Still holding my hand in his, he pressed an object, warm and hard and circular, into my palm.

I held a ring of ruby. The large oval stone was as red as a kiss and the shimmering diamonds encircling it were reminiscent of the petals of a flower. "You carried this ring to a murder trial?"

A flash of anguish crossed his face. "I have carried that ring every moment of the last twelve years. I bought it the day after I first saw you at the ball. The ruby reminded me of the rose gleaming in your black hair."

My heart thudded and my vision swam, yet a small laugh bubbled up from somewhere perverse. "Goodness. I truly made you pay for that 'transaction' remark, didn't I?"

He bowed his head slightly. "No more than I deserved."

He'd said he had a question for me. Looking down at the ring resting in the palm of my hand, I felt dizzy with the thing that I must now do. I reached for his hand and pressed the ring back into it. His fingers clung to mine as I pulled them away.

"Ophelia." His voice dropped to Sir's husky murmur. "I love you. I have loved you for a dozen years. After all, I followed you to this moment, didn't I?"

I drew back regretfully. "I have loved you all these years as well, but I cannot go back to that world. Being someone I am not nearly suffocated me during the trial." I took a single agonizing step away. "I cannot be your Lady Ashford."

He stepped forward, closing the distance between us. "Could you be Mrs. Harrington?"

I blinked. "Then who would you be?"

Malcolm took my hands and enfolded them in his own. "With two elder brothers with sons of their own, I am not in the line of succession to my father's title." He shrugged. "I will be Mr. Harrington." Then he grinned wickedly. "But you may call me 'Sir.'"

Forty-three

Boston

Piper sought out Brenna's beaming face, then Mick's sweet smile. She saw her parents' stunned expressions. She noticed Linc Northcutt hanging around the doorway, pure disgust on his face. It made her laugh.

"I am the one who's surprised," she managed. "I knew I had to the tell the truth about Ophelia, but I was convinced the truth would not be welcome here. It appears I sold Ms. Harrington-Howell short, along with the BMCS board of trustees, and for that, I apologize. I do hope you all enjoy the exhibit."

Piper began to slink away when Mick's voice boomed over the hum of the crowd.

"Just one more surprise, if I may!"

Piper's mouth unhinged as Mick jogged toward her. He came to stand at her side and addressed the thoroughly flummoxed crowd.

"I'll let you get to the exhibit in a flash, but first, there's something important I need to do."

Mick lowered himself on one knee and reached for Piper's left hand. Her head began to spin. This could not be happening. There was no way . . .

A ruckus rose from the crowd, but a few sharp *shh*-ings put an end to the noise, and the room went silent. Piper quickly glanced up at Brenna, who was crying. Piper had never once seen her best friend cry.

Suddenly, an elderly gentleman shouted, "This is the best damn Fall Gala I've ever attended!" As the laughter rose and fell, Mick continued to hold Piper's left hand, stroking her flesh with his thumb as he gazed up into her eyes.

"Oh my God," she breathed.

Mick grinned up at her, and she knew that if she hoped to remain standing she needed to focus on his handsome face, his soulful blue eyes, his perfect, smiling mouth.

"Piper Chase-Pierpont, I love you. You are the most incredible woman I have ever known."

As Mick pulled a dainty gold ring from his trouser pocket, Piper realized she was light-headed, that no oxygen was making it to her brain. She told herself to snap out of it—there was no freaking way she would space out during the most romantic moment of her life.

"Please marry me, Piper. Be my wife. Give me that honor."

She opened her mouth to speak. Nothing came out. Mick waited patiently, his smile never letting up.

"Yes," she eventually whispered. "Yes, yes, *yes*!"

VOLUME IV

Forty-four

Mick reached for the doorknocker, the solid brass of the lion's head shining in the morning sunshine. "Charming little hovel she's got here."

Piper chuckled. Claudia's Beacon Hill monstrosity had been the home she'd shared with her beloved Theron Howell, who'd owned a chain of New England sawmills. Though he'd long been dead, his money and Claudia continued on here. Piper smiled up at Mick, recalling how she'd been similarly wowed the first time she'd seen the place.

"Still no idea why we've been summoned to the manse?" he asked.

"Nope," Piper said.

The imposing door opened, and Claudia appeared in all her silver-headed glory. "Fabulous!" she said, ushering them in. "Let's have our little get-together in the parlor, shall we?"

Claudia gestured toward a set of gilded double doors. Piper felt Mick stiffen the moment they stepped into the room.

"Make yourselves comfortable. I'll be right back." She swooped out into the hallway.

Mick studied the heavy brocade drapes, the heirloom carpets, and the groupings of little straight-backed chairs and shook his head. "Where exactly are we supposed to get comfortable?" he whispered.

Piper elbowed him. "Whatever we're here for, I'm sure it won't take long."

He scoped out a dainty velvet love seat and settled in. Piper squeezed in next to him and clasped her hands in her lap.

Claudia reappeared, a silver tea tray in her hands.

Mick attempted to stand again. "Let me help you with—"

"Oh, don't be silly. You're my guests. Sit. Sit."

Within seconds Claudia had arranged the tray of cookies and tea things on a small table near the love seat. "Help yourself." She sprawled back in a chair, her silk drawstring trousers cascading softly around her long legs, one arm draped over the chair back. "Well, how are you two? Glad all the excitement is behind you?"

Piper sneaked a quick glance at Mick and couldn't help but giggle. Claudia's statement wasn't accurate by any stretch— their lives were a whirlwind of combining households, planning a wedding, and plotting out the first season of Mick's cable show. The producers thought Mick's profane ultimatum and return to Boston were part of the negotiation, and doubled his per-episode offer. Piper and Mick were set to meet the cable executives the following week—in New York. She didn't correct her hostess, however.

Claudia poured herself a cup of tea and added two sugars. "I wanted to talk to you about the board of trustees situation. You must know that Forsythe has been riding my ass nonstop since the exhibit opened."

Piper sat up straighter. "Uh, Claudia, I really don't have anything to do with—"

"Why would I want to be on that board? I plan to continue my travels and I certainly don't want to be tied down to insufferable meetings that only provide a venue for rich old men to drop names and get all tingly from the sound of their own voices."

"Actually—"

Claudia waved her hand through the air, stopping Piper.

"Oh, I know you quit your job. Good for you, though you'll be missed, I'm sure. I wanted to ask you to deliver this check to them."

Claudia reached for an envelope she'd tucked under the cookie plate and handed it to Piper. "They don't want me, anyway. They just want my money. There's enough in there to do something flashy—a new wing, a few new curators— frankly, I don't care how it's spent as long as the Ophelia Harrington exhibit is made permanent. Oh! And I want them to redo that phone operator show from last year— thought it was to die for!"

Piper considered the envelope, then Claudia, then Mick, and the envelope again. She didn't know which was funnier— that Linc Northcutt would be in charge of the Ophelia Har- rington exhibit—*in perpetuity,* no less—or that LaPaglia would have to restage the switchboard girls. Piper couldn't suppress her smile. "That's very kind of you, Claudia. I'm sure Mr. Forsythe will call you immediately."

Claudia let go with a dramatic sigh. "All right, kids. Now I can get to the real business at hand." She pushed herself up from her chair. "Don't go anywhere!"

After she'd darted from the room once more, Mick mumbled, "How much is in there?"

Piper peeked, reading the check upside down. She gasped. "Sixteen million."

"Dollars?" Mick squinted one eye.

Almost immediately, Claudia was back. She held a leather-bound book in one hand and a small velvet box in the other. Piper had no idea what the woman was up to.

She arranged herself comfortably again and held out an obviously old book. The tiny hairs on Piper's forearm stood straight up, like they'd been electrically charged.

"I thought you needed to see this," she said.

Piper accepted the book. It was just slightly larger than Ophelia's diaries had been, and featured a thick, masculine band of gilding along the edge. Slowly, it began to dawn on her. Could this really be . . . ?

"Before you read what's in there, I need to tell you a story." Claudia cleared her throat and raised her chin.

"When I was a small child, I was prone to spending hour upon hour by myself, playing with my dolls and making up imaginary friends and stories. I wouldn't say I was a lonely child, but I was left to fend for myself often." She stopped and pointed at Mick. "Dr. Malloy, you never got yourself a cup of tea."

Mick immediately reached for the teapot and poured.

"So, one of my favorite hiding places was the attic in my grandmother's house on Bowdoin Street—which was once Ophelia and Malcolm's home, as you know. One day right after the war, I found this journal in a trunk. If I'm not mistaken, it was the very same trunk I gave you, Piper, with the false bottom you discovered."

Claudia paused. "Anyone like a cookie?"

Piper and Mick shook their heads rapidly. The leather journal, now balanced on Piper's knees, felt like it was burning a hole in the top of her thighs.

"So I began reading this, and I must say, it was a story that changed my life. You see, I was quite susceptible to fairy stories and happily-ever-afters when I was a little girl, so I became fascinated with the lifelong love affair he described."

When Piper carefully lifted the front cover with a fingertip, a single line of scrawl was revealed: *"Malcolm Harrington."* Piper's mouth had gone painfully dry. "Is it really his diary?" she managed to ask.

Claudia smiled kindly. "Go ahead and open it, dear."

"I don't have any gloves!"

Claudia chuckled. "Sweetheart, I've been carrying that book around with me for seventy years and I've never worn gloves. It's old, yes, and I'll let you take better care of it from now on, but please don't worry too much right now."

Piper nodded. Mick scooted closer and helped support the spine as Piper slowly opened the front cover.

"You'll notice that all the pages are blank except for the

first few," Claudia said. Piper confirmed that and turned to the first page.

The writing was shaky, but broad and masculine all the same. It was not Ophelia's familiar script. There was no title page or introduction, and Piper noted that the first entry was dated just days after Ophelia's recorded death.

Suddenly, Piper froze. It hit her hard. These were Malcolm's words in her hands, what she had so longed to see. These were the thoughts and secrets of his heart, the heart of a man who could walk the earth as pompous Lord Ashford, Sir, and Mr. Harrington, all in the span of one lifetime.

And now, she would finally get to meet him.

Mick used his free hand to pat Piper's knee. "Shall I read aloud?" he asked. She nodded. Mick began, his Irish brogue soft and husky.

I am old and weary, but grateful for every day I've had. Ophelia has left me behind. She was always the first to leap. How empty the world seems. Her love never faltered and her lusty laughter never faded. I can hear her even now.

It is not every man who is fortunate to be loved as I was loved. Even in our wildest days, I treasured every moment with her.

It still stuns me that I nearly ruined my future with my arrogance. One night, I spotted an exhilarating creature across a ballroom and I had to possess her. When buying her hand in marriage didn't work, I sought to conquer her in secret.

It was I who was conquered. In just seven nights, that fledgling goddess not only discovered that I had a heart, but she stole it forever, then cradled it in the palm of her hand.

"Tissue?" Claudia asked, holding out a box to Piper. She hadn't realized she'd been crying.

"Thanks," she said, grabbing a handful.

"Nothing to be ashamed of, sweetheart. I've been reading this since I was eight and it breaks me up every time." Claudia sighed. "It spoiled me, you know. When I eventually went looking for a husband, I envisioned Malcolm Harrington. Ha! It certainly narrowed the field of suitors. Thank God I found my Terry."

Claudia stopped then, looking at Piper and Mick as if they'd been the ones to put a halt to the narration. "Well, continue," she said, relaxing into her chair again.

Mick cleared his throat.

Ophelia embraced her new life and moved on. For nearly twelve years I waited for her to be ready to settle her heart on me, not realizing that I was the one who did not yet know how to love without ownership, to adore without possession, to support without expectation.

My gut still goes cold when I remember the night I saw Lord B—— enter Ophelia's house. I was so racked with jealousy that I had already begun to walk away. But I turned around. I went to her because she needed me. Looking back, I believe that was the moment I stopped living like a reckless, self-centered fool, and began to live like a man.

Life is so fragile and happiness so fleeting. How fortunate I am to have had so much of both, on two continents. With my Ophelia.

We came to America and raised a family with love. We survived our brave William's death. We lived to see the emancipation through. Times have changed and they are changing still. The struggle for freedom, I suspect, will go on for many years. I do believe it is the central struggle of our time.

I have never forgotten Ophelia's call to arms. I watched as she stood before a crowd for the first time and delivered what would become her signature speech on the rights of all humans. Her passionate words burned. Her intellect defied their rules and smashed through their judgment. She was a woman, alone and in public, who dared to speak her mind. As her husband, I cared nothing for others' opinion of my decision to stand behind her as she took center stage. It was no sacrifice. It was my honor. That night, I saw her anew. I fell in love with her once more. That was the night she taught the world that it was impossible to own a human being.

Of course, I had learned my version of that lesson long ago. To have owned her would have destroyed her.

Piper blew her nose with enthusiasm, drowning out Mick's next words. "Sorry," she said, taking a sip of her tea. He repeated the sentence.

It is not difficult to understand why Ophelia worked so hard for the freedom of all human beings. Freedom has always been at the heart of everything she desired. She would smile at that and say, "Damn the cost."

Although Ophelia never regretted her life in London, she feared her past would detract attention from the cause, so her story has been hidden. I hope it emerges someday when the world is ready for a woman with a mind of her own.

Mick's voice trailed off. He examined the next few pages. Piper heard him sniffle. "That's it?" he asked, his voice plaintive and his eyes wide. "There isn't any more? It just ends like that?"

Claudia dabbed at her nose and nodded.

"He died that very night," Piper answered softly. "He must have finished writing in his new diary, gone to bed, and joined his Ophelia forever."

"Precisely," Claudia said.

The three of them sat in silence for a moment, Mick still staring at the book in his hands.

"May I?" Claudia reached out and Mick handed over the journal. She placed it on the table at her side. "Well, then, I know you two have better things to do than spend an entire afternoon with some crazy old lady, but there is just one more thing you might do for me."

Piper roused herself from her thoughts, her sadness, and her awe at what she'd just heard. "Of course," she said.

Claudia reached for the small velvet box. "Now, as you know, I am the last direct descendant of Ophelia and Malcolm Harrington. My husband and I were never blessed with children."

Mick and Piper shot each other a quizzical glance.

"I understand the ring you slipped on Piper's hand the other night was a loan for that rather spontaneous occasion." Claudia grinned. "My question is, have you selected a permanent one?"

Mick and Piper looked at each other again, this time with incomprehension.

"Uh . . ." Piper said.

Mick laughed. "We haven't had time, Claudia. We've barely had time to even discuss it."

"Oh goody," Claudia said. "If you are so inclined, then, I would like you to have this." She handed the box to Mick.

It balanced there on the center of his palm, but he didn't move, didn't speak. Piper held her breath.

"One of the many fascinating things I learned from Ophelia's diaries, Piper, is that this is the very ring Malcolm carried around in his pocket for a dozen years. My guess is that he had it engraved at a later date, perhaps even after they came to Boston, since the words reflect the nature of their hard-won love for each other."

Mick and Piper said nothing. They just stared at the box.

"Well, open it, for God's sake."

Mick looked up to Piper and she shrugged—she truly didn't know what to do at that point. He grabbed the lid and carefully pried it open, the velvet exterior and the satin lining shredded with time.

Piper sucked in air. Mick shifted on the love seat. Inside the box was a stunning oval-shaped ruby surrounded by more than a dozen small but blindingly clear diamonds, set on a substantial rose-gold band. It had to be worth a fortune.

"Claudia, this is so incredibly thoughtful of you, but this is a family heirloom and—"

"What? It should sit on a velvet cushion in a glass case and never ride again on the hand of a woman in love? Before you say no, remember that I have no one to pass it on to. Piper, you have shed light on Malcolm and Ophelia's story and it does not escape me that it took a great deal of courage to do so. I know of no other woman who should wear this ring, and, truly, I think Ophelia would want you to have it."

Piper's mouth fell wide, then snapped shut. "It's too much," she said. "I am flattered that you would want me to have it, but—"

"I'll buy it," Mick said simply. "Name your price and I'll pay it."

"Mick—"

"No, love. Claudia's right. You should have this ring. It's supposed to be yours."

"But—"

"Then that settles it," Claudia said, standing as if there were nothing left to discuss. "And my price is a dollar. Do you happen to have that kind of cash on you?"

Mick laughed. "By God, I believe you've caught me on a flush day," he said.

Claudia put her head back and roared. "Fine, then." She took a few steps toward the parlor door. "You two spend as much time here as you'd like. I have a few phone calls to return."

They both stood. "Thank you, Claudia—" Piper didn't even have a chance to finish her sentence. Claudia was already down the hall. They stared at the empty doorway for several seconds.

Eventually, Mick let go with a long, low whistle, then said, "Holy feckin' Jaysus H. . . ."

"On a pogo stick," Piper added.

They turned to each other, stunned. "What are we going to do?" Piper asked.

"I've got a great idea," Mick said, reaching into the velvet box. He placed the sparkling gold and jewels at the very tip of her ring finger.

"Wait!" Piper said.

"Ah, the truth comes out!" Mick said. "Which have you changed your mind about—the ring or wanting to be married to me?"

Piper laughed. "I just want to see the engraving inside."

"Right."

Mick leaned down near Piper's face, turning the inside of the gold band toward the light.

"Latin," Mick said.

"Una in sublime ferimur," Piper read.

Their eyes met. Piper saw everything she loved in Mick in that single shared glance—his intelligence, his humor, the depth of his understanding. She knew her smile was as big as his.

As he slid the ring down onto her finger, they spoke the English translation at the same time.

"Together, we soar."

Epilogue

Malloy's Pub buzzed with activity. The crew from Compass Cable Network were crammed into a semicircle in the bar's tiny dining room, along with their light stands, cameras, and endless bundles of electric cables. Though Mick could scarcely believe it, they were about to film the fifth-anniversary kickoff segment for *Digging for the Truth with Piper and Mick Malloy.*

Perched on their usual stools, their backs to the bar, Mick and Piper submitted to last-minute touch-ups. Piper shot a smile Mick's way, indicating that she was trying to be patient while the makeup artist powdered her cheeks and the hair guru foostered about with her long ponytail, draping it over one of her shoulders. Mick watched as the wardrobe stylist had a go at her next, doing his magic with safety pins and masking tape in an attempt to limit the way her shirt gaped at the neck.

Piper sighed. "Don't get stressed over this, guys," she told the stylists. "I'm only going to look sleek from the shoulders up."

"You're the most sleek, gorgeous, extremely pregnant woman I've ever seen," Mick assured her, reaching over and laying his hand on her protruding belly. "You are a fine creature, indeed, Mrs. Malloy."

Piper laughed. "Relax the cacks, Magnus. This is a family show."

Cullen suddenly hoisted himself up and plopped belly-first on the bar, shoving his head between them. He kissed Piper on the cheek. "They're lined up halfway around the block," he said, giddiness in his voice. "This is going to be the biggest send-off yet!"

Mick's brother slid back onto his mark behind the bar—center stage, as he called it—and began chatting it up with everyone in sight. Like every year, Cullen had ramped up his Irish accent for filming. He claimed it added ambiance and had helped make Malloy's Pub a Boston tourism destination. (Graciously, he admitted that four seasons on cable TV hadn't hurt, either.)

The director called for everyone's attention, and within minutes, the cameras were rolling.

"Thanks for joining us for another season of *Digging for the Truth*," Mick read off the teleprompter. "As always, Piper and I are celebrating our return to our home turf with a stop at Malloy's Pub on Broad Street in Boston."

That was Cullen's cue to stroll into the picture, slap a bar towel over his shoulder, and greet the audience as he pulled a pint or two.

Piper did her part next. "It's been an incredible year of adventure, discovery, and surprise for us—Peru, Istanbul, the snow-packed Swiss Alps, New Orleans, Mackinac Island, Michigan—we've covered a lot of miles this season, and we can't wait to show you what we've been up to."

Mick smiled. "Like we say every year, we've got the best jobs in the world!"

Piper nodded and smiled easily. "And this year, we managed to bring home the single greatest treasure of all." The cameras pulled back for a wider picture and Piper pointed to her baby bump.

Mick leaned in and placed a quick kiss on Piper's tummy. "Our little girl is already a seasoned world traveler, but we're almost certain the three of us met last fall, right here in good ole Boston."

"Go, Sox!" Cullen shouted out from behind the bar, which whipped the pub customers into a frenzy. As always, Cullen's off-script additions were what made these hometown kickoff shows among the highest rated of the season.

It took nearly two hours to wrap up filming, and by then Piper was clearly stiff and exhausted, though she tried hard to keep smiling. Mick helped her down from her stool while he rubbed her lower back. Though they had a few weeks before their daughter was due to make her grand entrance, Piper had been experiencing odd little tugs and twinges all week, making them wonder if Ophelia Malloy, like her namesake, might have already decided to do things her own way.

"I'll get the car," Mick whispered in her ear.

"No." Piper pulled at his shirtsleeve. "Let's walk. It'll do me good."

They made their way through the pub crowd, stopping to hug Cullen and Em and the kids and everyone else who wanted to give their congratulations. Once outside, they turned in the opposite direction of the crowd and made slow progress toward their parking spot four blocks away. Without planning it, they found themselves standing before the brightly lit windows of Beantown Books, the site of their first date. Their first kiss. Their first glimpse of what was possible for their lives.

Mick and Piper were quiet, the warm interior light spilling onto their faces, their arms around each other. Right there at eye level was a three-foot-long display banner that read:

UNBOUND
BY PIPER MALLOY AND OPHELIA HARRINGTON

Mick glanced down at his wife, noting the glow of satisfaction on her chubby cheeks. The bestselling hardcover had been on the shelves for months now, but like most everything in their shared life, the joy of Piper's success still felt brand-new.

"It's ironic, isn't it?" Mick asked, pulling Piper closer. "Ophelia once said she feared all the good literature had already been written, but here she is two hundred years later, an overnight success!"

Just then, a young, bespectacled woman inside the store strolled past the window display. She stopped, tucked a stray piece of hair behind her ear, and picked up a book.

Mick grinned at the innocent curiosity he saw in the girl's eyes, aware that he'd seen that expression somewhere before.

"It's weird, but I really want her to go home with a copy," Piper whispered.

"She reminds me of you a little bit," Mick said, placing a kiss on the top of her head. "You know, back when you took the ethnoarchaeology seminar just so you could stare at my ass."

"You wish," Piper said.

The young woman frowned as she carefully studied the cover, then turned it over to scan the back. She remained deep in concentration, her expression serious. Her eyes slowly widened and her lips began to spread in a sly smile. She looked around quickly, as if to make sure no one was watching, then tucked the book into the crook of her arm and headed toward the checkout line.

"Now you've gone and done it," Mick whispered, gently guiding Piper down the cobblestone sidewalk. "The poor girl will never be the same."

They continued in silent companionship for a few steps, then Mick felt Piper press tight to his side.

"Do you think they'll be writing about us in two hundred years?" she asked.

"Of course," Mick answered. "No one can resist a great love story."